CATE

AND

ERIC

A Novel by
Ronnie Morris

Copyright © 2013 Ronnie Morris
All rights reserved.
ISBN-10: 1480269301
EAN-13: 9781480269309

Forward

This story is set in Downriver. The term is used locally to describe the collection of small industrial towns that lie south of Detroit along the Detroit River. The cities of Allen Park, Grosse Ile, Melvindale and Trenton really exist. The characters, the city of Fairlane Hills, National Motor Car Company and Oak Grove Hospital are fictitious, however, and any resemblances to real people or incorporated businesses are purely coincidental.

Acknowledgements

To my wife Barb and her best friend Connie, thank you for your patience and love. To Cate Cassadea, a special thanks for making the story possible.

Prologue – July 1967

The radio was set to WKNR, 1310 on the AM dial. The four girls were crossing over the Detroit River on the county draw bridge headed to Looney Rooney's, a teenage hang out on the island of Grosse Ile. The song Go Now by The Moody Blues was playing and the girls joined the lead singer's laments about a lost love. During the next few years the girls would sing to other songs, but not together. They would sing individually, separated by great distances during more introspective moments.

The ambience in the car was a blend of their moods. Having just graduated high school, life was an adventure. Everyday was new and everything was fun. Though they hadn't spoken openly about it, the girls knew they soon must go separate ways. Linda was to be married the following weekend making the outing a bachelorette party, though bachelorette parties as such did not exist then. Cate would be moving to East Lansing to attend Michigan State University. Kathy, the driver, would leave for the University of Virginia. Jess was moving to California. While she wasn't sure what life held for her there, Jess knew it had to be better than suburban Detroit.

The girls finished the song and broke into hysterical laughter. Seventeen year old girls do that. Over the next forty years, they would learn such uncontrollable laughter was a gift. A gift sometimes lost too easily.

*Book One
Thirty-Eight Years Later*

*Episode 1
Plymouth, Indiana –
A suburb of Indianapolis*

Cate peeled off the hospital scrubs and left them lying on the floor where they fell. Opening the door to the shower, she noticed a small mildew spot on the ceiling and made a mental note to clean the stain with bleach and water. One more item to be added to the list of things that would never get done. Cate turned the knob to hot, closed the shower stall door and walked into the bedroom. Friday evenings usually called for her grey sweats, an ancient black tee shirt and an even older pair of black socks. Normally she would have completed the ensemble with a pair of fuzzy house slippers bought on a whim while visiting her daughter in San Diego. The slippers had seen better days and David occasionally threatened to add them to the Goodwill bag.

It had been a bitch of a week at the hospital and the last thing she wanted to do was go out with David's hunting buddy and his wife. At least not on Friday night. What Cate really wanted was to order Chinese, pour a glass of wine and read the novel she'd picked up at Walden Books during her lunch hour. As long as she was wishing for what was not to be, she'd add a few tokes on a skinny joint she'd hidden on the top shelf of her closet. It was the last of the stash she'd shared with her friend Missy. Of course that was before Missy moved to Idaho with her boyfriend. Thinking about her last joint, Cate wondered where a fifty-five year old nurse was supposed to buy a bag of weed in Plymouth. Their source had been some friend of Missy's in Indianapolis.

For a moment, Cate toyed with putting on the usual Friday outfit just to annoy David. She cast the thought aside and selected a pair of black slacks, a matching silk blouse and hung them on the door knob. Ironic she thought how black had become her favorite color. Was there some significance Cate mused, then retreated from that dead end.

The shower was still running and David insisted they share all the household expenses equally, even the utilities. Screw it, I'll stay in there as long as I damn well please, she thought or had she said it out loud, Cate wasn't sure. On her way back to the bathroom, Cate opened the dresser drawer, grabbed some underwear then closed the bath room door behind her. Steam rolled out of the top of the shower stall as she stepped over the discarded scrubs and opened the shower door.

Cate stepped under the spray. She wet her hair, then let the water cascade down her back. The heat felt good and eased the ever present stiffness in her back. Since the surgery, the twelve hour shifts at the hospital played hell with her lower spine. Cate had assured the surgeon she would take it easy but they both knew it would never happen. Before releasing her, Dr. Taj had recited the standard protocol following back surgery and provided a brochure itemizing the entire list of do's and don'ts. She had feigned interest, then put the brochure in the desk where it remained unread. She completed the physical therapy, however, which seemed a fair trade off. After thirty years as a nurse, she knew what to do, just not how make herself do them.

Episode 1 Plymouth, Indiana – A suburb of Indianapolis

Doctor Darpak Taj was the best orthopedic surgeon in the area and she was still surprised he maintained his practice in Plymouth. Cate knew he'd had several offers from larger hospitals in Indianapolis and could not understand why he stayed. Either he wanted to raise his children in a small town or just enjoyed being a big fish in a small pond. Whatever the reason, Cate knew she had been lucky to have him so close. Otherwise she would have had to go to Indianapolis and asking David to make that forty mile commute was not in the cards. David liked easy. Thinking of David jarred Cate from her daydream about Dr. Taj. During his rounds yesterday, he had reminded her again to rest her back. Hospitals and healing; an oxymoron if Cate had ever heard one.

Cate placed both hands on the wall in front of her and shifted her weight. The steamy water eased the tension in her muscles and she could feel her back beginning to loosen. Cate chastised herself for letting her mind wander to the subject of Doctor Darpak Taj. He was handsome she had to admit, even if it was in a swarthy, eastern sort of way. She thought he looked more Arabic than Indian and reminded her of a young Omar Shariff in the movie Funny Girl. She had mentioned this likeness once as they made small talk during his rounds. Doctor Taj was too young to have seen the movie, which was just as well, she certainly wasn't Barbara Streisand and would never sing and dance her way into the Zigfield Follies though today they were probably called the Rockettes. Now there was a thought, Cate said to herself, a fifty-five year old Rockette. What was Darpak Taj anyway, maybe thirty-five, he certainly wasn't forty. She'd already taken enough grief for marrying David and he was only ten years her junior. Cate sighed; being late for dinner would not be a good start to the weekend. Turning off the water, Cate grabbed the towel hanging over the shower stall and stepped onto the bath mat.

Episode 2
Plymouth Medical Building

Doctor Darpak Taj stood just over six feet; he was handsome and knew it. With his looks and intelligence he had once been considered a prize catch for any young woman in the Indian community. Cate Cassadea, the head nurse on the third floor had been correct when she told him he resembled Omar Shariff. Darpak had even white teeth and shiny black hair which he parted on the right, as opposed to the left so common in the United States. He always thought it odd the British men he had known in India, and he had known and hated many, showed no preference for which side to part their hair. While the Americans, first cousins to the pompous Brits, parted theirs predominantly on the left. It wouldn't matter which side Darpak chose, a thick lock constantly flopped over the middle of his forehead. The only thing that contained it was the surgical cap required in the operating room. He teasingly told his wife recently he was going to wear the hat all of the time. Ravenna laughed and ignored his threat by reminding him he could resolve the issue by simply shaving his head. Darpak ignored her suggestion by replying that a shaved head might elicit comments about a resemblance to Ben Kingsley which was not the same as looking like Shariff. The lock would stay.

Like most wealthy Indians, Darpak was a good bridge player. He also excelled at cricket. As a boy, he wanted to play for India's national team. He was such a good batsman, he came within a hair of making the team. A fractured ankle denied him the opportunity. Though disappointed at the time, it was the turning point in his life.

It was Friday evening and the staff had left for the weekend. Seated behind the desk in his office, Darpak was entering patient observations into the dictation machine. When he finished, Darpak got up and walked out of his office. After making sure the waiting area was empty, he returned to his office and locked the door. Before sitting at his desk, he fished in his pocket for the key to the bottom drawer. It was the only key and Darpak knew its location always. Inside the drawer was a grey lock box. Although it looked like an ordinary fire proof box available at Office Depot, it was anything but. The procedure for opening the box was precise. Any missed steps would be disastrous for the box and the person opening it. Inside was a phone, which like the box was anything but ordinary. The phone was connected to an encrypted satellite communications system. Darpak removed the phone and placed it on his desk. Turning it on, he waited for the call.

Episode 3
Allen Park, Michigan – A suburb of Detroit

Eric's head pounded. His eyes were bloodshot and both lids were swollen and puffy. Eric's face was bone thin and the dark rings under his eyes gave him a comical, raccoon like appearance. There was nothing funny, however, about Eric's physical state. He was exhausted and running on adrenalin. He needed to sleep, but there was too much to do before he could afford such a luxury. There were too many people counting on him. As he ran his tongue around the inside of his mouth, Eric noticed his tongue and teeth had an odd almost furry feel. It had been two weeks since he had brushed his teeth; even longer since he had bathed.

Though it was six o'clock on a Friday evening, Eric had no idea of the time or even what day of the week it was. It might be Thursday; but he wasn't positive. He had been working franticly for fourteen days developing the numbers and campaign strategy. Carrying Michigan was essential, if George was to have any hope of being elected President.

Traversing the twenty foot distance from the living room to the dining room required the balance of a tight rope walker. Eric was used to navigating around the clutter. The floor was strewn with districting maps, census reports, computer printouts, survey analysis and canvassing documents. The stacks were waist high. Glancing around the room, it appeared someone had thrown a truck load of maps and papers into the air and let them land randomly. Their order, however, made perfect sense to Eric. He could recite voting tendencies and local issues for each congressional district.

Since he was a boy, politics had been Eric's obsession. While his friends spent hours debating the Detroit Tigers chances against the Yankees, Eric thought about elections. He learned early, however, political discussions with his buddies were useless. Adults were not much better. The neighbors were not interested in interrupting their lawn mowing or leaf raking to discuss political issues with a twelve year old boy. The teachers at his school were also a disappointment, so Eric contented himself with eavesdropping when his father's buddies from the Downriver Democratic Club stopped by to drink whiskey, smoke cigars and discuss the world's problems.

While Eric liked playing sports and was an exceptional athlete, he never understood his friends' fixation on something as boring as baseball. Being the tallest boy in school, Eric played center on his sixth grade basketball team. Despite his size, Eric was extremely coordinated with lightening quick hands and feet. There were eight elementary schools in the district and each one fielded a team. During Saturday morning games at the high school, spectators were quick to notice the tall boy playing for Ina J. Mead elementary. The high school coaches kept an eye on the games and were drooling to get Eric.

When asked, Eric's mother attributed his agility to the dance lessons she forced him to take. Last year, she'd also added jazz and Adagio. Eric resisted initially, but knew his mother too well

Episode 3 Allen Park, Michigan – A suburb of Detroit

to believe he could buck her determined will. It was one more experience that added to his understanding as to why his parents eventually separated. Divorce was not the normal family arrangement in the 60s, and it was even more unusual for the child to live with the father. But Eric never held the estrangement against his mother and in truth, was just as happy to live with his dad. Alan's cooking wasn't bad and they had a housekeeper who came in twice weekly. The house was always neat and tidy and his dad was easy to live with. His mother, though a beautiful woman, was prone to bouts of depression and fits of anger. Even before the separation, she would go away for weeks at a time. And while he missed her during those absences, his grandmother would come from Arkansas to help out until his mother returned. When older, Eric would learn his mother's times away were spent at a hospital that treated alcoholism. Though it didn't lessen the loneliness he'd felt at the time, the knowledge did provide a basis for some forgiveness.

When his mother remarried, his time with her was limited to weekly dance lessons. She would pick him after school and after his lesson, they'd go out for dinner. Occasionally, Eric was allowed to pick the restaurant. When it was his choice, they went to Debby's on Allen Road or the Big Boy on Southfield Boulevard. Debby's had great meat loaf, one of Eric's favorites. At Big Boy he'd order the double decker hamburger, onion rings and a chocolate milk shake. He liked to dip the rings in ketchup and never failed to finish the entire order. His friends were envious. A maid and eating out were unheard of luxuries to kids growing up in Allen Park, but Eric would have traded them in a heart beat for a normal mother and home made meat loaf.

His only complaint lately had been his mother's arrangement for him and his dance partner, Peggy, to dance on television. The Captain Jolly Show was a locally produced weekly children's show that aired on Saturday afternoons. Captain Jolly, the host, wore a sailor's out fit, a blue baggy captain's hat and a fake beard. The show featured Popeye cartoons and local talent. Eric threw a fit when his mom told him he was scheduled to appear on the show, but the tantrum was to no avail. Once Nancy put her mind to something there was no deterring her. The Monday following the appearance had been awful; the teasing at school was relentless. It hadn't gone much better the following Saturday morning at basketball. Most of the boys on the other teams had seen the show and the black leotard tights and turtleneck. Only his size saved him from total humiliation. Every time Eric got the ball during warm ups, the players on the opposing team chanted homo, homo. The coach eventually made them shut up, but it was still humiliating.

Eric did not watch much television, with one notable exception. Though only twelve, Eric watched the 1960 presidential debates with a dedication equal to his buddies' following of the World Series. Seeing Nixon and Kennedy debate cemented Eric's desire to be involved in politics. His first memory of an election was in 1956 when Adlai Stevenson failed to unseat Eisenhower. Eric listened as his father, a stalwart southern Democrat, railed about the party's tragic waste of such a fine candidate.

That election was ancient history and nothing like that was going to happen this time. Eric was nearly ready to make his pitch to the committee. If his numbers were correct, Michigan could be delivered. If he was wrong, the state and maybe the whole election was lost.

Eric hadn't eaten in two days. Food was now a priority. Eric tiptoed around the stacks of reports, staying on the narrow path that led serendipitously into the kitchen. On good days, Eric could pull himself together enough to rinse the dishes and load the dishwasher. Occasionally he even washed the pans. He hadn't had one of those days in a while, however, and now dirty dishes filled the sink. On the stove two stainless steel pans were coated with rancid hamburger grease. On the counter an empty yellow Heinz mustard container sat next to a plastic bag that once held Wonder Bread hamburger buns. Eric picked up the bag noting the little red, yellow and blue balloons printed on the side. He hoped one of the buns had miraculously survived; a peanut butter and jelly sandwich sounded good. He set the empty bag down

Episode 3 Allen Park, Michigan – A suburb of Detroit

despondently. Eric had not shopped recently and his rations were desperately low. He reached for the refrigerator door and opened it. Grabbing a Smucker's grape jelly jar off the shelf, he unscrewed the lid. The jar also was near empty.

"Shit, don't even have the jelly, even if I had the buns," Eric said to no one.

He threw the lid on the counter and stuck his finger into the jar. Swiping the side, Eric managed to smear a small trace of jelly and stuck his finger into his mouth. He inspected the rest of the refrigerator as he licked off the jelly. Satisfied the refrigerator had nothing to offer, Eric closed the door and turned his attention to the cupboard. He hoped to find a box of crackers or a stray pack of Chips Ahoy. Eric loved Chips Ahoy. He'd bought three packs the last time he left the house but couldn't remember when that had been. Opening the cupboard door, Eric saw several boxes on the shelf.

"Now damn it, this is more like it," he chirped looking at the Ritz crackers, Premium saltines and Wheat Thins boxes. His elation turned to despair when he found the first box to be empty. Eric dropped the Ritz box on the floor and reached for the Wheat Thins.

"Screw those Ritz crackers," he grumbled softly. "They're overrated," Eric continued as he picked up the Wheat Thins box. The picture on the cover of a small whole wheat cracker topped with Swiss cheese made his stomach rumble.

Eric looked up from the Wheat Thins box. He remembered being hungry another time and rummaging through cupboards for snacks. But those cupboards had been at a different place and the memory seemed a mystery; he could only discern bits and pieces. He'd had the munchies after eating hashish laden brownies and he was not alone; there had been somebody else. There had been a girl. Eric closed his eyes in concentration; they were young and she was pretty.

The rest was obscured so he waited. After a few moments he began to see more. They had been laughing about something hysterically until she begged him to stop, saying she was going to pee her pants. Eric could see her cut off jeans. They were tight and cut very high emphasizing her trim body and narrow waist. He remembered watching as she slipped them on in the mornings, especially the little wiggle to get them all the way up. Why he could remember her now was unclear but that was how it worked. Memories of her, like so many others, came and went. There was no order or reason. Where the people in them disappeared to was unknown. They vanished as quickly as they appeared. When Eric looked into the empty Wheat Thins box again, tears welled up in his eyes. His life, like the cupboard, had become unbearably empty. There was no letting this box drop idly to the floor; Eric threw it against the wall.

"Damn it, Dad," he blurted. "Why would you put empty boxes back in the cupboard? Why the hell didn't you buy more ?" Eric added angrily.

Catching himself in mid sentence, Eric leaned against the wall as tears trickled down his cheeks. He brushed the tears with the back of his hand and knew the answer to his question before he finished it. Alan had been dead two years. Sometimes it felt like he was still there, still in the house they'd shared for fifty years. When his head cleared, Eric looked around the room and realized he'd have to shop for food. He hated going out and only did so when absolutely necessary but there was nothing left to eat nor anyone else to go.

Eric closed the cupboard door and walked to the back door where his hooded sweatshirt hung on a hook. Eric reached into the pocket, the keys were still there. He felt relieved because he couldn't always remember where he put things. The keys were there, thank God, so at least he wouldn't have to make the two mile walk to Kovalchek's Market. He was too weak for that. Closing the door behind him, Eric walked down the driveway to the van. He climbed behind the wheel and put the keys into the ignition. When the truck started on the third try, Eric backed down the driveway.

Episode 4
Grosse Ile, Michigan – An island in the Detroit River, 15 miles south of the city.

    Looking out the window, Ronnie watched the mammoth freighter preparing to dock. A worker on shore caught the line thrown down to him by the sailor perched on the bow. For the last thirty minutes, the ship had been fighting the current and shifting winds of the lower Detroit River. Ronnie knew the pilot would be in deep concentration maneuvering the ship to offset the variances of wind and water.

    The captain was seated in a big leather chair next to the ship's steering wheel. As the captain sipped coffee and smoked

Pall Malls or another of the unfiltered brand favored by old time Great Lakes' sailors, the pilot held the wheel with both hands, turning it ever so slightly.

The ship was completing its southbound journey from Calumet, Wisconsin to the McClouth Steel mill in Trenton, one of three remaining mills along the lower Detroit River. The pilot's name was Dennis Williams. Though Denny had navigated this landing numerous times, he still felt a twinge of anxiety. Every docking had its unique complexity. At a thousand feet in length and a cargo capacity of 800 tons, the Henry Ford II, was the biggest ore ship on the Great Lakes. She would be at dock for forty-eight hours to unload.

Though fifty-two years old, Denny retained a youthful look. He also retained a boyish disposition which helped explain his three failed marriages. When he was young, girls described Denny as cute. He still elicited such comments from barmaids and women at the pubs around the shipping docks. Though a few flecks of silver were beginning to appear around his temples, his dark brown hair was thick and curly. During the 60s and 70s he wore his hair in a fluffy afro but now kept it neatly trimmed. Of average height, Denny was fine featured with a thin nose and deep set, dark brown eyes. Exposure to wind and sun aboard ship had weathered his complexion. Wrinkles were beginning to etch deeper into his forehead and crow's feet around his eyes were becoming pronounced. When the ship eased to the dock, Denny turned to the captain.

"Permission to hand over the conn, Captain?" he asked.

It sounded like something from a Star Trek episode and reminded Denny that some of the best times of his misspent youth had been getting stoned on Friday nights with Eddie Wayne and watching Captain Kirk and Mr. Spock save the universe. He watched reruns on the Sci-fi channel occasionally in motels during lay overs. The program seemed so different now. No Eddie, no dope and no being sixteen.

"Permission granted," the captain answered.

"So," the Captain added, "how about dinner?"

Episode 4 Grosse Ile, Michigan – An island in the Detroit River

With the ship docked, the Captain's voice was more relaxed.

"Thanks, but I've plans," Denny answered, "got a buddy that lives not far from here. I told him the next time I was here we'd get together. I haven't seen him in a while and I do love the food over at Sibley Gardens. Never miss a chance when I make this run."

"Just thought I'd ask. Anyway, we'll see you Sunday evening then," the captain added.

As Denny turned to leave, he pulled his cell phone from his pocket and dialed Ronnie's number. Waiting for the call to go through, Denny opened the door and stepped out onto the platform next to the bridge. Standing next to the rail, he could see Ronnie's house directly across the river. He knew Ronnie would be watching. The phone rang twice.

"Hello," Ronnie said. Through his binoculars he could see Denny standing by the rail

"Hello, yourself you big pussy, can you hear me now?" Denny asked.

"Yes, I can hear you now," Ronnie replied mockingly.

Denny took a few steps toward the stern and spoke again, "Can you hear me now?"

"Yeah, I can hear you now," Ronnie answered.

Stepping in the opposite direction, Denny ended up where he stood originally, "How about now, numb nuts?" Denny continued.

"Hey, dumb ass, why don't you take about two steps forward and ask that question. We'll do a water test on your stupid telephone," Ronnie laughed at Denny's parody on the Verizon commercial.

"You'd like that, wouldn't you shit head. Kind of a payback for the time you fell off that dock you clumsy assed gimp," Denny answered.

The reference was to a camping trip to Canada thirty years earlier. Ronnie had gotten so stoned he fell off the fishing dock. After Ronnie's lectures about the risks of smuggling marijuana across the border, Denny promised not to bring any along. He had given Ronnie his solemn oath, no dope. At the campfire the first evening, Denny pulled out four joints.

"I don't see you for ten years, and you're still a big jerk off," Ronnie shot back. "Hey asshole, it's good to know some things never change."

Denny always brought out the worst in Ronnie. Time spent with Denny always bordered on the ragged edge of control making Ronnie wonder if maybe it was better Denny had fallen out of his life for a while.

"Well, get your asshole wallet and your asshole keys and drive your asshole over here in your asshole car and buy me an asshole dinner," Denny responded in staccato cadence.

"Hmmm, an asshole dinner, not sure they have them on the menu at Sibley Gardens," Ronnie answered. Ronnie noted he hadn't used such language since the last time he'd been with Denny. "Anyway, what is that, a French dish or something? I know they eat snails?"

"They're called escargot, numb nuts, and if you are lucky, I'll let your sorry ass buy me some and a few drinks. I know you can afford it, Mr. Retired Auto executive," Denny replied.

"Hey, I'm on a fixed income now, your ass will be lucky to be ordering a Big Mac with fries if I'm buying," Ronnie answered, "and the fries are negotiable."

"I've got your negotiable right here in my pants, now just get your ass over here. This steel mill stinks and I'm hungry as hell," Denny finished.

"Hey, Sibley's is just down the street from the mill, walk," Ronnie added jokingly.

"Shove your walk, just pick me up, I'll be out front," Denny replied.

"I'll be right there."

Ronnie set the phone on the table then walked into the kitchen. Reaching into the cupboard by the sink, he grabbed one of the snowmen glasses. Though ancient, they were his favorite. Beth'd tease him about using the snow men glasses year round. He'd tell her that they were second only to the Welch's Grape Jelly glasses with the purple and yellow dinosaurs. She'd bought them full of jelly when the boys were little. By some miracle, all

Episode 4 Grosse Ile, Michigan – An island in the Detroit River

four had survived. Their younger son tried to pilfer them during visits home. Ronnie considered giving them to him, but brushing his teeth with a jelly glass was a tradition Ronnie wasn't ready to part with. In all the years they'd been married, he'd never seen Beth use a glass while brushing her teeth, she scooped the water up with her cupped hand. Odd, he thought, to notice this little peculiarity now. She'd been gone two years.

Walking to his car, Ronnie heard the phone ring. He considered letting it go to the recorder but thinking it might be Denny, he turned back. At the door, Ronnie had trouble getting the key to turn the deadbolt.

"Getting old," he muttered as he struggled to get the lock to turn.

As he walked inside, Ronnie could hear his greeting telling the caller to please leave a message. If it was Denny, he'd pick up, if not he'd let it go to the recorder.

"Hello," a woman's voice said, "this is Amy Huber, er I mean, Irwin. I'm looking for Ronnie Harris," she continued. "If this is the correct number Ronnie, please call me at 422 6935, oh the area code is 313" she added. "I'd like to speak to you about Bobbie. It's important, please call me."

"What the hell," Ronnie whispered, "Amy Irwin?"

The message caught him off guard. "Why the hell is she calling?" Ronnie wondered aloud. "No way I can deal with whatever that's all about, at least not now," he added as he turned and walked out the door.

Episode 5
Fairlane Hills, Michigan – A suburb of Detroit.

Ahmed pushed the chair from the kitchen table and walked to the sink. He needed more water. His lips and tongue burned from the Frank's Hot Sauce he'd doused on his order of chicken. Ahmed knew it was a mistake to drink so much before the mosque. It was difficult enough to last through the entire Sabbath; leaving to use the bathroom was unthinkable. Even secularized Muslims, like himself, never exhibited disrespectful behavior.

Going to the mosque seemed such a waste of time. The incessant praying and kneeling while listening to some ancient Sheik was unbearable. It was tedious, there were so many better things to do Friday evening. He knew there were young people who might look forward to attending mass or temple, but he was not one of them. He'd had enough of that insanity in Afghanistan. He wanted to abandon his strict Muslim upbringing and be like many of the other young Arab Americans living in east Fairlane Hills. Some put on a show, but once out of their parents sight, they were no different from the young Christians in the west end.

From what Ahmed had seen, the young Arabs who attended Mosque seemed to do it out of fear, though he hadn't seen any of the corporal reprisals he'd experienced. To these young secularized Arabs, fear meant losing Master Card privileges or use of their new car. But he'd only been back in the States for a short while, so perhaps there was more to see. The women were not beaten in public here, so maybe martial discipline was kept behind closed doors.

Thinking about the mosque, Ahmed knew he had no choice. Attending was part of the deal. Kneeling on a hard stone floor seemed like torture though he knew it was not. On that topic, Ahmed could speak from experience whether it was techniques favored by al Qaeda or the CIA. He could talk about methods used to extract information or those used to extract revenge. It was just another part of the training camps. He'd also witnessed the CIA's versions at Guantanamo.

In the training camps, he was taught skills to resist torture, how to put his mind outside of his body. Reciting Koranic verses helped one distance himself from pain. To prepare for possible capture, he'd been blindfolded for days and denied food and water. Ahmed learned the impact solitude could have on those of even the strongest will. He knew how fear could grip your spine when electrodes were attached to your privates. He also knew the anxiety of waiting for pain to begin.

He'd also been taught skills to end pain permanently. Faithful Muslims knew suicide in the service of Allah provided a direct path to paradise and the virgins who waited there. He liked the idea of the virgins but secretly doubted it was true. Getting them required martyrdom, a hefty price to pay. It was too bad the reward for being wounded was not a few virgins. For such reward, he might be able to endure minor wounds. But he wanted no part of martyrdom, regardless of what his father and other fanat-

Episode 5 Fairlane Hills, Michigan – A suburb of Detroit.

ics believed. For them, martyrdom was the desired end for any warrior on jihad.

Putting aside the dilemma of the virgins, Ahmed turned on the cold water and filled a glass. As he drank he wondered what kind of god would create this madness. What kind of god would allow him, and boys like him, to see and experience the things they had.

It was not sane to create a world that allowed a seventeen year old boy to be beaten for possessing a bottle of hot sauce. How could God allow this to happen? Was a bottle of hot sauce really such a symbol of the satanic West? What kind of god allowed a young boy to be humiliated in front of everyone for hiding a bottle of hot sauce? Or beaten for drinking Coca Cola or buying a cube of ice for his tea?

His father had done this to him for one reason and one reason only. Haleem wanted to demonstrate to Osama he maintained control over his sons. Ahmed knew he had become an embarrassment to his father. He had always been the black sheep; the one who could never follow the rules. He was the son who would never be a true Muslim soldier. He was the cancer that must be cut out before his evil influence metastasized and ruined his brothers and sister. After their company had left, his father had told him just that. All because of a bottle of Frank's Hot Sauce. It was not sane.

His life could have been different had his father stayed in the United States. He could have made friends here and gone to school and enjoyed all the amenities of a Western life. But his father had to save the world. The great savior Haleem had to rescue the orphans of Afghanistan never caring that in the process, he'd sacrifice his own son's life. This had happened because his father had fallen under the spell of Osama. Ahmed despised Osama. Osama had caused the death of his father and brother. The great Osama, who had denied them the few simple comforts and joys Afghanistan had to offer was alive, while his father and brother were dead. Before Afghanistan, things had been so different.

Now here he was, back in Fairlane Hills. When he had last seen his father and brother, they were preparing to fight the American invaders. It was to be to the death and it had been. The Americans could just have easily killed him. How ironic it all was. Ironic or insane, he didn't know which because it was his love of western luxuries that had saved Ahmed's life. If he had not left the compound and snuck back to Kabul to watch videos with Omar, he'd also be lying dead. Or worse, he could be crippled like his youngest brother Caleb.

Ahmed set the bottle of Frank's back on the table and left the kitchen. He walked into the short hallway leading to the bedrooms. Though small by American standards, the apartment was adequate for his needs. He slept in the larger of the two bedrooms, using the other for storage though he really didn't have much to store, just a suitcase and a few clothes. The bed and dresser were purchased from Nasser's Discount Furniture on Greenfield Road. The living room furniture and kitchen table were bought at a second hand store on Warren Avenue. He really wanted a leather couch and matching chair. The CIA agent, however, warned him against such ostentatious spending. To maintain his cover, he had to project an image of a hospital janitor. After his assignment was complete, there would time to spend the five thousand dollars a month being put away for him. In the meantime, Ahmed was content with his large screen television defending the purchase by convincing the agent every Arab had one to watch Al Jazera.

There were so many good things about being back, like showers and reliable electricity. He could put ice in his tea anytime without being lectured about Western comforts making him soft and dependent. It was a wish come true but he missed his family and at times felt so alone. He had been away from Fairlane Hills for fifteen years and things had changed. While not a worrier by nature, Ahmed was concerned about how to end his relationship with the CIA. He wanted desperately to have a normal life. At twenty, he should be chasing women and having the time of his life.

Episode 5 Fairlane Hills, Michigan – A suburb of Detroit.

He hadn't had a choice when his father drug them halfway around the world to save Afghan orphans. He hadn't had a choice when his father sent him to the retched training camps. He hadn't had a choice when the instructors forced him to shoot AK47s and make bombs. He hadn't had a choice when the instructors blindfolded him and put him through simulated torture. None of these had been choices. The only choice he had been able to exercise, was refusing his father's request for him to become a suicide bomber.

Being an operative for the CIA had not been a choice either. He could have refused and been left to rot at Guantanamo or be killed by the guards or other detainees. If he was returned to Afghanistan, he'd be forced into Al Qaeda again. His only option had been to accept the offer from the Americans. His main concern now was surviving this devil's pact. In Afghanistan life was a day to day proposition so he was use to the uncertainties of life. He had to make the best of it until something turned up; it was just a matter of time. Ahmed slipped off his shoes, it was time to get dressed and leave.

Episode 6

Cate wrapped her hair in the damp towel then picked up the underwear laying on the vanity. Snapping the ends of her bra together, she caught a glimpse of her reflection in the mirror. The lightening fixture above the mirror contained several forty watt bulbs. It was original to the house and Cate had always hated it. David ignored her requests to install a new one saying he could not see any sense in wasting her good money.

Cate had turned fifty-five on Tuesday. The dinner tonight was a celebration marking, as David put it, her turning double nickels. Cate looked in the mirror again. Examining her reflection, she recalled the book Passages. She read the book years ago and was surprised how accurately it captured the essence of change each decade marked. As predicted, life in her forties had been a cruel emotional roller coaster ride. There was the divorce from Billy to begin with and there was the divorce from Billy to end with. The split could have occurred ten years ago or a hundred years ago, sometimes it felt like both. She still wasn't sure which Cate she was. Was she the hurt victim, the deserted spouse and mother who fell apart and had been on the verge of ending it all? Or was she the brave, independent woman, who kept the remnants of her family together and continued to create a new life for herself? Cate concluded long ago she was some god awful combination of weak and strong, independent and dependent, luster of life and suicidal all at the same time.

Though Cate did not consider herself conceited, she was pleased with what she saw in the mirror. Cate had always been striking. As a little girl, strangers would stop her mother on the street and comment about her beauty. The attention made her uncomfortable at times, she had always been shy. Her mother used to say she was born so shy the doctor had to slap her three times to get her cry because she didn't want any one in the room to know she was there. As she got older, the constant flattery, especially from her family and friends, exacerbated her shyness. Her introverted nature puzzled close friends and family. Cate wondered why people assumed beauty translated to self confidence in some kind of direct ratio. It always came as a shock when they found out it didn't work that way. People were also surprised she took anti depressants and her mother's friends would make comments like "I can't believe someone who's looks like you is depressed" or "honey, if I had your looks, I sure wouldn't need any medication for depression" or "why are you depressed, you can have any man that you want".

Even as a little girl Cate knew she was different. What had been thought of as an introverted childhood was really a symptom of a bigger issue, though calling it an issue was an understatement. Monster was a more apt description. As a child, that was what Cate called it. The monster would come and take over her thoughts and feelings. He would take her happiness away, rob her of her energy and make all of her fun go away. Cate hated the monster. She hated him for replacing joy with sadness and waves of foreboding. Sometimes the feelings were so foreign she would cry and not know why. The feelings scared her. So she cried because she was frightened and cried more because she was afraid to tell anyone.

She was eleven the first time the feelings came. At first her mother, Emma, thought it was the flu. Cate had always been a quiet, self reflecting child, but she still went to the park to play

Episode 6

box hockey, four squares and hop Scotch. She would never go by herself but as long as her best friend Kimmy came and got her, Cate would go. The two girls would laugh at secret jokes and came home sweaty and tired.

That day, however, had been different. Cate knew something was wrong but didn't know what it was. She couldn't describe how she felt. She hadn't slept well and woke up several times during the night. The next morning, she didn't want to get out of bed. She was tired and exhausted and sad. Her head didn't feel right and nothing seemed of interest. When her mom went into her bedroom to tell her Kimmy was at the door, Cate said that she didn't feel like going to the park. She didn't feel like eating or watching cartoons either. She didn't want to do anything except lie in bed.

Emma put a damp towel on her forehead and asked if she hurt anywhere. Cate remembered telling her mom that she didn't hurt, but just felt sad for some reason and then started crying. Her mom left her bedroom and returned with a bottle of St. Joseph Aspirin for Children. Her mom had given her two of the pills, a glass of water and strict instructions to take a good nap assuring her she would feel better.

Cate swallowed the two orange flavored tablets and fell asleep. When she woke up, she felt rested but the sadness remained. When her father, Louis, came home from his shift at the Ford Rouge Plant, Emma told him Catie had a mild touch of the flu.

Cate could hear her parents talking. A few minutes later Louis poked his head into her bedroom and asked how she was felling. She told him she was a little better and would be okay by tomorrow.

Cate knew her father loved her two brothers, but also knew she was his favorite. Maybe it was because she was the most like him, she had his aquiline good looks and sharp features. Cate also had Louis's fair skin, light hair and inquisitive mind. Most people were surprised when they heard his last name was Cassadea. Louis was quick to point out he was northern Italian.

Louis put his hand on her forehead and told her she didn't feel warm. He added that he agreed she would be better tomorrow. Kissing her lightly on the cheek, he asked if she wanted anything. Cate told him she was okay, she just wanted to rest a while more.

As he left her room, Cate knew what her father would do next. Grabbing the newspaper, Louis poured a cold beer and went on the front porch. If she was not at the park, Cate would sit on the steps and listen as he kibitzed with the neighbors who were usually sitting on their front porch. Redwood decks did not exist in their blue collar, working class neighborhood. Patio furniture was also sparse, but webbed aluminum folding chairs and metal gliders were in abundance on the neighborhood's front porches. On warm summer evenings, families sat outside sipping iced tea, lemonade or cold beer. Several of the homes on Cate's street had awnings that extended over the porches. The awnings usually matched the paint or aluminum siding.

Though unaware, Cate was experiencing her first bout of what doctors later diagnosed as intense juvenile melancholy. Cate just knew was she didn't feel like going to the park or sitting on the porch with her dad. The attack lasted the week but thankfully did't return again that summer.

Cate's thoughts returned to the present as she turned off the bathroom lights. In the bedroom, she selected a pair of panty hose from the middle dresser drawer then sat on the edge of the bed. The bedroom was spacious and easily accommodated the king sized bed, dresser and chest of drawers. She loved to curl up on cold winter mornings and gaze out the sliding glass door. It was cozy just to be there, feeling David's warm body next to hers. Cate would lie in a semi-conscious state lost in thought. David could sleep through a tornado and seldom awoke during early morning. He irritated her at times, was insanely jealous and overwhelmingly frugal but he had been there for her when Billy lost his mind and went middle age crazy. As she learned later, Billy had been middle age crazy even in his twenties.

Episode 6

Gazing out the door-wall, Cate loved the view of the back yard. The trees and dogwoods were fully leaved now. She worked for hours in the beds bordering their over sized lot. The house wasn't as large as the Cape Cod she and Billy had custom built in Michigan. It was a shame the marriage to Billy couldn't have been custom built with the same attention. That house had been so perfect, too bad Billy couldn't have been.

Cate glanced at the clock. It was almost five-thirty and she had to meet David at six fifteen. She finished dressing then walked into the bathroom to dry her hair. After applying her make up, she went into the bedroom and gave herself a final once over in the full length mirror. Deciding she passed inspection, Cate walked into the dining room. She'd let the dogs out when she had first come home but needed to put food in their bowls before leaving. She didn't think it would be a late night, but sometimes on Fridays, David could get a little over enthusiastic. After adding water to the dogs' bowls, Cate called the two West Highland Terriers into the house. Gucci, the older of the two, headed straight to his bowl. Duffy, who was not quite three, let Cate fuss on him before heading to his. Cate referred to them as her boys. Bending down, she gave each a pet on the head before heading out the door.

"You boys be good and keep an eye on the ranch while Jake and I are down at the Dry Bean. Don't let them Mexican rustlers come and steal all our cattle while we're gone," Cate said to the dogs. It was a line from the book Lonesome Dove she frequently quoted before leaving the house. Jake Spoon, a character described in the book as a leaky vessel, always reminded her of Billy. The description fit to a tee.

"I must be out of my mind," Cate uttered softly as she walked into the garage.

"It's been ten years, I'm on my way to celebrate my fifty-fifth birthday at the Outback Steak House for god's sake, and I'm thinking of Billy . Is there no peace?" Cate sighed as she closed the door behind her.

Episode 7

Eric backed down the driveway onto the street then stopped to shift the van into drive. When he pressed the gas pedal the big van lurched forward, hesitated then stalled.

"Shit," Eric said in a low guttural voice, "come on you piece of crap, don't pull that shit on me now."

"Just make it up to the market and I won't ask any more of you" he coaxed in a gentler voice. "Some times you just have to be gentle with 'em," he aded shifting the van back into park. When he turned the key again, the starter gave a muted groan but turned over the engine.

"Come on baby, you can do it," Eric pleaded. "Come on just one more time. Don't make me walk, please, just one more time."

Eric's stomach growled. He was losing patience with the truck. He let the starter grind another minute then turned the key to off. After letting the truck sit for a few minutes, Eric turned the key again. The engine turned over but would not fire.

"You piece of shit!" Eric exploded opening the driver's door and jumping out of the truck. Agitated, he abandoned his strategy of sweet talking and would let the truck know what he really thought. Eric slammed the door, walked to the front and opened the hood. He couldn't see any disconnected wires but smelled gas. Concluding the engine was flooded, Eric lifted the hood off the support bar and slammed it shut.

"Screw you National Motor Company," Eric swore closing the hood. He walked back to the driver's door adding, "and your shitty cars. It's no damn wonder you're losing market share."

Eric stopped in mid stride wondering where he'd obtained this last bit of information. Pausing, he squinted his left eye and scratched his right eye brow with the nail of his right pinky finger. It was a contemplative gesture he did unconsciously to help him focus his thoughts. When perplexed, Eric could lightly scratch his right eyebrow and the solution seemed to rise up from somewhere deep inside his brain. He really didn't know how it happened; it just did. His grandfather Harper T., a man he met only once, had the same idiosyncrasy. Nancy had never shared this bit of family history with her son. Harper T. was an attorney in Birmingham where Nancy was born. Given a choice, she'd have never left Alabama.

The family home had a large wrap around front porch with a swing where as a girl, Nancy took great delight reading Nancy Drew novels. She'd pass by her father's study and peer in on him occasionally on her way to the kitchen. One day passing by the study, she saw her father sitting behind his gigantic oak desk. He was leaning back on his leather chair, both feet resting on the corner of the desk. She noticed he was fervently scratching his eyebrow with the little finger of his right hand as he studied a legal document deep in thought. After watching a few moments, she continued to the kitchen.

"Why's daddy scratch his eyebrow so much?" she asked her mother.

Her mother set the sifting cup down then wiped her hands with an apron.

"Oh, he's just doing the Harper T. squint, honey," her mother laughed. "You've never seen him do that before?" she asked.

"Well yes, but why does he squint his eye up like that? How's he read with his eye all squished up?" She added.

Episode 7

"Honey," her mother answered, "he ain't reading, he's cogitating, as he calls it. All the Brohl men do that when they are trying to figure out something. He says it helps him think, but I don't know about that. Seems to me it would give you a headache."

Eric was sitting at the kitchen table working on multiplication tables when Nancy first saw him do the Harper T. squint. She had always known her only child was bright. Walking by the table, Nancy could see Eric was deep in thought. He had been staring at the worksheet for some time. Nancy could see the numbers, the blue mimeograph stood out vividly on the white paper. Nancy could see that he was stumped on the product of nine times six. It was not unusual to see her little boy in deep thought and knew Eric would eventually deduce the answer. What surprised her was he was working so diligently for such a long time. The problem should have been simple.

"Why Eric," she cooed in her thick Alabama drawl, "you know the answer to that little problem, honey."

The last syllable of honey was drawn out in a way that only women from the Deep South could. Eric missed few things about his mother, but the way she called him and his dad honey was one.

"You can think of it as being the opposite of six times nine, and I know you know your times tables up through six," Nancy added not liking to see her son struggle.

"Mom," Eric quickly replied, "I know the answer to the stupid problem is fifty-four. Anyone knows the answer to that. What I'm thinking about is how this whole stupid number system is based on multiples of ten. I'm trying to figure out if there is another multiple a number system can be based on."

Nancy cocked her head slightly as she considered Eric's reply. She hadn't expected the answer her ten year old son offered. She had never taken math beyond the one semester required at the University of Alabama, but considered herself numerically literate. Eric's reply left her speechless. She knew intuitively what he meant but couldn't get her mind completely around the idea.

"Well now honey," she said, "that's a right interesting idea but maybe you should just finish the problems on that paper for right now. Your daddy will be home shortly."

Sitting in the kitchen doing homework while his mom cooked had been better days, it was almost like his mother was normal. When Eric dreamed about her occasionally, she looked as she did that evening at the kitchen table. He'd see her auburn hair and clear hazel eyes that seem to change color with her moods. He could see the little crinkle that would form at the edge of her smile just before she would laugh. He could see her flawless complexion and swath of freckles that ran across the bridge of her nose, dotted her cheeks and spilled onto her shoulders.

During those times, Nancy's spells, as grandma Arnold called them, were not so bad. Eric always thought spells such a descriptive word. He quickly learned that southern women don't have mental illness, they have spells. Nor do they have premenstrual syndrome, they have lady spells. Postpartum depressions were baby spells. Instead of menopause or bipolar disorder, middle age southern women have elderly lady spells or up and down spells. When Eric was older, he would tell his dad Grandma Arnold didn't have dementia, she had confusion spells. His father had seemed comforted by Eric's diagnosis. At that time, his dad was still working at the National Motor's Engineering Center in Fairlane Hills Hills, a suburb of Detroit.

The thought brought Eric back to his present dilemma and reminded him of his anger toward the company. None of his father's bosses had even showed up at the hospital or funeral after his dad had given thirty-five years to the company.

"Not even a basket of flowers, you heartless pricks," Eric said kicking a tire as he walked past the front fender.

"All right, calm down now," he said to himself as much as to the van. Eric opened the door and climbed back into the driver's seat.

"Listen," he continued, "I lost my temper there for a minute. Sorry about that but I'm fucking starving. A little cooperation would be appreciated. I'm going to turn the key now, and if you start, I promise to behave better."

Episode 7

"Oh, yeah, I'm sorry about that kick, too," Eric added for good measure, "that won't happen again."

Eric kissed the palm of his left hand and pressed it gently on the dashboard as a final display of remorse. He turned the key and held the accelerator pedal to the floor, as his father had taught him when an engine flooded. After a minute of grinding, the van started. As Eric raced the engine, a black cloud emanated from the tail pipe. He let off on the gas, put the van into drive and pulled slowly away from the curb.

"Thanks for the help," he uttered aloud.

Eric inspected the houses as he drove. All the neat little brick bungalows and ranch houses looked no different than the first time he'd seen them as a child 1952. Allen Park, a mixed blue and white collar community just south of Detroit, never really changed which was good. Eric didn't like changes. He hadn't been outside in weeks because leaving the house made him jumpy. The difficulties with the truck hadn't helped. He was thankful none of the neighbors were outside and was especially glad that none of them had witnessed his temper tantrum. Eric didn't need any of the nosey dim wits to call the police and tell them he'd flipped out again. That would mean another trip to the hospital, an awful experience even when his father was still alive.

Eric made his way to Allen Road, the main drag through the city. Looking left, traffic was light with just a few cars and delivery trucks. He guessed some of the cars were coming from Inter City Baptist Church or the Thunderbowl bowling alley, both were just a quarter mile north. Their family attended the church until a deacon lectured Alan one Sunday on the evils of sipping Jack Daniel's and talking politics. Alan had replied sipping a little bourbon never endangered anyone's soul. Alan never returned though Nancy continued to take in services when not in the hospital. Eric hadn't seen the inside of the church since junior high, but had spent some time in the pool room in the bowling alley during high school.

Eric eased the van onto Allen Road and headed toward Kovalchek's Market.

Episode 8

When the cell phone rang, Darpak opened the cover.

"I'm not scheduled for surgery until Monday," he said clearly into the phone.

"Can your schedule be rearranged?" the voice inquired. "The patient is being be prepped for your arrival."

"I can be there by seven," Darpak continued, "have I examined this patient before?"

"No," the voice answered, "this is a new patient and her condition is somewhat worse than the last one."

"I understand," Darpak replied flatly then hung up.

He placed the box into the bottom desk drawer, slid it closed then locked it. The message instructed him to meet a female agent in Indianapolis. Male or female, it made little difference to Darpak. There would be nothing more to tonight's rendezvous than picking up the package. Despite his good looks, Darpak was not a lady's man. Though there had been opportunities, it was a rule he considered cardinal. Even if he was unmarried, there'd be no relationships inside the network. That could lead to attachments which impaired judgment.

Darpak put the keys in his pocket and walked to the coat rack in the corner of his office. After slipping on his suit coat, he went into the waiting area and walked to the door to the outer lobby. Making sure the lobby was empty, Darpak stepped out.

The Plymouth Medical Building is a three floored brick structure. Darpak shared the first floor with a gastroenterologist and two oncologists. He pushed open one of the double doors and stepped outside. After scanning the parking lot and walkway, he walked across the parking lot to his car. Like his office, home and wardrobe, Darpak's BMW sedan was immaculate. The vehicle was washed and vacuumed every week. Although it was two years old, the Beamer looked as if it had just been driven from the showroom.

At medical school, Darpak had taken much kidding about his compulsive neatness. Even after being on call for thirty-six hours, he looked like he'd stepped out of a fashion magazine. He always had at least one shower, a shave and two changes of scrubs during the shift. Darpak knew the others never understood his obsession. Then again, none of them had grown up in the filth and squalor in northern India. Darpak's deft in business was almost as good as his skill in the operating theatre. Among other assets, Darpak owned one-third of the medical building.

He pulled the key fob from his pocket and pressed unlock. The vehicle emitted a high pitched chirp as the door buttons popped up. Darpak got in, placed his brief case on the passenger's seat and closed the door. After starting the turbo charged engine, he let the car idle and took out his personal cell phone. He had not mentioned to Ravenna he would be late and though not on call, he had three patients recovering from surgeries. Having a back up plan in case the mobile phone's signal was down was another example of his obsessiveness. Attention to detail and thoroughness were traits that made him a good surgeon.

Darpak wanted to be a physician, even as a poor peasant boy in Kashmir. He was intelligent but poor nonetheless. The monks at the Hindu temple noticed his brilliance and provided educational opportunities available to young Indian children who met their criteria. Darpak met the criteria. He was brilliant, destitute,

Episode 8

and most importantly had experienced great suffering at the hands of Pakistani Muslims.

Darpak dialed the cell phone.

"Hello, Taj residence," Darpak heard Ravenna's voice.

"Is the handsome doctor at home?" Darpak teased.

"No, but his lovely, but lonely wife is here," Ravenna replied.

"In that case, is it safe for her lover to sneak over and see her tonight?" Darpak continued.

"It depends on which lover it is and what time he intends to sneak over. I expect my husband to be home about seven," Ravenna enjoyed the game.

"Well, I did not realize you had more than one lover, I am truly hurt. I thought I was the only one. Tell me, how many do you have? I hope it is not many. I don't mind sharing you with your husband because he truly is handsome. But I must say to share you with others, would be something that I could not tolerate. So tell me lovely Ravenna, with the raven hair and brown eyes, who are these other men?"

"Let me see," Ravenna replied softly, "there is the gardener, the pool boy and oh yes, there is my tennis instructor, and let's not leave out the check out boy at the super market. To be truthful, he is the most virile.

"Well, that hurts deeply" Darpak paused, "I was planning to sneak into your bedroom around ten o'clock tonight knowing your husband will be coming home late."

"Oh, Darpak," Ravenna said in a disappointed tone, "are you on call again tonight?"

"No, but there is some business I have to attend to in Indianapolis. I should be home before midnight. I'm not on call tomorrow, so we'll have a nice dinner and maybe catch a movie, I promise," Darpak replied.

"Okay, I'll try to stay up for you, but if I am too fatigued from the check out boy, it will be your loss," Ravenna teased. "Be careful driving home."

His decision to marry an Indian Hindu woman had been a good one. Ravenna understood the sacrifices necessary to maintain a medical practice. A surgeon's schedule could easily destroy a marriage. He'd seen the turmoil his colleagues endured with their spoiled American wives. In the Indian culture, there was an implicit understanding of how the welfare of the family revolves around education, hard work and sacrifice. Education was also a priority for girls and participation by females in the workforce at the highest levels was encouraged. Ravenna had been a student at The National Technical University when they met and pursued a post graduate degree in statistical analysis while Darpak had been in medical school.

She had also grown up in austere conditions, but never endured the hardships or violence that had engulfed his life. Ravenna was from a southern province, a tropical paradise compared to Darpak's Kashmir. Not only was the land in the lower altitude of Ravenna's home green and lush, the population was almost entirely Hindu. Strife between Muslims and Hindus existed on a much smaller scale there. She had witnessed famine and disease on the streets of Lamayuru, her home town, but had not experienced them herself. Darpak knew hunger and depravation on a personal level. His life had taken some fortunate turns and he often wondered if it was more than he deserved. Here he was, a poor fatherless peasant boy, living in the United States, driving a BMW and wealthy enough to buy or sell most of his neighbors.

His success had been accomplished through hard work, but there was more to it than that. Darpak realized almost everyone in the world works hard, yet the majority have to slave to just survive. There was a reason for his prosperity; a reason why he been given wealth and power. It was destiny that Krishna put him where he was, in a position to protect and preserve the tenants of his faith. And he would perform the duties even though they may be at odds with the oath he swore upon becoming a physician. These were vows he had sworn long before medical school. Vows people in western cultures would never understand. A pledge to protect his family, his home and his faith. It was an oath that many young Hindu boys in the windswept

Episode 8

mountains bordering Muslim Pakistan had taken before him. Kashmir would remain Hindu.

Darpak knew the world order had changed because of September 11. It had opened the Americans eyes. Now they too had experienced the wrath of militant Islam and could no longer ignore the atrocities his people had endured for decades. Americans now understood Hindu and Moslem animosities were not simply the result of two fanatical religious sects, in a far off corner of the world, killing each other for no reason. Americans were now forced to take sides. While unwilling to proclaim in public, those in power knew there was something to be gained by aiding the Indian Hindu's because their operatives were willing to do things Americans were not yet willing to do. The Americans now shared their objective; but only because September 11 had occurred in New York City instead of Bombay or New Delhi.

Darpak understood the grief of the families who lost loved ones on that day. His own father and uncle were murdered when he was nine. The Muslim militia who took their lives crossed the border thirty miles north of their home. When the fighting stopped, Darpak was left fatherless like so many other children in Kashmir. When he got older, it surprised Darpak how the world ignored the fighting in Kashmir. With India's and Pakistan's nuclear capability, such hatred and revenge, if left unchecked, could lead to landscape changes of unimaginable perspectives. It was this hatred that rendered Darpak fatherless, and it was the same hatred that had left his mother widowed and starving. The Hindu monks had capitalized on the situation. They knew Darpak was a commodity to be molded for their purpose. The monks provided him with food and shelter. They educated him and groomed him to attend India's highest technical school, then funded three years of medical school at Johns Hopkins. It had been a long range plan, something Indian's understand. Now there was a debt to repay; a blood debt.

"I'll be careful," Darpak told his wife then closed the cell phone as he turned onto Indiana Highway 36.

Episode 9

Ronnie walked to his Explorer and slid behind the steering wheel. He hesitated before inserting the key into the ignition.

"Amy Irwin, and Denny Williams, all in the same day," he said in disbelief. "Amy Irwin, what the hell?" he repeated. "How long has it been?"

Ronnie closed his eyes. He'd last been to the Irwin home when he was twenty-two, that had been thirty-three years ago. That night had not been pleasant. It was the last time he had seen Bobbie and their confrontation had been intense. They had only spoken once since; when Bobbie called from Tokyo while on leave between his second and third tours in Viet Nam. He had been drinking heavily. Venting his anger, he told Ronnie when it came to finding his next best friend, he'd try the Viet Cong. At least with the VC, Bobbie added, he knew what to expect. This last comment hurt deeply. Ronnie sat silently while Bobbie raged. There was no rationalizing the issue. There were no apologies to be offered knowing none would ever be accepted. It was a chasm that would remain; a gulf that could not be bridged.

Ronnie backed down the driveway and turned onto West River Road. Heading along the narrow two lane road, he remembered the road was closed at the water treatment plant. Getting to the county bridge would require a detour.

The island of Grosse Ile lies in the Detroit River twenty miles south of Detroit. Seven miles long and two miles across at its widest point, the population hovered around eight thousand. The Island was not as populous when Ronnie's dad had taken he and Bobbie fishing there as young boys. Then it was a quiet, secluded place with a boat launch near the best fishing holes in the lower Detroit River. As boys, Ronnie and Bobbie loved going there and had pledged they'd live there when they were grown ups. The Island's popularity had increased dramatically since then, but it was still a nice quiet place to live and raise a family.

When he reached Ferry Street, Ronnie turned left and continued to Meridian Road. Turning right, he kept his speed under the posted limit. There was a speed trap just ahead and he didn't want to be delayed. The trap was usually in place during early morning or late afternoons and was designed to catch unaware off Islanders. Ronnie spied the squad car concealed in its usual hiding place, a small clearing on the opposite side of the road. The trees and bushes had been removed just enough to accommodate the Crown Victoria Police Cruiser. The location was ideal, directly across the street from the elementary school. The speed limit dropped from forty to twenty-five miles per hour a hundred yards in each direction. Signs indicating the reduced speed limit were strategically placed making it near impossible to comply.

The school building sits a half mile back from the road and is served by a separate road so there is no real need for drivers to slow. To Ronnie's knowledge, no one ever contested their speeding ticket in court, most drivers were too embarrassed to explain to a judge why they were speeding in a school zone. The fines levied by the township were steep and a sore point for residents of surrounding communities who sometimes viewed Islanders as rich, elitist snobs

Approaching the school, Ronnie saw a glimmer of chrome from the cruiser's front bumper and waved at the officer. Officer Matt glanced up from his radar gun and waved back. Ronnie didn't know Matt's last name, everyone just called him Officer Matt. It was an improvement from his previous title of Oil Change Matt a nickname he'd gotten while working at the Island Shell station. Rita, who worked behind the counter, gave him the nickname because his mechanical skills were so limited, oil changes were the only repairs he was allowed to do. While Matt hated the nickname, it was a step up from Tow Truck Matt, Lawn Mowing Matt or Floor Washing Matt all of which Rita used as need arose.

The Island Shell Station is one of two gas stations on the Island. The other is a full service Union 76. Ronnie maintained the Island's demographics were pretty much defined by which station a person patronized. Long time, gentrified Island residents frequented the Union 76. The station had been owned by the Dickenson family for as long as anyone remembered and looked like something from a Norman Rockwell painting. It has such charm, Nissan Motors featured it one year in their televised advertisements.

Timbo Dickenson worked diligently to preserve the station's original character. At six feet two inches with his shaved head, Timbo intimidated the local high school boys who had called on his then teenaged daughters. Though the girls were now grown and gone, he had retained his image. His Union 76 also retains its 1950s gas station image both inside and out. Self service is not an option at Dickenson's.

Timbo and his employees start each day with immaculate uniforms. The shirts are egg shell white, heavily starched and pressed with first names stitched in red letters above their breast pockets. Though grease stains may be scattered across the shirts by day's end, the station is always spotless. The floors in the office and sales area are original hardwood and maintained in pristine condition. The candy counter also is original. The oak framing is polished and the glass wiped clean with Windex daily. The counter still stocks 5th Avenue Bars, Paydays and Wrigley Spearmint Gum.

The Island's other station, the Shell sits at the intersection of the Island's two main drags, Meridian Road and Macomb Street. It's a favorite hang out for local teenagers who gather under the pale yellow light cast by the giant illuminated sea shell to buy gas, cigarettes, Mountain Dews and Baffo pizza rolls from their buddies who work there part time. During the summer, cars line up two abreast at the pumps. Muscled boys wearing tight Abercrombie tee shirts flirt with shapely young girls, in pastel tube tops and low cut jeans. They lean out of car windows exchanging information about whose parents are out of town. Every town has a hang out, usually it's a fast food joint, but the Island's building code prohibits fast food restaurants. Burger King signs or McDonald's arches might mar the landscape so the Island Shell fills the void.

After passing the speed trap, Ronnie brought the Explorer to a stop at the traffic light at Macomb and Meridian. He could see Steve Hall, the owner of the station, standing under an older model Oldsmobile resting on one of the two hoists. Glancing down Macomb Street, Ronnie could see the downtown businesses. The Kroger Supermarket, Save-On Drugs, The Island coin car wash and Lloyd's Bar and Grill, the local watering hole, provided most of Ronnie's needs. Continuing down the one mile stretch is the hardware store, the bakery, Nate's Meat Market and two real estate offices.

When the light changed to green, Ronnie continued south on Meridian. He passed the new Police and Fire Station and noted a sign announcing a fire department open house. Catching the green light at Grosse Ile Parkway, Ronnie turned right toward the county bridge which connects the southern end of the Island to the mainland. While turning, he waved at a Grosse Ile Garden Club member pulling weeds from one of the flower beds planted on the four corners.

As he approached the draw bridge, Ronnie could hear a familiar hum resonate from the undercarriage of the Explorer as the tires passed from the asphalt pavement to the metal grated flooring of the bridge. The metal roadway is slippery when wet, especially during winter when conditions require strict adherence to the twenty mile per hour speed limit. It was late summer and not raining, so Ronnie maintained his speed at thirty-five.

Episode 9

Gazing over the guard rails, he could see small power boats making their way along the Detroit River. The pale aqua color of the water and set against the lush, green landscape of the shoreline was pleasant. Ronnie could see a large sail boat up river approaching the bridge. In a few minutes he knew the bridge would swing open to allow the sail boat to pass.

Ronnie still couldn't believe Denny was a Great Lakes Pilot. Then again, Ronnie sometimes found it difficult to believe he was fifty-five and living on the Island. It was even harder to conceive he was living without Beth. The thought reminded him about the call from Amy Irwin and a tinge of guilt ran through him. He and Bobbie had never planned it this way. Their dream had been so different. They were supposed to live in grand houses on East River Road and fish the river every chance they got. They were to spend their lives hanging out together. That was the pledge, to remain best friends for life. But none of that had happened.

Episode 10

Ahmed unzipped his blue jeans. His father would say they were a symbol of the decadent west. Haleem believed luxuries like blue jeans reflected an ideology of materialism which led to abandonment by Allah. So Haleem insisted his family dress in traditional clothes. Buying jeans had been one of Ahmed's first priorities and he had paid eighty dollars for them. It was an unimaginable sum to the poor in Kabul, but Ahmed didn't care.

Ahmed wore his pants slung so low the tops of his plaid boxer shorts showed. Today he'd added a pale blue Detroit Lions jersey with the number twenty and Sanders printed in silver letters on the back. Two gold chains and Dior sunglasses, completed the look. Ahmed flirted with the blonde girl who worked at Sunglasses Hut but nothing came from it. She was from west Fairlane Hills. Ahmed slipped off the jeans, pushed his Nike Jordan's aside with his foot then walked over to the small closet. He hung the jeans on a coat hook and the jersey next to the jeans.

In his boxer shorts and shirtless, Ahmed looked like any of the other young Arab men in east Fairlane Hills. At five foot eleven, he was taller than his father and towered over his uncles. He weighed one hundred and seventy-five pounds, little of which was fat. Ahmed's hair was very thick and worn in the quasi military cut popular with other young men in the neighborhood. Ahmed had a thin angular nose, like his mother, which made him look as much Jewish as Arab. Young men with his likeness were favored for reconnaissance and were sought after as suicide bombers. Ahmed was the only boy in his family to inherit his mother's Palestinian features. His brothers looked distinctly Syrian, they were heavier set and had their father's broad nose, low eye brow and kinky black hair.

Ahmed was clean shaven and had no intention of growing the full beard his CIA contact wanted him to have. Charlie believed the beard would help him connect with any members of Al Qaeda or Hamas living in east Fairlane Hills but Ahmed had convinced Charlie appearing like a young secular Muslim was a better strategy. Ahmed argued successfully he could better fit in and after making contacts, it would appear he had been persuaded into radical Islam.

It didn't take Ahmed long to discover fitting in was more expensive than anticipated. Baggy jeans and football jerseys were okay during the day, but nighttime was different. Hanging out at clubs and coffee bars required tight fitting shirts of silk or shiny polyester. Jeans were replaced by micro fibered slacks and black leather shoes with prominent heels. Gold chains were complemented with expensive watches, gold bracelets and rings. Expensive colognes were also required. It had taken some effort to convince Charlie to increase his stipend.

Ahmed took the dishdasha off the hanger and slipped the traditional Muslim robe over his head. After pulling it over his shoulders, the robe fell to full length with the bottom hem just above his ankles. The dishdasha was white with a high collar. It had intricate geometric designs embroidered into the upper half. Wearing the Islamic robe to Mosque was a concession he had made reluctantly to Charlie. Ahmed slipped his feet into the sandals and took his kufis off the shelf. He placed the prayer hat on his head and walked out of the bedroom. As he headed down the steps, Ahmed could feel the air wafting on his bare legs.

Episode 10

    He descended the stairs quietly to avoid disturbing the old woman who lived with her husband and adult son in the flat below. When he first met the elderly couple, Ahmed assumed they were probably near deaf allowing him to play music and his television as loudly as he wanted. Ahmed also hoped their adult son might provide some insight about night life around east Fairlane Hills. He had been wrong on both counts. The old woman had the hearing of an owl and the son was feeble minded. The old man suffered from kidney disease and spent most days sitting in a cushioned chase lounge by the garage.

    The two family flat sat on a double lot on a narrow residential street. The old woman meticulously tended a garden that took up most of the extra lot. A large trellis loaded with purple grapes sat next to the garage. The old man's chase was positioned by the trellis shading him from the afternoon sun. Ahmed watched one day as the old man moved from his morning settee to the chase. Changing locations required great effort and two canes. When the old woman came out to help him, she reached down and picked up the furry white cat that was constantly curled up in the old man's lap. It took five minutes of foot shuffling for the old man to traverse the thirty feet to the shady trellis. Watching his pained movements was so depressing, Ahmed vowed he would never become old and incapacitated. Better to die having fun in some reckless act of youth than to suffer that fate.

    Ahmed closed the door and walked to his car. Having a few extra minutes, he'd take the long way to the mosque. The less time spent at the mosque the better. Ahmed knew informants at the mosque would relay his arrival time to Charlie. To date, Ahmed had not been able to identify them.

    He turned right on Warren Avenue and drove through the commercial center of Fairlane Hills's Arab community. The six square mile section is home to thirty thousand Arabs, the largest population outside the middle east. The shops and markets provided an opportunity to check out girls as they shopped for Halal meats and vegetables.

The stores were a flurry of activity. Women were pushing shopping carts or carrying armloads of groceries in paper bags reminding Ahmed of the bazaars in Kabul. A good number of the women wore traditional head scarves but few were covered head to foot in burkas.

Ahmed still hadn't gotten use to women drivers, something never seen in Kabul where driving was as forbidden as reading for females. Getting caught doing either resulted in severe punishment or even death. Yet here in east Fairlane Hills, Muslim women freely drove cars without head coverings. Passing the Shatilla Bakery, Ahmed stole a quick glance toward the coffee shop. He planned to stop there after the mosque.

The El Baddar mosque, a large brick building that originally housed The Fairlane Hills Methodist Church, was just ahead. The Methodists initially tried to proselytize the neighborhood's growing Arab population, but eventually gave up and moved their soul saving operations to Detroit's western suburbs.

Ahmed pulled into the parking lot. Walking through the double doors, he returned two men's greetings with a wish for peace and prosperity also to their families, if it be the will of Allah of course. Ahmed removed his sandals and continued barefoot. He walked to the front and took a place where men were kneeling and preparing themselves for the call to prayer. He took a place next to an older man wearing a worn and tattered dishdasha. Ahmed placed both hands to the side of his head, then quickly glanced toward the women's section at the back of the mosque. Ahmed knew even secular women who bared their heads at the markets, would never attempt such liberties. While they may have driven themselves to the mosque with uncovered heads, such liberties would never be attempted here.

Ahmed felt guilty about having lustful thoughts in the mosque. While head scarves made it more difficult, he could still pick out the pretty ones. There were also certain things even traditional worship dresses couldn't hide from a young man's probing eyes. While looking at the row of women, a man's silhouette caught his eye. Ahmed wasn't certain if the dim light

Episode 10

had distorted his vision, but thought he recognized the man. Ahmed closed his eyes to make them more sensitive, but when he opened them the young man was no longer there. Assuming he was mistaken, Ahmed turned his head back toward the front as the Imam walked in. At the same moment, Ahmed felt someone brush against him. It was the young man and Ahmed had not been mistaken. He knew the man.

Looking down, Ahmed noticed the young Arab was missing his left hand; it had been amputated at the wrist. Ahmed remembered the day the hand had been lost. They had been thirteen year old boys. When the shell in the AK47 jammed, the boy had mistakenly placed his hand on the end of the barrel while he tried to clear the breech. The gun discharged. That had been seven years ago. Now here he was in a mosque half the world away. Ahmed turned to face the young man.

"Peace to you and your family, Ahmed," the voice was familiar. "May, Allah be with your father and brother in paradise."

"And peace to your family also," replied a surprised Ahmed, "if it be the will of Allah."

Episode 11

The speed limit on Allen Road is thirty-five miles per hour, but Eric kept the van at twenty. The Allen Park police are notorious for strict enforcement and Eric had never forgotten their injustice. As a high school senior, Eric had defended himself in court against them but failed to make his case. The ordeal only reinforced his determination to attend law school. Eric's father, Alan, paid the fine and court costs without complaint.

The speeding ticket infuriated Eric, because he had always been a safe driver. He was not a hot rodder and never took chances. Eric didn't even play the radio loudly which to his teen-aged buddies, seemed out of character. It was another example of his enigmatic puzzle.

The high school coaches also found Eric to be a conundrum. He had wonderful athletic gifts but possessed an independent spirit. Privately they believed Eric lacked commitment, discipline and desire. They were wrong. Eric possessed those attributes but simply exercised them differently. Eric loved competition, he simply chose to channel his passion into debate, forensic speaking and politics.

Eric's insatiable desire to excel in cerebral disciplines was beyond the coaches' comprehension. They would never understand him. He liked football, basketball and track, he simply didn't love them. The coaches believed he could someday play professionally but Eric made it clear to them he never planned to waste his life in such pursuits.

While dismaying to his high school coaches, Eric's intellect provided a gifted genius for strategic planning which became evident during his freshman year. Eric became obsessed with the television series Mission Impossible. He watched the show religiously every Sunday night and dreamed of leading his own Impossible Mission Force. Eric loved everything about the show, especially the beginning when a wooden match ignited and the flame was placed at the end of a fuse. As the hypnotic theme music played and the fuse burned, Eric waited anxiously to hear of the teams mission.

Eric idolized the lead character Jim Phelps who received his weekly mission from an audio tape. When the recording ended, the recorder would self destruct, leaving Phelps to grapple with accepting the mission. The missions were never turned down and were always completed successfully by his smart and savvy team members. Their ingenious plans were always a fraction of a step ahead of the bad guys' evil twists and turns. Eric desperately wanted to assemble his own team, but needed an impossible mission. His wish came true sophomore year when he decided to steal a set of the year's chemistry tests from his teacher's office.

To complete the mission, Eric planned to steal three keys and make duplicates. He would need a key to the school building, a key to the chemistry teachers office and a key to the file cabinet. Like Jim Phelps, Eric's first action was to select a second in command then assemble his impossible mission force.

After football practice Eric wolfed his dinner telling his father he had to study. In his bedroom, Eric pulled the previous years annual from his book shelf. Eric skipped to the pictures of the freshmen class and began reviewing them one by one. The choice for second in command was quickly obvious.

Episode 11

Eric knew Tom Allen was the only choice. He was high intellect and shared Eric's love of adventure. Tom was smart, shrewd and most importantly, had an independent air. It would be he and Tom who entered the school and stole the tests. If something went wrong, they also would be the ones holding the bag.

Eric knew his selection would hurt Wes's feelings. They had been best friends since kindergarden but team selection had to be based exclusively on talent. The team would only be successful if each member was perfect for his role. He would make it up later to Wes and the decision was for Wes's own protection. If they were caught, expulsion would be immediate. If that happened, Eric would never be able to enter Wes's home again. As much as he loved the challenge of stealing the tests, banishment from Wes's was something Eric could not bear. When his parents separated, he had lived with Wes's family while his parents sorted their lives one final time. Eric owed Wes's parents.

When Eric presented Tom with his idea, Tom's reaction was as expected.

"Cool, let's do it," had been Tom's casual reply.

There was no hesitation in his voice. Eric studied Tom's body language for any sign of doubt, but there was nothing betraying any lack of confidence. There had been no looking around in hesitation, just a calm reply of agreement. Eric would get the same cool reply years later when they roomed together at the University of Michigan and joined Students for a Democratic Society.

After two hours, the basics had been drafted. Mr. Drew's keys would be taken from the coaches locker room while he took his daily jog after school. Copies of the keys would be made at the hardware and the originals returned before Mr. Drew returned.

Eric and Tom agreed that team members with particular required skills would be recruited from their gang who hung out in Wesley's basement. With Tom at his side, Eric presented the plan to the first two candidates. Jack, who worked part time at the hardware and could make the keys, was a priority. Bobbie would be the runner from the school to the hardware. They would also have to find a role for Ronnie because Bobbie would never agree unless he was included.

After hearing the plan, Bobbie and Jack were receptive but apprehensive because of possible expulsion. At first, Bobbie seemed suspicious of Eric's motives. Bobbie couldn't understand why Eric would be willing to take the risk. When Eric asked if there were any questions, Bobbie focused on the issue.

"Jesus, Eric," Bobbie inquired, "you fucken' got an A on the first quiz no sweat, and didn't make anything but A's all last year. Why would you want to do this? What's in it for you?"

"The challenge, my boy, the challenge," Eric answered.

"Shit, Eric," Bobbie continued, "Ain't the class itself enough of a challenge for you?"

"Not really, Bobbie. Now what will be a challenge is not laughing out loud every time old man Drew passes out those pre-printed tests. He's such a lazy ass, sort of serves him right. I mean what kind of job is that when the teacher gets the tests from the book publisher. It shows a lack of originality. I can't respect anyone lacking originality," Eric retorted briskly.

"Hell, Eric," Jack interrupted, "you're the one with the most to lose if we get caught. You will never get into your beloved Harvard if we get caught." Jack interjected sarcastically.

"Ah now, getting caught," Eric spat back, "that's the operative word. First, we'd have to get caught. That just won't happen. It ain't in the stars, Jackie boy."

"Yeah, but Eric,' Bobbie replied, "you got a great plan for getting the key's, but you haven't said diddle shit about how we are going to get into the school without getting caught.'

"Listen up boys, you just leave that part up to me and ole' Tommy here, we got that all mapped out. You just deliver the copies of the keys Jack, and doctor the inventory logs. Bobbie, you keep old man Biondi distracted while Jack's doing his thing. The actual entry into the school will be Duck Soup.

"Duck soup, who the hell eats duck soup?" Jack asked.

"It's a figure of speech, moron," Eric retorted impatiently.

Episode 11

"You know, the Marx brothers, the movie, Duck Soup?" Tom added sarcastically, "don't be such a dip shit."

"Jesus, Tom, honestly are you the only one around here I can communicate with?" Eric said with a wry grin.

"So are you assholes in or out?" Eric asked flatly.

"This tape will self destruct at the end of this message. Remember Jim, if you or any member of your team is caught, the ambassador and the United States government will disavow any knowledge of your actions," Tom added. The line was from the show when Phelps received his mission.

"Well, are you guys in or are you a couple of pussies?" Eric asked.

Jack leaned back on his chair and stared up at the living room ceiling. While the other three wore beat up jeans and sweat shirts, Jack was dressed in pale blue Levis and a madras plaid shirt with a button down collar. Appearance was important to Jack. He supported his wardrobe by working part time at the hardware. Jack possessed a natural mechanical aptitude and loved to tinker with things. Eric understood the importance of Jack's role and was prepared to pull Jack aside and tell him that this was the first of several missions. Jack began flittering the tassels on his loafers. Tasseled loafers had replaced penny loafers and Jack had wasted little time in buying a pair.

"Seems like this plan pretty much depends on me making those keys," Jack uttered in reply. "So seems there should be something extra in it for me."

Jacks comments caught Eric and Tom off guard. The issue of negotiation had never entered their minds.

"What do you mean Jack?" Eric asked warily. "You are pretty damn lucky we included you at all. We have back up plans for everything Jack. Even the keys."

"I'm in,' Jack replied quickly.

"Count me in, too" Bobbie added, not wanting to be perceived as the only pussy in the group.

"Well boys, let's celebrate the occasion," Eric said pulling two bottles from his father's liquor cabinet. "I'll add water later to make up the missing amounts," he continued pouring shots of bourbon and scotch into four glasses.

"I like mine on the rocks," Eric added plopping ice cubes into his glass, "how about you girls or maybe you're straight up types."

"I'll take some ice," Bobbie answered not knowing what on the rocks or straight up meant.

Eric poured the drinks and handed each boy a glass. Jack took the glass and swallowed a small sip. The scotch burned his throat. His drinking experiences had been limited to beer. Being curious, Jack decided it an opportune time to exploit Eric's good mood.

"Okay, Eric," Jack interjected; "once we have the keys, what's the rest of the plan?"

"Just trust me Jack, you know all you need to know for now," Eric answered calmly.

"Well, I already agreed to do my part; I'd just like to know the rest," Jack replied taking another sip of liquor, "damned fine bourbon, I might add," attempting an air of sophistication.

"Well numb nuts, you didn't get bourbon moron, you got scotch" Eric laughed.

"Drink a lot of whiskey, do ya Jack?" Tom giggled.

Jack was embarrassed but stood his ground. Bobbie wondered if the alcohol was affecting Jack's thinking, it wasn't like him to be so assertive.

"What's your favorite brand?" Tom continued, "Maybe Eric can ask his dad to stock it for you next time?"

Bobbie laughed, everyone respected Tom's lightening quick wit. Bobbie hoped Jack's judgment wasn't impaired enough to get into a put down contest with Tom. At times, the best Eric could do against Tom was a draw.

"Well, asshole," Jack replied, "I have twice the risk everyone else has. While I've said that I am in, and I am in," Jack looked at Tom, "I think you should tell us the rest of the plan."

Bobbie's head was spinning from the whiskey and he couldn't follow Jack's train of thought.

Episode 11

"Why do you have more risk than the rest of us?" Bobbie inquired.

"Well, if we get caught, then I lose my job at the hardware and get expelled. Try that one on for size, Toothpick." Jack replied slurring Bobbie's nick name.

Bobbie recoiled, he was six foot two and weighed a hundred and fifty-five pounds. Everyone had always called him Stick because he was so tall and skinny. During a football game the previous fall, the quarterback said he would try to throw the ball to Stick down the right side line. Tom had remarked Toothpick would be more appropriate after the other team got through with him. From that day on Bobbie was Toothpick, a nickname his mom even used on occasion.

"Okay, numb nuts," Eric said to Jack, "here's the rest of the plan. After you make copies of the keys, we will break into the school at night. Old man Thacker, the janitor, goes home for lunch around eight o'clock. While he leaves, Tom and I will go in and lift the tests. We have a communication system set up. The Thacker's live two doors from Ronnie's. When he sees old man Thacker pull up his driveway, Ronnie will call the pay phone out front of the school. That will be our signal to go in. When old man Thacker leaves, Ronnie will call again. We'll have five minutes to get out. Toothpick, you will be out front listening for the call and will signal with a flash light to the lookouts at each end of the school. One lookout will run to the chemistry lab windows and signal Tom and me with a flashlight. If something goes wrong, say a cop drives up, or anything like that, Bobbie will signal the lookouts."

"Who will the look outs be?" Jack asked.

"Wes and Randy, now is that all, are we done?" Eric turned to Jack.

"Well, I have one" Bobbie said taking a swallow of liquor. He let the ice cube fall into his mouth. After swishing it around a couple of times he spat the cube back into the glass.

"This has to be good," Tom said rolling his eyes. When Bobbie flashed Tom the finger, they all started laughing.

"Okay, Einstein, what's your query?" Eric asked.

"Hey asshole," Bobbie answered with irritation. "I ain't no queer!"

"No, dip shit, query as in question. Tom, I repeat, are you the only one I can talk to?" Eric looked at Tom.

Tom laughed and poured another drink. Tom's alcohol tolerance was equaled only by Eric's.

"Okay, Bobbie, I'm sorry. Now what's your question?" Eric said earnestly.

"Okay, Eric. No offense taken. My question is, who's going to be the girl member of our IMF team," Bobbie asked with a deadpan face.

The other three boys burst out laughing.

"We're talking about stealing keys, breaking into the school, stealing tests. Possible juvenile court and expulsion and you're worried about who the girl team member is?" Tom asked incredulously.

"Well, all that shit you just said is possible," Bobbie said, "but I don't worry about that. I can only do my part is all. I want to know if we're gonna have some big tits to look at before and after. That's all I am saying."

The other three boys burst out laughing again. Bobbie's comment was prophetic. His attitude would serve him well years later in Vietnam. His ability to block out distractions would save his life. Eric wiped tears of laughter off his cheeks and looked at Bobbie.

"Sorry to tell you this, numb nuts, but there's no girls," Eric responded. "Why do you ask?'

"Well, on Mission Impossible, they have that blonde agent, you know, Cinnamon. Then there's that other agent occasionally with the black hair, the pretty one. So I thought we might have a girl on our team," Bobbie finished.

"Well, this is our first mission, so for now, no girls. Is that okay with you Agent Irwin?" Eric said.

"Who'd you have in mind anyway, Bobbie?" Jack asked.

"I don't have anyone for certain in mind, but I was thinking, how about Cate Cassadea?" Bobbie answered quickly.

"Cate Cassadea, Cate Cassadea! Is she all you ever think about? You been talking about her since seventh grade. Shit Bob-

Episode 11

bie, you've never even kissed her and you want her to be part of the team?" Jack shot back.

"Hell, Bobbie," Tom interrupted, "I wouldn't exactly say you're looking to add some big knockers to the team with that selection. She's damn near as skinny as your bony ass."

Jack and Bobbie started laughing again. Stopping to catch his breath, Jack noticed that Eric hadn't joined their levity. Jack also noticed a flash of anger at the corners of Eric's eyes when Bobbie mentioned Cate's name and recalled Eric's failure to join their banter about girls in their class that they'd like to bop. When Cate's name came up recently Eric acted strangely. While shooting pool in Wes's basement the prior week, they decided to list the top ten girls they'd like to have one shot at. Everyone had Cate near the top of their list but when they asked Eric, he replied that it was a stupid game and he would rather just shoot pool. It was apparent Eric had something for Cate, then again they all'd had crushes on her at one time or another. Besides being knock down gorgeous, she might beat out both Tom and Eric for valedictorian. So Eric had it bad for Catie. Interesting, Jack thought deciding to put that little nugget away for later use.

"Bobbie, your choice is a little surprising, considering the make out session you had with Beth McGowan last weekend. Didn't seem like you were thinking 'bout Catie then. Did you decide to change the menu from Italian to Irish or what?" Jack asked.

"Screw you, Jack Off," Bobbie shot back angrily, "let's not talk about Beth. Let's leave her out of the discussion. She's a non topic, okay?"

"Okay, man you don't have to be so sensitive, I was just giving you some shit. Hell you can dry hump with Bethany M all night for all I care," Jack replied with a loud laugh.

"Enough girl talk, and mission talk, let's get some pizza. All this drinking made me hungry," Bobbie added.

"Oh, you mean your one drink, Bobbie. Are you sure you can stagger down to Marino's?" Tom replied sarcastically.

"Fuck you Tom," Bobbie answered, "give me another shot; I can handle it, no sweat."

"Maybe we better get down to Marino's quickly, Toothpick, those zits on your face need an oil change and Marino's is just the answer," Tom kept up his barrage.

"You can be such an asshole, no make that such a big asshole," Bobbie retorted.

Though angry, Bobbie knew he was no match for anything physical with Tom.

"Come on Bobbie, lighten up. Hell, I'll buy you the first slice when we get there," Eric interjected.

Jack was relieved Eric had come to Bobbie's rescue. Because Bobbie's parents were divorced, Jack assumed Eric felt some kind of bond because they were the only ones from broken homes.

Coming out of his daydream, Eric stopped the van at the light on Allen Road and Hanford. He looked over at Marino's Bakery & Pizza and saw four teenaged boys walk out the door carrying two pizzas.

"I wonder if they are going to Wes's to shoot pool?" he asked himself aloud, but knew that wasn't possible. Wes had been gone for twenty years. Eric always knew nothing good came from reckless driving but had never been able to register that point with Wesley. It was one mission in which he had failed miserably.

Episode 12

Cate pushed the garage door opener button and waited. As the door lifted from the floor, she surveyed for anything that looked out of place. Cate's therapist said her compulsions were based on reasonable fear and were normal. That'd been thirty-five years ago. Cate was better now, but would never be cured. Though she'd learned to control her fears, they were always there just beneath the surface.

Before Kelly's death, Cate didn't fear dark, empty places. On occasion, when walking alone into an empty place, her mind would flash back to the fall of 1969, the last time she had seen Kelly alive. It had been a beautiful fall day. The trees were a barrage of colors, the air was crisp and they had been young and full of energy. Kelly and Brad had driven to visit her in East Lansing. From Cate's apartment just off campus they had walked to Varsity Pizza. Kelly loved their roast beef sandwiches. Cate and Brad ordered Italian subs and fries. The waitress brought their order in white paper bags with three large Cokes tucked into a corrugated drink carton. They had taken the food to Michigan States Botanical Gardens for a picnic.

Sitting under a sprawling oak tree, they talked about nothing and laughed about everything. They were close to the football stadium and could hear cheers erupting intermittently. They planned to walk to the stadium for the second half but never got around to it. Autumn Saturdays with Kelly were always such fun; then again any time with Kelly had been fun.

Kelly, her freshmen year roommate, had grown up on a family farm in Grand Haven, a small town on Lake Michigan. Barely five feet tall, Kelly was a tiny firecracker with auburn hair and blazing green eyes. She had a wicked sense of humor, a malicious smile and a razor tongue. They had hit it off immediately and their freshmen year had been incredible. Life was endless adventure. They were eighteen, away from home and coming of age at a time when so much was changing. Cate wondered if those years with Kelly had been the only time she had ever been truly alive.

They had smoked pot for the first time together at a fraternity party just before Thanksgiving break. Everything seemed so hysterically funny. When they went back into the party, they'd laughed so hard Cate was certain she'd peed her pants several times. The music sounded better; and the snacks even tasted better. Potato chips tasted like thinly sliced wafers of ambrosia, pretzels were culinary delights prepared by a master chef.

They stayed at the party for a while blowing off preppy dressed frat boys with stylish hair and even white teeth. After an hour, they left and walked to Grand River Avenue. The street seemed a cornucopia of delights. There were tacos and burgers. There was pizza and subs. After debating McDonald's versus Burger King, they settled on Big Macs. Trying to order, they found themselves nearly mute when the boy in a maroon shirt with a golden arch on his breast asked them what they wanted. They looked at each other blankly before degenerating into muffled giggles; it was such a deep philosophical question. They eventually managed to articulate their desires. When the young man slid the Big Macs, fries and orange drinks across the counter, the girls felt proud they'd maintained sufficiently to find a place to sit.

The next morning, they pledged to spend the rest of their Saturday nights together. Their covenant remained in tact until fall semester of their sophomore year. They had been sipping beer from plastic cups at a house party, making cutting comments about several boys standing by the keg when Kelly's eyes flashed in recognition. One of the boys looked in Kelly's direction. By his wide smile it was obvious he also recognized her.

Brad was a pretty boy with long chestnut hair parted in the middle. While long past summer, he still had sun streaks in his hair. He was wearing a blue University of Michigan tee shirt and a pair of bell bottom Levis with a peace sign embroidered on the left thigh. When he spoke, Cate knew instantly she was going to like him. He had a confident air but even with his good looks, Cate knew he was not conceited. It was obvious he had eyes for no one in the room but Kelly. When he walked up to them, Kelly spoke first.

"Nice shirt asshole, lost track of where you are Brad?"

Typical Kelly, Cate thought, go immediately for the jugular.

"Hey, Kelly, way to greet someone from your home town. Could you be at least a little cordial? I came all the way up here from Ann Arbor just to see your snotty ass," Brad replied.

"Bite me Brad; you came up here cause all the good looking girls are up here. You're just tired of tending the barn down in Ann Arbor," Kelly retorted.

"Damn, Kelly, do you always have to be so nasty?" Brad responded with a wide grin.

"Well, I'll tell you what, Brad Warner, this is my friend Cate Cassadea. We'll both keep you from getting your ass absolutely kicked because of that stupid tee shirt if you go fill up our beer glasses," Kelly added smugly.

"Anything your highness wishes. It's nice to meet you Cate. Though I can't say much about your choice of friends," Brad added taking their cups.

"I take it you know him?" Cate asked while Brad walked toward the keg.

"Oh yeah, Brad Warner, my big heart throb in high school," Kelly answered.

"You never mentioned him before," Cate continued.

"I don't know, we just never connected. If I was available, he'd be with someone, or vice versa. He was two years ahead of me. There was always something there, it just never happened," Kelly responded. "Sort of like you and that boy, what's his name, you know Eric. There was something there but it just never took off. Same with Brad and me."

"There's something there now," Cate replied. "I think he's smitten."

The following weekend Brad came to East Lansing again. The weekend following, Kelly went to Ann Arbor. Brad graduated in the spring and went to work for his father's chain of auto parts stores. Shortly after, they were married. Though happy for Kelly, it meant they wouldn't share an apartment the next year as planned.

Brad and Kelly moved into a farm house near Grand Haven. In the late fall while Brad was in Traverse City on business, Kelly was brutally murdered. Her killer broke in and hid in a closet for hours until Brad left. The police never caught the psychopath and neither Brad's nor Cate's lives were ever the same.

When the depression reared its ugly head again after Kelly's death, Cate dropped out of Michigan State and returned home to Melvindale. Six months later, she enrolled at Wayne State University, in downtown Detroit.

Needing something to fill her days until the semester started, Cate looked for a part time job. Kimmy's mother told her the Ramada Inn was looking for help in the lounge. Cate drove there, applied and was hired on the spot. When she told the manager she wasn't experienced, he replied there was a book of drink recipes behind the bar.

Leaving the lounge, Cate stopped at the coffee shop. A cup of coffee and some solitude sounded good so Cate selected a table by the window. While waiting, she pulled out a pack of Marlboros from her purse. After taking a deep drag, Cate let the smoke drift slowly from her mouth. It seemed there were times now when a cigarette and gazing out the window were the

Episode 12

only things she had wanted. The waitress brought her coffee and asked Cate if she was the new girl that was going to work in the lounge. Cate told her yes while taking a sip of coffee. She didn't feel like talking, but did her best to be cordial. When the waitress asked if she wanted anything else, Cate thanked her then stared out the window again.

The last time she had been in the coffee shop had been when her high school class met there for breakfast the morning after senior banquet. Now it seemed the things she once enjoyed so much made little sense. Tee peeing the principal's house, dumping soap suds in the fountain at Hart Plaza or food fights at the Embers restaurant after Sadie's seemed so naively innocent. The bad things felt so senseless. Kimmy's dad dying of a stroke or Kelly's violent end lent such a random spin on life.

She smoked several more Marlboros contemplating how she had ended up at the Ramada Inn wondering what to do with the her life. Cate wasn't sure how long she sat there looking out the window and was startled when a male voice shook her from her solitude.

"Cate Cassadea, what the hell are you doing here?" the voice asked.

"Drinking coffee and figuring out my life." Cate answered. "Something, I imagine you've never had to do Eric. You've always had all the answers," she continued sarcastically.

"Whoa, hold the phone. Maybe I should just get my coffee to go and leave you alone. Just thought I'd say hello, that's all," Eric turned to walk away.

"Sorry, Eric," Cate said grabbing his arm.

"What can I do to make up for being so rude?" Cate continued.

Eric looked at the pack of cigarettes.

"How 'bout you give me one of those," Eric pointed at the pack, "and buy me a cup of coffee."

Cate slid the pack of cigarettes across the table as Eric sat down across from her. He flipped open the box, pulled out a cigarette and stuck it in his mouth. Fishing in his pocket, Eric

71

pulled out a chrome Zippo. After taking a deep pull, he exhaled the thick smoke toward the window then turned to Cate.

"I was heading to Ann Arbor, but I am in absolutely no hurry. So tell me, what's got the brilliant Cate Cassadea so perplexed?" Eric asked sincerely.

The story about Kelly poured out of Cate in more detail than she intended. It was soul cleansing and soul blending all at the same time. They spent the next two hours smoking, sipping coffee and talking. When they finished Cate's pack, Eric went to his car and they finished his. They laughed about smoking the same brand and talked about stupid immature things they had done. They got giddy reliving the night of senior banquet, especially how they ended up making out in the back seat of Kimmy's car. They even laughed about Cate beating him for valedictorian and mutually admitted neither of them ever figured out why their relationship had never continued beyond that one encounter.

Eric asked if he could come by when her shift ended. They went downtown to Lafayette Coney Island, his father's favorite place to stop with his Democratic Club buddies.

Reflecting on that chance meeting with Eric, Cate wondered if there was some truth to the saying when one door closes another opens. When a door with Kelly had closed, a door with Eric had opened. He was attending the University of Michigan and living with Tom Allen. They had become very involved with the anti-war movement and SDS. Ann Arbor was only a forty minute drive from her parents house, so he'd occasionally pick her up after work. Other times she spent weekends in Ann Arbor.

During February, Cate's life took an unexpected turn. She always hated cold weather and it had been a miserable winter in Michigan with record snowfalls and low temperatures. Before meeting Eric, she had planned to go to nursing school in Miami, Florida after a semester at Wayne State. The admission officer at Wayne had been snooty when telling her several classes from Michigan State wouldn't transfer. Cate found herself telling the admissions counselor to shove it and stormed from his office. She drove to Ann Arbor and told Eric she was enrolling at the University of Miami the following fall. Cate was in love with Eric but she knew he was scheduled for an internship in New York in the fall. The following year was an election year and Eric had already talked about his plans for the Democratic campaign and law school at Harvard. Cate couldn't put her life on hold waiting for him.

Eric supported her decision and they vowed to make the most of their time together. After Eric finished the campaign, they'd find a way to be together even if it meant law school in Miami instead of Massachusetts. There was always Christmas break, somehow they'd make it work.

Cate left for Miami the the same week Eric departed for New York. They were inseparable the spring and summer before they parted. A couple of Eric's buddies had refurbished an old Chris Craft cabin cruiser and they spent long evenings on the boat and even longer, lost weekends in Ann Arbor.

Cate loved Miami; Eric didn't. He enrolled at Miami for law school but he was unhappy. Miami was not where Eric wanted to be. Years later Cate understood Miami wasn't really the reason they went separate ways. It wouldn't have mattered where they lived; Eric's issues were deeper than geography. The break up was difficult for both of them. Cate knew that for a specific time in their lives, each was exactly what other needed and while bitter sweet, that time was over.

Cate shook herself from the daydream and walked to her car glancing into the back seat to make sure it was empty. It was not compulsive, it's just good security she reassured herself as she unlocked the '95 Buick Rivera.

David called her car the Beast, it was an apt nickname. At first Cate had been irate with him for buying the giant, gold colored tank, but now had somehow become attached to the damned thing. The previous Halloween, David dressed as a pimp for a costume party and insisted Cate go as a prostitute. They drove the Beast to the party where she had to tell David twice to quit referring to her as the lead bitch in his stable.

Cate backed the car down the driveway. She certainly never considered the Outback Steak House fine dining, and reminded herself it was the thought that counted. She would have preferred to stay home but felt compelled to try to be a good sport and enjoy the evening.

Cate found a parking place near David's Chevy Blazer. Walking into the restaurant, Cate reminded herself to not be uppity, as her mother would say. She saw David sitting at a booth. Don and his wife Charlotte were seated opposite him. David waved to her as she made her way to them.

"Here's the birthday girl," David stood and kissed her.

"Hey, birthday girl, you're looking great," Charlotte added.

"Double nickels, Catie girl," Don said holding up a glass of beer.

"Don't remind me, Don. I'm trying to forget," Cate answered.

Don and Charlotte were nice people. They were sociable and Don and David spent a lot of time hunting together. Charlotte wasn't exactly a deep thinker, but she was honest and good natured. After spending time at hospital gatherings with doctors and their spouses, Cate valued honesty and humility.

The waitress came and asked Cate if she'd like a drink. Before Cate answered, David surprised her by saying that she didn't have time for one because they weren't staying and asked the waitress to just bring them their bill.

"What's this all about?" Cate asked.

"Well, Little Darlin'," David said in a fake western drawl, "we done decided that us Indiana hillbillies need a little culture'en up. We're leaving this here steak house and heading for a mysterious dining adventure over in the bustling mee-tropolis of Indianapolis. We're heading to the unknown and are gonna eat us some of that fereign food."

"What are you talking about, David?" Cate continued.

"I've got us reservations at the Peacock," David replied.

"Yeah, and Charlotte and I are going to see what it's like to eat cat," Don laughed.

"Don!" Charlotte exclaimed poking him in the ribs with her elbow.

"That's okay," Cate laughed. "Besides, Indians don't eat cats. That's the Chinese."

Episode 12

"Are you serious, David?" Cate continued. "Are we really going to the Peacock?"

"That's right Little Darlin'; I know you've wanted to go there for the last couple of months, ever since you read that review in the Indianapolis Star. That's where we're aheadin', that is, if you don't mind bein' seen with us country folks," David added.

"This is so sweet, I don't know what to say," Cate answered.

"Don't say nutten', just do the ordern' when we get there. We'll take the Beast, and you can drive Little Darlin," David finished.

David laid a twenty on the table as they left. Entering the interstate, a silver BMW passed Cate in a hurry. The BMW had been tailgating the last few miles and the drivers behavior was grating Cate's nerves. Not knowing what possessed her to such an impulsive action, Cate gave the driver the finger as he flew by. It might have been her difficult week at work or the thought of being fifty-five or maybe just life, Cate didn't know.

"Oh, shit," Cate said in a muffled voice.

"What the hell?" David exclaimed, "Did you just give that guy the finger?"

"Yeah," Cate, answered in an embarrassed tone, "and the driver is Dr. Taj!"

"Damn it!" Cate added, "He's been on my tail like some Kentucky hillbilly and you know how I hate tailgaters."

David burst out laughing.

"Serves the prick right," Don chimed in. "Them Indians may know how to cook exotic food and practice medicine. But they don't know shit about driving. Assholes come over here, make a fortune, buy a Mercedes and think they own the damn road."

"Guess he won't be a ridin' your ass no more Little Darlin," David laughed.

"Don't worry about it, Sweetie," Charlotte tried to comfort her, "he probably don't even know it's you."

"Yeah," Don added, "it's not like you drive a recognizable car. There's loads of 1995 gold Buick Rivera's on the road."

David and Charlotte burst out laughing again.

"Oh, brother, he knew it was me," Cate replied, "this will make for an interesting Monday morning."

"Water under the bridge, McCassio," David said in an Irish brogue. David's grandparents were from Ireland and he would call her McCassio after a few drinks.

Pulling into the Peacock's parking lot, David announced they'd splurge on valet parking. Inside, a dark skinned woman with a jewel embedded on the side of her nose led them to their table. The waitress approached and asked if they wanted to order drinks while they were waiting. David asked if there was such a thing as Indian wine. When the waitress answered there was, David told her to bring them a bottle of their best.

Charlotte said she needed to use the restroom and asked Cate if she'd like to go with her. As they made there way down the aisle, Cate stopped abruptly. Directly ahead of them Dr. Taj was seated across from the most beautiful Indian woman Cate had ever seen. Cate was certain the woman was not his wife. When Darpak glanced up from his menu, a look of surprise registered on his face. Recapturing his composure, he looked directly at Cate.

"Hello, Nurse Cassadea," he said. "I thought that was you on the interstate. I wasn't positive until you waved. That was a wave, I take it," he finished with a faint smile.

Episode 13

It was a mile further to the market. Besides clammy hands and a knot in his throat, Eric felt under control. Swallowing hard, he relaxed his grip on the steering wheel. After wiping his right hand on his thigh to dry the sweat, he repeated the motion with his left.

With his hands returned to the ten and two positions, Eric passed Rita's A&W Root Beer Stand and was almost abreast of Allen Park Drugs. He and Wes always rode their bikes to the root beer stand after little league games. Wes would order a drink made of half orange, half root beer with two dill pickle slices floating on the top. Eric tried to remember what Wes called the drink.

Seeing the drug store sent a surge of despair through Eric. It would always be a place of evil. The store's name and phone number had been printed in dark blue letters on the labels attached to his mother's little prescription bottles. Eric sometimes wondered if Allen Park Drugs were the first words he'd learned to read. After a few of his own melt downs, his father would stop there on their way home from the hospital. Eric wondered how two buildings that evoked such opposite emotions should be located next to each other.

Mad Dog, the name of the drink Wes loved, popped into Eric's mind making his gloom lift. Mad Dog was what should have been printed on his prescription labels because that's how he felt after taking the assorted poisons packed in them. Lost in thought, Eric nearly missed the turn into Kovalchek's Market. In reaction, he slammed on the brakes making the tires screech as he completed the turn.

"Damn," Eric muttered, "that could have been disastrous. Gotta get a grip here, quit daydreaming and focus."

Eric crept down the aisle of the parking lot until he found a spot big enough to accommodate the van. Opening the door, he stepped out.

As a child, Eric had often accompanied his mother to Kovalchek's. Just a small butcher shop then, it now carried a full line of produce, canned goods, and specialty items and had a package liquor license.

As Eric entered the store, the automatic door opener clicked and the metal door swung open. He remembered what a big deal it was for a store to get an automatic door opener. The day Kovalchek's installed one, Eric and Wes stopped by while on one of their bicycle odysseys. Wes walked back and fourth several times to determine how the electronic eye worked. After a while, Old Man Kovalchek finally came out and told Wes to stop. When they got back home, Wes asked his dad if they they could have one put in their house so he wouldn't have to open the front door anymore. Sipping a bottle of Stroh's beer while reading the Detroit Times sports section, his dad laughed and replied who knew what the future held.

Eric could remember something as insignificant as Wes's dad reading the Times, yet other memories were lost in a foggy haze. The disturbing thought left Eric as quickly as it came and he selected a shopping cart. Deciding what to buy was more important now, he'd let the other stuff go. By the time he reached the meat counter, his cart was full of jars of peanut butter, boxes of cereal, cans of tuna, potato chips and Campbell's soup.

Eric's patronage had become a quandary to Stanley Kovalchek's oldest son who operated the store. In his eighties, Stanley still came into the store but infrequently. Gary, wanted to ban Eric from the store, believing his presence was bad for business. Gary explained to his father Eric looked like a homeless waif. His clothes were filthy, his oral hygiene was non existent and his hair was almost down to his shoulders. To make things worse Eric occasionally had body odor.

Stanley would hear none of his son's protests. As long as it said Kovalchek's on the sign, Eric would be welcome if he didn't harass other customers or steal. Stanley reminded Gary they were Catholics, helping the infirm was their duty. Gary knew how stubborn Polish people, especially those who had lived in the old country, could be. They were compassionate. Gary had witnessed his father's benevolence, especially during recessions. What Gary didn't know was his father's empathy for Eric was based on something else. As a young man, Stanley had been in love with Eric's mother.

Nothing ever came of Stanley's infatuation, other than innocent flirtation whenever Nancy came into the store. Though Nancy had been gone for a long time, Stanley still carried a torch and seeing Eric reminded Stanley he had been young once.

Gary was working behind the meat counter when Eric pushed up his cart. It had been a decent day and Gary decided not to spoil it. Getting Eric to articulate what he wanted required more patience than Gary possessed so he decided to make Jessica take Eric's order.

Gary looked over at her. He knew there was some connection between the two. What a match, he thought, Eric the smelly vagrant, being waited on by Jessica, the ex-heroin addict. Jessica had been a pleasant surprise though and he to admit, he had been wrong about her. Gary thought his dad had stroked out when Stanley announced Jessica would be coming to work for them.

Jessica's father had been a judge and until his death, a frequent customer. In their discussion about hiring Jess, Stanley said they owed Judge Olson. The Judge had been very instrumental in getting their package liquor license and building permits for the store. Gary also knew the Judge was also a regular member at his father's weekly poker game.

So far Jessica hadn't missed a day and was clean and sober. She also hadn't robbed them or brought any junkie friends to the store. Gary believed her behavior had something to do with the two women who had just come into the store. The blonde woman's name was Kathy and Jess called the other woman Linda A. They were friends from high school.

"Hey Jess, here comes your buddy, Eric" Gary said, "you wait on him; I can't deal with him today."

"Sure, Gary," Jess replied, "go take care of what you need to do. I'll help him out, no sweat," Jess picked up a dish towel from the counter and wiped mayonnaise from her hands. She'd been mixing a batch of bologna salad.

Eric stood about ten feet down the aisle. Jess knew it would take him a few moments to make it to the meat counter. She looked over at Kathy and Linda who were standing by the produce bin.

"Hey Linda, Kathy, get over here," Jessica said in a loud whisper motioning to them.

Eric reached the counter at the same time as the two women.

"Eric," Jess said in a friendly tone, "do you remember Kathy and Linda?"

Eric looked at the two women with a blank stare. There was some connection but he couldn't place them. The blonde woman looked friendlier than the one with dark hair. She was shorter and had large pale blue eyes with a slight upward slant. Her eyebrows also arched higher. The dark haired woman wore tight blue jeans and a low cut blouse. Her hair was longer and pulled back. It was held in place by some kind of clip. Her breasts were also larger. Eric didn't quite understand what to make of this last observation and decided it was of no importance.

Eric struggled with Jessica's question for a minute. Feeling uncomfortable, he wanted to answer but couldn't find the right words. Kathy was the first to speak. Having been a school teacher for thirty years, she could sense Eric's panic.

Episode 13

"It's okay Eric, if you don't remember us," the blonde woman said softly. "I'm Kathy Mac, we went to school together. We went to Mead elementary and then Dasher Junior High. After that, we went to high school."

Eric stared at Kathy momentarily then looked down at the floor.

"Hey, Eric," she continued, "it's okay, it's been over thirty-five years since high school. Don't feel embarrassed if you don't remember."

"Yeah, Eric," Linda added hoping to ease the situation. "Maybe it's just 'cause we're so much better looking now than back then."

Eric turned his attention back to meat counter. He recognized Jessica only because she had waited on him the last several months. She bore little resemblance to her high school days. Her even, white teeth had been replaced with poor fitting dentures. Her face had a narrow and sunken look where there had once been a flawless completion and full checks. Jess's arms were bone thin which added to her overall worn appearance and made her look much older than her friends.

"Can I have some hot dogs and ground beef please?" Eric asked ignoring Jess's question about the two women.

"Sure enough, Sweetie," Jessica answered. She scooped ground beef into four small cardboard containers then wrapped them in brown butcher's paper. After wrapping a dozen hot dogs, she set all five packages on top of the counter.

"You want some bologna salad Eric, it's fresh. I just made it," Jess added with a smile.

"Just the hamburger and hotdogs," Eric answered meekly.

"Hey Eric, you gonna make chili over mashed?" Linda asked.

Chili poured over mashed potatoes was a main stay at their high school when lunches were made from scratch by a half dozen hair netted women in white uniforms. It had been Linda's favorite.

Eric gave Linda another blank look and picked up the packages. He thanked Jess then turned to leave. Pausing, he knew he should say something to the two women and finally managed, "It was nice meeting you two," then walked toward the cashiers.

"Chili over mashed! Linda what the hell is wrong with you," Kathy scolded her friend.

"He didn't even tell you how much he wanted," Linda said to Jessica ignoring Kathy's admonishment.

"Hell, Lind, he didn't how much to ask for," Kathy interrupted

"Then how did you know how much to give him?" Linda questioned Jess again.

"Been there Sweetie, been there in spades," Jessica answered making a head motion indicating she had to take care of a customer at the other end of the counter.

"I'll be back in a minute. It always picks up just before quitting time. It's like everyone realizes they might want to eat the next day," Jess said walking away.

Linda and Kathy looked at each other. Eric's shocking appearance had unsettled them and neither knew how to articulate their feelings.

"Can you believe that was Eric?" Kathy said breaking their silence.

"You know," Linda added, "I wasn't trying to be mean with that chili over mashed comment. Just thought I'd lighten the moment and who knows, maybe jar something loose in his head. I'd like to have some chili over mashed myself right now, I'm starving."

"And the little bread and butter sandwiches on the side with some cole slaw," Kathy responded.

"I gotta say, seeing Eric Arnold looking like that freaked me out. He was so handsome in high school. He had those dark eyes and a great body. Is there anyone from our class that isn't a total fucking loony tune?" Linda asked.

Kathy was surprised, she expected Linda to be more empathetic in her reaction to Eric's mental state. Linda had barely known her father, a hopeless drunk who drifted in and out after her mother had been institutionalized leaving Linda to be raised by her aunt. Kathy knew Linda was no novice in dealing with off centered lives. Linda reached over and grabbed Kathy's arm.

Episode 13

"Yeah, but my god, Lind. Eric Arnold, jeeze is no one safe. If someone as smart as him can end up like that, what does this mean for us?" Linda added.

"Maybe, that's the good part, Lind. Maybe we're dumb enough to get a freaken' chance," Kathy answered with weak smile.

"I don't know about that, but if I wind up there someday, at least help me keep it together enough to take a bath and brush my teeth once a year," Linda replied.

"We'll make a pact. I'll keep it together enough to buy the soap; you keep it together enough to buy the toothpaste."

"Then what, we brush each others teeth?" Linda said between nervous giggles. "Hell, by that time, we'll be taking them out to soak; we won't have to worry about brushing them."

"Shit Lind, just promise me you'll remind me to put them in every morning."

When Jessica told them about Eric's appearances at the market, they hadn't taken her seriously. Jess's life had been a tumultuous mixture of drugs, rehab centers and abusive men.

Once, when she had been beaten nearly to death, Jess had given the hospital Linda's name as next of kin. Growing up next door to each other, they had always been closer than sisters. Like all long time best friends, their friendship had its ups and downs which became mostly downs after Jess's heroin addiction. Jess had always been there for Linda when she returned from visiting her mother at the hospital. Though her aunt had called it a hospital, even as a child Linda knew it was not a regular hospital. It was not a place where people go to have their tonsils removed or broken legs set. Her aunt said it was a place where people went when their brains didn't work right. Linda was to learn patients at the Brain Hospital seldom got well and returned home to stay. At least her mother hadn't. Seeing Eric, Linda knew he had spent considerable time in the Brain Hospital and probably needed more time there. It reminded her they both had grown up without a mother at a time when stay at home moms were the norm and she decided to say a prayer of thanks before going to sleep that night.

Linda had always thought Cate and Eric would end up together. In her naïve teenaged dreams, Linda imagined heart surgeon Cate would someday marry Senator Eric. They'd live a story book life of saving lives and the country while living in Washington D.C. She knew part of the dream came true for Eric and Cate but it certainly didn't end happily ever after. Cate hadn't become a heart surgeon, Eric hadn't become a senator and Jess, though she spent a lot of time in court, never became a judge like her father.

Over the years Linda and Kathy occasionally complained to each others about opportunities missed. The encounter with Eric reaffirmed Linda's belief they hadn't come off too badly. After working summers as a car hop at Rita's Root Beer Stand she married the owner's son. They now owned a small trucking company and while not rich, they were not hurting. Kathy finished college and became a teacher. Her marriage to a singer in a local rock band was a failure, but Kathy had managed to land on her feet. Linda watched Eric as he made his way into the parking and thought about the direction her own life could have taken. The vagaries of life, she said to herself.

"Shit," Linda muttered, "we dodged a big bullet there."

"What'd you say, Lind, I missed that?" Kathy asked.

"Nothing, Kath, nothing, at all."

"He's just pitiful. What am I going to say to Cate? Eric was one of her two big loves you know," Kathy asked.

"Why say anything at all?"

"You're right, Lind, guess I'll just let that one lie."

Looking out the door, they watched Eric loading grocery bags into the back of his van. After closing the cargo doors, he got into the truck and drove out of the parking lot.

Buoyed by his success with grocery shopping, Eric decided to stop at the Big Boy on his way home. It hadn't occurred to him a bath and clean clothes were in order before going into a restaurant. He was oblivious to such minor details. After all,

Episode 13

he'd driven all the way to the store, shopped and paid the clerk without dropping his wallet. Though it had been one of his best days in a very long time, it bothered him he couldn't place the two women. At least he'd remembered the woman behind the counter. Her name was Jess. Eric took comfort in being able to remember that much. Maybe the other women's names would come to him; maybe not. The dilemma became less important as he continued driving.

The Big Boy was just ahead on the corner of Southfield Boulevard. Eric didn't like driving such busy roads and avoided them when possible. The restaurant was on the right side of the road, however, so he could get there without making a left turn. Lefts were difficult. Getting home from the restaurant would be doable, he could make rights all the way.

The thought of a double decked hamburger, onion rings and a milk shake captivated Eric. He hoped to catch the traffic light green so he wouldn't have to stop at the intersection. Voran's Funeral Home was there. Like the drug store, it was a building that gave him bad feelings. Alan had been there. It seemed all the people he loved ended up there eventually. Wes had been there and so had Nancy.

Finding himself sitting in the parking lot, Eric got out of the truck and walked toward the restaurant. Several patrons gave him disparaging looks as they walked to their cars. Eric ignored their looks.

The hostess was a young college student and noting Eric's appearance felt apprehensive. She didn't want to tell the raggedy man to leave and was about to talk to the manager when an older waitress named Rudy approached her. Rudy whispered to her that she'd take care of everything then told Eric to follow her. She led him to a booth near the back of the restaurant. Rudy had known Eric since childhood. She had waited on him during his infrequent visits over the last twenty-five years but hadn't seen him lately. Rudy knew she should have left the place years ago, but like the rest of her life, it had become comfortable and she had to pay the bills. There hadn't been many options.

After a few minutes, Rudy returned to Eric's table carrying a large serving tray. She set the double decker hamburger and onion rings in front of him then reached over, picked up the frosted glass of vanilla milkshake and slid it in front of him. The shake was so thick the straw stood straight up. Eric removed the paper covering from the top of the straw and took a drink.

"What about my mom's food?" Eric asked. "She'll be here any minute and you know she doesn't like to wait."

"Oh, don't worry yourself about that Eric; her order will be right up. You go ahead and finish yours. We'll keep hers in the back so it'll stay warm. If I remember rightly, Nancy hates cold food. She told me that the last time she was here. Said if it was cold again, she'd just head on down to Debby's next time. We don't want to piss off your mom, do we Eric?" Rudy finished.

"No mamn." Eric said then took another drink.

Eric finished his burger and onion rings and a few minutes later Rudy walked to his table and handed him a paper bag with another burger and onion rings.

"Looks like my mom won't be coming after all," Eric said to Rudy as he took the bag, "and I have campaign things to work on. It's an election year and George is counting on me for help."

"Are you working for George Bush's campaign this year Eric," Rudy asked.

"George Bush, are you crazy, he's a Republican. Afraid not," Eric responded, "I only work for Democrats. Alan would lose his mind if I ever worked for a Republican. Besides George Bush isn't running for anything, he's head of the CIA for President Nixon. We're going to unseat that lousy Nixon. I'm working for George McGovern, and when we get him in office, we'll get out of this lousy war. You can take that to the bank," Eric's thoughts were now coming in lucid streams.

"Well, good luck Eric, hope the election works out okay for you. You come back and see me real soon. Don't worry about paying. Your mom stopped by earlier and left the money with me. I'll take it to the cashier for you," Rudy gave Eric a smile as he got up to leave.

Episode 13

"See you soon, thanks," Eric said holding the carry out bag, "oh, yeah thanks for the order for my mom. I'll give it to her when I get home."

"I'm sure you will. Tell Nancy I said hello when you see her."

One of the younger waitresses had overheard their conversation and walked over to Rudy.

"Wow, is that guy whacked or what?" she asked popping a wad of grape bubble gum. "Who is George McGovern? I never heard of him."

"Who's George McGovern?" Rudy replied watching Eric make his way to the front of the restaurant, "Oh, he's only the best president we never had."

"Best president we never had, I don't get it, what the hell does that mean?" the waitress asked with a quizzical look.

"Nothing, Sweetie, like just about everything else in life, it means absolutely nothing. I'm going on break to have a smoke. Cover my tables for me?" Rudy replied.

"No problem," the waitress answered popping the gum again.

The smoke was an excuse so Rudy could make sure Eric made it to his car okay. Taking care of Eric made her feel good. Kind of makes up for skipping mass last week Rudy told herself as she returned to her station.

Episode 14

Driving past pristine farms with freshly painted houses and immaculate barns, Darpak thought how different the terrain was from Kashmir. The soil here was loamy and black compared to the arid, mountainous landscape of northern India.

Traffic was light on the four lane road. Most commuters from Indianapolis were home by now, quelling frayed nerves with martinis or cold beers. After which would follow barbecued steaks and complaints about bosses, ex-spouses and late child support payments. Even later, would be the woeful Cubs blowing another game. Darpak was not surprised, most Americans were so enamored in the minutiae of their own lives they were oblivious to the conditions in other parts of the world. Darpak knew recognition of pain and suffering was only possible when it happened to you or those close to you. For a while, the events of September 11 brought to America what most of the world already knew, but things had slowly crept back to normal.

Americans were incapable of hating anyone for long. Teddy Roosevelt had been right when he characterized the American spirit by saying the business of America is business. Viet Nam was an example of this mindset. America waged a long and pain ridden war against the Vietnamese in the 1960s, then found a way to rationalize building automobile assembly plants for them in the 1990s.

Darpak doubted any of the commuters along Indiana Highway 36 would understand what he was about to do. They would be quick to tell him as a doctor he had sworn to save lives, not take them. Though most Americans would contend any action that rid the world of Muslims was a good thing, they'd be quick to add replacing them with Hindus was not much of a gain. They preferred both groups stay on their own side of the planet.

While they went ahead with their picnics and little league baseball games, he'd continue with his own plans. There were Hindu children orphaned every day who would never get a chance to play baseball or go on a picnic. So if reducing the number of Muslims reduced the number of Hindu orphans, it was an equitable trade off. There were risks involved, but he'd decided long ago to accept those risks; too much of his family's blood had already been invested.

The entrance to the interstate was just ahead. For the last ten minutes he had been stuck behind an older model Buick barely maintaining the speed limit. He'd have passed the gold antique but a tandem trailer blocked the left lane. The Buick hadn't increased its speed even when he had nearly driven on top of the vehicle's bumper. Reluctantly, he stayed behind the Buick until the entrance ramp for the freeway.

Darpak assumed the driver was some blue haired senior citizen on her way home from an early bird special. The front passenger was constantly turning toward a couple in the back and engaging in a very animated conversation. When both vehicles veered right to enter the on ramp, Darpak pressed harder on the accelerator. As he inched closer, he noticed a parking sticker in the back window and recognized the car. To his surprise, it was Nurse Cassadea's old Rivera.

When the on ramp curve ended, he deftly steered around the Buick. Darpak glanced to his right and was surprised when the driver extended her middle finger at him. Darpak chuck-

Episode 14

led, apparently Nurse Cassadea had not appreciated his driving skills. He let off on the gas keeping an equal pace with the Buick. When Nurse Cassadea turned her head, an expression of surprise registered on her face. Darpak laughed out loud, knowing it would make interesting conversation during rounds on Monday. When Darpak pressed the gas pedal to the floor, the BMW shot by the Buick.

Darpak turned his thoughts to his meeting at the restaurant. The agent would be wearing a dark blue suit and a red scarf. She would recognize him from photographs. He would take a seat at a separate table. When the agent was sure neither of them had been followed, she would ask him to join her. At first they would make innocuous small talk for the ears of any diners seated close by. After dinner, Darpak would leave with two small brushed aluminum cases. In one case would be surgical instruments. In the other would be several vials of what was labeled as a newly developed antibiotic. It would be Darpak's responsibility to get those vials to Fairlane Hills, Michigan.

Darpak entered the restaurant through heavy glass double doors and gave the hostess his name. While she examined the reservation list, Darpak surveyed the restaurant for any changes to the exit locations since his last visit. A few moments later the hostess led him to a table. While he was waiting, a waitress came and asked if he would like a drink. Darpak replied a Perrier with a twist of lime would be fine. Darpak saw his contact at a table nearby and was briefly taken back by her beauty. The agent glanced around the restaurant then got up and asked Darpak to join her.

"Will there be other people joining you, sir?" the waitress asked upon returning and noting Darpak's change of table.

"No," Darpak answered, "it will be just the two of us."

"Fine sir, then when you are ready to order, just let me know and I will come back."

"Are you ready?" Darpak asked the agent, "Or would you like more time?" The waitress waited to hear the woman's reply.

"I think I'm ready," the agent answered.

"Fine, then," the waitress said, "may I start you with an appetizer?"

"How is the Aloo Bonda?" Darpak asked, referring to the small balls of mashed potatoes fried and seasoned with cumin, mustard seeds and fresh green chiles.

"Oh, it is very good," the waitress continued in a Hindi accent, "we serve it with either tamarind or green chutney, you have your choice."

"The tamarind will be fine," Darpak replied.

"Do you want to order your entree now or after I bring the appetizers?" the waitress continued in her polite voice.

"I think we can order now," Darpak replied raising his eyes from the menu and looking at the agent.

"Certainly," she answered," I'll have the Shami Kebab and the vegetables Gujarati."

"An excellent choice, the Gujarati here is superb," the waitress replied.

"Your choice sir?"

"I'll have the same," Darpak answered.

"Your meals come with Rajasthani Pilau," referring to the festive spiced rice from the state of Rajasthan. "I'll be back in a moment with your appetizers," the waitress finished and left the table.

While waiting for their food, Darpak continued to make small talk. He asked about conditions back home. The agent answered by telling him sales were increasing and that good progress was being made in research and development. The answer let Darpak know more deliveries were to come soon and that revisions to the formula were still in process. It appeared that everything would continue as planned when Darpak caught sight of familiar profile.

"We may have a minor situation," Darpak said in a low tone

"What is it?" the agent asked.

"I know one of the women walking towards us. She's a nurse at the hospital. There's another woman with her that I don't know," Darpak responded.

"Which of the two do you know?"

Episode 14

"The blonde woman, her name is Cate Cassadea. I'm not going to introduce you unless it's necessary. The quicker they go and the less they know, the better."

When the two women reached their table, the agent noticed a look of surprise on the blonde woman's face. The agent glanced at the two brushed aluminum cases on the table and casually slipped her napkin over them. It had been a natural reaction, but a mistake. Darpak averted his eyes from the cases.

"Hello Nurse Cassadea," Darpak said when the women were directly in front of them," I thought that was you on the interstate but I wasn't positive until you waved. That was a wave, I take it?"

"Doctor Taj," Cate said her face turning crimson. Cate hadn't recognized the doctor until she and Charlotte were almost on top of his table.

"Yes that was a wave I gave you," Cate laughed and rolled her eyes. "Well, a kind of wave anyway."

"We have similar waves in India, though I must say, I've never had a chance to use them here. I'll stop by your station Monday morning and maybe we can discuss international sign language," Darpak replied with a faked smile then turned his attention back to his drink.

"Sorry about that. I thought you were someone else," Cate said feeling awkward. She was about to say goodbye when Charlotte began talking.

"Say Doctor Tajsh," Charlotte slurred, "I don't really know you, but have seen you around town. To be honest, we have never eaten Indian food and I wondered if you could recommend something. We don't want to make a mistake and find out later that it was something that we weren't comfortable eating."

Cate was caught off guard at both Charlotte's question and her level of inebriation. She had failed to see Charlotte sneak a Valium from her purse in the back seat on the way. First I give the doctor the finger and now Charlotte insults his culture, Cate said to herself. Damn it Charlotte, Cate pleaded in her thoughts, just shut the hell up and maybe we can get out of this with some amount of dignity.

"Well, if I were you, I'd order the Tandoori chicken. It's made with strips of marinated white meat, skewered on bamboo sticks and barbecued. It's quite tasty," Darpak smiled pleasantly. "I think you will enjoy it."

He turned to his drink again hoping his comment would get the two women on their way. It appeared the women were about to leave when the drunk woman began talking again.

"Thanks Doc, 'cause I really don't want to order something and then find out tomorrow, that I had eaten Lassie or something." The valium combined with the alcohol had rendered Charlotte nearly incoherent.

"What was it, this Lassie thing? I don't understand?" Darpak replied.

"Well, Lashie was," Charlotte slurred again when Cate cut her off.

"Lassie was something we'll talk about another time, Doctor," Cate interjected. "Sorry Charlotte, but we need to get to the lady's room now."

Cate grabbed Charlotte by the arm and tugged her away from the table.

"I'll see you at the hospital, Monday Doctor," Cate added turning her head back toward the table.

"Thanksh for the tip, Doc," Charlotte added over her shoulder as Cate led her away.

"Christ, Charlotte!" Cate whispered in the restroom as she washed her hands, "What a thing to say."

"Oh, you mean that Lashsie, comment?" Charlotte laughed as she pulled a tube of eye liner from her purse.

Cate watched as Charlotte fumbled with the tube. She couldn't get the top off and held the tube closer to her face to make sure she was turning it the right way.

"Yes, I mean the Lassie thing," Cate shot back as she grabbed the tube from Charlotte's hand, "For the love of God, Char, here let me help you."

Cate unscrewed the top then handed it back. Charlotte tried to apply the make up but her hand trembled causing her to

Episode 14

apply a smear of eyeliner to her eyelid midway between her eyelash and eyebrow.

"I think I mished," Charlotte laughed then tried a second time.

An unsuccessful second swipe left a trail of mascara about a half inch below her lower lash.

"Well, thish ain't gonna work," Charlotte giggled. "Do you think you can help me out here again, Sweetie?" she asked. "Guess I shouldn't have taken that valium back in the car."

"Jesus, Charlotte, what the hell were you thinking. How much did you take?" Cate asked in a concerned voice.

"Oh, I just took a fiver; I'll be all right in a little while, honey. Just need to get my bearings and have something to eat, that's all. Help me get this shit off my eyes and I'll be okay. Can't go back to the table looking like half of a raccoon you know, because who knows in a place like this, with all these turban heads. You walk around looking like a raccoon, and these fuckers will try to cook you, as well as those Lashies and Sylvesters they got roasting in that kitchen back there. Chicken Tandoori, my ass, Tweetie Tandoori's probably more like it," Charlotte began laughing. Small tears streamed down both cheeks. In an effort to wipe them away, Charlotte smeared the mascara even more.

Cate wanted to be angry, but after Charlotte's remark and the ridiculous looking make up on her face, Cate began laughing at the lunacy of the situation. What a way to celebrate a fifty-fifth birthday, she mused.

"Here let me help you," Cate said wetting a paper towel to wipe the make up off Charlotte's face.

"Oh, yeah, by the way, that's not Doctor Taj's wife," Cate said to Charlotte.

"No shit, sweetie. That was obvious from across the room. I may be a little drunk but it didn't take much to figure that out. Men are so transhparent. Anything I can't stand, it's a cheating man. Don't care if it says doctor in front of his name or not. It don't make that shit right. His wife's probably home taking care of the babies, and he's out with Ali fucking Baba's beauty queen, doing who knows what," Charlotte looked at Cate. "You ever have a man put that kind of hurt on you, sweetheart, you'll know what I mean."

"Ali Baba was Arabic, not Indian," Cate corrected Charlotte attempting to change the subject.

"Same shit. Oh wait, Cate, are you saying just because them Arabs don't eat pork, they ain't pigs like the rest of the men in this world?" Charlotte replied with a laugh.

"Don't kid yourself, honey," she continued, "even them Muslim pricks with their three or four wives are cheating sons of bitches. Hell, you could give most men a hundred wives, and you know what them lousy bastards'll do the first chance they get? They'd sneak off with the first set of willing tits that walk by, and come up with some lame excuse why they need number one hundred and one. Fuck 'em honey. Listen to me, they're all the same."

"You know Char, this may be one of our better nights," Cate responded.

"Let's go eat Lassie, before the poor over worked bitch gets called on to rescue Billy from the well," Cate added feeling a new bond with Charlotte. Leaving, Charlotte paused in the doorway.

"Don't you mean Timmy, Cate?" Charlotte asked. "Timmy was the boys name in Lassie, not Billy."

"Timmy, Billie, what's the hell's the difference, let them both drown," Cate answered. "Like you said Charlotte, they're all the same."

"But Timmy was only twelve years old in Lassie, Cate. He didn't do anything wrong."

"Oh, that's only 'cause he's only twelve," Cate answered, "he'll be a lying, cheating bastard like the rest of them, Char, when he's old enough. There hasn't been one born yet who either hasn't, or won't be when they're old enough for their balls to drop. You know the old saying, God gave men a brain and a dick, but only enough blood to operate one at a time."

"Amen to that sishter," Charlotte slurred, "let's go have some of that Indian wine."

"I think maybe you are done with the wine tonight Char," Cate answered.

When they returned to the table, Cate drank one glass while Charlotte helped Don and David finish another bottle. After dinner and espressos they left the restaurant and walked to valet parking. David fumbled in his suit coat pocket and handed the valet their ticket. The evening air felt good against Cate's flushed skin. The porter brought their car and opened the driver's door. Cate got behind the wheel as Charlotte and Don collapsed noisily into the back seat. David lowered himself into the passenger seat and leaned his head back.

"Put on your seat belt, David," Cate said. When it appeared he had not heard her, she leaned over and nudged him.

David grabbed the seat belt but had trouble clasping the buckle.

"Think I may need some help with this, babe," David answered.

"What a fucking crew," Cate muttered as she leaned over and buckled David's seat belt.

"What'd you say, Catie my dear," David relapsed into his Irish accent.

"Oh, I just said, that's what I do," Cate answered.

"Yes," David answered with a giggle, "that's what you do."

"You're a good lass Catie McCassio," he added.

"Yeah, and look what it's got me," Cate said sarcastically shifting the Buick into drive.

"What'd you say Catie girl?" David asked.

"I said, that's what my mom taught me," Cate answered.

"Take a nap, David," she added in a tone indicating she was done talking.

Cate pulled out of the parking lot. Turning her head to look for oncoming traffic, she saw a man crossing the street. She recognized Doctor Taj and noticed he was carrying one of the cases the woman covered with the napkin. Seeing the cases, she'd assumed it was some promotional item the doctors were always getting from drug company reps. Like they don't have enough money to begin with, Cate said under her breath. The drug companies ought to be sucking up to the nurses, she continued, we're the ones who make most of the key decisions anyway. What do we get, she added, maybe a dozen doughnuts and free coffee. Maybe it was some type of electronic organizer. What a waste, Cate thought, most doctors she knew were unorganized scatter brains. Well, Cate added with a wry smile, maybe the case contains a vibrator. From what she'd heard, at least that would be something doctors' wives could use. With a muted laugh Cate pressed harder on the Buick's gas pedal.

Episode 15

When the Imam began the prayer, Ahmed turned toward the front of the mosque. He knelt forward and pressed his forehead onto the floor. His mind was spinning. Ahmed could see the small, scarred twist of flesh at the end of Kamal's stump and wondered if he used some type of prosthetic device. Ahmed also wondered if having only one hand would hinder Kamal's sexual capabilities. Fondling a girl's breasts would still be possible but only one at a time. Ahmed was so engrossed with the concept he failed to notice the prayer had ended.

"I see you still have problems focusing during prayer," Kamal whispered then nudged Amend gently on the shoulder. "You have not changed much."

Ahmed wanted to ask Kamal where he had been since their sweltering hot summers in North Africa. He hadn't seen Kamal after the injury. The young Palestinian seemed to have disappeared. Ahmed thought of the boy who'd lost his hand whenever he watched an Al Jazeera newscast about a suicide bombing or other acts of terrorism. He wondered if such a deformed limb also limited Kamal's fighting capacity. Kamal's mention of his father and brother, however, indicated he was informed about events in Afghanistan.

"After the service," Kamal whispered into his ear, "go to Al Borduni's restaurant. There will be a man in the third booth. His name is Mahmood. Listen very closely to what he tells you. This is serious, Ahmed, not a time for jokes."

"Will you be there?" Ahmed asked.

"I will be in the restaurant, but I will not be joining you," Kamal answered.

As Ahmed started to leave, Kamal grabbed him by the elbow, "Ahmed, I'm serious. Please, no kidding or joking around," he repeated.

"Why am I to talk to this Mahmood?" Ahmed whispered back.

"This is not the place for that conversation," Kamal answered.

Kamal broke their embrace and turned to the next worshiper offering a greeting of Allah's blessing. Ahmed did not greet other worshipers, he was too perplexed about Kamal's instructions and uncertain as to his next move. When he left his flat earlier, he assumed it would just be another Friday evening wasted at the mosque.

The previous weekend, Ahmed had gone to some clubs with a group of young men he'd met through his friend Ali. Ali had been a patient at the hospital where Ahmed worked. While cleaning Ali's room, they'd begun talking. Having moved to Fairlane Hills from Syria with his family, Ali sympathized with Ahmed about the difficulties of moving to a new country. Ali kept in touch with Ahmed after he was released from the hospital. There had been drinks and introductions to young women making Ahmed look forward to tonight.

"Damn it," Ahmed cursed under his breath walking out of the mosque. "Just when it looked like maybe my life would get normal, fucking one handed Kamal appears out of nowhere. Fuck him."

Ahmed was upset that his plans had been ruined. He felt sorry for Kamal when he saw his mutilated hand, but now felt little pity for him. The loss was obviously not enough to persuade Kamal to forget all the craziness they'd been exposed to as boys.

Episode 15

"I should have left the mosque the minute I saw him," Ahmed heard himself say as he walked to his car. "Dumb ass, nothing but a big fucking dumb ass," he continued his self flagellation. "Did you really think you'd be free of them, Ahmed. All I really want to do is drive this car, go clubbing and chase women. I don't give a rip about the rest of their bull shit, why can't they just leave me alone?" Ahmed continued while starting the Pontiac.

If he could finish this business quickly enough maybe he could hurry home, change and still meet Ali. Driving on Ford Road, Ahmed saw a familiar car in his rear view mirror. He half expected Charlie to pull him over, but knew he wouldn't do anything so obvious.

Catching the yellow light on the corner by the restaurant, Ahmed made a quick right. The sign said no turn on red but his hopes the sign would deter Charlie were dashed when Charlie reappeared in the rear view.

"Screw you, fat ass," Ahmed said aloud putting on his left turn signal before turning into Al Bourdini's parking lot. Charlie didn't follow. Tailing him from the mosque was just Charlie's way of letting him know he was being watched. Ahmed parked his car, got out and walked into the restaurant.

The building originally had been home to Fairlane Hills Pizzeria during a time when few Arabs ventured so far into west Fairlane Hills. During that time, the neighborhood had been Fairlane Hills's little Italy and Schaefer Road was the unofficial boundary. Arabs were free to do business of course on either side of Schaefer; but they didn't own businesses or live so far west. The demographics changed in the 70s when a few Italian families sold their homes to Arabs at inflated prices.

Ahmed waited for the hostess, an attractive Lebanese girl with dark eyes and a small mole on her left cheek, to seat him. Her hair was pulled back and she had on tight black slacks and a white blouse. If Mahmood didn't show up soon, Ahmed decided he would make a move on her. As he was ready to initiate a conversation, a tall, thin man approached and told the hostess Ahmed was with him. Ahmed followed the man to a booth and took the seat

101

opposite him. As Ahmed sat down, he looked to his left and saw Kamal seated at a large corner booth next to a young and very pregnant woman. Another couple was with them. The women wore head scarves and simple Palestinian Sabbath dresses.

A waitress came to their table and asked Mahmood if they wanted drinks. Mahmood ordered juice from oranges and pineapple. Ahmed ordered a Coke. The waitress was not as pretty as the hostess but still looked inviting in her tight black pants. If things didn't work out with the hostess, Ahmed decided to try the waitress.

Ahmed became lost in a fantasy about the hostess when he realized Mahmood was glaring at him. The man's intense stare reminded Ahmed how irrational religious fanatics were. He wondered how Mahmood could not also be engrossed with the hostess's shapely rear end. Ahmed wanted to tell Mahmood he didn't care about jihad. The only holy war he wanted to wage was one where he ravaged the hostess's voluptuous breasts.

"I take it you are Mahmood," Ahmed began the conversation.

"Some people know me as Mahmood, but I have had other names," the rail thin Arab responded.

Ahmed would have laughed at Mahmood's cheesy melodrama if the man wasn't so scary. He had intense eyes with narrow eyebrows and a thin beak-like nose. His hair was thinning in the front and he looked to be in his forties, but Ahmed was not a good judge of age. Anyone over thirty looked ancient. Most people that old were not much fun; they tended to take life too seriously and it appeared this man was no exception. Mahmood resembled an animal Ahmed had seen on the National Geographic channel recently. The show had been about ferrets and that's what Mahmood reminded him of. A very big and very ugly ferret. Ahmed suddenly had a sinking realization this meeting would not be their last.

The waitress set their drinks in front of them. Smelling the orange fragrance from Mahmood's drink, Ahmed wished he'd ordered something from the juice bar and considered changing his order but decided otherwise. It might make the meeting last

Episode 15

longer and no amount of juice was worth spending another minute with a man with so much hatred burning in his eyes.

"Ready to order?" the waitress asked.

"Yes," Mahmood answered without picking up the menu.

She pulled a small green order pad and a Bic pen from her apron.

"Okay, what would you like?" she asked looking at Mahmood.

"I'll have the chicken gaylia," he answered.

"I'll have the same," Ahmed told the waitress. He loved the thin strips of chicken cooked in spiced tomato sauce with onions, green peppers and mushrooms.

"The meals come with rice and fattoush. You also have a choice of either humus or baba ghanoush," the waitress said still looking at Ahmed.

When she finished, she gave Ahmed a hint of a smile revealing an even row of porcelain white teeth. She was wearing red lip liner which contrasted nicely with her teeth. Maybe she wasn't so plain after all, Ahmed concluded, maybe it was just the hostess was such a knock out, even a pretty girl would appear less so.

Ahmed decided on baba ghanoush. He loved the ground eggplant seasoned with garlic, olive oil and lemon. The waitress closed her order pad and walked toward the kitchen

"Now, Ahmed," Mahmood said, "tell me how you are back in the United States."

"What do you mean?" Ahmed asked, "I just got tired of life in Afghanistan and decided to come back here. This is where I lived before." The core of his reply was truthful but divulged only what was necessary.

The waitress returned carrying a large black tray and began placing small bowls in front of them.

"For you sir, the humus," she said setting a bowl in front of Mahmood, "and for you the baba." The waitress smiled again at Ahmed.

Smelling her perfume, Ahmed felt slightly irritated. This girl is hot for me and I am going to get nowhere because of this Ferret, he said to himself. Ahmed had always been good at hanging nicknames on people and wished there was someone to share this one with.

Mahmood pulled a saucer filled with pickled turnips and yellow peppers closer to him. He took two turnip strips and placed them on his plate then picked up one of the peppers by its woody stem and plopped it in his mouth. Ahmed noticed the stem protruding from Mahmood's lips and concluded he looked even more disgusting. Mahmood tossed the stem on his plate. His beady eyes darted around the room as he took a piece of pita bread from the basket and tore it in half. Dipping the bread into the humus, Mahmood scooped up a large dollop and crammed it into his mouth

Ahmed often wondered where the line of demarcation lay between religious fanatic and psychopath. In Mahmood's case, it was apparent the line had been blurred long ago. Ahmed had seen his type at the camps. He'd often wondered whether the Mahmoods of the world were psychopaths first who became religious fanatics, or simply religious men whose fanaticism drove them to be psychopaths. In the end it didn't matter. What mattered was what happened when the Mahmoods found a home where their psychotic behavior was sanctioned. Mahmood had found such a home; fanatical Islam. Ahmed knew there wasn't anything innate about Islam to elicit such behavior, any faith or belief could be a channel for such fanaticism, there were countless other examples.

"So, it's just that simple, you got tired of living in Afghanistan. You just packed up and came home to Fairlane Hills?" Mahmood asked sarcastically.

"Well, it wasn't that simple, I had to make some stops along the way. The important thing is I got home," Ahmed answered again with kernels of truth.

"And did one of the stops along the way include a stop at the interment facilities in Guantanamo?" Mahmood continued eating.

Before Ahmed could answer, the waitress came to their table and placed a bowl of fattoush salad in front them, brushing against Ahmed as she turned to leave.

"There was a brief stay at the facility. It was only a short lay over. I had become separated from my family when the war

Episode 15

started. The Americans picked me up near Kabul. They took me to Guantanamo," again a mixture of truth and caution.

Mahmood appeared ready to continue the interrogation when the waitress approached with their main course. She set steaming platters in front of them along with bowls of rice. Though the chicken and vegetables smelled good, Ahmed's appetite had diminished. Mahmood spooned heaping quantities on his plate and began eating vigorously. Trying to keep his emotions in check, Ahmed filled his plate but found it difficult to eat.

After stuffing down several mouthfuls, Mahmood drank some water then looked up at Ahmed. A trickle of the gaylia sauce dribbled from the corner of Mahmood's mouth as he speared a mushroom from his plate. Hesitating momentarily, he held the fork motionless midway to his mouth as he picked up the white napkin lying in front of him and wiped off the sauce. After cleaning his chin, Mahmood continued eating the mushroom.

"You are not hungry?" Mahmood asked. 'tis a sin to waste food," he added in his heavy accent. "In the camps, did they not teach you to eat when food is available? The next meal may never come."

"Yes," Ahmed answered, "they taught us many things that I would just as soon forget."

Ahmed surprised himself with his answer. Mahmood was a dangerous man, but Ahmed had become annoyed by of all of this questioning. Whatever Mahmood wanted, it was better to get it out in the open quickly.

"Well for you, young man, I hope more things are remembered than forgotten," Mahmood tore another piece of pita and scooped up the last of the humus.

"I was never that good of a student," Ahmed replied.

Ahmed knew he was on thin ice but hoped to somehow wriggle out of the situation. If he could convince Mahmood he was incompetent, maybe the Ferret would look elsewhere.

"I know you were a disappointment to your father," Mahmood continued, "and I know your father and brother were martyred."

105

"Then you know how they died. They were very brave, sorry but am I am not like them."

"So, you have no desire to avenge their deaths? You will just let their blood be for nothing? You will let those that kill your family to continue killing your Muslim brothers and sisters? You are content to do nothing?" Mahmood asked wryly.

"My father's blood was not spilled for nothing. There were some ideals of his that I share. There were some things he did that I admired, but we are different, or maybe I should say were very different. I know he was disappointed in me but I want to live my life in a different way." Though trying to contain his emotions, Ahmed's voice became shaky.

"Yes, I know how you want to live your life. You want to drive fast cars and listen to western music. And you want to chase after American whores. I see the way you look at the waitress. There are more important things in life. Muslims are being persecuted and killed all over the world. You of all people, Haleem's son, should want to do something about it. Your father and brother are martyrs. Your mother is willing to be martyred, and she is but a woman."

"My father and mother accomplished some very good things. I know that. I believed in what they did with the orphanage. They saved children that would have died and I thank Allah for those good things they did. I tried to help in those things. I helped build the orphanage, and I helped care for the children. I played games with them and held them when they were frightened. Those are things I could do. I could make them laugh and be happy at least some of the time," Ahmed couldn't believe the words coming out of his mouth. It was as if he was someone else watching himself debate this man.

"And you could sneak off to Kabul with your useless friends, and listen to decadent music and watch useless movies. That is what you did best. Now you have a chance to make up for that. Now you have a chance to make your father and mother proud," Mahmood's eyes seemed to bore directly into Ahmed's very soul.

"I had these arguments with my father. That is why I left Afghanistan. That is why I am trying to make a new life for myself

Episode 15

here. I am not interested in any opportunities you may have for me," Ahmed set his fork down and picked up his glass of water. He took a drink then set the glass down.

"No, Ahmed that is not why you left," Mahmood placed his hands on the table and leaned forward.

"You left because the Americans offered you a way out. A way to the life you desired. So now you are here, at their behest doing their work and turning your back on your Muslim brothers," Mahmood continued in a low voice.

"I am doing no work for them. I hold American citizenship, I was born here. When they arrested me, they soon found that what you say about me is true. I was of no value to them. As you said, all I wanted to do was hang out with my useless friends and listen to music and watch movies. They knew I had nothing to give them and as an American citizen they had to return me here," Ahmed answered, pleased he had been able to control his anger.

"So, the CIA just brought you here. Somehow you had enough money to pay for a place to live and find a job. How stupid do you think we are?" Picking up his fork, Mahmood continued eating.

"Look, my friends and I had some money put away before the Americans came. We were saving it. When we had enough, we were going to buy plane tickets and come here. We got the money smuggling movies and cigarettes. We also dealt in hashish and other businesses my father never knew about. When the Americans came, we surrendered rather than being killed fighting, I admit that. When they figured out I couldn't help them, they let me go. I had some extra money to get the apartment and establish myself. The job, I got through the Fairlane Hills Arab Council. You can check that if you like. The records are there." Ahmed was pleased with his rebuttal, most of which was truth with the exception of Charlie arranging the job at the hospital.

"So, it appears that you have finally attained this life that you always wanted. You have your car and your western clothes and money. It all came at a price. Now we are going to give you an opportunity to repay those you owe," Mahmood signaled to the waitress.

"Is there something more I can get for you?" she asked.

"My friend and I are ready for coffee," Mahmood answered.

The waitress left then quickly reappeared with two small cups and a porcelain pot of Turkish coffee. She poured a cup for each of them then set the pot between them. Mahmood added two teaspoons of sugar to his cup and took a sip.

"The coffee is very good, Ahmed," he said, "you should have some."

Ahmed picked up the cup and took a drink.

"There, I drank the coffee; it's very good just as you say. Now what do you mean an opportunity to repay? I don't owe anyone, anything," Ahmed replied.

"You owe many people. You are just not aware of it quite yet," Mahmood said refilling his cup.

"Who do I owe?" Ahmed asked.

"Well, to begin with, you owe your father. You owe your mother, and you owe your brother who was brave enough to find his way to paradise."

"I owe my father and mother for feeding me and clothing me? That is a parent's responsibility. It says so in the Koran," Ahmed added smugly.

"Oh, so now you are going to lecture me on the Koran? Someone who cannot stay awake during prayers?" Mahmood shot back. "Let me tell you someone else you owe. You owe Kamal, sitting over there. If it were not for him, you would not be sitting here right now. He is the only reason you are alive. He convinced us you could be of some benefit."

"What do you mean, some benefit?" this last exchange had become unsettling. Ahmed felt himself beginning to perspire.

"Well, your job at the hospital, to begin with. I heard your story about how you got it. I do not believe it. We know there is something going on at Oak Grove Hospital and we want to know what it is." Mahmood answered.

"What good can I be?" Ahmed asked, "I am just on the janitorial staff. I mop floors, I empty waste baskets. How can I be of any help?"

Episode 15

"We want you to keep your eyes open. We want you to keep us informed of anything unusual. We want you to tell us if anyone approaches you and asks you for information about any of the patients. There is something else that Kamal is working on. In time, you may be called on to assist him," Mahmood answered.

"If I say no, are you and Hamas or Islamic Jihad or whoever you are connected with going to come and kill me?" Ahmed whispered.

"Who I am associated with is unimportant. Killing you would be counter productive so no, we will not come and kill you if you refuse. As you said you are an American citizen, and have rights. You have the right to protection from the American government while you are on American soil. So no, we will not kill you, Ahmed. But let me ask you a question," Mahmood said his black eyes locked onto Ahmed's.

"What question is that?" Ahmed answered.

"Is all of your family here on American soil, or are some still in Afghanistan?" Mahmood picked up the cup and finished his coffee.

"Are you talking about my mother and sister?" Ahmed asked guardedly.

"I just asked if your family is all here or are some still back there," Mahmood answered.

"Real Muslim fighters don't kill innocent women and children," Ahmed responded. "You of all people should know that."

"Lecturing me again on the Koran?" Mahmood asked sarcastically.

Mahmood slid out of the booth and motioned to the waitress. The waitress brought the check and handed it to him. Mahmood glanced at the check then walked toward the cash register.

Ahmed slumped back in the booth and looked over at Kamal. Kamal looked up from his food momentarily then nodded his head. Ahmed slid out of the booth and walked to the door. As he opened it, he looked back at the waitress. The meeting with Mahmood had dampened his spirits and he had lost interest in pursuing her signals.

Ahmed walked to his car and opened the door. He put the keys in the ignition and started the Pontiac. Before he could put the car in gear he heard a phone ring. The sound was disorienting. Ahmed thought it was his own phone and hoped it was Ali. He pulled his phone out of his jacket pocket but the ringing continued. Realizing the tone was different, he listened for the source. Opening the top of the center console, Ahmed saw a metallic blue phone.

"Damn it," Ahmed said out loud pounding the steering wheel with the palms of his hands, "that's just what I need right now, Charlie on my ass."

Ahmed flipped open the phone.

"Yes, Charlie," he said in a disgusted voice.

"This isn't Charlie," the gravelly voice replied.

Ahmed's heart froze. It was the Ferret.

Episode 16

The low pitched hum resonating from the Explorer's undercarriage stopped as the road changed back to asphalt. Having crossed the bridge, Ronnie was now in Trenton and the entrance to the Elizabeth Park Marina was just ahead. The county owned park sprawls along a three mile semi-circular canal connected to the Detroit River. The canal provides boaters with access to park's picnic areas, walking trails and soft ball diamonds. There are also launching ramps and a concession stand with tables where old timers gather to sip coffee and exchange fish stories.

Nearing the entrance, Ronnie saw several vehicles pulling trailered boats. The lead rig was a blue Sea Ray cutty cabin pulled by a Dodge pick up. The driver looking to be in his thirties, had long black hair cut in a mullet and wore silver wrap around sun glasses. His sleeveless tee shirt revealed a large tattoo on his left shoulder. A heavily made up blonde woman sat in the passenger seat with a vacant look on her face. As Ronnie came abreast of the truck, she removed a cigarette from her lips and flicked it out the window. Ronnie knew the odds were good a bucket of chicken and a bottle of Tequila were stashed somewhere in the Sea Ray. They were probably headed for Crystal Bay to hang out and blast Jimmy Buffett from the Sea Ray's sound system. After a few shots of tequila, the blonde might even be coaxed into removing her bikini top and join other brazen young women flashing other partying boaters. It was this kind of behavior that led Ronnie's yacht club neighbors to complain how much better boating was before it became affordable to the peasants.

The Sea Ray reminded Ronnie of times he and Beth had beached their own cutty on Sugar Island. There wasn't enough tequila in the world to ever get Beth to remove her top in public but she never looked down on people like the Mullets. Though they may not eat brie or sip Pinot Noir, she'd say they were usually quick to share their beer and Buffalo wings.

Beth could eat an enormous amount of chicken wings, then again Beth could eat an enormous amount of everything. It had been that way since their first date in 1965. They'd gone to a dance after a football game. After the dance, they and two other couples loaded into Ronnie's powder blue 1960 Ford Falcon and drove to the local Big Boy where she consumed two burgers, fries and a hot fudge sundae. It had exhausted Ronnie's allowance for two weeks.

She was a little wisp of girl with long brunette hair pulled back in a French braid. Her hazel eyes were complemented by her flawless complexion. Ronnie was smitten and knew immediately he would marry her someday. Her last name was McGowan, so he assumed she was Irish. He was half right. She had her father's quick Irish temper which Ronnie experienced often over the years. It was offset by her quick Irish wit; Beth laughed easily.

Her voracious appetite was one of the things Ronnie missed most. Before the cancer, she'd have eaten the Mullet couple's Buffalo wings and then found a way to polish off their entire KFC bucket. She'd also make them laugh as she downed their Bud Lites; a quality Ronnie loved most about her. While her temper sometimes made her act first and think later, she could be at home with anybody. Beth could laugh and joke with Mr. Mullet about NASCAR, and an hour later discuss Tolstoy.

Episode 16

She was the single most loving person he had ever known and he was lost without her. There were very few Beth McGowans in this world and he had been lucky enough to spend thirty-five years with her. Beth's temper was scary, but even scarier was never seeing her smile again or hearing her laugh again. She loved life and had shared hers with him. Ronnie often wondered what the odds were of meeting someone at seventeen that could still complement you at fifty. They were slim. He knew he had been lucky.

Behind the Mullet couple was a green bow rider pulled by a Dodge Durango. The driver looked somewhere in his forties, as was his pudgy, red headed wife. There were three boys in the back seats. The middle one had the mother's carrot topped head.

Two bass boats were next in line. They were low profile professional models with metal flaked paint that matched the pick ups pulling them.

Last was an ancient yellow fiberglass tri-hull, with an outdated Chrysler outboard resting on the stern. The rig was towed by an even older model Chevy pickup that had been painted green at one time. Driving the pick up was a large black man with silver hair and a thin goatee. His partner, a diminutive man, wore a Detroit Pistons baseball cap with the bill pointed to the right. Ronnie had seen them several times fishing the cut by the power plant. Ronnie waved at the men as he passed. Removing the stump of an unlit cigar, the driver waved back.

At the stop light, Ronnie turned right on West Jefferson Avenue and noticed a sign in the window of the dry cleaners announcing sweaters were half off. He wondered who cleaned sweaters in late summer; but maybe autumn was not that far away. Beth had been so good at planning for those kinds of things. The canal was off to his right and Ronnie could see several boats on the grass bank. Ahead was the Tourist Lodge, a rustic red brick building with a high roof and tall windows where unfortunate souls performing community service met on Saturday mornings.

Behind the Lodge was a picturesque clearing with an old wooden foot bridge spanning the canal. Near the bridge sat a covered pavilion with picnic tables and barbecue grills, a favorite location for weddings pictures. A chauffeur was standing by a stretch limo idling in the parking lot while a young bride and groom posed on the bridge. It was such a splendid evening, Ronnie considered pulling into the lot and watching them. Beth would have insisted. Though direct at times, she had a soft spot for young people filled with hope and anticipation. Seeing the wedding party increased Ronnie's feelings of melancholy knowing Beth would never see her boys marry.

Beyond the tourist lodge, West Jefferson makes two ninety degree turns before reaching Trenton's business district. At the second turn, an A&W Drive In sits on one corner while an ice cream stand is on the other. The road widens there, becoming a boulevard with a paving stoned median. Retro street lamps, trees and cement benches line the median. Ronnie continued past Elliot's Bakery and Gerry's Five and Dime. Beth was a sucker for dime stores. Trips to any city always included a stop at the local five and dime. She maintained her love for them was a carry over from childhood shopping trips with her mother. Ronnie passed The Grand Hotel where the marquee read Congratulations Thomas and Jennifer. Ronnie wondered if it had been Thomas and Jennifer taking pictures on the footbridge. He wished the sign could have read Congratulations Ronnie and Beth.

Leaving downtown, Ronnie saw the silhouette of the steel mill ahead. The exterior was an intertwined mixture of corrugated steel and brick, with windows that looked to have been last cleaned during the Great Depression. Ronnie assumed there was some architectural design to the place reflecting the manufacturing process for steel, but other than the four large smoke stacks rising above everything else, the layout made little sense. The railroad tracks winding around the plant looked to have been laid when steam engines were the modern mode of transportation. The grounds around the mill were always covered with a thin layer of soot.

The entrance was a quarter mile ahead and Ronnie could see the guard shack where he was to pick up Denny. Getting closer,

Episode 16

Ronnie saw Denny standing next to a security guard seated behind an elevated desk. They were smoking cigarettes. Denny saw the Explorer and opened the door to the shack. It struck Ronnie how professional Denny looked in his khaki pilots uniform. He carried a small green duffel bag in his left hand and his pilot's hat in his right. The last time he had seen Denny had been a few years before Beth died and she had been gone two years. Denny looked the same, just a little older. He was a few pounds heavier and his hair now had touch of silver. Denny flashed the same shit eating grin, as Beth had called it, and opened the rear passenger door. He set the duffel bag on the back seat.

"Sisification!" Denny said with a mischievous laugh, sending a smile across Ronnie's face.

Denny opened the front door and climbed into the passenger seat. The familiarity of his greeting lightened Ronnie's melancholy. Denny had been good at blowing off emotional land slides. It was one of the things Ronnie envied, though he knew Denny had navigated some turbulent personal waters of his own.

Denny had been married to Beth's younger sister Carol. They'd met as teenagers during the summer of 1969 when they worked aboard the Columbia, one of two Bob Lo Boats. Bob Lo Island, an amusement park on the Canadian side of the lower Detroit River, lies just due east of Grosse Ile. When the park was a thriving business, Grosse Ile residents could see roller coaster cars whizzing along the rails of the white latticed structure. If the wind was right, they could even hear passengers scream as their coaster cars rocketed down several steep inclines.

Visitors to Bob Lo Island were transported to the park by a pair of triple decked, steam driven ferries. Built in the 1930s, the Columbia and St. Claire were painted gleaming white. With their wide open decks, they were as much a part of Detroit's heritage as Vernor's Ginger Ale and Tiger Stadium. From downtown, the nineteen mile trip on the Detroit River took about an hour and was a tradition for Michigan families every summer.

The amusement park had been family owned until inheritance squabbles and poor management led to bankruptcy.

When Bob Lo was finally sold to real estate investors, summer mansions and condominiums replaced the Wild Mouse and Log Ride. The Columbia and St. Claire with their dance floors, concession stands and cotton candy machines were also sold ending another Detroit way of life. Moon light cruises, where passengers sat on wooden slated chairs feeling the moist breeze flow across their cheeks while listening to big band music, ended forever. There would be no more steamy Kowalski Franks topped with spicy yellow mustard and sweet onions. There would be no more cold Stroh's beer sipped from frosty brown bottles while the Detroit skyline faded into the distance. Hearing the Bob Lo boats would be shuttered, Ronnie lamented there would be no more first kisses stolen by giddy teenagers on the top deck. Before she died, Ronnie confided tearily to Beth he'd give everything he owned, and all he could borrow, to be a teenager and kiss her one more time on that deck.

When Denny was promoted to first mate on the Columbia, he married Carol. She had never been very stable, even as a child. To complicate things, shortly after the wedding Denny's father died suddenly. His mother never recovered from the loss and committed suicide shortly after. Before his parents' deaths, Denny's drug use had been recreational. Afterward, it turned into a self medicating nightmare. The marriage to Carol lasted eight tumultuous years.

It seemed every ounce of anger Denny felt toward his mother, became directed at Carol who was too fragile to cope with even the emotional requirements of a normal marriage. She melted under the weight. To cope, Carol turned to prescribed medications but unlike Denny she could not turn it on and off with the boating season.

Carol had intended to finish her art degree after they were married. It never happened. Following the divorce she spent the next twenty years bouncing from one addiction to another. During that time, Denny married twice and had two daughters. Ronnie and Beth got the odd Christmas card from him over the years but in an unexplainable way, they both missed his bizarre

Episode 16

yet entertaining sense of humor. Denny did not attend Beth's funeral but called with condolences. The call was the last time Ronnie heard from him until the one recently saying he would be at the mill in Trenton and wanted to meet for dinner.

"Sisification yourself, ass wipe," Ronnie said as Denny closed the passenger door.

It was a standing joke between them. When they were young, Denny often called Ronnie a sissy for refusing to hang out with him and his buddy Eddie Wayne. Denny announced one day he'd created a new word, sisification, to describe Ronnie's cowardice

"I was impressed with the way you docked that freighter," Ronnie said easing the Explorer back onto West Jefferson. "Oh, and by the way, why'd you put your fagotty little captain's hat in the back seat?" With Denny it was better to be on the attack.

"Oh you like that, do you?" Denny grinned and looked out the side window.

"Yeah, why don't you reach back there and put that little fagotty hat on your pube head," Ronnie added with a smile.

"Pube head! Like you of all people should be calling anyone pubic head. Wait, your hair is so grey, you look like Grandpa Pube," Denny countered.

"At least I don't try to hide mine with some fagotty hair dye, Mr. Grecian Formula," Ronnie shot back.

Denny's unpredictability was one of the traits Beth liked most about him. She never carried a grudge against Denny for the divorce maintaining there were so much missing in both of them, that together they added up to less than a whole person. She'd defend her lack of resentment by adding one had to value what little Denny and Carol had to offer because it was all they were capable of. Beth could capturing a person's essence in simple terms, a skill Ronnie never possessed.

"I don't use any queer assed hair dye, numb nuts. I'm like Ronald Reagan, I just have hair that stays dark naturally," Denny grinned.

"Yeah, well maybe you do but Reagan didn't keep his shaved off to stop people from calling him pube head," Ronnie replied.

"Well, Reagan and I have so much in common, maybe I should run for president."

"Yeah, do that Denny. When you get elected, I'll call you President Pube. Besides, you already have Alzheimer's from all those drugs during your wanton youth. You've got a head start on being the next Ronnie R."

"That was cruel. When did you get so cruel? I always thought you were just a big sorry assed wuss," Denny countered.

"It just comes with the age, Denny. The boys maintain I've turned into a crotchety old bubble head."

"Well, I don't know about all that bubble stuff, but I'd agree you are a crotch head," Denny replied.

Distracted, Ronnie nearly missed the turn into Sibley Gardens. He hit the brakes while turning the Explorer steeper than intended.

"Nice turn, keep driving like that and next thing you know, you'll be living in Sarasota wearing striped shirts, plaid Bermuda shorts and knee high black socks with your sandals and cataract sunglasses. By the way, what the hell is a bubble head?" Denny asked as Ronnie parked.

"That's what my boys call old guys who wear those baseball caps with the plastic meshing around the sides and back. You know the ones without any curve to the bill," Ronnie answered as they got out of the truck.

"Oh yeah," Denny said, "they're usually wearing those pale blue jeans and have really big glasses that are tinted grey even when they're inside."

"I hadn't noticed the glasses thing 'till you just said it, but yeah they do," Ronnie agreed.

"Well come on you bubble headed sissy, you're gonna buy me some calamari," Denny replied nearing the restaurant's entrance.

"I'll buy it, but I ain't gonna eat nothing with tentacles and suction cups," Ronnie answered.

Walking into the restaurant, Ronnie thought of how Beth characterized Sibley Gardens as Downriver cozy. It had been one of her favorite places. First time patrons are usually pleasantly surprised to find such superb Italian dining in the middle of a heavy industrial area. The exterior is an eclectic mixture of construction materials. The cinder block walls are painted light grey while the front is a combination of field stone and stucco. Inside, the bar is paneled in dark wood with red leather upholstered booths. The dining room has booths along the outer walls and oaken tables in the center. The tables and booths are always covered with immaculate white table cloths.

The hostess, a pretty girl in her mid twenties greeted Ronnie by name and asked if they would preferred the dining room or bar. Ronnie told Denny to decide. Denny chose the bar.

"How nice to see you again Mr. Harris," Denny said in a high pitched imitation of the hostess as they slid into a booth near the back.

"Be a gentleman, Denny," Ronnie replied reaching for the bread basket.

The waitress came to their table. She was tall and slim, had dishwater blonde hair and looked to be in her late thirties.

"Good evening gentlemen. Can I bring either of you a drink?" Her name tag read Darlene.

Denny smiled and ordered a Heineken. Ronnie ordered a Labatt's. The waitress returned Denny's smile with a small tilt of her head and said she'd be right back with their drinks. Ronnie noticed Darlene's quick inspection of Denny's left hand and guessed the absence of a wedding ring had prompted the head tilt. He wondered how many times this scene had played out in Denny's life of boats and bars. Denny was supposed to spend the night and return to his freighter the next day. Ronnie was pretty certain Denny would be piloting the freighter tomorrow, but surmised spending the night might have become iffy.

"Looks like you've become a regular. Has Sibley's become Ronnie's Cheers, where everyone knows his name?" Denny asked.

"No, but I do come in here from time to time," Ronnie replied.

"Well, seeing the hostess, I can't blame you."

"Denny, she went to high school with my sons," Ronnie answered.

"Yeah, and like you don't see those big firm ta tas," Denny replied flashing a grin.

Darlene appeared with their beers before Ronnie could reply.

"A Lebatt's for Mr. Harris, and a Heineken for Commodore Perry," Darlene said setting the drinks before them.

Ronnie laughed at the remark. It was clear the comment also surprised Denny. Ronnie knew it would be an interesting evening.

"So, have you decided what you want?" Darlene asked.

Denny answered first, "I'll have the calamari."

"Do you want pasta or a baked potato?"

"I'll have the pasta and the salad with the house dressing," Denny smiled as he set the leather bound menu on the table.

"And you Mr. Harris, what can I bring you?" Darlene asked politely.

"Well, better company for dinner, but you can't help me there," Ronnie answered. Darlene laughed as Denny took a drink of his beer. "So, instead, I'll have the Lasagna. I'd also like a cup of minestrone and for a salad, the Michigan Cherry," Ronnie replied. "Try the minestrone Denny, it's really good," Ronnie added.

"I've had it here, but I was going to ask Darlene if they had any oysters on the half shell," Denny looked up at Darlene.

"Well, Commodore, oysters are out of season. They are only available during months that have an R in them," Darlene answered.

"Well," Denny shot back, "this is Argust, isn't it?"

Darlene laughed softly.

"I'll be back in a minute with your salads," Darlene added then left.

"Well, landed on your feet again there Mr. Williams. It appears you still have the touch," Ronnie lifted his glass in salute.

They each took a drink of beer as Darlene approached their table with the salads and soup.

"So what's it like living in the Pagoda House?" Denny asked.

"Mr. Harris, you live in the Pagoda House?" Darlene interjected.

Episode 16

"Well, at least for the last few years," Ronnie replied. "The Commodore here is spending the night with me while his ship is docked over at the mill."

"You do know who Commodore Perry was, don't you sweetheart?" Denny asked Darlene.

"I do," she answered, "I've read Shogun. He opened Japan to trade during the 1700s."

"Ahhh, very good," Denny replied, "he was an adventurer of sorts who liked to explore."

Ronnie leaned back in his seat. This was Denny at his smooth talking best.

"So I've heard," Darlene answered with a smile.

"So, Darlene, do you like exploring?" Denny took their exchange a little further.

"Sometimes," she answered, "I'll go explore the kitchen and see how the natives are doing with your entrées."

Darlene winked at Ronnie as she left the table.

"Denny, you are still the master of the ladies," Ronnie said as he added grated Parmesan to the minestrone.

"Just a matter of practice," Denny chewed a forkful of romaine. "And some natural talent," he added with a laugh.

The two men made some small talk, commiserating about the Tiger's dismal summer and the Lions upcoming season. It was safe conversation; they the avoided topics relating to Beth or Carol.

Darlene brought their dinners. When they finished, she asked if they wanted coffee. Ronnie told her they'd have coffee at home but asked her to pack up a couple of cannoli to go. Taking them home had been a tradition with Beth. Darlene said she'd have them ready in a minute and took Ronnie's Master Card.

"So, the Pagoda House? I've always wondered what that place looked like on the inside," Denny said as Darlene returned and handed Ronnie a white bag.

"Let's set sail, Commodore," Ronnie answered. As they walked toward the parking lot Denny stopped abruptly.

"I think I left something," Denny said looking back at the restaurant. "I'll be back in a minute."

"The only thing you left in there, Denny, was Darlene. I'm not a moron you know," Ronnie added.

"No, just a big fucking Sisification," Denny replied with a hardy laugh.

Episode 17

Pulling up the drive way, Eric noticed he'd left the garage door open. Stacks of old newspapers and magazines were strewn around worn out tires, lawn tools and garden hoses. The only functional item was the red Snapper lawnmower. Eric kept enough space clear to access the mower when Inspector Larry from the Department of Public Works stopped by. The visits happened regularly during the summer when Eric's elderly neighbors called city hall to complain about his failure to mow the grass, or mixture of weeds as they described it.

Eric noticed Inspector Larry had taken a softer approach and his requests had become gentler. He had even helped Eric get the ancient mower running when it failed to start. Inspector Larry had loaded it into his yellow pick up and taken it to Marv's Fix-It Shop

Marv's was one of Larry's favorite stops. Located next to Celia's Sub Shop, it sat across the road from Thunderbowl Lanes where Larry and his wife Martha had bowled on Friday nights. When Larry pulled into Marv's parking lot that day, the work shop door was open. He could see Marv working on a mower. Marv looked up, saw Larry's truck and walked outside. Marv was the most squared looking man Larry had ever seen. Every feature of Marv's physical presence seemed to have a ninety degree angle. His shoulders were square, his jaw was square; even his head was square. Marv's close cut, flat topped hair cut only added to the angular illusion. He had served two tours in the Marine Corps and it showed.

"Hey, Inspector," Marv said wiping his hands with a salmon colored rag pulled from the back pocket of his overalls.

"Trouble with this Snapper?" Marv added looking at the mower in the bed of the pick up.

"Yeah, it won't start. The plug may be bad. I was hoping you could take a look," Larry answered.

"No, problem Inspector, drop that tail gate and we'll take her in the shop and find out in short order."

Larry lowered the tail gate and they unloaded the mower. Marv pushed it over to one of the work benches.

"Thought you were a Toro man, Larry. When'd you pick up this antique?" Marv asked as they lifted the mower onto the bench.

"Oh, it's not mine. Just trying to help out a needy citizen," Larry answered.

"Anybody I know?" Marv asked pulling the ignition wire off the spark plug. He grabbed a wrench lying on the work bench.

"Belongs to a fella named Eric over on Keppen Street, you probably don't know him," Larry leaned against the workbench.

"Oh, you mean Crazy Eric?" Marv asked as he removed the spark plug and held it up to examine the firing tip. "Plug's bad, probably needs a tune up."

"So you know Eric?" Larry asked in return.

"Inspector, I grew up here in Northern Allen Park. I went to high school with him at Melvindale. I graduated three years ahead so I didn't know him real well. He was a year ahead of my little brother. Not many people around here I don't know. People stay here long enough, something they own eventually breaks," Marv said picking up an air hose and blew grass clippings off the Snapper.

Episode 17

"Well, then you probably know he has some issues," Larry raised his eye brows.

"Yeah, I know about those, thought maybe he'd gone the same way as some guys I served with in Nam," Marv said putting down the air hose.

"So is that what happened to him?" Larry asked, "You never know with people like Crazy Eric what's the right or wrong thing to say. Just thought I'd help him out a little. If his grass gets long, his neighbors complain, mostly 'cause they have nothing better to do."

"Well, I really don't know all of it. I wasn't around here all that much when my brother played ball with him. He was a hell of a football player you know," Marv said walking to the other bench for a screwdriver.

"Who your brother?" Larry asked.

"No, Eric. Hell of a basketball player too," Larry answered, "but better in football. He was an all state tailback in 1967. My brother played defensive tackle."

'You're kidding," Larry replied incredulously. "Hell, I played against him. I graduated from Allen Park High in '69. But I was just a sophomore then, didn't get into the games much."

"Smart as hell, too. Didn't play football in college though. He went to Michigan. I think old Bump Elliot wanted him to play before he got the boot and Bo came in. He was class valedictorian too I believe. Maybe it was drugs or whatever that knocked him off his rocker. Couldn't say, but I heard he did a couple of years at Harvard Law or something. My brother knew him better and told me that one time. Crazy Eric walked by while we were chewing the fat one afternoon," Marv said unscrewing the oil plug. Dirty oil spurted into a catch pan.

"Not smart enough to change the oil though," Larry smiled as he pointed at the thick black sludge.

"Tell you what Mr. Good Samaritan. It's almost lunch time, you go next door and get us a couple of cheese steaks, I'll do the tune up for free, if you buy the parts," Marv said. "I feel sorry for ol' Eric. On second thought, I'll spring for the parts too, gotta watch out for a fellow Cardinal. Can't let you Jaguars say we don't take care of our own," Marv added with a laugh.

"That's a deal," Inspector Larry agreed. "What do you want on yours?"

"The works, tell Celia extra peppers. I got a couple of Cokes in the fridge, drinks on me."

Larry walked across the parking lot to Celia's Sub Shop. He took a seat on a stool at the counter and ordered two Philly cheese steaks subs to go. The young girl working the counter wrote his order and placed it behind several others on the small wooden ledge in front of the grill.

Inspector Larry remembered when the place had been Ted and Celia's Sub Shop, until Ted allegedly took up with one of the young waitresses. He'd also heard Celia's lawyer was a barracuda and Ted was lucky to leave the court room with his pants. He'd never had a chance to verify the rumor about the courtroom drama, but it made for a good laugh.

Celia's real name was Cecilia, but nobody ever called her that. She was a good business woman and continued running the shop. Celia was standing at the grill in front of a steaming pile of shredded flank steak when Larry walked in. The steam had saturated her hair and the two soggy locks hanging down on each side of her head reminded Larry of the Orthodox Jews he and his wife had seen during a vacation to New York City. Celia liked Inspector Larry. She knew about his wife's condition and respected his devotion. Most men, Ceil contended, would have signed the consent to end life support so fast it would make a person's head spin and found a replacement before the ink was dry. She believed men of character, like the Inspector, were rare.

"Well, if it isn't Inspector Larry," she said with a broad smile. "All the trash bins are covered, the drains all work properly and we wash our hands after using the bathroom."

Celia took the dish towel draped over her shoulder and wiped the sweat from her forehead.

Episode 17

"Hey Ceil," Larry said turning toward the short dark complexioned woman. "It's not an official visit. Just grabbing a couple of subs for me and Marvin."

Before Celia spoke, Larry had been looking out the window towards the bowling alley. He and Marty had been regulars at the sub shop after bowling. Larry would have a cheese steak and Marty would eat pizza. She maintained it was the best Downriver. The pepperonis were thick and plentiful. They curled up around the edges making miniature grease cups. Marty had a cast iron stomach and sometimes ate four pieces.

Friday nights weren't the same now. He'd joined a men's league and while it helped pass the time, it left him feeling empty. Then again, little in his life had remained the same. Maybe it would have been better had Marty's stomach been fragile. Maybe she would have avoided pizza and the stroke. Hell, Larry said to himself, who really knew, maybe she would have had the stroke even if she ate tofu and sprouts. Or died of breast cancer like Marv's wife.

"Marv's?" Celia asked, "What are you doing over there? If you're buying him a sub, you're certainly not writing him a citation I take it. That would be cruel and unusual punishment, especially if he's buying," she finished with a laugh.

It had been a while since Larry had been in the shop. Celia had lost weight. Her eyes looked puffy with remnants of black circles under them. Probably the stress of the divorce, he thought. As she spoke, Larry noticed tiny bits of white saliva had gathered at the corners of her mouth. Marty would have been tickled, she often referred to her as Swallow Your Spit Celia. Now that Celia was free, Larry wondered if there was an opportunity for Marv to ease some of his loneliness. Larry chuckled aloud at the thought.

"What's funny, Inspector?" Celia asked.

Larry hadn't realized he had laughed out loud and was lost for words. He finally managed a reply.

"Oh, nothing Ceil, I just told myself a joke I had never heard before, that's all,"

"Oh, very funny Mr. Inspector," she replied. "I'll just take it that was a private moment and leave it at that."

"So what are you doing over at Mower Marvin's anyway?" Celia asked with a sly grin.

"You know he hates that nick name," Larry replied.

"Sure, why do you think I call him that?" she answered maintaining the grin. She had white Mediterranean teeth. Larry liked her smile even with the two white flecks at the corners of her mouth. She was genuine; Larry knew there was no harm intended. Calling Marv, Mower Marvin was just her way of spicing up the day.

"Oh, just dropped off a mower for Marv to do a minor repair on is all," Larry replied.

"Now Inspector, you know using your city truck to transport personal property is against the law," Celia winked at Larry then walked back to the grill and flipped the pile of sizzling steak with a large metal turner.

"Oh, it's not mine, Ceil, just trying to help one of AP's needier citizens. That's all."

"Take over on this grill for a minute, hon," Ceil said to the teenaged girl who'd walked in from the back room. Celia walked to the counter.

"Yeah, who's the lucky citizen that's getting such royal treatment? Must be some big shot buddy of the mayor," Celia asked pouring Diet Coke from the dispenser. She handed the paper cup to Larry.

"Hardly," Larry answered taking a sip of soda, "it belongs to a fella over on Keppen Street. Crazy Eric, if you know who that is."

"Yeah, I know him. He's that homeless looking guy. He's walks by on occasion. That's real Christian of you Larry. Why's he so special?" Celia asked.

"I don't know. When I have to go write him up for not mowing his lawn, he just seems so damn pitiful that's all. If his mower doesn't run, then he can't mow the lawn. Then the neighbors have an excuse to try to get him evicted. Maybe I should just let

Episode 17

nature take its course. I really don't know why I do it, Ceil to be honest with you," Larry finished.

"Add a third sub to that next order, hon." Celia barked to the young girl working the grill.

"I'll be right back with your order, Inspector," Celia walked back to the grill where the young girl was putting Larry's subs in a white paper bag. Celia waited until the third sub was completed and stuffed it in the bag with the other two. She walked back to Larry and handed him the bag.

"What do I owe you Ceil?" Larry asked reaching for his wallet.

"It's on the house Inspector," she answered with a wink.

"Hold it Ceil, you know I can't do that," Larry answered then opened the worn leather billfold and pulled out a crisp twenty. "I just printed this one this morning, careful you don't get ink smudges on your hand," he added.

"Hey, since when can't a shop owner give away free samples," Celia persisted, refusing his money.

"Since it says City Employee on my paycheck. Come on Ceil, you know that," Larry said as he handed her the twenty. "And there are three subs in this bag Ceil, I only ordered two."

"The third one's for Crazy Eric, and that one I insist on buying. The guy's pitiful. Maybe he can use his own money for some new clothes. Heaven knows he could use them and a hair cut and bath while he's at it," Celia replied handing Larry his change.

"Thanks Ceil, now we both can say we don't know why we do it," Larry said as he took his change and walked out.

"Because you're a man of integrity, Inspector Larry and there's too few of you around,"

she said after the door closed.

Larry walked back to Marv's carrying the white paper bag in one hand and the styrofoam cup half filled with Diet Coke in the other. Marv finished the repair and told Larry to have a seat at the bench while he washed his hands. The two men ate their subs talking about the upcoming football season.

After unloading the repaired mower, Eric was surprised when the Inspector handed him a paper bag containing a cheese steak sub. They sat on the back porch in silence while Eric ate. After thanking the Inspector, Eric started the Snapper. Larry said he'd be back in a few days to make sure everything was okay. A week later, Larry returned with a paper bag containing subs and diet cokes which the two men ate on the back porch without exchanging a word. Subs eaten in silence became a weekly occurrence.

Eric had no idea why the Inspector had become so nice. He also had no idea the Inspector's wife had suffered a stroke over the winter and was in a nursing home. After receiving a huge dose of life's realities, Larry understood the precarious nature of a person's sanity. After thirty years, he'd retired from Ford Motor with plans of traveling and enjoying life. Marty's stroke had changed all that.

When he sat beside her at the nursing home, Larry knew his girl Marty was locked in that body somewhere. She couldn't speak, but some days he thought he saw a flicker of acknowledgement in her opaque blue eyes. He swore she would squeeze his hand slightly when he kissed her and told her he'd be back tomorrow. Sitting with her one day, he thought about Eric and wondered if maybe like his Marty there was a different Eric trapped in there someplace. Larry decided he'd do what he could to give the other Eric a chance.

****

Eric got out of the van and opened the rear cargo doors. Grabbing one of the grocery bags, he carried it into the kitchen then walked back to the truck and brought in the other two bags and the bag Rudy had given him at the Big Boy. It still bothered him that he couldn't remember the two women at the market. It might come to him later, he could never predict such things.

Looking around the kitchen, he couldn't recall the last time he'd cleaned. It had been such a good day, he decided to straighten up after putting the groceries away. He piled all the dirty dishes on the counter next to the sink, then put the stopper in the bottom. After adding dish soap, Eric turned on the hot

Episode 17

water and as the sink filled, he put the groceries away. When the sink was full, he added the dishes and grabbed a dish cloth off the rack. After washing the dishes, he picked up the two frying pans, scraped the grease into the disposal then set the pans into the sudsy water. While they soaked, Eric dried the dishes and put them away. It took some scrubbing to finish the pans but he finally got them semi clean.

Pleased with his accomplishments, Eric made his way through the living room dodging the stacks of newspapers and magazines. He walked into his bedroom where bath towels lay crumpled on his bed. Dirty socks, with holes, were stacked high on the dresser and tattered blue jeans were strewn on the floor of the closet. Eric decided to pile all of them in the hallway until he could find a basket to carry them downstairs to the laundry.

As he picked up a pair of jeans from the closet floor, something on the bottom shelf caught Eric's eye. He could see four large books. Eric set the jeans in the hallway then returned to the closet and the books. The titles were written in gold embossed letters along the bindings. Two of the books were bound with red covers; one had a white cover while the book to the far right was green. All four books were titled The Cardinal Echo. Eric grabbed the green book and turned it over to so see the cover. In gold letters printed diagonally across the front were the words Melvindale High School 1967. Eric tossed the book onto his bed. It landed next to a pile of boxer shorts and what had at once been white tee shirts. He grabbed the other three books and set them on the floor next to the bed. Picking up the shorts and tee shirts, Eric added them to the stack in the hall way then walked back into the bedroom. The high school annuals had triggered something. There was a connection he couldn't quite put together. He paused and while looking at the ceiling his right index finger found it's way to his right eyelash as he stood in thought.

"That's it," Eric said aloud as a fleeting memory raced through his brain.

"That's how I know those women," he added in euphoric disbelief.

131

"They're in these books," Eric continued as he turned on the reading lamp next to his bed.

Eric noticed his hands were trembling as he collapsed backward on the twin bed. He felt confused about which book to open first. He decided on the green covered book with the year 1967 printed below the title, it was the most recent.

Eric sat up and changed position. He turned so his back was against the wall, then grabbed a dingy pillow and placed it behind his back. Bringing his knees up, Eric opened the green book and placed it on his lap. Opening the first page, he felt a sense of deja vu as he stared at the two page panoramic picture of a high school gymnasium. Eight girls in cheerleader outfits were caught in some kind of synchronized motion. Behind them, Eric could see bleachers filled with students. In the top right, there was a group of boys sitting together wearing red jackets with white leather sleeves. There was a block M on the front of their jackets. Most of the boys wore short cropped hair and had thick looking necks and wide shoulders. Some looked serious; others were smiling. Two boys in the bottom right of the picture appeared to be caught in the act of exchanging some kind of secret. The boy on the left was saying something into his friend's ear. The secret must have been humorous and meant only for his friend because the first boy had cupped his hand and pressed it against the other boy's ear. The other boy was laughing. Eric held the book closer and stared at the boys' faces. He recognized them but couldn't remember their names or that he had shared their joke that day.

The joke was about the blonde cheerleader standing in front of the two boys. Just before the picture had been taken, she'd completed a cartwheel and her cheerleading skirt had flopped down at the height of her acrobatic maneuver. The boys had gotten a peek of her bared butt cheek when her brief had ridden up. Though he didn't remember, Eric overheard their comments and could barely keep a straight face.

To the right of the bleachers, a tall dark haired boy stood behind a podium. He was dressed in a dark suit with a white shirt

Episode 17

and a green paisley tie and was speaking into a microphone. Above the bleachers, several paper signs were attached to the gymnasium walls with slogans written in red paint about taking back the Little Brown Jug. The picture had been taken from the top level of the gymnasium during a pep rally in the fall of 1966. It was Eric's senior year before a football game against their arch rival Lincoln Park High. The shot had been taken with a wide angle lens; if it had been taken with a telephoto, Eric might have recognized the seventeen year old football captain behind the podium as himself.

As Eric scrolled through the book, the bedroom began to feel stuffy. He set the book on the floor, stood on the bed and slid the window open. It was a balmy summer's evening. The white cotton curtains ruffled as the breeze poured into the opened window. Looking at the twilight sky, Eric sucked cool air into his lungs. It was starting to get dark and he saw two faint stars peeking through the hazy air. He remembered a time when the stars hadn't been so hidden. He and Wes would lie in the damp grass and the night sky had been full of little bright pin points. Sometimes they would sleep in Wes's Davy Crockett pup tent. Maybe that was where Wes was now, Eric thought. Maybe Wes was up on one of those stars driving a Corvette. He loved Vettes so much. Wes had finally gotten one, only to end up at the bottom of a canyon outside of Los Angeles. Eric wondered whether his mother had been right when she warned about getting what you asked for. Then again, maybe Wes wasn't up there in the stars at all. Maybe he was locked somewhere in the picture at the front of the high school annual. Maybe they were all locked there and everything that had happened since was just an illusion.

Eric looked at the clock on his dresser. It read nine-thirty. He knelt down on the bed and turned the book over. Eric stayed in that position staring at the pages until his knees began to ache. Lying down again, Eric balanced the book on his stomach and continued flipping pages. He looked at the pictures and read captions. Though he had no clear memories, a sense of longing floated through him. When Eric reached the individual snapshots of the senior class, he spent ten minutes staring at the picture of a boy with dark hair and high cheekbones. The caption read, Eric Arnold: Co Salutatorian, Captain Football and Track Teams, Captain Debate Team, State Champion Forensic Competition, voted Young Man Most Likely to Succeed.

Eric continued scrolling through the pages. He stopped when he got to the students whose last name began with C. He seemed mesmerized by a picture of a blonde girl with a Mona Lisa smile. The caption below her picture read Cate Cassadea, Valedictorian, President National Honor Society, President Latin Club, and voted Young Lady Most Likely to Succeed. Something seemed to stir in his soul, making him feel uneasy. It had been so long since he had even remotely felt anything. Seeing the girl's picture jarred something. He flipped back to the section of students whose last names began with A. He stared at the picture of a girl on the page directly opposite of his picture. Her name was Linda Alten. It was one of the women at the market; the tall dark haired woman with big breasts. He continued looking at the rest pictures until he came to a picture of a girl named Kathy Mac-Connell. It was the other woman.

Eric finished the book and set it on the bed. Four hours later he had finished the other three books. He opened the 1967 book again. He looked at the picture of Cate Cassadea for a moment then laid the book face down on his chest. Eric closed his eyes. It had been a very long day. Eric sensed his life was about to change. It was his last conscious thought before drifting into a dream filled sleep.

Episode 18

Hearing Mahmood's voice was a shock. Ahmed leaned back into the bucket seat, closed his eyes and took a deep breath.

"How did you get the phone into my car?" he asked calmly.

"Come on Ahmed, you know how simple that is. Who is this Charlie?" Mahmood continued.

"Charlie is a guy I met last week at a club. I thought maybe he left his phone in my car by mistake," Ahmed doubted Mahmood would believe his story.

"I don't believe you Ahmed. Anyway, here's another demonstration so you understand my capabilities better," Mahmood replied as Ahmed's own cell phone began to ring.

"How did you get my cell number?" Ahmed asked trying to mask his surprise because Charlie had provided the phone.

"That is not important, is it?" Mahmood shot back. "What is important, Ahmed, is that I have it."

"I thought I made myself clear in the restaurant," Ahmed replied.

"Consider this a demonstration, Ahmed. Just as easily as I obtained your phone number, I can find your mother and your little sister," Mahmood continued. "Have I made myself clear?"

"I understand. Exactly what do you want me of me?" Ahmed asked in a strained voice.

"We'll let you know the details later. What I want you to do for now, is to continue going to mosque. Kamal will be your contact there. Do as he requests and your mother and sister will be safe," Mahmood answered.

"Then what?" Ahmed asked tersely, "After I cooperate this time, what next?"

"You just do as Kamal asks, that is enough for now. Our conversation is over, so please get out of your car and put the phone under your front wheels. As you leave, back over the phone and leave it on the ground where it lies. Do you understand, Ahmed?" Mahmood asked in his gravely voice.

"Yes, I understand," Ahmed scanned the parking lot but couldn't see anyone. He looked toward the houses and apartment buildings behind the restaurant but saw nothing.

"In the future, this is how we will communicate. If I need to speak to you I will provide a secure phone. Afterwards, you will dispose of it.

"Yes, I understand," Ahmed replied trying to maintain control.

"Oh, by the way," Mahmood interjected. "I assume Charlie is your contact from the American government. For arguments sake, we will assume he is CIA. You will use him, or help us use him. Then if you are very good, when we are all done with him, we'll give you the pleasure of killing him. Would that please you?"

Ahmed remained silent.

"You didn't answer Ahmed, so I'll just assume that is acceptable to you. By the way, if I am not mistaken, your little sister's birthday is next week. Would you like us to relay your best wishes to her? How old will she be Ahmed? I've forgotten, is it eleven or twelve?" Mahmood's voice sounded so evil it made Ahmed's skin crawl.

"You seem to know so much, I have to believe you know her age," Ahmed spat back angrily.

"Well, Ahmed let's just hope she lives to see her twelfth. Then she will be almost old enough for marriage. Behave, do as we ask,

Episode 18

and perhaps we'll let you participate in the selection of a prospective husband," Mahmood voice now a near hiss.

"I'll do what you ask. Just don't hurt my sister," Ahmed answered.

He hadn't seen Aaliya in over nine months. In his mind's eye, she remained a whimsical little waif of a girl with long black hair and dark brown eyes. Aaliya had his sense of humor and shared his careless wit. Ahmed was determined to find a way to get her away from the madness in Afghanistan. He hadn't mentioned anything to Charlie yet, but the timetable was drawing near. He had to get her out before their mother married her to some zealot. Once that happened, she would be condemned to a life shrouded in a burka like some captive slave. Aaliya's quick laughter and innocent smile would be gone as would her inquisitive mind. Her bright eyes and quick smile would be replaced with the same droll, resolute complacency common to the Afghan women Ahmed pitied.

"Just see that you do, Ahmed and who knows, we may even be related someday. Would you like to have me for your brother in law?" Mahmood hung up before Ahmed could answer.

Ahmed realized he would have to kill Mahmood. It was that simple. Ahmed got out of the car and placed the phone under the front wheel. Backing over the phone, he heard a sharp crunching noise. As he left the parking lot, Ahmed glanced at his rear view mirror and saw a figure dart out of the shadows and pick up the the phone.

When he got to Ford Road, Ahmed pulled into a gas station. In the restroom he splashed cold water on his face and feeling calmer walked to the cooler and grabbed a bottle of Gator Aid. When the old Arab behind the counter asked him if there would be anything else, Ahmed answered two packs of Marlboros and handed the old man a twenty. Pocketing his change, Ahmed left the station.

With shaky hands he opened the Gatorade and took a drink. He felt the cold liquid settle in his stomach and opened a pack of Marlboros. Ahmed placed a cigarette between his lips. As he lit it, his cell phone rang. Great, Ahmed thought, now what? Was it Charlie with more of his bull shit, or was it the maniacal Mahmood again. It really didn't matter, Ahmed didn't want to talk to either. He let the phone ring as he took a drag on the cigarette. Feeling angry, Ahmed picked the phone up off the passenger seat, and flipped it open.

"Yeah," Ahmed said flatly.

"What's up? You coming tonight or what?" Ali was barely audible over music and voices in the background.

"Where are you?" Ahmed asked.

"We're at the Traffic Jam over by Wayne State. There's a really good band playing and there's some hotties here, dude with your name written all over their tight little butts," Ali added.

"I don't know, I just left the mosque. I have a headache and feel beat," Ahmed replied.

"Ahmed, come on now. Don't be a pussy," Ali continued. "It's Friday man, they got some nice squeeze here."

"I'll need to go home and change first," Ahmed asked reluctantly.

"No sweat, unless one of these babe's decides she can't wait any longer, then I may have to bounce," Ali answered.

"I'll be there," Ahmed replied.

"We'll be looking for you," Ali laughed then hung up.

Driving toward his flat, Ahmed's mind buzzed with anxiety about his sister and excitement from Ali's call. When he arrived home, Ahmed locked the doors to the Pontiac. As he walked toward the flat, Ahmed saw Sammy, the old couple's son sitting on the front porch. His real name was Sameh, which meant forgiven in Arabic, but everyone called him Sammy. He was reading a porn novel and smoking an unfiltered Lucky Strike. Several bugs flittered around the yellow light bulb hanging from the bare socket. Grey smoke swirled around Sammy's face. Sammy was so engrossed in his book, he barely noticed until Ahmed reached the top step.

"Hey, Sammy," Ahmed said slipping his key into the lock.

The porch was large. There was room for Sammy's lawn chair and two guest chairs, though Ahmed had never seen him

Episode 18

entertaining friends. Sammy looked up from his reading. He wore horn rimmed glasses with black frames and lenses so thick his dark eyes were magnified to nearly twice their size. Sammy had a thick mustache that was in constant need of trimming. His mustache and lips were heavily nicotine stained. It hadn't taken Ahmed long to conclude Sammy was learning disabled. Ahmed had seen numerous people like Sammy in Afghanistan, harmless souls trudging through life as best they could. Sammy was capable of work though, and had a job at a local discount store.

"In for the night, Ahmed?" Sammy asked as he pulled the cigarette from his mouth.

He flicked the ash into a blue coffee can sitting next to his lawn chair. A small piece of cigarette paper stuck to Sammy's lower lip which he removed with his little finger.

"No, just home to change then I'm heading out," Ahmed replied as he unlocked the door.

"Need some company?" Sammy asked.

The question startled Ahmed.

"I don't think so, Sammy," Ahmed answered. "I fly solo. Besides, I'd just slow you down."

"I was thinking about heading over to the York. I thought maybe you'd like to go with me," Sammy said as he placed the Lucky Strike back into the corner of his mouth.

"The York? Never heard of it," Ahmed didn't want to be rude, but he didn't have time for a long story. "What's that a bar or something?"

"It's the oldest cat house in Detroit," Sammy said with a lopsided grin. "The York Hotel, it's right off the freeway over on Visgar Avenue. You can get what you want at the right price. I had some great tang two weeks ago for forty bucks."

"I, uh, I think I'll take a pass, Sammy. I already got some plans. Hey, maybe next time," Ahmed replied politely. Ahmed stopped just as he got through the doorway. It was a mistake but curiosity got the better of him. It was a failing his father had pointed out frequently. Ahmed leaned back and stuck his head just outside the door.

"Tang, Sammy. I just gotta ask, what the hell are you talking about?" Ahmed wondered if he'd misunderstood Sammy's comment.

"You got a lot to learn there, young man," the cigarette bobbed up and down as Sammy spoke.

"Tang, you know as in poontang," he added with a laugh.

"Think I got your drift there, Sammy. Maybe next time," Ahmed replied and bounded up the stairs laughing.

Ahmed changed quickly letting his dishdasha lie on the floor where it fell. He slowed down long enough to brush his teeth and gargle mouth wash before running back down the stairs. Sammy was still sitting on the porch reading his book though he'd gone into the house for a glass of iced tea. Taking a drink, Sammy looked up as Ahmed continued down the porch steps.

"Later, Sammy," Ahmed said over his shoulder before driving off.

It was after nine when Ahmed walked into the club. Ali was seated at a table with a dark haired girl. Her chair was close to him and they were in close conversation. Ali saw Ahmed, flashed a smile then motioned for him to come to the table. He introduced Ahmed to the girl and explained she was with her girlfriends, students at Wayne State. When Ali asked her to bring them to the table, she got up, walked over to a table nearby and said something to the three girls sitting there. The crowd at the table soon grew to about a dozen. Ahmed spent the rest of the night sipping beer and talking to a girl named Stacey.

Ahmed stayed until closing. Before she left, Stacey gave Ahmed her number and told him to call. Pulling in front of his flat, Ahmed was relieved to see Sammy had taken his reading indoors. On his way to the club, Ahmed had passed the York Hotel. He'd seen the building dozens of times but never given the old structure a second thought. When asked about living in the Mid East, Ahmed often answered by saying there were parts of Detroit that looked worse than Baghdad. Though said in jest, the area around the hotel was a prime example.

Ahmed climbed the stairs to his apartment. After throwing his clothes on the floor, he pulled the covers down on his bed and collapsed on the sheets. Lying in his boxer shorts, Ahmed

Episode 18

turned out the light then stretched out placing both hands behind his head. The pillow case felt cool on his forearms. Somewhere down the block a dog began barking. A male voice yelled an Arabic obscenity telling the owner to shut the dog's mouth. The dog immediately quit barking. Ahmed was almost asleep when his cell phone rang. After fumbling in the dark, he finally located the phone. Hoping it was Stacey, Ahmed answered in anticipation. His hopes were soon dashed.

"Ahmed," Charlie said in his nasally Michigan accent.

"Fuck me, Charlie do you know what time it is?" Ahmed asked in an irritated voice.

"Yes, Ahmed. Among other talents, I can tell time," Charlie replied. "You're on my clock buddy, not your own. You do remember our deal?"

"Yeah, a pact with Satan is more like it," Ahmed muttered laying back on the bed. "Next time I'll turn my phone off before bed," Ahmed continued.

"Yeah, well I can come over right now and pack your little camel jockey ass back to Kabul if you want to be cute. Besides, if you turn your phone off, how will Mahmood get in contact with you," Charlie shot back.

Ahmed sat up.

"What's that supposed to mean?" he asked apprehensively.

"It means, meet me tomorrow at noon," Charlie replied.

"I have to be at work by three, how am I supposed to get there on time if I meet you?" Ahmed asked.

"Just be there," Charlie said before the phone went dead.

Ahmed set the phone on the floor. He'd drunk several beers and just wanted to sleep. Placing his hands behind his head again, Ahmed looked out the window. He thought about Aaliya. She would be twelve next week and he would not be there for her birthday. Her name meant gift in Arabic and it pained Ahmed that he would not be there to give her one. Ahmed felt a breeze flutter through the window and drift over his shoulders. The quiet and fresh air was a pleasant change from the smoke and noise at the club. Ahmed closed his eyes and saw Stacey's face as he drifted off to sleep.

Episode 19

Ronnie knew it wouldn't take Denny long to make arrangements. Denny was fast with women; always had been. Ronnie lowered the windows in the Explorer and leaned back in his seat. He had eaten too much and felt drowsy. The evening air felt good. A small breeze kicked up and washed moist air across his face. He could smell the river. Eating the lasagna reminded him how much Beth loved Italian food. Of course she loved any kind of food. Before she'd gotten sick, Beth had developed a taste for several ethnic cuisines. She loved Tai with all of the exotic spices and coconut milk sauces. She'd introduced Ronnie to Lebanese food at restaurants scattered around east Fairlane Hills. They had become regulars at Pegasus's in Detroit's Greektown. One time, she even drug him to an Ethiopian restaurant. His smile grew wider as he thought about Beth's remark during that meal. She said that de vuelta, the spongy textured bread served with their dinner, had a texture similar to a corpse's skin. He'd had difficulty finishing his food after the remark but Beth's appetite hadn't diminished in the least.

When first married, their favorite restaurant was Major's, an Italian place in southwest Detroit. At the time, the neighborhood was home to a large Italian community and there were several restaurants and pizzerias. Gonella's Market, with its hanging salamis, strings of garlic, and white aproned proprietor, would have been at home in New York's Little Italy. The Oakwood Bakery, just down the street, sold the best hard crust Italian bread in the city. When they could afford it, he and Beth would go to Major's on Friday evenings. Mary, a friend of Beth's from high school, waited tables and always slid a few extras their way.

On Saturday afternoons Ronnie and Beth went to Gonella's for subs, then stopped at the Oakwood Bakery to pick up bread. There was a little court yard out front where the Italian women would sit and escape the heat from the large ovens. They wore dark dresses and rolled their nylon stockings below their knees. Elderly Italian men gathered by the bocce ball court and sipped wine from green bottles without labels.

Lost in his day dream, Ronnie didn't notice Denny open the passenger door.

"Hey you old bastard," Denny said with a smirk, "did somebody miss nappie time?'

"Screw you smart ass," Ronnie responded, "buckle up and let's go."

Neither of them said anything until they were in downtown Trenton. Ronnie finally broke the silence.

"So, you all set with Darlene or what?" he asked.

"Yeah, she's going to come by after she gets off work if that's okay with you," Denny replied.

"No problem for me, hell, you guys can just stay at my house tonight if you want."

"We'll see how things go, she may feel a little funny about that. You know how women are," Denny answered.

"Well, tell her I'll put on my ear muffs, if that provides any more comfort to the situation," Ronnie said with a laugh.

"Well, you are so old, I'll just tell her you're almost deaf, she'll have no problem believing that," Denny replied.

"You're just cruel, anybody ever tell you that Dennis Williams?"

Episode 19

"Oh, once or twice. I never listened," Denny responded. "Hey, by the way, what were you thinking about while you were lost in space back there in the parking lot? You had a big assed smile on your kisser and seemed a million miles away."

"Not a million miles, Denny. A million years maybe, but not a million miles," Ronnie answered. He caught the red light at the corner by the frozen custard stand. A small crowd was milling around eating cones and enjoying the summer evening.

"Hey, pull in this ice cream place and let's get a cone," Denny said in a near excited voice.

"What the hell, Denny? We just ate a huge dinner," Ronnie replied. He was stuffed and didn't feel like anything else. "Besides we got connoli."

"Screw those connoli, we can eat them later, let's get a cone. What the hell, don't be a dried up old shit. You know, if Beth was here, we'd be stopping," the reply jumped off his tongue making Denny wonder if his glib comment might put a damper on the rest of the night.

"Okay asshole," Ronnie said with a smile, "you're right. But if Beth was still here, I wouldn't be sitting in my car with Commodore Perry on a Friday night."

Ronnie pulled into the lot and Denny got out of the Explorer. Ronnie heard a faint buzz emanating from the incandescent flood lights as he watched a steady stream of cars and motorcycles leaving Elizabeth Park. As he watched two vehicles, loaded with teenagers, pulled into the A&W Root Beer stand across the street.

Ronnie counted four boys in the Ford Taurus. The other vehicle, a white minivan, had six girls the same age. As Ronnie watched, two boys jumped out of the Taurus and ran up to the minivan. The boys had on blue University of Michigan tee shirts. One of the girls, wearing a Central Michigan tank top, got out of the van and embraced the taller boy. Ronnie assumed they had run into each other at the park and were saying goodbyes before heading off to college. Ronnie wanted to jump out of the Explorer, run over and tell them to hang on to every second; it all would go by so quickly.

He realized there was no way to impart such wisdom to an eighteen year old because only in retrospect can anyone understand what has just passed. Denny returned with two cones. He had a vanilla custard with toasted coconut sprinkles and a vanilla and chocolate twist. Vanilla with coconut sprinkles had been Beth's favorite. Ronnie wondered if Denny remembered or if it was just a coincidence.

"Hey, thanks," Ronnie said taking the vanilla ice cream from Denny's outreached hand. A few of the sprinkles fell off and dropped onto the Explorer's seats.

"I'd say I'm sorry about the spilled sprinkles, but you never really gave a shit how the inside of your car looked anyway," Denny said licking his ice cream.

"Well, I cared. It's just that Beth never did and it was too small of a battle to fight," Ronnie took a bite and remembered he hadn't had a cone since Beth died

"Doesn't really matter, you'd have lost that battle along with the rest," Denny said as he took another swipe at his cone. Ronnie noticed the dark and light streaks of Denny's ice cream had run together where he had taken the last lick. "Really not your fault though, you were over matched from the beginning." Denny added. "So, what were you thinking of back there in Sibley's lot? From the look on your face, I couldn't tell if you were having a wet dream or just passing gas. You looked so contented I figured it had to be one of the two," Denny finished with a smirk.

"Ha, ha, very funny, Denny. You know, you shouldn't waste your time on the boats, you should just go buy a ticket right now, fly to Vegas and become a comedian, you are so fucking funny," Ronnie said with faked sarcasm while pulling out of the lot. "See those two car loads of kids over there," he pointed his cone in the direction of the A&W.

"Yeah, the girl by the door has great tits. I noticed them when I was in line for the ice cream. So it was a wet dream, need my handkerchief?" Denny asked.

"Jesus Denny, in your whole life, have you ever thought of anything else? The world doesn't revolve around big tits you know," Ronnie replied in mocked disgust.

"No, but they do sort of help give it the spin, don't you think?" Denny answered quickly.

"Denny, sometimes you are just unbelievable. Are you ever going to slow down?"

"Only when they bury me. Anyway, when they do, I won't have grey hair like yours from all that backed up semen," Denny winced at his choice of words. He'd hoped to stay clear of comments about death or dying until he had a chance to at least let Ronnie know how bad he felt about Beth.

"Grey hair from backed up semen, that's a good one Denny," Ronnie said with a smile. "I'll have to remember that one for the boys at the bakery."

Denny was relieved his comment had been taken so well recalling how his own sarcastic approach to grief hadn't been very cathartic after the drugs and anger ran their course. They were nearing the Elizabeth Park Lodge and the cold ice cream tasted good. Ronnie remembered Beth believed ice cream to be the perfect dessert. No matter how full you were, you could always wedge down some ice cream to smooth things out a bit, as she put it.

"So, shit head," Denny started up again, "what were you thinking about back there at Sibley's or is it some big mystery." He had finished the ice cream and was crunching on the cone.

"Oh, I was just thinking about old times at Major's Restaurant. Mary would wait on us. Sometimes she'd come over to the flat after her shift and she and Beth would drink wine and smoke dope."

"Boy, Mary Hooper. Now there was one great set. She was way ahead of her time. Now days, a skinny girl with big hooters is very common. Mary had those back in the 60s. Didn't see that very often back then. I'd have liked one or two grabs at those babies."

Ronnie started to laugh but swallowed at the same time and was nearly choking on the frozen custard. The cold sent a sharp pain to his temples. He winced and momentarily let go of the steering wheel to squeeze the bridge of his nose with his thumb and forefinger. It was trick Beth had taught him.

"What the hell, you stroken' out on me here?" Denny asked.

"No, just swallowed the ice cream too fast," Ronnie answered in a croak.

"I can drive if all this fun is too much for an old man like you," Denny added.

"No, I can drive okay. It's just, geez Denny, is there nothing sacred to you?" Ronnie replied smiling again.

"Yeah, like you never noticed Mary's zoomers, give me a freaking break here mister saint. Those skinny legs and tiny waist. Hell, if it wasn't that Beth would have beat the ever loving shit out of you, you'd have made a run or two at those zoomers yourself."

"You know it's funny, 'cause I really do miss Mary. She died you know, about a year before Beth."

"I didn't know that, what the hell happened?"

"Lung cancer. Lived Downriver like the rest of us. Stay here long enough, hard to dodge it."

"What a shame. Man I really I liked her," Denny looked out of the passenger window.

"What the hell do you think it is that makes all these young girls have big ones these days?" Ronnie asked changing the subject. The mood in the truck dampened after he told Denny about Mary. "Do you think it's the hormones in the food chain?" he continued in a serious tone.

"You see Ronnie, that's your problem right there. You think too much. Instead of wondering what causes young girls to have big tiddies, you should look at 'em and just enjoy 'em. Who gives a shit how they get 'em? As long as you get a chance to get at them, who cares how they got there. That's beside the point. Hell, maybe they are all filled with fucken' silicone. Who really cares, except some retard like you." Denny picked up a napkin off the seat and wiped his hands.

Episode 19

"Well, I think our time has past Denny, when it comes to the getting at them part. That boat sailed a long time ago. I have to say, with all that's wrong with the world, guess it makes you feel kind of good knowing the young boys today at least have that bright notion to look forward to."

"Well, this boat is still in the dock and ready to sail, baby, and I still try to get at 'em when I get a chance, even if half of them are surgically enhanced," Denny replied emphatically.

"Yeah, maybe you're right, about that. If it is silicone, then maybe we ought to be looking into Dow or Dupont stock. Maybe we're missing a big investment opportunity," Ronnie replied.

"You know, I never looked at it that way. That's something to consider. I'll call my broker Monday morning and tell him to look into the latest market data on fake tits."

The Elizabeth Park Lodge was just ahead reminding Ronnie of another shared memory.

"Remember when we used to bring the dogs up here, Denny?" Ronnie asked seriously.

Denny and Carol had a Boxer named Ginger. Ronnie and Beth had an Australian Shepherd. After Labor Day, when the park closed for the season, they'd let the dogs run free. They would bring charcoal and roast hot dogs for a picnic lunch.

"Oh, yeah, I remember that. I really liked it best in the fall. The leaves would turn and the dogs would run and play. Carol and I would sneak off and smoke a couple of joints, you'd get all freaked out that the cops would come and we'd all get busted," Denny said with a smile.

"Well, I was just starting at Ford," Ronnie answered quickly. "I had a lot to lose."

"Yeah, you were a major pussy."

"Still am."

"Always will be. Good thing you had me around from time to time to bring a little excitement in your life.'

Ronnie knew there was truth in Denny's statement.

"Anyway, yeah I remember those days. Carol wasn't so whacked then. We could still have fun together."

"Well, those times were good for all of us. None of us had a cent to our name, we were broke all the time, but hell when you're young, you don't need much to have fun."

When they had reached Grosse Ile Parkway, Ronnie turned left. As they approached the County Bridge, Denny reached into the storage compartment and picked up Ronnie's cell phone.

"Mind if I make a call? Mine's in my bag in the back seat."

"Nah, just leave a quarter in the tray," Ronnie replied. "Used to be a dime."

"Oh, you'll pay me for this call," Denny answered. "Just want to show you a little something. You'll get a kick out of my awesome display of power."

Denny dialed the phone then held it up to his ear.

"Hey, Ray," Denny said into the phone, "this is Denny. I'm in the tan Explorer just going over and I want to impress my buddy. Can you swing this baby open after we pass?"

"Watch this, Ronnie," Denny said returning the cell phone to the storage tray.

When the Explorer hit the metal grating, the alarm lights began flashing. A few moments later the barrier arm dropped closing the bridge to traffic in both directions.

"What the hell, Denny. How can you do that when you're not piloting a boat?" Ronnie asked as he stopped the Explorer to watch the bridge swing open.

"Some of the bridge operators are retired river pilots. We have a connection at the union hall." Denny answered. "That's my plan, too. In a couple of years, I'll just move in with you, and work on the bridge," Denny continued with a laugh. "Well, I won't really move in with you. I'm going to look for a place on the Island or in Trenton."

"So we'll be neighbors?"

"Maybe, if everything works out?"

"There goes my property value," Ronnie teased.

Ronnie turned onto West River Road and drove along the shoreline passing old palatial houses with large covered porches and well groomed grounds.

Episode 19

"You know, add a little Spanish moss and some Cyprus trees and this place would be a replica of Savannah," Denny commented.

As they passed West Shore Golf and Country Club, Denny saw the Pagoda House ahead. He had seen it from the river several times but this was his first view from land. He was familiar with the home's history; courtesy of a captain of an ore freighter who knew a good bit about the buildings along the river. The captain told Denny the house had been designed and built during the 1920s for Harry Bennett, Henry Ford's thug of a general manager. According to the captain, Bennett visited the Emperor's summer palace in China and liked the architecture so much he used it as a template for his summer home. The captain wasn't certain who'd nicknamed the place The Pagoda House, but noted it was fitting. He told Denny what he'd heard about the Pagoda's construction including the security features because the union had made several attempts on Bennett's life. According to the captain, the house had secret doors and escape tunnels.

As they approached the house, Denny could see the it was perched on the river's edge. Half of the house sat on land while the other half extended out into the River. The house was painted white and had a red tiled roof. The roof lines tapered down on all four sides and then pirouetted up at the corners common to Chinese architecture. An attached garage, with identical roof lines, was positioned toward the rear of the house and extended into the water. On closer inspection, Denny could see that the garage was actually a boat house. The house itself had several large windows and a balcony extending from the back. The front of the house sat so close to the road, Denny wondered how there was any room for parking. As they rounded a small bend, Denny got a better look at the grounds and saw a large clearing across the road with a garage that matched the house. Ronnie pulled into the parking area in front of the garage and shut off the Explorer.

"Well, Denny, here we are. What I call home," Ronnie said stepping out.

"Wow, cool place, Ronnie," Denny said as they stepped into the foyer. Denny set his bag down and looked around. The great room to his left was very large and had two windows along the far wall separated by a fireplace. The windows looked out on the road and shoreline. In the distance, Denny could see a line of cars making their way across the bridge. The floors where polished hardwood planking and in the middle of room sat an over stuffed couch and matching love seat. Three pictures were on the fireplace mantel along with a pair of candelabras and a white porcelain bunny. Denny walked closer to the fireplace. There were pictures of Ronnie and Beth's sons along with a large picture set in a gold frame of the extended family gathered in front of a Christmas Tree. Denny took the picture off the mantle. He assumed it had to be at least two years old because Beth was in it. She looked thin and pale. He recognized Beth and Carol's older sister, Ann and her family. There were several small children in the photo Denny guessed were grandchildren. I could have been in this picture, Denny said to himself.

"I'm putting the connoli away, you want a drink," Ronnie yelled from the kitchen.

"Yeah, I'll have a beer if you have one."

"Lebatt's okay," Ronnie yelled back.

"I prefer Heineken, but your lousy Canadian stuff will do," Denny answered absently.

Ronnie carried two long neck bottles into the great room and handed one to Denny.

"Dude, a lot of kids," Denny said as he delicately placed the picture back onto the mantle.

"Yeah, that was taken the Christmas before Beth left us," Ronnie said looking at the photograph. "Those are Ann and Frank's grandchildren. They have ten of them now. They're quite a crew."

"So you and Beth still had Christmas every year?"

"Well, not the last one. I couldn't do it without her. The boys live out of state now, so Ann had it at her house. Come on, I'll show you around. The bedrooms are upstairs, we'll take your bag up after the tour," Ronnie said leading Denny into the nook.

Episode 19

The nook was immediately behind the great room and held a small round table with four chairs. There was a window to the left of the table that provided a panoramic view of the river. To the right of the nook was a large kitchen with maple cabinets, granite counter tops and stainless steel appliances.

"Nice kitchen," Denny said, "who picked out all this stuff?"

"Beth and I both sort of, it made for some good arguments," Ronnie replied with a soft laugh.

"Most of which you lost, no doubt," Denny took a drink from the long neck.

The dining room was to the right of the kitchen. There was a long table with six chairs neatly in place. Several old pictures were hung on the walls. Denny recognized the pictures, they were of Beth's mother's family; he'd seen them before. Behind the dining room table was a butler's table holding several framed photographs. To the left of the table was a large sliding glass door leading out to the balcony. The door was open and the air smelled of open water.

"Nice place Ronnie, how did you end up here?" Denny asked.

"Well, you know Beth, she loved this place from the first time she saw it in high school. Come on we'll get your stuff situated in the bedroom and then sit out on the balcony," Ronnie added heading back into the great room.

Denny picked up his bag as they made their way to the stairway. Ronnie told Denny to go ahead because it would take him a little longer now to climb the stairs. Denny looked back on his way up and noticed Ronnie climbed the steps by putting his good leg up a stair and then bringing his bad leg up afterward. Denny reached the top of the stairs and waited.

"It's the second room to the right," Ronnie said.

Denny walked into the room and put his bag on the antique bed. The room was not very large, but big enough for the undersized double bed and the matching chest of drawers. Denny recognized the furniture, it was the same set Ronnie and Beth had at their flat as newly weds. A window across from the bed looked out on the river. It was open and the curtains were pulled back to let the breeze in. The room had a cozy feel.

"Sorry 'bout that, the stairs take me a little longer," Ronnie said from the hall. "Will this work okay?" he added as he walked to the door.

"Looks good to me," Denny answered, "I recognize the furniture."

"Yeah, that was Beth's grandmother's. Ben used this room. It faces the river, I thought you might like it to keep an eye on your boat," Ronnie said pointing toward the open window.

"Get your stuff situated, the bathroom's right across the hall. The towels are in the linen closet next to the bathroom door. By the way, I'll be sleeping in the room next door. If Darlene decides to stay here, just put a tie on the door knob," Ronnie added with a laugh.

"Tie on the door knob, I don't get it?" Denny replied.

"Oh that was just a thing from college. If you had a girl in the room, you put a tie on the door knob so no one would barge in."

"Oh, sorry, Mr. Rich Fraternity guy, I didn't go to college." Denny said with feigned sarcasm.

"Yeah, right, like anyone in Melvindale was rich. Even the mayor was poor, you lived there long enough to know that. Anyway, I'll be down on the balcony," Ronnie turned toward the stairs.

"If you're as slow going down as you were coming up, I'll probably be there waiting for you," Denny teased.

"Always breaking my balls, Denny. Some things never change. With Beth gone, I guess someone will have to take her place. You're a poor excuse but better than none at all," Ronnie finished and walked down the steps.

Denny could hear the thumping on the wooden stairs as Ronnie started down. He took his shaving kit out of the overnight bag, walked into the bathroom and set it down on the large double sink. He washed his face then walked back to the bedroom deciding to leave the rest of his gear in the duffel bag. If he ended up going to Darlene's for the night, he'd just have to repack.

Denny found Ronnie sitting at a patio table on the balcony which ran the entire length of the house. It extended outward about twenty feet out from the house and had a wrought iron railing around the perimeter. At the far end was a green Weber

Episode 19

gas barbecue grill. To Denny's right was a plastic storage box with a life ring attached to a rope. A small sign reading, For Emergency Rescue Of Drunks and Other Fools was attached to the railing next to the life ring. Four canvas director's chairs were placed along the wall to the left of the patio table were separated by pots of flowers. Directly across the River Denny could see the freighter moored by the mill. He walked to the railing and looked down at the fifteen foot drop to the water.

"You don't want to get too loaded and fall off here!" Denny said in jest.

"Aw, you'd do okay Denny," Ronnie replied, "you're fat enough now; you'd float."

"Oh, that was mean," Denny said with mock hurt taking a drink from the bottle of Lebatt's.

"Just kidding," Ronnie answered and took a sip of his own.

Denny walked back to the patio table and took a chair to Ronnie's right. Both men sat quietly for a few minutes sipping beer and looking out on the river. A full moon had risen, casting a pale halo over the open water. As they watched, a small powerboat making its way up river turned on its running lights. The sound of the boaters voices carried over the water.

"How's your dad?" Denny asked breaking the silence.

"Oh, Big Red?" Ronnie answered using his father's nickname. "Oh, he's just fine. Over eighty years old now. Still fishes the River three or four times a week. The boys call him the machine, because he just keeps going like the Energizer Bunny."

"The man's a legend no doubt," Denny said finishing his beer.

"You want another?" Ronnie asked.

"No, think I'll hold off for a while. You know the old saying, drink one, piss six," Denny replied.

"I can make us some coffee if you want," Ronnie offered. He'd been nursing his own beer.

"Maybe in a bit. I should switch to the coffee though. When Darlene gets here, I don't want to fall asleep," Denny answered.

"Well, I'll make us some coffee then. I've 'bout had enough beer to hold me."

Ronnie went into the kitchen, put on a pot and returned to the table. He was carrying a tray with two cups, a sugar bowl and a cream pitcher.

"It'll be done in a few minutes. You take cream and sugar as I remember," Ronnie said.

"Yeah, and a little Viagra would help," Denny answered with a wink.

Ronnie assumed Denny's response was a joke, but wondered if there was a kernel of truth buried somewhere in his reply.

"Yeah, it'd be a pain to drink all that coffee to stay awake and then not be able to do anything about it," Ronnie said in jest. "Denny Williams is not having performance anxiety now is he?"

"Well, not really. A couple of times lately, let's just say the mouth wrote some checks the body couldn't cash."

"Dude, don't sweat it. It happens to the best of us, at least as best I remember, it does," Ronnie answered. The aroma of freshly brewed coffee drifted out onto the balcony. "Let me get the coffee and you can tell Doctor Ronnie all about it."

Ronnie came back carrying a pot of steaming coffee. He filled both cups and handed one to Denny. Denny added cream and sugar then leaned back in his chair. Holding the cup in both hands, he turned his head to look up the river. Denny tried to compose himself to speak but struggled.

"This isn't the Denny Williams I know," Ronnie said as he picked up his cup and took a sip.

I really don't know what's wrong with me," Denny replied. His lower lip quivered as he tried to maintain composure.

"I just look at my life and wonder where the hell it's gone," Denny added a flood of tears welling in his eyes.

"Hey, welcome to fifty," Ronnie said. "What, you think you are the only one who feels like this?"

"Yeah, but it's different for you. You had a marriage and you have your boys," Denny stammered.

"You have two daughters Denny."

"Yeah, I have two daughters who want nothing to do with me. I've been married three times. Now here I am wait-

Episode 19

ing for some waitress to show up so I can feel like I'm twenty something again."

"Darlene isn't just some waitress. That's one of the other benefits of passing fifty, those kinds of things tend to lose their value somehow."

"You're missing the point," Denny said then looked down. "You had a good marriage, to someone you loved. At least that's how it looked from the outside."

"There were tough times, there Denny. It wasn't always a love fest around here you know."

"Yeah, but you two found a way through all of that, and I don't think you did it solely for the kids."

"No, but I guess what I'm saying Denny is that maybe there can still be something like that for you."

"I don't think I'm capable of that, Ronnie. Sometimes it seems there's something missing in me, and I don't know what it is. With Carol, what the hell, I don't know. We just weren't right for each other or something. We were young and I don't know, I just couldn't make it work."

"Carol had some shortcomings of her own, Denny. Still does for that matter. You two were just not a good fit. You were both young and who knows why people do the things they do when they're young. Hell, it's all a crap shoot at that point in life."

"Then I found Janet and we had the girls, and I thought this was it. I'd be happy. Then what do I do, I start chasing around and ruin it all. What the hell is wrong with me? I just can't seem to keep things from getting screwed up." Tears streamed from the corners of Denny's eyes. He wiped them with one hand while holding the cup of coffee with the other.

"Well, I blew that one big time. My girls think I'm a psycho. Then I marry Marsha, and lord knows why I did that. She made Carol look like the rock of Gibraltar. Now here I am, fifty years old, alone and hitting on waitresses and barmaids."

"What happened between you and Janet?" Ronnie asked wondering how the evening had taken such an unexpected turn.

"Guess the short story there is, Janet wanted me to be like her dad. He has that business you know, and they always had a stable, secure life. Shit, I was gone on the boats all the time. She wanted me to quit sailing and learn her father's business. That's the last thing in the world that I ever wanted to do."

"Well, I don't see you as an accountant, that's for sure."

"So, you don't think I could do that?"

"That's not what I'm saying. Look, you're bright enough Denny. You don't pilot a vessel like the one across the river without a good measure of mental competency. It just wouldn't have been a good fit, that's all. Janet was just looking for something you couldn't give her. That's not anyone's fault."

"I don't know, I just feel so alone some times. You have no idea what that's like." Denny blurted, then felt embarrassed. Beth's absence still didn't seem real.

"Oh, I think I do, Denny. I think I do," Ronnie said softly.

"Sorry, I should have thought a little better before I spoke," Denny took a sip of coffee. "Maybe I should have stuck to talking about sports and women," he added in a weak attempt to lighten the conversation.

Ronnie picked up the pot and poured more coffee into Denny's cup.

"Now I know you're fifty," he replied with a wink.

"Why do you say that?" Denny asked.

"'Cause if you were under fifty, you'd have said you should have stuck to talking about women and sports. The order of priority changes when you become an official old fart. Sports takes on a higher priority," Ronnie replied laughing.

"I just don't know anymore. Sometimes none of it seems like worth talking about," Denny's eyes welled up again. Ronnie had never seen him so emotional and knew something was really eating at him.

"What's going on, Denny? There's something that's really tearing at you. Hey, it's okay to talk about these things. You can't keep it all bottled up forever. Do you still keep in contact with your buddy, Eddie Wayne? Do you ever talk to him or maybe your brother about how you're feeling?"

Episode 19

"No, Eddie's life is a bigger mess than mine."

"So what's making you feel this way? Is it something you can put into words?"

"It's everything and nothing," Denny answered looking at the night sky. "I guess it's mostly my girls. Janet asked a couple of years back if I would let her husband adopt the girls. I refused of course, but it really hit me the girls would even want him to adopt them."

"How do you know that?"

"They told me one night when I took them to dinner."

"Was that the girls talking or Janet talking through the girls?"

"No, it was clear they wanted Craig for their legal father," Denny replied.

The tears began flowing from Denny's eyes. Ronnie leaned over and handed him a napkin. Denny wiped his eyes then blew his nose.

"Having your girls say that had to hurt. Hell, no wonder you're such a mess. You said that happened a while back. Why all the grief now?"

"I don't know. I thought I was stronger than this. Then when Marsha walked out two months ago. I don't know. I couldn't even hang on to a loser like her, what does that tell you? I don't know, Ronnie, I just don't know," Denny said between sobs. He set his cup on the table and bent forward in the chair holding his head in both hands.

"You don't know about what, Denny? What is it you don't know about?" Ronnie coaxed.

"I just don't know why the women in my life, I mean why do the women in my life." Denny stopped talking; unable to finish. Ronnie saw he was in anguish.

Ronnie leaned forward on his chair and put a hand on Denny's shoulder.

"What about the women in your life, Denny? What about them?" he asked.

"They just leave me. I know I give them reason to. I don't mean to be what I am. Some part of me just can't seem to be normal. Some part of me makes me do things that drive them all away."

"Listen, Carol, was so unstable Denny. You have to admit you two were never right. Janet, well she was from a wealthy family. At least as wealthy as anybody Downriver can be and no, you'd never be like her dad, Denny. It wasn't fair of her to expect that. Marsha, well I never knew her, so I can only go by what you said about how she made Carol look like the Rock of Gibraltar. Shit, anybody who made Carol look stable, had to be so fragile that any ripple in the water would tip her canoe over."

"Yeah, but what about Theresa?" Denny asked in a whisper.

"Theresa? I never knew you were involved with a woman named Theresa?" Ronnie asked letting go of Denny's shoulder.

"Theresa, was my mom, Ronnie," Denny lifted his head. "I wasn't enough to keep her in this world."

"Jesus, Denny! You can't think that way. Your mom was sick. She really didn't know what she was doing. God Denny, don't blame yourself for that," Ronnie added firmly.

"Think about it Ronnie, I wasn't enough for my mom to go on living for."

"You weren't the only one she had to live for Denny. What about your brother?"

"He was older. He was married and had kids of his own. He had his own family then. He had something to hold on to. I was just out of high school. Why wasn't I enough for my mom to hang on to? Why am I not enough for anyone to hang onto? Not Carol, not Janet and not even Marsha," Denny answered. Breathing deeply he sagged back into the patio chair.

"Seriously, have you and your brother ever talked about this?" Ronnie asked wondering how the conversation had gone to such unexpected levels.

"I tried once. Sometimes I think he's so much like our mom. He lives for Evelyn and his kids. Guess maybe he's not so much like

Episode 19

my mom. All she ever lived for was my dad. At least Jeff lives for his kids."

"Maybe Theresa only lived for Theresa, Denny. Maybe she really only ever lived for herself."

"Shit, I don't know Ronnie. Damn, I can't believe I'm falling apart like this. I'm really sorry, I really am. It's just, I don't know. When I saw the picture it really hit me."

"What picture Denny? What do you mean?"

"You know the picture of Christmas of the whole family on your mantel. I should have been in that picture. If I was halfway normal, I'd have been in it."

"Denny, that wasn't all your fault. We both know that."

"I should be in some Christmas picture someplace, Ronnie. At least with my own girls. I just feel like time is running out, and I'll never be enough for anyone to hang around for. Not even my girls. Hell, I wasn't enough for my own mother."

"What about your brother? You don't spend Christmas with his family?

"Not the last couple of years. They hated Marsha. Besides, last year they went on a cruise at Christmas. We weren't invited."

"What about Eddie Wayne? What the hell has he been up to? What did he ever do about that insane girlfriend of his, what was her name, Candice? Yeah, that was it, Candice. She was a stripper or something, wasn't she?" Ronnie asked trying to change the subject and allow Denny time to gather himself.

"Oh, no. If you ask her, she was an exotic dancer," Denny replied with hollow laugh.

"So what happened to them?'

"Well, that crazy ass Eddie Wayne married that even crazier bitch. Somehow or another the two of them are still together. Go figure, see what I mean. Those two lunatics have managed to stay together. Though there were some times when I didn't know which of them would kill the other. There were fights with black eyes and police and trips to the emergency room. She even stabbed him one time. Crazy bitch. But he took her back. Not to say he didn't beat the shit out of her a few times afterwards, but damn, they're still together."

"Is that what you want Denny? You want to trade places with Eddie? Maybe no relationship is better than one like that."

"No. What I want is what you and Beth had. A home, kids and a life together. Maybe she's gone now, and I know you are still hurting, but you had it all. At least you have Christmas pictures. Having had it all, is one hell of a lot better than never having had it ever. Fuck me, I don't' even know if what I just said makes sense."

"Having had it all, just makes it a little harder when some of it goes away. Yeah, there is a feeling of comfort that comes after the really hard part is over. I don't know what it is really. Maybe it's just a feeling of having no regrets, maybe that's what makes it easier. Maybe it's just looking back, and though you know there were some little things you would like to do over, the big things were in place. So you only end up with a few small regrets. The truth is you tend to not dwell on them, 'cause you know the big ones were so good. Now who's not making sense?"

"Hell, sometimes I even think I'd take what Eddie and Candice have. Compared to what I have, at least they have something."

"So where are those two love birds?" Ronnie asked with a short laugh.

"Believe it or not, they're at my place, but you can't say anything to anybody."

"Why?" Ronnie asked in surprise.

"Eddie got into some bad shit down in Florida. He and Candice have been staying at my place, really hiding out is more like it. They owe some people money. This is some very serious shit 'cause the people that are looking for them are bad people. Very bad. Luckily they don't know about me. That's why Eddie and Candice are here."

"So, are you afraid for them or something?

"Well, you know I'd do anything for Eddie Wayne, he's my oldest and best friend. We go back to when we were kids

Episode 19

in Tallahassee. You don't know what it's like to have a friend you go back with that long who's in big trouble. I mean hell, Eddie and I have been best friends for forty years. He's more like a brother than a friend. You have any idea what that's like?"

"Yeah I do understand what that's like, more than you know. I had a friend like that once, but that friendship went away," Ronnie said refilling his cup. "You want some more coffee?"

"Screw the coffee, give me another beer."

"You sure? Maybe you should layoff the alcohol for a while. Darlene, remember?" Ronnie responded.

"Yeah, you're right," Denny said after a few moments. He took another deep breath. "I feel better now. Now tell me about this buddy that you had."

"Oh, it was like you and Eddie. His name is Bobbie," Ronnie said taking a drink of coffee. Ronnie wondered if he'd never get to sleep after all the caffeine but knew it was too late to worry about it.

"Wait a minute, Carol told me about this a couple of times. He was like your best friend or something but was dating Beth and you two had some kind of falling out."

"Well, something like that. Bobbie was my first friend when we moved to Melvindale. Bobbie's family moved into their house the same day we moved in ours. I had just turned four and we were best friends from that day until 1970."

"So what happened?" Denny sat up in his chair looking relieved.

"Well, he was engaged to Beth then. He was in the service. In Nam. I was home from Michigan State and Beth and I ran into each other. Things just happened."

"Fuck me, that's classic Hollywood," Denny replied.

"Yeah, it was ugly. In all fairness, though, I saw her first. Beth and I were an item before she went with Bobbie."

"So what drove you two apart?"

"You mean me and Beth, or me and Bobbie?"

"Well, obviously you and Beth, you moron," Denny forced a grin.

Feeling relieved to see Denny smile, Ronnie continued his story.

"Some of it was that lightening quick Irish temper of hers. Hell, you experienced some of that if memory serves me. Mostly it was just that we were so young. We split up and she and Bobbie started going out. I never stopped loving her, though."

"You were okay with your best buddy dating your ex girlfriend?" Denny asked.

"No, but I had too much pride. Bobbie asked me if it would be okay. I told him I didn't give a shit, but that wasn't how I really felt. Hell Denny, remember what it's like to be eighteen and have your balls stepped on? You just grin and bear it. I didn't think it'd last. I really didn't think they would get engaged, but they did," Ronnie said picking up his coffee cup again.

"So you two met up again. How'd that happen?"

"I went to a party. She was there, one thing led to another. I told her I still loved her but wouldn't stand in the way with Bobbie."

"What'd she do?"

"Hell, you knew Beth! She said she still loved me and asked why I didn't say no to Bobbie when he asked me if it was okay to ask her out."

"If she was going to marry Bobbie, she had to be some in love with him?" Denny replied.

"Yeah, but we all grew up together. Kids did that in Melvindale. I suppose they do that in all small towns. Maybe there's a sort of a love that grows out of familiarity. It's hard to explain. Maybe it's a comfort thing or shared background. Hell, I don't know, maybe you had to be there in the late 60s or something. People got married because they were expected to or something. Damn I'm not being clear about this. Let's just say Bobbie and Beth loved each other but not like Beth and I loved each other, if that makes any sense at all."

"You're right, I'm not sure I completely understand. Go on. What happened when she broke it off with Bobbie? That had to be intense."

Episode 19

"Yeah it was. Beth and I both felt terrible."

"So what happened?"

"Well, Beth wrote to Bobbie to tell him the engagement was off and she was going back with me. When Bobbie got leave he called me from Japan. He was angry. He came home about five months later and I went to see him at his house. I was stupid enough to think we could work it all out. I was wrong."

"So you guys have had no contact since?"

"Strangely enough, not until today. His sister left me a message on my recorder. She called just before I left to pick you up."

"What'd she want?" Denny asked.

"I don't know, but she left her number."

"So, what are you going to do? You going to call her?"

"I haven't decided," Ronnie replied.

"So what ever happened to Bobbie?"

"He made a career out of the Army. Three tours in Nam, I know that much. I heard he stayed in 'till the first Gulf War. That thing with Bobbie really hurt my dad."

"Really, he and Big Red were close?"

"Yeah, Bobbie's dad walked out on them when we were in third grade. Bobbie kind of looked to Big Red as a father figure. My dad loved Bobbie, too. That was the really hard part. It's kind of like that ripple thing. You know how when you throw a pebble in the water and the rings begin to spread out in ever increasing circles. Melvindale was like that puddle of water; the ripples hit a lot of people."

"Fuck me, I gotta piss. All this emotion and sincerity has my bladder exploding," Denny said. As he stood up, the door bell rang.

"Who the hell is that at this time?" Ronnie said. He got up with Denny and walked toward the foyer. Denny went into the bathroom while Ronnie continued toward the door. There was a narrow full length window parallel to the door where Ronnie looked to see who was on the porch. Darlene was standing there, dressed in her black and white waitress uniform holding a small paper bag. Ronnie opened the door.

"Darlene, this is a pleasant surprise. Thought Denny was picking you up at the restaurant after your shift? Come on in."

"The crowd thinned out and Rudy asked if anyone wanted off," Darlene said stepping into the foyer, "I hope it's okay. I was so excited about seeing your house; I told him I could use the time off. Believe me, I put in enough hours this week."

"Sure come on in. Denny's in the bathroom, I'll tell him you are here. Have a seat," Ronnie closed the door as Darlene took a seat on the sofa.

"Wow, really cool place," she said looking around.

"Thanks," Ronnie walked to the bathroom and knocked gently on the door.

"Hey, Denny," he said in a loud whisper, "Darlene's here, she got off early."

Denny opened the door quietly.

"Can you entertain her for a minute? Sorry 'bout this, I need a little time to group my poop as we used to say. Would it be okay if I took a quick shower and shaved? It'd help me get my shit in order?"

"No sweat, I'll give her the extended tour. Get yourself organized, we'll be on the balcony," Ronnie answered.

"Thanks."

Ronnie walked back to the great room where Darlene was sitting. "Denny's going to take a quick shower if that's okay."

"Sure, no sweat. Oh, the wine's for you," Darlene said handing Ronnie the paper bag.

"Thanks, you didn't have to do that, that's so nice," Ronnie replied, "can I pour you a glass?"

"Sure, as long as you have one with me."

"Okay, I'll go open it up. Either sit, or if you want; walk around. Make yourself at home," Ronnie said.

Ronnie walked to the kitchen, opened the bottle and returned with two glasses. As they sipped wine, Ronnie took her downstairs and showed her the boat house where the Four Winds sat cradled in the hoist. Darlene asked if he took the boat out often, Ronnie answered he hadn't since Beth died.

Episode 19

After an awkward silence, Ronnie showed her the escape tunnel that led from the house, went under West River Road and came out at a place in the woods beyond the garage and parking area. Darlene said she had heard there was a tunnel but hadn't believed the rumors. They returned upstairs in time to meet Denny coming down from his shower, his hair still wet.

"Get the grand tour?" Denny asked taking the wine glass from Darlene's hand. He took a small sip.

"Yeah," Darlene answered excitedly, "Ronnie took me down to the boat house and showed me the tunnel and everything."

"Hey, I didn't get to see them. Maybe you can show them to me a little later," Denny took another drink of the wine, then handed the glass back to Darlene.

"You smell good," she said, "wish I'd have stopped at home to shower before I came. Should have thought of that before; I smell like the restaurant,' she added.

"Hey, just take one here," Denny suggested, "Ronnie won't mind, will you?"

"Hey, help yourself, me casa, sue casa, or what ever the hell the saying is," Ronnie knew the wine was taking its toll.

"Uh, I don't have anything to put on. Maybe next time," Darlene said as she walked into the kitchen and poured another glass.

"Hell, Ronnie must have something you can put on," Denny added.

"Sure, I have some sweats and stuff," Ronnie offered feeling a little uncomfortable.

"Have some boxers and a tee shirt?" Darlene asked.

"Sure, no problem. Denny, show Darlene the bathroom and I'll be up in a minute to get you something to wear. It takes me a while to climb the steps."

Taking their wine glasses, Denny and Darlene headed upstairs. Ronnie followed and gave Darlene a pair of boxers and a green Michigan State tee shirt.

"We'll be down on the balcony, come on down when you're ready."

A few minutes later Denny appeared on the balcony and took a seat on the patio chair.

"Hey thanks for listening tonight."

"No problem," Ronnie replied, "but you should find someone to help you work through all this."

"I'll be okay," Denny added.

The two men sat in silence until Darlene walked out on the balcony. Sitting at the table next to Denny, she looked refreshed. It had been a while since Ronnie had sat on the balcony with a woman in boxer shorts, with wet hair and wearing a tee shirt. It was one of Beth's favorite ensembles. We didn't get quite enough evenings on this balcony, Ronnie said to himself, there should have been more.

"So how did you come to live here?" Darlene asked breaking the silence.

"Oh, it was one of those fluke kind of things. Beth always loved this place. I told Denny earlier this evening, she wanted to live here from the first time we saw it as teenagers," Ronnie set his glass on the table.

"You didn't grow up here?"

"No, we grew up in Melvindale. We used to come out here in the 60s to a place called Looney Rooney's," Ronnie answered with a smile, "but that was another time."

"Hey, I heard of him," Darlene said, "no kidding, my aunt used to talk about him. My grandparents still live in Allen Park and my mom's older sister used to talk about him."

"Who the hell was Looney Rooney?" Denny asked over the rim of his wine glass.

"Denny you'd have loved this guy," Ronnie said with a spark of excitement. "He was this really mellow old recluse. His house was just down the road and he had this big porch where he'd let teenagers come and party. He'd play guitar and sing on that big old front porch. It was really a gas. Really a gas, now there's one that gives away my age."

"So kids would just show up at this crazy old guy's house?" Denny asked.

Episode 19

"That's pretty much it. Anyway, Beth, Bobbie and I came out here all the time. It was really cool," Ronnie answered.

"So what happened to him?" Darlene asked.

"Oh, I think the township forced him into a psychiatric hospital or something. The house was torn down years ago and some doctor built a mega mansion on it. I'll show you the spot some time. Great memories, bring your aunt out some time Darlene, we'll swap Looney Rooney war stories," Ronnie said. "On that note, think I'm going to turn in. I'm bushed. If I stay up much longer, I'll turn into Looney Ronnie. Just make yourself at home."

After changing and brushing his teeth, Ronnie climbed into bed. He could hear Denny and Darlene from the balcony speaking in muffled tones. Ronnie hoped the wine would put him to sleep right away; Denny's revelations had given him head spins. Ronnie remembered something he'd read about survivors of suicides feeling guilt and anger. He had never considered someone perceiving themselves as another person's sole reason to live. He turned the idea around in his head for a few minutes wondering if guilt could outweigh anger. It was too complex of an issue and too late, he'd pick up the threads in the morning. Ronnie took a deep breath and looked at the ceiling. A breeze came through the window as he pulled the sheet over his chest. Somewhere in the distance, he heard the sound of a freighter blowing it's horn. Must be over in the channel Ronnie said to himself. He thought of how Beth loved the sound of the freighters' horns, especially on dark foggy nights. Tomorrow has to be better, Ronnie said to himself as he rolled over and fell asleep.

Episode 20

 Traffic on the interstate was light. Setting the cruise control at sixty, Cate relaxed her grip on the steering wheel. David had reclined his seat and was snoozing comfortably. Cate knew he would sleep all the way back to Plymouth; David could sleep anywhere.
 A full moon had risen casting a shimmer of soft light on the rural Indiana countryside. After conversations spoken too loudly and the clatter of busboys clearing tables, the quiet felt pleasant. The two cups of coffee after dinner had thankfully counteracted the affects of the wine. Cate felt she could drive indefinitely through the pale moonlight.
 Cate glanced into the rear view mirror to make sure Charlotte was still breathing. Cate noticed Don had slid to the corner of the back seat. His head was flopped over and nestled in the small crack between the door and the seat, his right cheek pressing against the window. His head would roll one way and then sway back as she changed lanes. Charlotte was leaning against him with her head on his shoulder. The palm of her right hand was under her cheek and Cate could hear her deep rhythmic breathing during pauses in Don's snoring. Cate felt envious of her passengers. They looked cozy and content as the big Buick floated along the freeway.

Seeing them, Cate recalled how she and her brothers would sleep in the back of the family station wagon during trips to the their summer cottage. Louis and Emma bought the tiny summer place in Leamington, Ontario when Cate was just a baby. Her parents had saved and scrimped to get the money to buy the place, but it had been worth the effort. Cate loved the cottage. They spent most summer weekends there. In those days, the drive took three hours, if traffic on the Ambassador Bridge was not backed up. Three or four times each summer, Louis would drive the family up on Friday, stay for the weekend and then return home alone on Sunday night. Cate, her mom and two brothers would stay at the cottage for the week while her dad worked.

Summers in Canada were magical. Theirs was one of the small beachfront cottages that lined the road leading into the Pointe Pelee Provincial Park. It had one bedroom, a living room and kitchen on the first floor. There was a loft on the second floor where Cate and her brothers slept. Her friend Kimmy was allowed to come along two or three weekends a year. Cate's brothers had each other for company.

Once or twice during the week, Cate and her mom would walk to the Bay View Market pulling Cate's red wagon. They'd buy milk in quart bottles and baked goods for dessert. Emma was particularly fond of the little butter tarts. They were like tiny pecan pies, but had raisins mixed into the filling instead of pecans. After the first bite, the sweet gooey filling would run onto Cate's hands. Cate and her mom would pile the bags of groceries into the wagon and make the return trip along the blacktop road that bordered the Lake Erie shoreline.

There was a dance hall about halfway into the park. It was an ancient log cabin building with a little snack bar where she and Kimmy would buy hamburgers and fries for lunch. Cate had eaten burgers in many places since those summers but hadn't found any that compared to the Dance Hall's. It might have been the Canadian sweet relish piled on the burgers or the vinegar sprinkled on the fries that made them taste so good. Or

Episode 20

maybe it was because she was ten years old and had spent the day swimming and riding a zillion miles on her bike leaving her so hungry everything tasted good.

Sometimes the taste of a vinegar laden French fry at the Indiana State Fair would send her mind reeling in memories of a time when things were less complicated. There was no television at the cottage, her parents had been stern about that. There was no washer or dryer either. Dishes were washed at the sink where conversation was shared with the person standing next to you. There were comic books, however, and Nancy Drew novels and Mad Magazines. Cate always felt cozy, snuggled into her bed after bathing in the lake. She'd read 'till her eyes got too heavy. The lapping of the waves against the sandy beach lulled her to sleep before she ever finished a third comic.

There was no furnace at the cottage; it was strictly a summer place. It was a place of sunshine, waves and sand. A simple place in a much simpler time. Lately, Cate felt she'd give anything to be ten years old again and have one more summer there. She had been so immersed in thoughts of the cottage, Cate hadn't noticed the silver BMW in her rear view mirror.

****

As he walked to his car, Darpak saw the big Buick leave the restaurant. Running into Nurse Cassadea had been a surprise. Before leaving, he had tucked the aluminum case into his pants and buttoned his suit coat. He would spend tomorrow with the family then drive to Detroit on Sunday.

After merging into traffic, Darpak passed an elderly couple poking along in a Ford Crown Victoria. The driver was a diminutive man with wisps of grey hair and thick glasses. Darpak wondered what would bring such an old couple out on Friday night. He was considering their possible destinations when he spotted the Rivera ahead. He thought briefly about staying behind Nurse Cassadea all the way back to Plymouth, but dinner with the beautiful agent had put other ideas into his head. He eased the BMW toward the Buick then changed lanes when he closed the gap. As Darpak pulled abreast of the Buick, he glanced to his right.

****

Coming out of her day dream, Cate noticed headlights in her side view mirror. Looking to her left, she was startled to see Doctor Taj. A faint smile crossed his face. The doctor gave her a quick wave and pulled away. Cate waved back and thought about their encounter. She wondered whether her appearance had spoiled a secret rendezvous. Doctor Taj caught Cate's smile and wave just before exiting the freeway. Assuming there were no delays, he'd be home in forty-five minutes.

Cate took the same exit. She looked at the moonlit landscape and it reminded her of the road leading to the cottage. Both roads meandered through expansive corn and wheat fields separated by barns and old farm houses. Cate hadn't been back to the cottage in years. After Louis died, she'd sold her part of the place to her brother Frank. At the time, she and Billy needed money to build their dream house. She rationalized the sale by telling herself the extended family had gotten too large to fit in the tiny place anyway. There had been some talk of expanding it and making the second story bigger but somehow it had remained just talk. After the divorce from Billy, she'd gone to the cottage once with her daughters. She found it cramped and wondered if the place felt that way to the adults when she was a child. After spending three nights with her brother and his family, Cate left feeling like one of too many sardines.

Lately she thought about asking David if he was interested in getting a place in Canada. She knew it was pointless, he'd said when he retired, their next move was to the sunshine. She didn't like to think about David retiring. By that time, she would be seventy, a notion too depressing to dwell on. David would only be sixty. Up to now, their age difference hadn't seemed like a

Episode 20

big deal but she wondered how he would feel then. You could lift a chin and remove a frown line easily enough, but how do you tummy tuck a sagging spirit or find a Botox that erased the mileage on your soul. Cate looked at David. He wasn't a Billy or even an Eric; those kinds of love are relegated to certain times in life. David had been there, however, when she needed someone. Cate saw the Plymouth sign and was surprised the time had gone by so quickly.

****

Darpak was ahead of schedule. As he made the turn into the sub division, Darpak felt a sense of satisfaction. He owned one of the largest and most expensive homes in town. He pulled up the driveway, pushed the button for the garage door opener then eased the BMW into its spot. After shutting off the engine, he reached under the seat and extracted the aluminum case. He entered the house and stopped in his study to lock the case in his desk.

****

As Cate passed the city limits sign, she nudged David and told him they were in Plymouth.

"What's up?" David asked rubbing his eyes.

"Hey," Cate joked, "don't you know that will give you wrinkles."

"The hell with the wrinkles," David responded. "Are we home?"

"Almost," Cate answered, "why don't we drop off Don and Charlotte, then just head home. We can pick up your truck tomorrow."

"Hell, no," David replied in a good natured voice, "I don't want to leave my Blazer there for some drunk to ram into or some teenager to hot wire and go joy riding. Swing by the Outback, I'll take Don and Charlotte home."

"I don't know David," Cate answered doubtingly. "You've had a lot to drink. Maybe you shouldn't be driving."

"Maybe I didn't drink as much as you think," David answered putting his hand on Cate's thigh.

"Hey stop that," Cate whispered motioning her head toward Don and Charlotte in the back seat.

"Hell," David replied with a laugh, "they wouldn't know it if you pulled the Riv over right now and we did it on the hood."

"Well, I know Charlotte wouldn't, but Don holds his liquor better," Cate answered.

"Let's put it this way, he had a couple of belts of Scotch while you and Char were in the lady's room. We could invite him for a threesome right now and he'd think we were talking about golf," David smiled.

"David!' Cate admonished, "What a thing to say."

"Well, tell you what Cate. You drop me off at my truck. Then you drop off Don and Char. I'll go home, let the dogs out and be ready for you when you get there. We'll celebrate your birthday in the appropriate fashion." David replied with a grin.

"Well, I'll run them home," Cate said. "You let the boys out and if you aren't passed out by the time I get there, we'll see about celebrating.

"I'm fine. I didn't drink all that much. Besides, I had a good nap. I'll be fine," David rolled down his window.

"David," Don asked in a sleepy voice, "where the hell are we? Montana? We gonna shoot some elk now?" he added.

"No, numb nuts, we're in Plymouth. You know the bustling, one horsed, metropolis where you've lived your entire waste of a life," David answered with a laugh.

"Okay, I was just wondering," Don added then leaned his head back.

"We're just about at the Outback. Cate's going to drop me off, then cart your drunken asses home," David replied.

"Sounds good to me Captain, carry on," Don gave David a mock salute and closed his eyes.

Cate could see the Outback ahead on her right. She slowed the Buick and turned into the parking lot. When Cate pulled up

Episode 20

to David's SUV, he unbuckled his seat belt and leaned across the driver's seat and kissed her lightly on her cheek.

"See ya at home, babe," David said climbing out of the Rivera.

"Let the boy's out, I'll be right home," Cate replied. "Be careful driving," she added as David closed the door and walked toward his truck. Cate watched to make sure he got there okay. She looked in the back seat again. Charlotte had stirred a little but didn't wake from the lights of the Outback's parking lot. Don seemed to have recovered.

"We at the Outback, Cate?" he asked groggily.

"Yeah, I just dropped David off at his truck," Cate answered as she pulled around the restaurant heading toward the road. "We'll have you home in a minute," she added.

Cate drove a couple of miles before stopping at a traffic signal where the red light seemed to take forever.

"Ain't that always the way of it," she said out loud, "whenever you're in a hurry, it seems like the red lights last at least three times as long as normal."

When the light finally changed, Cate drove another mile then turned right. Don and Charlotte's house was a short distance ahead. Cate pulled into the driveway.

"Hey, Char, come on, wake up now, we're home," Don nudged her and Charlotte started to come to. Looking around the inside of the Buick, she struggled to get her bearings. A momentary look of bewilderment crossed her face as she looked at Don.

"Where are we?" she asked.

"We're home hon. Can you walk to the house?"

"Yeah," Charlotte slurred, "I can make it. Just help me out of this car."

"Hang on there hon, I'll come around and open the door," Don answered.

"I think I better help you, Don," Cate said. She got out of the Rivera muffling a quiet laugh. "I can steady her on the porch while you get the door unlocked. We don't want her doing a header off the porch.

Cate opened Charlotte's door while Don made his way around the car and helped get Charlotte to her feet. Cate considered telling Don to keep a close eye on her because of the valium, but decide against it. They finally got Charlotte to her feet and onto the porch. Cate kept her steady while Don opened the door.

"I can take it from here, Cate. Thanks," Don said.

"Okay then, see you over the weekend," Cate replied and walked down the steps.

It was a short drive home from Don and Charlotte's. Cate put the radio on a soft rock station then rolled the windows down to purge the blend of alcohol, curry and stale perfume from the car. The fresh air felt good as she pulled up her driveway and opened the garage door. David's Blazer was not in its usual spot and a feeling of uneasiness ran through her. The feeling remained as she opened the door to the house.

****

After locking the case in his desk, Darpak climbed the stairs to the second floor and quietly opened the door to his daughter's bedroom. Devmani was curled up on her stomach and fast asleep. Her long dark hair had fallen over her face and her right thumb was stuck in her mouth. Darpak thought about removing the thumb but didn't want to wake her.

When Darpak looked into his son's bedroom, Javesh was also asleep. He was not a stomach sleeper like his sister and lay spread eagled diagonally across the bed. He'd kicked off his covers and the pillow was on the floor. Javesh was wearing a Cubs tee shirt. He was tall like his father and would be handsome. Ravenna maintained he would break a few hearts along the way but in the end they agreed he would marry a Hindu woman of their choice. Little Devmani would also marry the man they chose. Darpak pulled the sheet over his son and walked out of the room.

When he walked into the master bedroom, Ravenna was lying in bed reading a textbook.

Episode 20

"Reading the latest Cosmo?" Darpak teased as he walked toward the bed and bent down to kiss her.

"Yes, I'm catching up on the latest fashion in multi variant regression analysis," she answered setting the book on the night stand. Ravenna wrapped her arms around Darpak's neck.

"Well, I'm impressed. Did you have a good evening?" he asked.

"Yes, it was a pleasant enough. We ate dinner then watched a video, but I think I'm ready for a little grown up entertainment," Ravenna returned Darpak's kiss.

"Well, let me clean up a little and I'll see if I can't be of more interest than Shark Tales," he had seen the DVD case on the coffee table.

"Very perceptive Doctor," Ravenna replied letting her arms fall from his neck.

"I don't miss much, Doctor Taj," Darpak answered. She had a PHD but rarely went by her title.

"Well, hurry up in the shower, I can't stay awake all night," Ravenna teased then picked up the book.

"I'll be right back and then we'll work on your regression," Darpak teased back. Darpak took a hot shower and shaved. After slipping on his bathrobe from a hook on the back of the door, he walked back into the bedroom.

****

Cate walked into the house. The dogs heard her pull into the garage and were waiting by the door. Gucci sat patiently waging his tail in controlled moderation, while Duffy spun around in circles.

"You boys need to go out?" Cate asked petting Gucci on the head then picked up Duffy and hugged him. "Okay, come on."

The dogs followed Cate to the sliding glass door and bounded outside. They ran around for a minute sniffing for just the right place.

"Seems like one spot would be as good as the next," Cate said aloud to distract herself from the concern she had felt since pulling into the garage. Maybe he stopped for gas, she told herself. Hopefully he'd not been pulled over. She had their only cell phone. She wanted them each to have one but David refused saying the pager he wore at the plant all day was enough electronic tethering. She decided to give him ten more minutes, if he didn't show up, she'd go looking for him.

****

Darpak's body was covered with sweat. He was slightly out of breath and felt a little dizzy from their intense lovemaking. The dinner with the agent had stirred him more than he realized. He closed his eyes and was just drifting off when the telephone rang.

"I thought you were not on call tonight," Ravenna said in husky voice.

"I'm not," Darpak replied. For a moment he thought the call might be connected to his meeting with the agent, though she wouldn't contact him this way. He also knew there were contacts within the American government protecting their interests. It had to be the hospital; maybe one of the attending surgeons became ill or something. Darpak reached for the phone on the night stand.

"Hello. Yes, this is Doctor Taj," he said then paused. "Yes, yes, I'll be right there," Darpak added in a controlled voice. After setting the phone back on the receiver, he sat up.

"Was it the hospital?" Ravenna asked.

"Yes, I'm going to have to go in. There's been an accident. Several people were injured."

"Can't someone else go in?" Ravenna asked. Rolling over to face him, she put her hand on his shoulder.

"This is very bad, Ravenna. Six people were injured. We're going to work on four of them here. The other two are going to be air lifted to the burn center in Indianapolis."

"Be careful Darpak. It's late and it's Friday night, people will be driving home from the bars."

Episode 20

"I'll be okay Ravenna," Darpak answered. He dressed quickly. After kissing her, Darpak hurried to the garage. It was going to be a long night which might make the drive to Detroit on Sunday difficult. He didn't want to delay the trip.

****

Cate sipped a glass of water while sitting at the dining room table. She watched the dogs in the back yard and after a few minutes, called them back into the house. She tried to control her emotions, but knew something was wrong. David should have been home by now. She gave the boys two dog treats each, knowing Duffy would beg for more. Cate looked at the clock again; ten minutes was up. She told the boys to behave themselves and grabbed her purse off the kitchen table. She had walked to the garage and pushed the opener button when she heard the phone ring. Cate bounded through the door and across the kitchen to the wall phone. She picked it up before the third ring.

"Hello," she said anxiously, noticing her voice had a higher pitch than normal.

"Is this Mrs. Warden?" a man's voice asked.

"This is Cate Cassadea," she replied.

"Is Mrs. Warden there?" the man asked.

After the divorce Cate had taken back her maiden name. It was one of the few conditions she insisted upon when she agreed to marry David. After Billy, Cate vowed to never take another man's name. She'd remain Cassadea or she'd remain single. David had agreed reluctantly.

"I'm married to David Warden," Cate answered trying to clarify things.

"This is officer Shatzer, from the Plymouth police department," the man answered. "I hate to tell you this, but your husband has been in an accident. He is at the hospital."

It was as if a lightening bolt had come out of a perfectly blue sky on a perfectly normal summer's day and struck Cate in the middle of her perfectly normal forehead. She felt paralyzed. She tried to talk but it was as if she had been thrown into a scary dream where she screamed for help but no sound came out of her mouth.

"Ms. Cassadea, did you hear me?" the officer waited for a reply. "Are you okay? You need to get to the hospital. Can you drive, or do you want us to send a car for you?" he added when Cate didn't answer.

****

When Darpak arrived at the hospital, he entered through the emergency room, wanting to get a feel for the situation. Outside, the hospital was a buzz of flashing police cars and ambulance lights. It looked like something from a war zone. The surgical chief of staff was already in the emergency room supervising triage. Darpak approached him.

In his mid fifties, Dr. Harold Hartig was a physical giant of a man. He was a competent surgeon, good administrator and an even better politician. He also was a home grown product whose father had been the only surgeon at the hospital when Plymouth was just a small farm town. Harry was tall; every bit of six feet five. He had been a local basketball hero and played one year at Indiana University. Harry had a full head of bushy hair that was now salt and pepper. His eyebrows were also thick and bushy. He was a good surgeon but knew Darpak was better.

"What are we looking at, Harry?" Darpak asked intensely.

"A total disaster, Darpak, a total disaster. I haven't seen anything like this since the tornado hit back in '62. I was only fourteen, but I still remember my dad trying to deal with all the injuries. Anyway, enough of that. We've got six major injuries. We have two teenaged kids with second and third degree burns over extensive portions of their body. We're trying to stabilize them. The helicopter will be here shortly to take them to Indianapolis. We've got a forty year old male with major brain trauma. The pictures on him are waiting

Episode 20

for you. He's in really bad shape. We've got three teenagers, one male, and two females with assorted broken bones, a broken pelvis and one with internal bleeding. Roger is going to take the girl with the internal bleeding first. I want you to take the older male with the head injury. Let's talk on the way up," Harry said as they walked toward the elevator doors. They boarded the elevator where Doctor Hartig pushed the button to the second floor. The elevator door closed in front of them.

"Anything else I should know?" Darpak asked.

"Yeah, depending on what you run into, you may have to operate on one of the teenagers after you finish with the head trauma. I've got a call into Bainbridge to see if they can spare anyone. Hell of time for Geof Bush to be out of town, but everyone needs time off. I'm going to assist Roger. When Tim gets here, he'll assist you. We just gotta do the best we can," Harry said as they entered the locker room to change into their scrubs.

"So that's it then?" Darpak asked as he began peeling off his clothes.

"There's one more thing. The man you will be operating on is Nurse Cassadea's husband," Doctor Hartig said pulling up his green scrub pants.

"Damn," Darpak mumbled lowly.

"I'll switch with you if it's a problem, but you're the best neuro we have. He doesn't have much of a chance from what I saw in the ER." Doctor Hartig pulled a matching green top over his head.

"No, we're not friends or anything. It's just, well, we had dinner in the same restaurant tonight over in Indianapolis. I ran into them. We talked a bit, that's all. I'll do the cutting," Darpak replied then walked to the sink and began scrubbing.

****

Cate sat next to the priest in the surgical waiting room crying intermittently. The priest would console her and she'd pull herself together only to find herself sobbing again minutes later. She knew the priest, but not very well. She would find out later that he and two other clerics had been called into the hospital. The hospital chaplain was a young Methodist minister who took rotations one weekend a month. When summoned to the emergency room, he took one look and called for reinforcements. The priest knew Cate from his hospital rounds and admonished her occasionally in a good natured way to attend mass more often.

The priest sat with her a while, then excused himself saying he needed to go to the emergency room to check on one of the injured girls who was from from the parish. Cate told him she would be okay. Cate sat slumped and watched him walk somberly to the elevator. The night's events had been a real soul searcher even for the priest. Explaining God's infinite wisdom to the families of the teenagers had been trying. How could anyone understand why the kids who had not worn their seat belts were expected to survive because they had been thrown from the car while the ones who were belted ended up trapped inside the burning vehicle. Their chances of survival were dismal at best, and even if they did, more surgeries were yet to come.

Cate glanced at the middle aged woman in charge of the surgical waiting room. She assumed Cheryl had been called in when the multiple surgeries were scheduled. It appeared she had rushed to the hospital, her hair was lopsided and her make up askew. Cheryl walked over and took a seat next to Cate and did her best to fill in for the priest. Cate apologized about not being able to get a better hold on herself. Why did she let David drive, she asked Cheryl. He'd had trouble even buckling the seat belt before leaving the Peacock, she added. Why did they have to go all the way to Indianapolis for her birthday dinner. Cheryl did her best to convince Cate it was nobody's fault, David had just done a loving thing taking her to Indianapolis for dinner.

Episode 20

Cate had no idea how long she had sat there. She thought about calling someone, but what was she to say. She knew she would have to call David's family but was confused about what to tell them. It didn't make sense to call Don and Charlotte. There was no way those two could drive. She decided to wait until she had more definitive news but knew it could be hours. As she sat there looking down at the floor, Cate realized Cheryl had said something to her. Looking up, she saw Doctor Taj walk into the waiting room.

"Cate," the doctor said softly.

He still had his surgical cap on. His face mask dangled at the side of his head with a trap looped over his left ear. She was surprised to hear his voice and from the the look on his face, knew it was not going to be good news. She'd seen that look on too many doctors' faces.

"Yes, doctor," Cate answered then stood on unsteady legs.

"We did all we could, Cate. We really did," the doctor said in a sympathetic voice.

"Oh, my God," Cate said with anguish. The room seemed to be spinning. This is just a bad dream, Cate thought, this isn't real. David's not dead, he can't be, not now. Cate collapsed on the chair. Holding her head in both hands, she began sobbing.

"I'm so sorry Cate. I wished I could have done more. There was just so much damage, Cate. So much damage," Darpak repeated placing his hand on her shoulder.

"I know you did your best," Cate said between muffled sobs.

Cheryl pulled her close and began rocking her in a gentle back and forth sway. Cate had done the same thing with her girls, after they skinned a knee or bumped their heads.

"I'm sorry, I know I'm a nurse. I know I should have a better grip," Cate cried, "but it's just so hard."

"I'm sorry too Cate. I have to go back into surgery shortly. One of the girls has a broken pelvis. Another has internal injuries. I wish there was more time. I am truly sorry for your loss," Doctor Taj patted her on the shoulder then walked back toward the operating room.

"Cate, I'm going to call down to the E room for the priest," Cheryl said sympathetically.

"Okay," Cate answered. Her voice sounding like it was coming from somewhere outside her body.

The priest returned in a few minutes.

"Cate I'm so sorry. David's with God now, he's not suffering," the priest said. Though he was sincere, his condolence sounded hollow in his own head. "I've arranged for an officer to drive you home and one of the sisters to meet you at your house. She'll stay for the night if need be."

"Thanks, Father," Cate answered in a horse whisper. It was the best reply she could muster. "I'd like that," she added after taking a couple of deep breaths.

Cate was surprised she was able to respond with any sense of coherence. She suddenly felt guilty about not being a good Catholic the last few years. She had engaged in sharp disagreements with Emma about the Church's treatment of women and felt this sudden kindness was more than she deserved. Going home alone right now was not something she could bear.

Cate didn't remember the ride home in the squad car. The next thing she knew she was standing next to the police car on her driveway. She also had no idea what time it was. The sun was starting to come up so she assumed it had to be close to five. A nun was waiting on her porch along with another woman. The nun introduced herself as Sister Margaret. She was older than the other woman who looked to be about Cate's own age. Sister Margaret looked sturdy. Nuns always looked that way to Cate; very plain, very sturdy. Maybe it was all the clean living or the absence of make up, Cate was never sure. The other woman introduced herself as Joan. Cate didn't catch her last name and didn't ask her to repeat it. The nun told the officer he didn't have to stay; they'd call if anything was needed.

Cate unlocked the door and the three women walked into the house. Duffy was barking and Cate was afraid he'd wake the neighbors. As usual, Gucci sat complacently while Duffy spun in circles. Gucci was more perceptive. His tail dropped imme-

Episode 20

diately when Cate reached down, swooped him up and hugged him tightly. Duffy was too busy running around the feet of Sister Margaret and Joan.

"I think I better put the boys out for a while," Cate said walking toward the sliding door in the dining room.

"We'll let them in, Cate," Sister Margaret said. "Why don't you go up and lie down for a while. You need to rest."

"Thanks sister," Cate said as she opened the door wall. The dogs went into the back yard. Duffy took off like a flash, while Gucci stayed by the patio, not letting Cate out of his sight.

"Did the doctor give you anything to help you sleep?" Sister Margaret asked.

"No, but I have something here to take if I need it," Cate replied as she caught a glimpse of her reflection in the door wall. She was suddenly aware of how disheveled she looked and felt embarrassed. "I look a shambles," she said to the two women. "What does it really matter, my life is a shambles. I might as well look the part," she added. It took what little strength she had to not break down again.

"Well, dear, if I were in your shoes, I'd take something and get some sleep. Joan and I will be right here if you need us. We'll be praying for you, dear."

Cate thanked the two women and walked to the bedroom. She suddenly felt so very tired. She filled a glass with water at the bathroom sink and took a bottle of Xanax from the cabinet. She popped one of the white tablets on her furry, coffee stained tongue and drank the entire glass of water. Cate walked to the bed and pulled back the duvet. She opened a window to let some fresh air in then sat on the edge of the bed and slipped off her shoes. As she collapsed on the bed, Cate could hear a cardinal join the choir of other song birds in their welcome to the morning sun. The cardinal's whistle was familiar and comforting; he'd woken up her often during the summer. She listened to the other birds chime in. Cate didn't know if it was the Xanax or the stress, but she could almost hear the sounds of waves lapping onto a beach. I must be hallucinating Cate thought. It sounds just like the cottage, with the birds and the waves. I'll wake up tomorrow she thought, and this will all go away. Cate heard the cardinal whistle one more time before the tranquilizer took its toll and she fell into deep dreamless sleep.

*Book Two
Home Again*

Episode 21

Cate placed the last suitcase into the trunk of the Rivera. It was a warm morning for September. She was wearing jeans and a sweat shirt when she began loading the car but the sweat shirt had been shed twenty minutes ago. She took a deep breath and sat on the steps of the front porch next to Gucci. He could always sense when she and David were about to leave on vacation. Maybe it was the suitcases that tipped him off or maybe dogs really did have some kind of sixth sense. Whatever the reason, he always became mopey when she and David were going away.

Cate hoped by letting Gucci be part of the packing process, he'd be less freaked out about moving from the only home he'd ever known. It was a ridiculous notion, Cate admitted, to treat a dog like a person but who really knew what went on in their furry little heads. Sometimes it was as if Gucci could read her mind. Cate laughed softly, here she was, recently widowed and psychoanalyzing her dogs like some old crazy lady. She had heard veterinarians were now prescribing Prozac for dogs and wondered if she could dose Gucci with Prozac while measuring out her own Wellbutrin.

"Duffy, come on now," Cate yelled to the little white terrier who'd wedged his way between two evergreens below the bay window. He was sniffing around a place where a squirrel had dug a small hole to bury a hickory nut.

Duffy gave up his search and ran up to Cate. He strutted up the steps as Cate opened the door. She stood in the middle of the great room and gave it a quick inspection. Everything seemed in order. She walked up the steps and did a quick tour of the bedrooms and bathrooms. Seeing nothing had been missed, she turned and went back down the steps with the dogs following closely behind.

"Yes, Guch, I have the food and water bowls," Cate said in a condescending voice.

After setting the lock, she walked outside and stood on the porch in silent reflection looking at the for sale sign. Cate surveyed the yard. She had vowed not to cry and so far she had kept her promise. Her roots were not in Plymouth, though she wasn't certain they were still in Melvindale either. She hadn't lived there since the fall Kelly was murdered. The town had changed. Some changes were physical, others went beyond that. Cate found it ironic that thirty-five years later, she was grieving another loss and moving back to a gritty little town that mostly held memories and ghosts.

The idea of moving back home had come up unexpectedly after the reception following the funeral home visitation. Standing on the porch, Cate's mind drifted back to the reception. She was still surprised Kimmy and her mother had come all the way from Melvindale. Kimmy called and told her they were coming; no arguments accepted. They'd booked a room at the Holiday Inn and intended to leave immediately after the service but Cate insisted they come by the house and have something to eat. They stayed for two hours.

Just before leaving, Kimmy's mother walked into the kitchen and told Cate she should move back home to take care of Emma. Kimmy's mom had always been the queen of guilt. Cate said she intended to stay in Plymouth because of her job. Kimmy's mom replied that with the insurance money she was about to receive, Cate probably wouldn't have to work anymore. Embarrassed, Kimmy whispered to Cate they were

Episode 21

leaving before her mother said anything else so crass. Cate told Kimmy not to go too hard on her mom as they walked out the door. When she walked back into the kitchen, Kathy and Linda were still sitting at the table.

"And she wonders why Kimmy always runs off with any guy that shows the least bit of interest," Linda said.

After the caterer finished cleaning, the four women changed into pajamas and gathered in the family room. Kathy and Cate took places at opposite ends of the couch. Jess plopped on the love seat, her legs elevated over the arm while Linda headed toward David's lazy boy. A bottle of wine had been opened and three glasses poured. The women sat silently for a few moments, each searching desperately for the right thing to say. As teenagers, the same scene had played at countless sleepovers. Cate finally broke the silence.

"What a fucked up day," she sighed and took a sip of wine. "No, I take that back, what a fucked up two weeks."

"Amen, sister," Kathy said and raised her glass toward Cate.

"So, now what?" Linda asked, reclining the lazy boy.

"Hell, if I know," Cate said. A small tear began to gather at the edge of her right eye.

"Hey, it's okay," Jess said. "It's us Cate; you don't need to hold anything back. We've all been through a lot together."

"I'm sorry," Cate said dabbing her check with a Kleenex.

She hadn't seen Jess in long time and was surprised at the toll the years had taken. Sitting in the living room with her old friends was the best therapy possible and she'd had enough to know. There was a certain comfort in just being with them.

"This may sound stupid," Kathy said with the hint of a smile, "but maybe Kimmy's mother was on to something today."

"What?" Jess replied setting her Diet Coke on the end table, "that Kimmy should give up men and join a nunnery."

The women began laughing. Jess sarcasm had always been biting and painful.

"No," Kathy replied taking a sip of wine, "what she said about you moving back home, Cate."

"Yeah," Linda added, "maybe that's not such a bad idea. We could all be together again. Why not, what the hell is there for you here, now?"

"Well, my job for one thing," Cate answered. "Don't listen to all that stuff Kimmy's mom said. There may be some problems with the insurance companies."

"Honey, you don't have to decide on this right now," Jess replied sincerely. "Anyway, you have enough on your mind. We don't have to talk about all of this stuff now."

"No, that's okay," Cate replied. "I need to talk to someone about this stuff."

"Okay, Cate," Kathy said petting Gucci on the head. He had snuggled up close to her. "Tell us anything you want, but if it gets too hard, just forget about it and we'll talk about something else."

"Well," Cate stammered, hesitated and then started again. "There could be some complications. David's blood alcohol was just under the minimum for a DUI. One witness at the accident scene claims David had the yellow light and was not at fault. The kids in the car he collided with were leaving a party and had been drinking. Another car was sort of chasing them, and the kids in the car that ran into David may have gone through the light while it was still red. It's a mess. The police are still investigating. I should never, I should never," Cate paused. "I should never have let him drive home," Cate said and began crying. Kathy moved down the couch and hugged her.

"Listen Cate," Jess said, "this was not your fault in anyway. You asked David to leave his truck, but you know how men are about their vehicles. Their truck is like their penis. You can't tell them anything about how or when to operate either one."

Cate smiled.

"Amen to that one," Kathy interjected.

"Those kids had no business chasing each other up and down the roads, though heaven knows we did the same thing," Jess said turning to look out the window. "Who knows why these things

Episode 21

happen," she added. "We got lucky that's all. Those kids didn't. It certainly wasn't your fault Cate. So take yourself off the hook."

"One of the kids that got burned is not expected to make it. And I feel so terrible about that," Cate said as tears poured down her cheeks. "I look at my girls and think how I would feel if it was one of them. I don't think I could take that, and and,"

"It's okay, Cate," Kathy said holding her hand. "Let it out if it will make you feel better."

"I just want it all to go away, and it won't," Cate finished and leaned her head back on the pillow.

"Cate," Linda interrupted, "this is going to take a very long time. Why don't you think about coming home. Hell, you can work anywhere. They're begging for nurses. You could work at Oak Grove Hospital tomorrow. Then we'd have sleep overs on weekends and hang out. It'd be like the old days."

"Sometimes I wish we could have the old days back. But they're gone. Sometimes I feel a million years old," Cate said. She picked up her glass, took a sip and set it back down. "Anyway, the police told me to see an attorney."

"Why would they say that?" Jess asked.

"They said if one of the kids dies, there could be criminal charges. The kid's parents could sue or something."

"But you have insurance, so why do you need an attorney?"

"I didn't ask. I have an appointment with one Monday." Cate answered.

Cate returned to work the following week feeling it was best to get on with life. It had been a miserable week. Two of the kids in the accident were on her floor. After the second week Cate realized she could no longer live in Plymouth, there would always be too many reminders. When one of the burned teenagers died, Cate decided to move back to Melvindale. Cate called Kathy after making her decision and interviewed at Oak Grove Hospital two weeks later and was offered a position.

Cate brought herself back to the present, stepped off the porch and walked down the sidewalk. She looked back at the house then continued to her car. "This has been one crazy two months," Cate said to Gucci as she opened the driver's door.

Several minutes later she was back on Highway 36; two hours later she entered Michigan on eastbound I-94. The drive was going better than expected. Gucci had jumped into the front passenger seat, was curled up and was asleep while Duffy scurried around the back seat.

Cate stopped at the rest area just past Marshall, Michigan. She and Billy would often dine at the Win Schuler's restaurant there. After another hour of driving, Cate was near Ann Arbor. Thoughts of her quiet life married to Billy switched to a miss spent youth with Eric. She had cried momentarily at the rest area by Marshall. The Ann Arbor sign elicited more tears. She considered taking the State Street Exit to the University of Michigan campus but decided she was not ready.

She wondered how Eric's life had turned out. Kathy told her little snippets here and there; things Jess relayed when she saw him at Kovalchek's Market. Jess hadn't mentioned anything about him the night of the funeral. Cate knew there was the possibility of running into Eric after moving back home but decided she'd cross that bridge if she ever got to it.

Cate could see the giant Uniroyal tire next to the freeway welcoming visitors to the Motor City. Seeing the Melvindale exit sign hit Cate stronger than she anticipated. Second thoughts began gnawing at the back of her mind as the emotions of finality and uncertainty rushed through her. This was not going to be just a weekend back home with her mother and her memories. She was back where she started and wondered if the last thirty years had been for nothing. On life's board game, she had been sent back to start without collecting two hundred dollars.

Cate exited at Oakwood Boulevard. As she passed the Ramada Inn where she tended bar after Kelly died, Cate could see several faces through the coffee shop's window. She wondered if a young girl was sitting at a table smoking cigarettes and sipping coffee with an old flame she'd bumped into unexpectedly. She also wondered if there was a middle aged woman sitting alone

Episode 21

at the counter staring into an empty coffee cup wondering how her life had slipped by so easily. Cate cast both thoughts aside. A right turn at the next stop sign would bring her full circle. She found the thought depressing and decided to focus on good things. Her daughters were healthy and she had three close friends waiting to have dinner with her tonight. There would be more bumps in the road, but two healthy daughters and three good friends was probably more than most people in this world had. She wondered if it was more than she deserved.

Cate turned right and saw the Welcome To Melvindale sign. The Little City With A Big Heart and The Honorable Daniel A. Killard, Mayor were written along the bottom in smaller letters. Daniel was in her graduating class. Now all these years later, he was the mayor. Danny would always be the big football player who drank a little too much beer at float parties. Cate wondered if he had similar thoughts about her.

As a child, Melvindale had been the center of her universe. It had been her world. The intersection of Oakwood Boulevard and Allen Road encompassed downtown. The four corners were a bustle of activity, especially on Saturdays. Eason's Department store was on one corner and the Mel Theatre sat across the street. City Hall, a large grey cement building, and the Rexall Drugstore occupied the other two corners. Every Saturday, Cate and Kimmy would walk several city blocks from her home on Flint Street to the theater. They'd join the pilgrimage of other kids headed to the movies. Admission was twenty-five cents and most candies could be had for a dime. Popcorn was fifteen cents; adding butter was another nickel.

When she entered junior high, the attraction became more than just the movies. Sometimes they'd meet with boys from school and Kimmy would spend little time watching the screen. Cate was more reserved. Though she'd sit next to one of the boys, that was as far as things were allowed to go.

As Cate approached the intersection, she looked over to what had once been Meri Dot's Beauty Shop. The building was still standing though it now housed a floral shop. The salon was always busy on Saturday mornings, especially around homecoming and prom. Frank's White Grill, a hamburger joint, was next door to the Rexall Drugs. Chili and greasy little burgers with fried onions were the specialties. Cate loved the burgers and Louis would occasionally bring home a bag of them as a special treat.

It all looked so different now. The theatre had been razed years ago when family movies lost their appeal. In the theater's place was a CVS Pharmacy. The old city hall building also was gone and a McDonald's sat on the corner. Cate could see paper hatted teenagers in burgundy uniforms dispensing Happy Meals where Jess's father spent a life time dispensing justice. Eason's Department Store was also gone. The big Protestant church had been removed to make room for the Walgreens parking lot. Cate remembered she had graduated with the pastor's daughter. Cate wondered if she had become a missionary and lived in some far off place.

Cate caught the traffic light at Prospect Street. At one time, Dasher Junior High sat on the corner but it also had been razed after the new junior high was built. With Dasher gone, Cate had an open view of the football stadium. The high school was down the block from the stadium. The yellow brick building looked the same except for the windows. The big metal framed windows had been replaced with wood siding; only two small windows per classroom remained.

Looking out from the second story classrooms had been one of Cate's favorite pass times. The building was set back from the road and the expansive lawn had several oaks, elms and maple trees that turned vibrant colors in the fall. After the leaves fell, the marquee to the theater could be seen over the roof tops of the nearby houses. When it snowed, Cate would watch the little flakes drift down or swirl in the wind. The spring rains and heavy thunderstorms also provided a diversion. It saddened her to think the students would now have only the tiniest little glimpse of the outside world. The school saved on energy costs no doubt, but how could the students look out and dream.

Episode 21

When Cate saw the green street sign with Flint printed in neat white letters a lump swelled in her throat. Her mouth felt dry and cottony. She made a left turn and drove two blocks. The house looked the same. Her father, like the rest of the homeowners, had been fastidious about his home's upkeep. The lots were small and the houses were packed very closely but most lawns were mowed twice a week and were always weed free and dark green. Before the blight, huge elm trees lined the streets and their branches spread out and interlaced with the trees on the other side of the street. During the fall, great mounds of yellow and red elm leaves were raked into piles in the streets. Cate and Kimmy would ride their bikes through the big piles while neighborhood boys played touch football games. The pungent smell of burning leaves drifted across town during late October.

As Cate pulled in front of her mother's house, Duffy became eager to get out of the car and bounced around the back seat like a maniac. Gucci put his paws on the dashboard and was checking out the neighborhood. Looking around, Cate noted most of the houses on the block were still well kept.

Cate opened the car door and let the boys out. Duffy headed directly to the big maple and lifted his hind leg. Gucci stayed close to Cate. Duffy followed Cate and Gucci to the fenced backyard. As Cate opened the gate, the yard seemed smaller.

"You boys stay back here in the corral," she said to them in a soft voice. "Emma won't tolerate any silliness, so you're going to have to learn to behave. And that means you Duffy." Hearing his name, the little white terrier stopped his investigation and looked up. Determining treats were not forthcoming, he turned back to nosing around several tomato plants staked along the fence line.

Emma walked to the back door just as Cate stepped inside. Her mother had on the Capri blue jeans Cate bought for her last spring and a yellow short sleeved blouse partially covered by her ever present apron. Though she owned several, the white one with the big yellow sunflower embroidered on the front was her favorite. Years ago, the apron pocket would have contained a turquoise leather cigarette case holding a pack of Kent cigarettes. The case had a chrome metal border with two little latches that snapped together with a distinctive click whenever her mother opened or closed it. Besides time shared at the cottage, smoking cigarettes with her mom on the front porch was one of Cate's favorite memories. That didn't happen of course until after she had come home from college. On warm summer evenings, they would sit on the front porch, sip cold Pepsi Colas from glass bottles and smoke cigarettes until after dark. Those were peaceful evenings filled with nothing more than watching cars go up and down the street.

"Hey, Catie," Emma said as she hugged her daughter then kissed her on the cheek. "Why didn't you come in the front door? It's open."

"Oh, I wanted to take the dogs out back and let them run for a while, mom. They've been cooped up in the car and needed to stretch their legs."

"Especially that Duffy," her mom replied with a smile.

"Yeah, especially him," Cate answered as she followed her mom into the tiny kitchen.

Cate looked around the house. It was the only place her parents had ever lived after they married. The small kitchen and nook sat directly to the left of the front entrance. A short hallway led out of the living room past the doorway to the basement. At the end of the hallway was her parent's bedroom. To the left was Cate's bedroom and the bathroom. Her brothers had occupied the upstairs bedroom. When Cate returned home following Kelly's death, she moved to the upstairs bedroom and decided to sleep there again during this stay.

"Come on in and have something to eat. I made spaghetti," Emma said as she walked to the stove and stirred a pot of sauce simmering on the vintage Kenmore gas stove.

The sauce smelled delicious making Cate feel a little torn. She didn't want to spoil her appetite for dinner with the girls but she hadn't eaten since breakfast. Seeing the heavy aluminum pot of boiling pasta made her think of her father. Louis

Episode 21

shared her love of spaghetti. Emma always made it the first night they were at the cottage. Everyone was always starved by the time they arrived. After helping unload the station wagon, Cate and her brothers would run down to the lake for a quick swim while Emma got dinner ready.

"Get the salad out of the fridge and put the dressing on it, dear. I'll get our plates ready."

Cate opened the refrigerator and took out the Tupperware bowl. As always the lettuce, cucumber, celery and tomatoes were cut into neat and precise little squares. The slices of green onion looked like they had been prepared by a NASA scientist, each piece an exact replica of the next. The salad reflected her parents approach to life; simple and neat.

Emma took her customary seat facing the window. Cate sat to her right. The seat to Emma's left had always been her father's place. Though he had been gone five years, his place would remain. Little things in life can run so deep, Cate reflected. The two women ate their dinner at the little round table with its crisply pressed, pastel table cloth. Cate got up once to let the dogs in. It was a leisurely meal filled with conversation about neighbors both alive and long gone. When finished, they set their plates on the counter.

Emma suggested they have coffee on the front porch. Taking their cups, they walked outside. Cate sat down in the familiar plastic furniture and thought how a cigarette would have completed the ambiance, even one of Emma's dreadful Kents. Emma sipped her coffee and completed her commentary on the neighborhood's latest news. Hips had been replaced, stents had been placed into arteries, children had been divorced and spouses had died.

Cate and Emma finished their coffee then washed the dishes by hand. Emma would never have an automatic dishwasher, a fact Cate grudgingly accepted. Emma offered to finish, if Cate wanted to unload her car. Cate accepted the offer and managed to get everything out in five trips. Some of the boxes she took to the basement; the rest were taken upstairs.

Book Two Home Again

Cate set the last suitcase on the floor and looked around the bedroom. It was the biggest in the house and had very short side walls to accommodate the steep roof lines giving the room a mini A frame appearance. The slanted side walls and small ceiling gave the room a cozy feel, especially during thunder storms. A double bed sat on the right side of the room with a chest of drawers and a small desk directly across from it. Cate set her make up bag and lighted mirror on the desk. She placed her electric curlers on the dresser to leave room on the desk for her laptop computer. She unpacked the suitcases then told her mom she needed to lay down for a while before meeting Kathy and the girls for dinner. Cate laid down cross ways on the bed on her stomach, reached over and picked up her Ipod. She put on the ear phones, pushed play and waited for Smoky Robinson's smooth voice. Cate decided the only thing missing was a few zits on her forehead. Other than that, it could still be 1966. Cate drifted off and was awakened by the sound of her mother's voice echoing off the barren stairway walls.

"Thanks, mom," she called down, "I'm up now."

Cate grabbed her robe and headed down the stairs to the bathroom. She adjusted the water and climbed into the shower. As she washed her hair, Cate noted the ceramic tiles surrounding the tub. The tiles were original to the house, yet there wasn't a spec of mildew on them.

Cate finished bathing and went back upstairs to dry her hair and dress. She picked out a deep blue pants suit and complemented it with a cream colored silk blouse. Cate added a string of pearls and put the final touches on her make up. She went back downstairs where Emma told her how beautiful she looked. Cate took the boys out to the backyard. After a few minutes, she brought them back in. Emma was watching a Lawrence Welk rerun on PBS. Cate kissed her mom goodbye, walked out and got into her car. Cate looked around the big Buick and laughed. All decked out and heading off for a night with the girls. Cate asked herself how forty years had passed by and remembered

Episode 21

how her father had told her shortly before he died that life was indeed a mystery.

Ten minutes later, Cate was in Fairlane Hills and saw the Hyatt Hotel it in the distance. The hotel was a semi circular design with an exterior of bronze colored glass. Adjacent to the shopping mall, there had been a monorail at one time connecting them. Cate pulled into the valet parking area where a young uniformed man gave her a claim ticket.

"Sweet ride mamn," he said before driving away.

Cate walked into the lobby. It was not much different from other large hotels. She wandered around the lobby looking at framed art hanging from the walls then decided to sit and people watch until her friends arrived. Cate took a seat on one of the couches and hadn't been there long when a familiar looking profile passed by. Two dark complexioned men, dressed in expensive suits, approached each other from opposite sides of the lobby. She didn't recognize the shorter man walking from the right but knew he was Indian. Cate turned her head again toward the man with the familiar profile. Her view was partially obstructed by the railing dividing the sitting area of the lobby from the front desk. Cate got up from her seat to improve her sight line. Feeling a bit silly, she approached the two men from behind a pillar to obstruct their view. Cate could see them perfectly. The man on her left was Doctor Taj. The men shook hands then walked toward the elevator.

Cate didn't know what prompted her behavior other than simple curiosity. She followed the two men toward the elevator. She noticed Doctor Taj was carrying a brushed aluminum case in his right hand, identical to the one he carried from the Peacock restaurant the night David was killed. She wondered if Dr. Taj was shilling for a pharmaceutical company on the side.

The two men stood talking in front of the elevator doors. The other man turned to look in Cate's direction. Cate didn't know why, but she stepped behind the pillar again and remained there for a moment before looking out. The man had turned back toward Doctor Taj as they continued their conversation. Just as she was checking the elevator's position through the transparent shaft, someone touched her on the shoulder. The unexpected contact startled her.

"Jesus, Kathy!" Cate exclaimed as her left hand flew up to her chest, "You almost gave me a heart attack." Her face turned bright crimson.

"Cate, what the hell are you doing?" Kathy asked removing her hand from Cate's shoulder.

"She's checking out those two good looking camel jockeys," Jess interjected with a laugh.

"Well, my, my, my," Linda added in a hushed voice. "What'd we have here? Little Cate the voyeur."

The women began giggling.

"Shssh," Cate said to her friends, "I think one of those men is Doctor Taj from the hospital in Plymouth. And they're not camel jockeys, I mean Arabs, Jess, they're Indian."

"Which one is he Cate? The tall good looking one or the shorter good looking one?" Jess asked.

"If it is Taj, he'd be the taller one."

"Then, why don't you just go on over and say hello?" Linda asked.

"I don't know, they're probably talking business or something, I don't want to interrupt."

"What's the big deal?" Jess interjected, "They may be doctors, but in the end, they're just a couple of rich towel headed curry breaths, who're probably waiting to pick up a couple of white hookers."

Kathy and Linda began laughing at Jess's coarse comment. Cate looked at her three friends. Not much had changed; nothing of substance anyway. A few more lines on their faces and hair not quite as shiny as when they were teenagers, but deep inside they were the same as ever.

"Well, I truly doubt that, Jess. But they are probably both loaded. At least I know Taj is, he's big into real estate and owns

Episode 21

about half of Plymouth. I don't know why, but I just as soon not go over and talk to him. Let's just go eat dinner."

Guillo's was on the second floor just a short walk from the elevator. It was a small, cozy place with Italian décor. The Maitre D seated them and a wine steward came over to take their order. Kathy ordered a bottle of Sauvignon Pinot for the table and Jess ordered a diet Coke. It was a relaxing time of intimate talk sprinkled with occasional laughter. After two hours they decided to drive to Richie's, a jazz and piano bar on Michigan Avenue. As they were leaving the hotel, Kathy asked Cate if the man walking a few yards ahead of them was the same man they had seen earlier with the doctor she knew. Cate had already spotted him but hadn't said anything. She'd acted foolish enough for one night and didn't want to reinitiate any conversation about her odd behavior. When they got to the valet parking area, the man was fishing in his pants pocket for the claim ticket. As he did, Cate caught a glimpse of something shiny tucked into his pants. He had the aluminum case Doctor Taj had been carrying. The man finally located his ticket and handed it to the valet. He then quickly buttoned his coat. When the valet brought up the man's car, he got into it and left. When the valet brought the Buick, they left for Richie's.

At the club they nursed two drinks each until Linda said she'd was tired and wanted to call it a night. Cate said she'd drop Kathy at home and the four women exchanged hugs. It was a quiet drive back to Melvindale. Cate mulled over the encounter with Doctor Taj. She knew it was her imagination, but couldn't help wondering about the cases.

"What the hell, Cate," she muttered aloud, "have you lost what little mind you have?"

When Cate reached her mother's house, she locked the Buick and walked up to the back door. Cate opened the door and tip toed up the steps. As she stepped through the door, Cate stopped in mid step.

"Oh, my God, mom!" she screamed and rushed toward her mother who was lying on her side at the end of the hallway. Cate knelt down to see if she was still breathing. She was, but just barely. Cate took her mother's pulse and reminded herself to remain calm. Her nurse's training helped her control her emotions but not much. Cate ran to the phone and dialed 911.

Episode 22

From his balcony, Ahmed had a panoramic view of his east Fairlane Hills neighborhood. The satellite dishes attached to the roofs made the neighborhood look like a field of giant sunflowers. The view reminded Ahmed of the poppy fields in Afghanistan.

Ahmed sat on an aluminum patio chair with his feet propped up on a large wooden spool. At one time the spool held forty gauge electrical wire but now served as the center piece of his patio set, though Stacey maintained it was a stretch to call the menagerie of mismatched furniture pieces a patio set. The quality of the furniture was less than what Ahmed desired but every penny saved could be put toward other priorities.

Ahmed didn't intend to be a janitor at Oak Grove Hospital forever. Hanging out with Stacey only added to his desire to attend college and become an engineer. He was mechanically gifted which was evident early on in the camps. There were few others who learned to break down and reassemble weapons so quickly. Ahmed frustrated his instructors because his aptitude was accompanied by such little dedication. He also was talented with electronics and had a knack for being able to improvise on the spot, which enabled him to excel with explosives. Though he had no desire to harm anyone, Ahmed enjoyed the challenge of designing and detonating bombs. He realized enrolling in engineering school could only happen after his commitment to Charlie was fulfilled and he hadn't figured out how to manage that. The entanglement with Mahmood also added to his dilemma.

The unseasonably warm September weather made it feel like August. He still had on his soccer uniform and was sipping a can of Arizona Iced Tea. He was thirsty from the exercise and the cold tea tasted good. Through Ali's connections, he had joined an organized team that played games on Saturday mornings at a pitch in west Fairlane Hills. After the games, Ali would retrieve a cooler of beer from the trunk of his car and carry it to one of the picnic tables where the game was discussed with teasing and laughter.

The sun felt good on his face and Ahmed wished he didn't have to go into work. Through Charlie's connections, his normal workweek was now Sunday through Thursday. He worked from three thirty until midnight. Friday was left open so he could go to the mosque. Saturdays he was free to mix with other young Muslims in east Fairlane Hills.

Lately Charlie had been very demanding. Ahmed had the feeling Charlie believed he was holding something back, which was partially true. Charlie contacted him the night he met Mahmood and requested they meet. Ahmed divulged almost everything Mahmood said at the restaurant and used Mahmood's threat against his sister as a reason to ask Charlie about getting her out of Afghanistan. Charlie agreed to do his best. He told Ahmed the timeliness of the assistance would be in proportion to how much information Ahmed provided. It was a trade off with his sister's freedom as the prize. Ahmed couldn't help but loathe men who would use a twelve year old girl's life as trade bait in a struggle of geo politics.

Ahmed hadn't revealed Kamal was his contact at the mosque; thinking it better to keep some things to himself. Ahmed also hadn't revealed to Mahmood the details of his work for Charlie.

Episode 22

Playing both sides against the middle made Ahmed feel at times like a human pawn in an international chess game. He understood pawns were expendable and would tell Charlie as little as possible. He would deal with Mahmood the same way.

Since meeting with Charlie, Ahmed had recognized two other men at the Mosque. He also kept that information to himself. Ahmed didn't have anything new to offer Mahmood either. He'd made a couple of interesting observations at the hospital but needed time to gather more information. His work had mostly been as the emergency room custodian. At Charlie's instructions, he was to wander around the hospital and look for anyone he recognized from the training camps or Afghanistan. If he spotted anyone familiar, he was to call immediately. He was also to make contact if he recognized anyone at the mosque. On the other side, he was to inform Kamal if he saw anything at the hospital that looked suspicious.

Ahmed was walking a tight rope. He had to tell each of them enough to satisfy, but not enough to exhaust his value. Once he was of no further use to either, his days would be numbered. While he didn't think Charlie would kill him, Charlie could send him back to Afghanistan and had threatened to do so occasionally.

Though he hadn't mentioned it to either Charlie or Mahmood, a recent observation warranted more investigation. When a young Arab in the emergency room was being moved, Ahmed had followed the gurney and stepped inside the service elevator. The nurse wore a surgical mask and told Ahmed to use another elevator because the patient might be contagious. As he left the elevator, the nurse pushed the eighth floor button.

An hour later, Ahmed got back onto the elevator with his cleaning cart and pushed the button for eight. When the elevator stopped, he pushed his cleaning cart out and started mopping. A stern looking nurse approached him and asked what he was doing. Ahmed pretended he didn't understand and answered in heavily accented, broken English. He listened with a perplexed look on his face while the nurse explained the area had already been cleaned. Ahmed explained in broken English he had been sent to clean the tenth floor. The nurse informed him in a condescending tone he must go up two more floors.

Feeling he was being hurried away, Ahmed noticed that the other nurse at the station was male, very big and muscular. The female nurse watched him as he boarded the elevator and pushed the button to ten. When the elevator stopped again, Ahmed got off with his cart. He knew it was the psychiatric ward. He looked at the nurse's station and noticed the entry doors to both sides of the floor were locked. It occurred to Ahmed the doors leading to the rooms on the eighth floor were also locked. Ahmed pushed the cart back onto the service elevator and returned to the fourth floor.

When Ahmed asked who cleaned the eighth floor, his boss replied eight was a secured area for infectious disease and there were protocols to maintain negative pressure so contaminated air wouldn't leak into the rest of the hospital. The boss added their department did not have responsibility for the floor. Ahmed planned to keep an eye on future patient movements from the emergency room.

Ahmed finished his iced tea and stubbed out the cigarette. After showering, he put on his custodian uniform and left for work. He entered the parking garage and found a spot on the third floor. He took the stairs down to the basement, pulled his time card from the rack and punched in. Ahmed loaded his cart with cleaner, rubber gloves, disinfectant and headed to the emergency room.

Though it was late afternoon, the emergency room was nearly full. There was the typical collection of feverish looking young children and teenagers with sprains and broken bones. Ahmed knew there would be ambulances with elderly patient with cardiac problems as well as traffic accident victims, allergic reactions and stomach flu sufferers. The latter of which, seemed to continually miss their little throw up trays.

It was after eleven when he was emptying the waiting room waste baskets that two ambulances arrived within minutes of

Episode 22

each other. The first was from the Melvindale Fire and Rescue. After backing up to the double entrance doors, the driver jumped out to open the back of the ambulance. His assistant adjusted an oxygen mask pressed closely to the patient's face as they wheeled the stretcher toward the entry doors. An attractive looking middle aged woman walked beside the stretcher holding the patient's hand. As they rushed by him, Ahmed could see the patient was an elderly woman who'd had a stroke. Her face was twisted to one side and her right hand was drawn up, almost claw like and pressed against her chest. An IV was inserted into her other arm. At least it wasn't another stomach flu patient Ahmed said to himself. He knew it was not a sensitive thing to say, but he had already put in eight hours, a good portion of them cleaning up after patients with abdominal cramps. He assumed some kind of virus was going around, because several patients suffering similar symptoms had been admitted. The attendants rushed the elderly woman into the back of the emergency room while the doctor barked orders to the staff.

Ahmed watched for a few moments and then continued cleaning. He glanced up in time to see the next patient being unloaded from the City of Fairlane Hills Ambulance. The patient was a young male about his own age. As the stretcher wheeled by him, Ahmed's heart skipped a beat. He knew this young man from the camps. The patient was lying on his side with his legs up toward his stomach. He was in great pain. Ahmed took a few steps closer. The man's name was Raheem and he had been in the barracks with Ahmed in western Pakistan. Ahmed watched in fascination as the young man was taken back to the examination rooms. He followed the stretcher at a distance. Ahmed didn't think Raheem recognized him, but he wasn't taking any chances. Ahmed watched as Raheem was taken to an examination room near the elderly woman.

Ahmed had to decide whether to call Charlie and tell him a trainee from an al- Qaeda camp had been wheeled into the emergency room or contact Mahmood and give him the same information. Ahmed decided to do both.

Ahmed left the emergency room and walked outside as he pulled the cell phone from his pocket. After dialing, Ahmed waited for the call to be routed through the Pentagon or wherever it was that housed Charlie's chain of command.

"Yes," Charlie said flatly. Ahmed decided to be brief.

"I've spotted someone I know," Ahmed said as he walked away from a group of smokers gathered outside the entrance. Seeing them made Ahmed want a cigarette.

"Know from where?" Charlie asked in a business like voice.

"From my childhood vacations," Ahmed answered.

"So you spent some time with this friend? Are you one hundred percent sure?"

"Yes, and on more than one occasion," Ahmed answered.

"Where is he now?" Charlie asked.

"His name is Raheem and he just arrived at the E room."

"Anything else we should know?" Charlie asked coldly.

"Other than he looks very ill, no," Ahmed answered.

When the other end of the phone went dead Ahmed walked toward the crowd of smokers. He found a young couple and asked politely if he could borrow a cigarette. The young man handed him a pack of Newport Lights and a lighter. Ahmed pulled the smoke deeply into his lungs and handed the lighter back. He thanked them then walked a few yards away to smoke in solitude. Ahmed finished the cigarette and dropped the butt on the cement.

Back inside, Ahmed walked to his cart and pushed it into the examination area. The emergency room was divided into two areas. For critical patients, there were four enclosed rooms with glass paneled walls and doors. The rest of the examination rooms were separated with curtains. Raheem had been taken to one of the curtained rooms. Ahmed continued down the aisle pausing long enough to inspect each room. He still hadn't located Raheem as he walked toward room sixteen. The curtains had been pulled but were not completely closed on one side. Ahmed could hear male and a female's voices coming from the room so he paused to listen.

Episode 22

The elderly woman with the stroke was lying in a bed in the glass enclosed room across from Raheem. The middle aged woman was standing by the door while a doctor attended the old woman. The middle aged woman was smartly dressed and wore nice jewelry. She had short blonde hair and the bluest eyes Ahmed had ever seen. He concluded she must have been a looker in her day because she was still attractive. Ahmed found it unsettling that he could think of anyone her age as being attractive, but she was none the less. Just as he started to strike up a conversation, Ahmed was called away. Twenty minutes later he returned to find the doctors and nurses were gone. The blonde haired woman was sitting in a chair next to the bed.

"Excuse me, is it okay if I empty the trash?" he asked pointing to the trash can.

"Sure, no problem," the woman answered. "Here, let me move out of your way," she added getting up and walking toward the door.

"Oh, that's not necessary, stay seated," Ahmed said as he picked up the trash can and emptied it into the basket on the cart.

"Is she your mother?" Ahmed asked motioning his head toward the elderly woman.

"Yes," the blonde woman replied sadly, "she's had a stroke. The doctor said she'll be okay but it'll be a while until she recovers. They are getting a room ready for her."

"Sorry to hear that," Ahmed said. "How old is your mom?"

The blonde woman seemed very upset and there was an air of sadness about her. Ahmed decided to keep the conversation going. She seemed glad to have someone to talk to and it provided an opportunity to see what had become of Raheem.

"Oh, she just turned eighty," the blonde woman added dabbing at a tear running down her cheek.

"Are you here alone?" Ahmed asked.

"Yeah, but my brother is on his way. He should be here shortly. The staff is taking good care of her, I just wish they could get her up to her room."

"Yeah, I know what you mean. There's so much commotion around here. It certainly isn't a good place to rest. There's a cafeteria on the first floor. They don't serve hot food this late, but they have packaged sandwiches and coffee."

"Thanks, I'm okay for now. I think I remember where the cafeteria is. I'm supposed to start working here Monday," Cate said. "But now with my mom like this, I don't know."

"Really, where are you going to work?" Ahmed asked.

"I am supposed to be the afternoon nursing supervisor on the sixth floor," Cate answered.

"Well, I don't clean six regularly, but I do get sent there sometimes if someone is on vacation. It's a good place to work. I think you'll like it. My name's Ahmed by the way."

"Oh, mine's Cate. Cate Cassadea. Thanks for the concern. I appreciate it."

"Ahmed, we've got a geyser down in eight," one of the nurses said walking by the room. "You better come down real quick."

"Sorry, gotta go. Hope your mother gets better soon," Ahmed said as he left.

Cate looked up at the monitor. The staff had worked quickly and Emma would survive. The doctor wouldn't comment about any quality of life issues saying those would sort themselves out in the next few days.

Cate sat in the chair for a while then decided to stand up and walk around. She took a few steps out of the examination room and rolled her head from side to side to loosen the muscles in her neck. She was about to go back into her mother's room when she stopped in mid stride. Walking directly toward her was the man she had seen with Doctor Taj earlier at the Hyatt. He wore a white hospital coat and was reading a chart as he walked toward her. For a moment Cate thought he was going to walk up to her and ask her why she had been hiding behind the pillar in the hotel lobby. Her cheeks flushed as she turned and stepped into her mother's room. She wished she had a magazine or newspaper to cover her face. Cate turned her head and looked at her mother. After a couple of minutes Cate looked up. She hadn't

Episode 22

heard the doctor pass by and was confused how he could have just vanished. Stepping into the aisle, Cate looked both ways and wondered if her eyes had played tricks on her. She was exhausted and needed sleep but doubted the adrenalin in her body would allow such a luxury. Cate turned to walk back into her mother's room when she caught sight of the doctor.

The reason she hadn't seen him became obvious. He had walked into the examination room directly across from her mother's room. A separation in the curtains allowed Cate to see his profile. She watched in amazement as the doctor reached into his medical coat pocket and pulled out a brushed aluminum case. It looked like the one she'd seen tucked inside of his suit coat at the Hyatt. Cate stood mesmerized as the doctor then took a small vial from the case and inserted a syringe into the top then drew out a small amount of liquid. The doctor purged the air inside the syringe and inserted it into the young Arab's arm. Looking up, the doctors eyes met Cate's and he abruptly closed the curtains.

His motion jolted Cate out of her near hypnotic trance. Cate quickly turned and reentered her mother's room. What she witnessed was not standard protocol. Bringing something in from the outside was not something she had seen at any hospital. Cate reassured herself, the doctor didn't know she had spied on him at the hotel, and there wasn't any way he could know of her knowledge about the case being from Doctor Taj. I'm making more out of this than there is Cate told herself. I'm tired, my husband died recently, now my mom's had a stroke. That should be enough cause to be seeing things that are not really there.

"Mrs. Cassadea," a voice called from nowhere.

Cate was sure it was the Indian doctor telling her to follow him to a padded room on the tenth floor. Cate looked up and was surprised to see a tall Caucasian doctor. He had dark hair and was her age. Cate recognized the face but couldn't recall his name.

"Sorry Doctor, but it's been a long night."

Book Two Home Again

"That's okay; you've had a rough time. My name's Doctor Nolen. I'm in charge of the emergency room. My first name is John. People in high school called me Johnny, that was back at MHS. That's where I believe we know each other."

"Oh my gosh, Johnny Nolen. I remember you; you were a year behind us. You played basketball, I remember that."

"Yeah I did, and my father still never lets anyone forget it," he said with a laugh. "I just came on duty. I looked at your mother's chart and thought that it must be you with her. They'll be coming to get her in a minute. It looks like she will be okay. If you need anything just ask."

"Thanks, I appreciate that."

"Are you living in the area now?"

"No, well, yeah, I just moved back from Indiana. I'm a nurse and am supposed to start working here on Monday."

"Listen don't hurry it. If you want, I'll put in a good word for you if you need a couple of days delay. I've been here forever and there aren't too many people I don't know and even fewer who don't owe me some favors."

"Thanks I'll be okay. By the way John, do you also have a practice? Now that I'm back, I'll need an internist."

"No, I strictly do ER. Running this place takes all of my time and then some. I've been doing it since I graduated med school at Wayne State."

"That's got to be tough; these hours are a killer. Why'd you decide to go this way? I did one year in ER and thought I'd gotten a commuted sentence when I was moved out."

"Believe it or not, I like it. Always have, it's sort of my mission."

"Mission?" Cate asked.

"I was going to be a missionary but somewhere along the line I decided I could do a mission right here. It sounds odd I know. Anyway I need to get going on my rounds but it was nice to see you."

"One quick question?" Cate asked as he started to leave.

She wanted to ask him some other questions but was afraid he'd go into an are you saved or born again speeches. Cate had no idea what her mission in life was, but lately it seemed to be

Episode 22

to have things get screwed up as much as possible. She was still angry at the universe and it's creator for what had happened to David. A sermon about it all being part of some grand plan was not what she wanted to hear. She was curious about what she had seen in the room across from her mother. Cate decided to take the risk.

"From professional curiosity, the young man in the room across the aisle, what's the matter with him? I didn't recognize the symptoms. It looked like appendicitis but I couldn't tell for sure, maybe gall bladder?"

"I haven't studied his chart. He's being attended to by Doctor Nakshatra. I know he's being moved up to the eighth floor, must be viral. That's our infectious disease floor now."

Thanks John," Cate replied as Doctor Nolen left the room.

Episode 23

Ronnie poured a cup of coffee and looked out the dining room window. Scott Brown, his next door neighbor who had moved to Grosse Ile from Boston, always raved about autumns back in New England. Ronnie would match October in Michigan with Vermont any day. The Northeast may have more maples but Michigan had its share and when their leaves changed color, nothing was more beautiful or majestic than a Michigan oak or ash.

If there was one Michigan shortcoming where Ronnie agreed with Scott, however, it was moving the Tigers out of Tiger Stadium. According to Scott, Red Sox lovers would never have let their team leave Fenway with its historic Green Monster outfield wall. Ronnie and Beth went to the last game at Tiger Stadium and like the rest of the fans, left misty eyed with a deep sense of melancholy. It was the stadium of Cobb and Greenberg..

It was the destination each spring for Detroit area grade school boys and girls. They'd pile off big yellow school buses with brown paper bags full of peanut butter and jelly sandwiches and march up endless cement ramps to dark green, wooden slated seats. The boys would tote in Al Kaline signature model gloves hoping to catch a foul ball that seemed to float endlessly in the

Book Two Home Again

late spring Michigan sky. They'd entice opposing batters by yelling swing batter, batter, batter in high pitched staccato voices. After the game, they'd pile back into their yellow school buses for the bouncy ride home. They'd run excitedly to tell fathers, who'd just put in a shift at an auto plant or steel mill, about their odyssey to Tiger Stadium.

There was no way anyone could convince Ronnie a trip to Comerica Park with its luxury suites and ferris wheels could ever compare to Tiger Stadium. Comerica Park just didn't have the feel of a classic ball park. Baseball wasn't about gourmet food or ferris wheels. It was about summer days, Ball Park Franks and Stroh's beer. It was about peanuts in the shell bought from a vendor hawking his wares or leisurely walks from the Holy Redeemer Church Parking lot.

Strolling through Corktown only added to the anticipation of seeing the emerald green grass and the immaculate Georgia red clay infield. It was a walk Ronnie had taken with his father and Bobbie countless times. Somehow, Detroit never figured out how to hang on to the things that made the city so special. Tours of the Vernor's ginger ale bottling plant were gone, as was the Stroh's brewery, the Wonder Bread Bakery, and the Sander's Ice Cream Shops.

Thinking of Tiger Stadium rekindled another issue that had been churning in Ronnie's mind. He'd done nothing about returning Amy Irwin's phone call. It was football season now and watching University of Michigan and Detroit Lion's games also stirred up memories. His father, who everyone called Big Red, had taken him and Bobbie to U of M's stadium every fall. They would sit in the back of Big Red's Chevrolet and talk about the game all the way from Melvindale to Ann Arbor. Big Red's best friend, Woody, would ride shotgun and pack a few beers to drink on the way. Catching a game at The Big House was an annual tradition until Bobbie left for Viet Nam.

Amy's call was still on the recorder. All he had to do was dial the phone. Then what, Ronnie asked himself. People don't track you down after thirty-five years to tell you good news. It was as

Episode 23

simple as saying hello to someone he'd known since he was four years old and as complex as reaching into his soul. It had been nearly two months since Amy's call. Ronnie knew it was time to face whatever truth awaited. He pushed the replay button and waited for Amy's voice to pierce the silence. Ronnie wrote the number on a yellow post-it then picked up the phone and walked to the balcony. He sat on one of the patio chairs and looked out over the water.

He took a couple of deep breaths pulling the crisp air into his lungs. It was a bright sunny day and the Michigan sky was clear and blue. It seemed a shame to throw such a beautiful day to chance. Ronnie considered pitching the post-it into the wind and letting the breeze whisk it into the river where the current would carry it away. Maybe he should just forget it all, grab his golf clubs and play one more round. What difference could a phone call make anyway. What was there to say? Beth was gone; would that make everything all right between them. Would a phone call repair a lifetime of friendship thrown to the wind because somewhere it had been decided they should both love the same girl.

"Screw it," Ronnie said aloud and dialed Amy's number. He'd give it four rings, if no one answered, he'd hang up. It would be the ideal outcome. His conscience would be appeased, he would have done his duty and avoided the whole ugly issue. No one could ever say he'd dodged it, at least no one but himself. As he was about to press the off button, the phone stopped ringing

"Hello," a woman's voice answered. He knew instantly it was Amy.

"Uh, hello," Ronnie replied. His voice sounded strained within his head and his throat tightened.

"Who is this?" the woman asked.

"Uh, Amy?" Ronnie asked.

"Yes, this is Amy," the woman replied.

He found it strange how mature her voice sounded. It seemed out of place. Amy would always be Bobbie's little sister. She was still the skinny little girl with strawberry blond hair and freckles, running around in plaid shorts and white tee shirts. Of the four Irwin kids, she and Bobbie looked the most alike. All of them had stand on end, bushy strawberry hair and freckles, but Amy had Bobbie's nose. The other two boys had their father's steel grey eyes. It struck Ronnie how much Amy sounded like her mother. That hadn't come through on the recorder. It was like rewinding the clock to 1952 and hearing Lisa's voice again. He and Bobbie had been four then. Amy was in diapers, Teddy was just shy of two, and Jimmy Jr. was five. Ronnie wondered if Lisa was still alive, he hadn't laid eyes on Bobbie's father, Jim Sr. since he walked out in 1959. Ronnie suddenly regretted not going to play golf.

"Amy, this is Ronnie Harris. I'm returning your call."

There was silence from the other end.

"Listen, I'm sorry I didn't call sooner. This was very difficult for me to do. It took me this long to work up my courage."

"I understand and thanks," Amy replied. "Sorry, but hearing your voice again is kind of emotional for me, too. Bobbie really wants to see you, Ronnie. If you can manage it."

"Is Bobbie okay? Sorry, but when I got your message, I just assumed it was not good news. At this age, voices from the past seldom bring good tidings."

"To be honest with you, no, it's not good news."

"Is everything okay with Bobbie?" Ronnie asked.

He looked down at the water. Two fishermen in a small aluminum boat were jigging for walleyes. Ronnie wondered if he and Bobbie could have been like the two men.

"Bobbie has cancer Ronnie. I hate to blurt it out like that, but the prognosis isn't good. He's at Oak Grove Hospital. He'd like to see you."

Ronnie felt his heart sink. Oak Grove Hospital and cancer, he didn't know how to respond. He had vowed to never set foot on the fifth floor again. Now he was being asked to return and watch his one time best friend mark time until the end mercifully came. Ronnie had seen that ending once, a second time wasn't fair to ask. They had been like brothers from the age of four until

Episode 23

twenty-one. He was being asked to say good bye twice to the boy he'd played with in the sand pile next to the house. He was being asked to say goodbye twice to the friend he'd shared his first beer with, the boy who was in the front seat when he'd felt his first breast at the drive in movie. Ronnie wondered how he would say goodbye to the best friend who had lived with them after Jim Sr. walked out on his family. Those goodbyes were said thirty-five years earlier. Now Amy was asking him to do it all again.

"How bad is it Amy?" he asked in a low voice.

"Very bad. Bobbie says it's from the Agent Orange in 'Nam."

"When can I see him?" Ronnie asked as he slumped over holding the phone in one hand and his head in the other.

"Anytime, but the sooner the better. He's coherent now. He gets a pain shot every few hours, in between his mind is pretty clear."

"Amy, I am so sorry. I don't know what to say."

"Just say you will go see him. I know things got messed up between the two of you. None of that can be changed now, but it will do him a world of good to see you."

"I feel like such an ass for not calling sooner. I really do," Ronnie said; his voice little more than a whisper.

"Look, I know you must have gone through a lot with Beth. I wish this could be easier," Amy added.

"Can I go today?"

"Sure, I'm going to drop by there around three. If it makes it any easier, come when I'm there. That might be a good way to start. He'll eventually be moved to hospice, but there's some time yet before that happens."

"You won't tell Lisa, Bobbie and I were drinking will you?" Ronnie asked with a soft laugh. When he and Bobbie had gotten drunk during freshmen year, Amy told her mother on them.

"No, I promise," Amy answered with a smile. "Anyway, mom wouldn't much care now. She has dementia. I'm going to the nursing home after the hospital."

"Sorry to hear that Amy, looks like you have your share of trouble."

"Kind of comes with the age."

"Amen to that one."

"Okay, Ronnie. See you about three then?" Amy replied.

"Yeah, and thanks Amy. I know it wasn't easy for you to make the call. I just want you to know I appreciate it."

"You're welcome Ronnie. See you at the hospital then. Good bye."

Ronnie sat in the patio chair and watched the fishermen. The spot they were fishing was a good one. He'd fished it with Big Red several times during the summer. Ronnie decided to head to the golf course, play a few holes and have lunch before going to see Bobbie. He needed a distraction.

Ronnie loaded his clubs then drove to the course. As he got out, Ronnie could hear the screeching of conveyor belts carrying coal from two huge mounds next to the power plant across the river. Sprinklers were spraying water on the coal piles. After three holes, he rode back to the clubhouse and took a seat by the window. The waitress, a dark haired woman came to take his order. Ronnie ordered a chicken salad sandwich and a glass of iced tea. He forced himself to eat half of the sandwich then sipped the tea and looked out at the water. Lost in solitude, he sat by the window picking at his food. After an hour, he placed a ten dollar bill on the table and left.

Thirty-five minutes later, Ronnie turned into the hospital's service drive. The ten storied red bricked building had been built in the early fifties and two large wings had been added over the years. Though the bricks used to build the wings were close in color to the original building, they weren't a perfect match. When Beth was diagnosed, Ronnie urged her to get treatment at the the Karmonos Cancer Center in downtown Detroit. But she elected to go to Oak Grove, insisting it was as good as Karmonos and closer to home. Besides, she added, everyone from Melvindale goes to Oak Grove. If she was going to die someplace, she'd sooner die with people from her home town than a bunch of strangers.

Located in the city of Fairlane Hills, the demographics at Oak Grove Hospital had changed since she'd given birth to their boys

Episode 23

thirty years prior. With nearly thirty thousand Arabs now living in the city, Fairlane Hills was now home to the largest Arab population outside of the middle East. There was even a Halal menu at the hospital to accommodate Muslim patients. Beth loved Arabic food but the menu had done her little good as the radiation and chemo took their toll. Her loss of appetite had been very hard to witness; nobody loved to eat as much as Beth.

Ronnie turned into the parking structure and found a parking spot on the second floor between a red Chrysler Caravan and a blue Ford Crown Victoria. Parked in a spot next to the entry door was an older model Buick Rivera. It was in mint condition and dwarfed the Crown Vic. The Rivera looked like it had just been driven out of the show room. Ronnie paused to peer inside. The leather upholstery was beautiful. Whoever owned the Rivera had the last classic GM built.

Ronnie smiled at the woman behind the information desk and she returned his smile. Though it had been two years, she looked the same. He continued to the elevators. The cafeteria was just down the hall. He'd eaten countless meals there and wondered if any of the cashiers he knew were still working. The soups were good as were the stuffed peppers. The hamburgers he had tried only once. Miller's Bar, just down the road had the best burgers in the Detroit area. Miller's had been a regular stop after visiting Beth. A cold beer had been a welcome respite after time spent on the fifth floor.

He'd sent the women who worked at the cafeteria two large boxes of chocolates the first Christmas after Beth died. He'd also given Earl the bartender at Millers a nice tip. Earl didn't seem the type to enjoy chocolates. Both gifts were given in earnest gratitude. They all had been very kind. The nurses on the fifth floor got both chocolates and an arrangement of flowers. Ronnie wondered whether this visit would end with another round of chocolates and flowers.

The elevator doors opened. Ronnie boarded with several other people. Someone had already pushed the button for five. He made his way toward the back and took a place next to a heavily perfumed elderly woman. Beth wore no perfume. The old woman's perfume reminded Ronnie of the girls at Melvindale High in the 1960s. They wore one of two fragrances; Ben Hur or Taboo. Today he'd probably dislike both as much as whatever it was the woman next to him was wearing. Ronnie smiled recalling the fragrances he and his buddies had worn. The interior of his 1960 Ford Falcon must have smelled like a French brothel after a night at the drive in. First there had been Jade East, then English Leather, then British Sterling, and then Brut. Ronnie remembered Big Red saying anyone who paid five bucks for a bottle of after shave must be out of their collective minds when you could get Old Spice for ninety nine cents.

The elevator stopped at the third and fourth floors. Ronnie could feel his emotions build with each successive stop. When it reached five, an intense feeling of deja vu permeated through him. He stepped off the elevator and looked at the nurse's station. The woman's overpowering perfume might be a good thing, maybe his sense of smell would be deadened. He wouldn't notice the haunting smell of antiseptic, medicine and hopelessness that permeated the fifth floor. He didn't want to remember that smell, but it came rushing back anyway.

Ronnie looked at the nurse's station. He didn't recognize any of the women on duty and found relief in that fact. A trip down memory lane would only add to the burden. He really didn't want to smile and tell everyone he was fine and how his life had returned to normal. He wasn't fine.

The only girl he'd loved, since he was old enough to love, was gone and there was never going to be anyone who could replace her. He'd brought her here to be healed then take her home to cuddle in the cabin of their Four Winns. They were supposed to sleep over in the bay. She'd drop him off at the dock just after sun rise so he could hike to the bakery for glazed doughnuts. He'd buy coffee from smart mouthed Nadia and a newspaper from the little red stand. They'd beach the boat at Sugar Island and divvy up the doughnuts. She'd eat her two then eyeball his. They'd lick the glaze off their fingers and

Episode 23

bitch about Nadia's coffee. That had been the plan. None of it ever happened.

The oncologists hadn't healed her and trying didn't mean much in a fight against cancer. Ronnie wanted to tell the doctors there was no prize for second place in a cancer marathon. All they really did was pump his wife's body full of poison, shoot her full of opiates, then ship her emaciated body out in a plastic bag to Voran's Funeral Home. Voran's completed their part of the bargain by vaporizing the only woman he'd ever loved. His part of the deal had been to scatter the contents of that tiny box around Crystal Bay and the beach at Sugar Island. There'd be no more glazed doughnuts or Nadia's lousy coffee.

Now it was time for round two. He'd find Bobbie's room and start the process again. In truth, what Ronnie really wanted to do was run, to sneak back into the elevator and push the first floor button. He would sprint to the parking structure and never return to this place of pain and suffering. At the nurse's station, Ronnie's hopes of making it to Bobbie's room unrecognized were dashed. Nurse Phyllis came out of the back room as the nurse was about to give him the room number.

"Mr. Harris," Nurse Phyllis said with a broad smile. She was carrying two Dixie cups, each holding different colored pills. Nurse Phyllis set the cups down and marked something in a chart.

"What a nice surprise," she added looking up. Her dark hair was pulled back and she wore little make up. Handsome best described her looks.

"How have you been?" she asked. "We've missed you around here, it's nice to see you."

"It's nice to see you too Nurse Phyllis," Ronnie replied in his best, courteous tone.

He wanted to get this part over as quickly as possible. The staff had always gone out of their way for Beth and he felt guilty about his desire to get away unnoticed.

"By the way, Mr. Harris, thank you so much for the candy and flowers. That was very nice."

Book Two Home Again

"You're welcome," Ronnie answered, surprised she's remembered.

"I'm here to visit a friend of mine named Bobbie, I mean Robert. His last name is Irwin. Can you tell me what room he's in?"

"Sure, he's in number 547 B. It's just down the hallway to your right."

Beth had been just across the hall. Ronnie had hoped Bobbie would be in the other wing. At least it wasn't the same room, he added, searching for some comfort.

"Thanks Nurse Phyllis," Ronnie said and started to walk away.

"I don't know why you won't just call me Phyllis,' she replied before he could get away.

"I don't know why you won't just call me Ronnie," he answered.

They had exchanged the same lines numerous times when Beth had been on the floor. When she'd asked him to drop formalities, he always replied it was a southern thing. People from the south always used titles, out of respect.

Walking down the hallway, Ronnie wondered if Amy was already in the room. When he was a room away, Ronnie stopped to brace himself. Taking a deep breath, he walked into the room.

The middle aged woman sitting in the chair across from the hospital bed was Lisa Irwin rewound forty years. When had the little skinny girl morphed into her mother? Ronnie cleared his eyes to make sure he wasn't dreaming. Amy looked up from her magazine and motioned her head toward the man lying asleep in the bed.

Ronnie fought hard to control his emotions. It was an older version, but it was Bobbie. Despite his best efforts, tears welled up anyway. Ronnie looked at his childhood best friend. It had been such a simpler time. Trite, but true all the same. Neither of them would have thought a day like today would ever come. What a wonderful time it had been. A time when summer evenings were warm and humid and air conditioning only existed at the Mel Theater. Lightening bugs were caught and put in bottles. A glass of Faygo Rock and Rye soda was a treat to savor and relish. It was a time of pick up baseball played in a vacant lot. It was endless games of hide and seek until the street lights came on signaling everyone was allie, allie in free. Ronnie looked at his friend. He knew that it wasn't going to be allie in free for Bobbie. Not this time.

Bobbie had always been the tallest boy in their class. He was six foot three when they graduated and very long legged. As kids he'd been so skinny his nickname was Toothpick. Bobby's right foot protruded from the hospital sheet and Ronnie could see the two middle toes were webbed. Ronnie knew three toes on the other foot were also webbed. They had been the object of many jokes when they had gone swimming.

Ronnie stepped closer. If Amy had turned into Lisa, Bobbie had become a clone of his grandpa Stamper. Most of Bobbie's strawberry hair was gone and his face was thin, but then it had always been so. He was pale, but Bobbie had always looked like an albino with freckles anyway. Ronnie swallowed hard and eased into the chair next to Amy.

"Hey, Amy," Ronnie said softly, "Has he been asleep long?"

"He was out when I got here," Amy replied in a whisper.

Ronnie had to look away to compose himself. Hearing her voice was like a flash back to the 1950s. "They gave him a pain shot before noon, he'll be coming around in a little while. Thanks for coming, it'll mean a lot to him."

"Thank you for calling."

Ronnie knew Amy had sensed his feelings. He wanted to add something about it being about thirty-five years too late but decided not to. Bobby opened his left eye. Regaining consciousness, he tried to determine if the short man with gray hair was real or an apparition. Bobbie lay motionless for a few moments then opened his other eye.

"Roaney Eugene," he said with effort and smiled weakly.

Bobbie pronounced Ronnie's name with a hard o and a heavy southern accent. It was the way Ronnie's hillbilly family pronounced his name. Adding Eugene accentuated Bobbie's faked Appalachian drawl. It was a good impersonation. It struck Ronnie that when Bobbie was gone, only his dad would be left to call him Roaney Eugene.

Book Two Home Again

"Roaney Eugene, don't you go down by them trees" Bobbie said in a horse whisper. He laughed softly. "I knew you'd come," he added.

The trees was their name for the little gully next to the train trestle bridge across the road from their houses. It provided a secluded refuge from the open fields. Because the trees were so close to the river, they were off limits. Of course they headed there every chance they got. On occasion, they'd walk across the train bridge to the fields and woods on the other side of the Rouge River. Bobbie's mention of the trees, sent Ronnie's mind back to the summer of 1959. He could see his mother standing on the front porch and hear her calling him home for dinner.

He and Bobbie had been playing in the open field across the street from their small frame houses. All of the houses in the tract were identical except for color. Ronnie heard his mom call for the third time and knew he'd have to get home for dinner. Dinner was promptly at four-forty five unless Big Red was working overtime. This week his dad was working eight hour shifts. It wasn't smart to be late for dinner. Any delay would result in a stern rebuke.

As much as he wanted to stay and play with Bobbie, Ronnie didn't want to risk angering Big Red again by being late. He knew better than make his giant of a father track him down in the fields twice in one week. Pulling that kind of stunt would end up in another whuppin'. Ronnie knew he wasn't the lone recipient of corporal punishment in the neighborhood, even the northern kids got spanked.

"I gotta go now, Bobbie" he said laying down the toy rifle, "My mom's calling."

"Oh man, can't you stay for a little while longer?" Bobbie asked. "Maybe we can find Sonny and Henry and a few more guys. Maybe we can have a battle."

Playing army had been major activity that summer. Sides were chosen, one team would take off and set up an ambush while the other waited and planned an attack. Play guns were used and

Episode 23

dirt clots functioned as hand grenades. Rocks were generally forbidden, but had been thrown on occasion.

Interest in playing war had waned lately. Ronnie and Bobbie had discussed this phenomena several times the last few days. After lengthy analysis they concluded some of the blame could be laid on the Compton sisters who had moved in with Jimmy P's family. The girls were also shirttail relatives of the Caudills who lived three houses from Bobbie. Jimmy P was also related to the Caudills though the entire family tree wasn't entirely clear. Jimmy P lived with his dad in an old flat roofed house that sat by itself on the opposite side of the road. It was a tiny place that had been painted pink at one time, but the paint had faded years ago. How the twins fit into the two families wasn't clear. They just showed up unexpectedly that summer. Nothing was ever said about their mother or father. Nobody ever asked either.

Ronnie's mother stepped out on the front porch and yelled his name again and added his middle name as a point of emphasis. In southern families adding a middle name generally indicated you were in trouble.

"I better go, Bobbie. My dad was really pissed off Monday when he had to come get me. I don't think I want to piss him off again, not just yet anyways," Ronnie answered as he shook his head. "He told me if I was late again this week, he'd take off his belt and make it so I wouldn't forget again."

"I don't get it, why the hell should parents get so pissed off just because you're late for dinner. Why the hell can't they just go ahead and eat their fat asses off. Shit, it's not like they have anything to say that I want to hear. So why the hell can't they just shovel it in and set mine to the side until I'm damn well ready to eat," Bobbie retorted with a stinging vengeance. The tirade of swearing included in their speech was a recent addition that summer.

"Well, I'll see ya after dinner, Bobbie," Ronnie added as he walked away. "Maybe we can play hide and seek or frozen tag. Anyway, I'll come over."

Book Two Home Again

While Ronnie's family, like most of the other families on the street, had come north to find work in the auto factories, Bobbie's parents were native Detroiters who had grown up on the east side. The Irwin's had moved to Melvindale because of the affordable housing and because Bobbie's dad was an appliance salesman at a store in nearby Fairlane Hills. Bobbie's parents considered the west side just a stop over. It was only temporary until Jim Sr. could save up enough to open his own store, then the family would head back to the east side. For the next few years Jim Sr. and Lisa would save what they could and put up with living in the cramped little frame house with their four small children. Relief was just a few short years away.

Bobbie watched Ronnie walk away from the underground fort they'd built in the field. It had been one of many building projects that summer. The fort had been dug out of the side of one of the hills from piles of dirt dumped from the footings of new houses. The roof was constructed from scrap lumber then covered with dirt and camouflaged with weeds. The fort could hold five or six boys and provided good cover during the battles.

In the future, Ronnie would tell his sons how kids made their own fun in the fifties. Between playing box hockey at the park and exploring the open fields and woods they were never bored.

Bobbie leaned back against a two by four that formed part of the fort's pillared entrance. He plucked a stalk of wild grass growing by the doorway, stuck it into the side of his mouth and began to chew. When he could taste the stem's bitter sap, Bobbie removed it and spit into the dirt. He didn't know it then, but he would have another occasion to sit in a similar bunkered fort. He'd be wearing a US Army Airborne 101 Screaming Eagle patch on his shoulder and wishing like hell he was back home throwing dirt balls and learning new swear words from older boys.

Bobbie looked up and saw his mother on the back porch saying something to his little brother Teddy and his sister Amy. From his position, Bobbie could see both front and back porches. The

Episode 23

Irwin's ate dinner around six-thirty unless it was Thursday night when the appliance store was open until nine. His dad worked late that night, so he and his siblings ate earlier. Lisa would wait and eat with their dad.

Bobbie was the second of four Irwin children. Jimmy Jr. was ten months older. Teddy was two years younger and Amy came a year after Teddy. Though younger than Jimmy Jr., Bobbie was taller. By the time he was ten, Bobby's three inches height advantage had become a sore point between them.

Jimmy Jr. rarely hung around with the neighborhood kids that summer. He had begun running with a gang of boys from Robert Street. Ronnie and Bobby were careful to steer clear of that group. While they all went to the same elementary school, there wasn't much interaction between the two groups. Robert Street Boys enjoyed different pass times. Pick up baseball and make believe battles were not on their short list of things to do. Their preferences ran more to shoplifting, sneaking cigarettes, breaking street lights and performing acts of sadism on stray cats. Occasionally Jimmy Jr. still played baseball in the empty lot. Ronnie knew it had been a difficult decision for Jimmy. Though he relished his tough guy act, Jimmy Jr. also loved to play baseball and was easily the best player in the neighborhood.

While shorter than Bobbie, Jimmy Jr. domineered his younger brother. Bobbie had never won a fight despite his size advantage. Ronnie fared little better though recently he'd managed to salvage a draw of sorts during a touch football game. Jimmy had slipped on some loose gravel allowing Ronnie to get him in a headlock before any punches were thrown. It was a rarity. Jimmy Jr. normally would have continued the fight but Bobbie told his brother that he'd side with Ronnie and it would be two against one. Bobbie's siding against his brother wasn't a surprise, everyone knew of Jimmy Jr.'s past cruelties and the bond between Ronnie and Bobbie.

"Hey, Roaney Eugene," Bobbie said startling Ronnie from his daydream. "Are you with us here?" Bobbie asked in a raspy voice as he sat upright.

"I'm the one on morphine here and you're the one who's tripped out," Bobbie continued with a quiet laugh.

"Sorry, Bobbie, just kind of got lost in a thought there. Jesus it's good to see you," Ronnie said extending his hand.

"Forget the handshake, you short shit, give me a hug. I may break eventually, but not yet. Or so says the quack who poses as a doctor in this hell hole."

Ronnie got up from the chair and leaned over the bed. He hugged his childhood friend though it seemed awkward for both of them.

"Hey sis," Bobbie said to Amy. "What'ya think Ronnie? Ever think you'd see little Amy all grown up?"

"No, I didn't Bobbie. And I bet she hears this all the time, but damn, does she look like Lisa or what?"

"No, shit, Sherlock. Got that same grating voice too," Bobbie winked at his sister.

"Yeah, well it wasn't only mom's voice that she used to keep you in line. And if you don't start listening to the doctors, I'm going to beat you with one of those little paddles she kept around."

"Remember those Ronnie. Remember those little paddles. She had those, oh you know, what the hell, I can't remember shit any more, you know the ones that you bought at the dime store. The ones with the ball at the end of the rubber band but the ball and the rubber band were gone. Instead of seeing how many times she could hit the ball, sometimes I think Lisa counted how many times it took to make us cry," Bobbie replied with a smile.

"Yeah," Amy said, "and it didn't take many to make you cry, Bobbie. You'd be howling like an Iraqi woman the first time she hit, you. Damn," Amy said looking around. "Guess I better watch what I say, there's a lot of Arabs at the hospital now."

"Screw 'em, little sis," Bobbie said, "say what you want. What the hell, what are they going to do ask us to leave? Nothing more I'd like to hear."

Episode 23

"Speaking of leaving, you two need to catch up, and I need to get going," Amy said getting up from her chair. She leaned and kissed Bobbie on the forehead.

"We're not supposed to do that. Have to watch about giving Bobbie an infection but sometimes we break the rules, 'ey big brother?"

"Yeah, and now that this little curly headed crippled boy is here, we're going to do all kinds of things that are against the rules. Ain't we Roaney Eugene?" Bobbie said in his southern voice again. "Hell, we might even go down to the trees and play by the river."

"Or we might break into a party store and drink some Ripple," Ronnie added.

The remark referred to Bobbie's failed attempt to break into a local party store during their junior year in high school. The owner of the party store had been wounded in a hold up attempt and the store had been closed while the owner recovered in the hospital.

"Guess you'll never let me live that one down, will'ya ass hole?" Bobbie retorted.

"It was a classic."

"Well, you two butt heads behave yourselves. That's probably too much to ask. Anyway, see you tomorrow Bobbie," Amy said.

"Now listen Amy, you don't have to come back tomorrow. You got a life and a family to take care of," Bobbie protested.

"See you tomorrow, Bob. Hope to see you again real soon Ronnie," Amy said then left the room.

Ronnie sat down in the chair. Neither man said anything for a few moments. Finally Ronnie broke the silence.

"She seems like a great sister," he said attempting to make small talk.

"Are we going to address the elephant in the room now or later?" Bobbie asked looking Ronnie directly in the eyes. It was obvious Bobbie wasn't going to agree with his attempt to bypass the issue. Ronnie didn't reply right away and both men sat quietly.

"I take it you're referring to Beth," Ronnie answered softly.

"Yeah," Bobby replied, "I think we should talk about her first. There'll be plenty of time for you to tell me about your job at Ford's and for me to tell you about my life in the Army." Bobby's comment reminded Ronnie how people Downriver referred to Ford in the possessive. They did the same with General Motors, National Motors and Chrysler Corporation. Ronnie always assumed it was a throw back to when Henry Ford owned the company.

"We need to get it out of the way, don't you think, Ronnie?" Bobbie added earnestly.

"Okay, if you want to," Ronnie said looking down at his feet. He'd hoped to avoid the topic but knew they needed to cross that bridge.

"What can I tell you Bobbie that you don't already know?" Ronnie asked.

"Not too much, really," Bobbie said. It was Bobbie who was now looking down.

"Was she on this floor?"

"Yeah, she was Bob," Ronnie said in a near whisper. "She was right across the hall."

"I thought so. You'll think I'm whacked, but it was almost like I could feel her here in some way. Sounds kind of nutty, I know."

"Nothing about this whole process sounds nutty to me Bobbie. Who really knows what this is all about or how it works. It just is, that's all that I know. There are no reasons or logic to it. It just is, that's all." It was one of Beth's favorite euphemisms. "So if you tell me you feel her here, then you do."

Both men sat again in awkward silence. Bobbie spoke first this time.

"This may not sit well with you, but do you want to know how I see it?" Bobbie asked.

Ronnie didn't reply. His head had been spinning since he'd pulled into the parking structure. His mind was a swirl of memories of their childhood and the woman they had both loved, then lost. Though they lost her in different ways, they'd both

Episode 23

lost her just the same. Ronnie looked at the best friend who suddenly and unexpectedly reentered his life. It didn't seem fair that in the end he'd have to let Bobbie go again. Opportunities taken and opportunities missed will define your life. Big Red had told him that years ago. At the time Ronnie had been deciding about taking a new job at Ford. He slumped forward in his seat and put his head into his hands. His cheekbones were pressed against his palms and his elbows were digging into both thighs.

"Yes, I suppose I do Bobbie. Though maybe some things are best left unsaid. The last time we tried, or I guess I should say the last time I tried to do something like this, it didn't work too well. So I gotta tell you, you're kind of scaring me here. We're not twenty-two years old. So we may need to talk about it, but I don't want it to cut what little string that's still binding us. It sounds like you need to get this off your chest though, or whatever it is you're trying to do. So tell me what you want to say?" Ronnie said not looking up.

"Well, that being said, here's how I see it. You dated her first. I slept with her first. You married her. Now I'm going to see her first on the other side. Guess that makes us even."

"Bobbie, don't say that. You're going to get better, and get out of here and then we're going to try to make up for lost time."

"I wish you were right, Ronnie. We both know better than that. But I do have some time left, and you're going to have to help me do a couple of things."

"What are you talking about Bobbie?" Ronnie asked. Ronnie guessed Bobbie was right about never getting better and the conversation about feeling Beth's presence was not surprising. Ronnie knew many people had similar experiences when the end was near.

"We'll talk about that stuff later," Bobbie answered. "How are the boys?"

The question surprised Ronnie. He felt relieved. Ronnie sat up in his chair and looked at his old friend. Bobbie was right, they needed to get that out of the way first.

"They're good Bobbie. The older one is his mom made over," Ronnie said. "The younger one looks like me but has his mom's appetite. He's kind of goofy though, probably gets that from his dad."

Both men laughed.

"Ah, a dreamer then," Bobbie said looking up at the ceiling.

"Yeah, a dreamer, you could say. Or ADHD or whatever label people want to put on it."

"Next time you come, bring a picture of them. I've never seen them you know." Bobbie choked up and looked away to regain his composure.

"I know, Bobbie," Ronnie answered. "I know."

"Okay," Bobbie said. He seemed relieved. "We've gotten the hard part over. We'll talk more about all that stuff, too. But later. Right now, I have a little surprise for you."

"What's that, Bobbie?" Ronnie asked.

"I want you to go down to the nurse's station and tell them you want to take me on a little wheel chair adventure."

"What the hell, Bobbie? Are sure you're up to it?"

"Yeah, but they'll give you a little shit and try to say no. Tell them we'll only be gone for ten minutes."

"Okay, I'll give it a try. I know one of the nurses pretty well. Do you know nurse Phylis?" Ronnie asked.

"Yeah, she's real nice."

"I'll talk to her. She and I got to know each other really well. Beth just loved her."

"Well, go put the hillbilly charm on her and get a chair. I guarantee it will be worth the sweet talk."

"Okay, I'll be back in a minute. What about your IV and all that stuff."

"She can help us there, too."

Ronnie returned in few minutes after promising Nurse Phyllis to be careful and to be back in ten minutes. She even helped Bobbie into the wheelchair and pushed him to the elevator. Bobbie told Ronnie to push the sixth floor button. When the elevator door opened at six, the other passengers moved aside to allow Bobby to pass by.

Episode 23

"Okay, dude, where to?" Ronnie asked.

"Forward, Muldoon," Bobby said pointing to the nurses station on their left.

It was an expression Big Red had used often, his standard answer when they had been walking into the University of Michigan Football Stadium and the boys would ask which way.

"Are you sure you're up to this Bobbie?" Ronnie asked again.

"Don't worry about the mule, Ronnie, just load the wagon," Bobbie replied with a laugh, using another Big Redism. Ronnie laughed with Bobbie and pushed him toward the nurse's station.

There were two nurses sitting at the desk and a third with her back to them. Ronnie wondered what Bobbie was up to. As they approached the station a young thing who looked no older than a Candy Striper asked if she could help.

"No, young lady, you can't," Bobbie answered in a cheery voice. "But that good looking nurse behind you sure can."

Hearing the comment, the nurse with her back to them turned around and broke into a broad smile. She looked older than the last time Ronnie had seen her, but there was no mistaking those blue eyes and that smile. There was only one person he had ever known that had eyes that color. It'd been fifteen years since he'd seen them but it wouldn't have mattered if it had been fifty, he'd have recognized them instantly.

"Cate Cassadea," Ronnie said.

Episode 24

At least he still had Fridays off, Ahmed thought while changing into his dishdasha. After the mosque, he planned to meet Ali at a club near Wayne State University. Stacey would join them after she got off work. Ahmed hoped he could persuade her to stay over. They could go to breakfast, then hang out together until he left for work.

Ahmed slipped on his shoes, grabbed his prayer hat and bounded down the steps.

"Damn," he said as he reached the bottom, he'd forgotten his jacket.

Ahmed raced back up the stairs, grabbed his leather jacket and ran back downstairs. Opening the door, he saw a young man walking away from his car. He had just upgraded the Grand AM's sound system and wondered if the man was checking it out for theft. Seeing Ahmed, the man walked away with his face turned the other way. Ahmed slung the jacket over his shoulder and continued walking towards his car wondering if the man was connected to Mahmood or Charlie.

To date he'd heard nothing more about Raheem. All Ahmed knew was Raheem had been taken to the eighth floor. One other unusual event, however, had taken place that evening. After cleaning a blood spill, he returned to the area where Raheem was being treated and ducked into the room kitty corner to Raheem's where an elderly man had been admitted for chest pains. The man was sedated so Ahmed moved quietly to the corner and had a perfect view of Raheem's room. Ahmed expected to see Raheem being treated by Dr. Nakshatra. What he observed was an empty room that didn't stay that way. As Ahmed watched, the blonde woman, whose mother had been admitted for the stroke, entered the room. It wasn't by mistake, because she had surveyed in both directions before entering.

Ahmed watched in captivation as the woman removed something from the medical waste container. The woman had carefully lifted the top off the medical trash bin with the yellow triangular sign and Biological Hazard printed in red and had taken great care in her method. The woman removed a pair of surgical gloves from the box on the table and put them on before lifting the top of the waste basket. She then took a third glove from the box and held it in her left hand. With her gloved right hand she retrieved a small plastic vile then placed the vial into the third glove then double tied the end. She repeated the procedure with another glove to provide a back up in case the first glove was compromised. Afterwards, she returned to her mother's room and deposited the vial into her purse. Ahmed was befuddled and wondered if she was some kind of quasi agent like himself. She might have been working for Charlie, but that wasn't logical and any connection to Mahmood seemed even more unlikely.

It had been over a month since he had watched Nurse Cassadea take the vial from the trash and he still had no idea why she would want the empty vial. Maybe she was a drug addict and hoped to glean remnants of Demerol or morphine from the vial. It was the only line of reasoning that made sense and it might also explain why she changed jobs. To keep an eye on her, Ahmed stopped by her station occasionally. The first time, he said it was just to welcome her and ask if there was anything he could do to

Episode 24

help. He had gone to her floor twice more but never observed anything suspicious.

Ahmed got into the Grand AM and drove two blocks when he heard a phone ring. After his first meeting with Mahmood, he'd checked the middle console for planted phones but lately had become careless. He cursed himself for his laziness as he lifted the console door. To his surprise it was empty. After three more rings, he realized the phone was under his seat. He understood now what the man he'd seen earlier by his car had been doing. Ahmed pulled the Pontiac to the curb and put the driver's seat as far back as possible. As he bent forward and reached under his seat, the steering wheel pressed against his chest.

"Damn that Mahmood!" Ahmed swore out loud as he continued groping. Finally his fingers wrapped around the phone.

"Yes," Ahmed said flatly into the phone.

He hadn't seen Mahmood since their first encounter and had hoped he'd never see the beady eyed ferret again. Ahmed heard Mahmood's irritating voice.

"You will receive instructions from Kamal today at the mosque. Give the phone to him and then do what he tells you." Mahmood said then hung up.

Episode 25

Cate sat at the desk which now served as her make up vanity. The desk had been her birthday gift freshmen year in high school. Louis never understood his daughter's request nor her determination to go to college. Girls didn't need college to become good wives and mothers and he had told his daughter as much. Cate thought of her father as she dried her hair. When she got older, they hadn't agreed on much. Her mother always maintained it was because they were too much alike. Cate applied her make up then paused looking in the lighted mirror. She knew the toll could have been worse.

She had been back to Plymouth twice. The first at the request of her lawyer. The investigation into the accident was continuing at a snail's pace. She had already given a deposition and couldn't understand why an investigation was needed. David had died and so had one of the teenagers. She didn't understand what difference her testimony could possibly make. David was dead. How could you try a dead man; none of it made any sense.

The second trip was to sign real estate papers. The buyers asked for a contingency if their house didn't sell. Cate could have refused but resigned herself none of it really mattered. If it took more time, she had nothing to lose. She had settled in at her mom's and had nothing but time. Her plans depended on Emma's progress. Her mother's odds of getting out of the nursing facility were slim so she could put everything on hold until after the holidays. Her life was now an emotional roller coaster, though merry go round was a more apt comparison, everything seemed to be spinning round and round.

There were many options to consider. She thought about moving to California after everything was settled. One of her daughters lived there. Maybe she'd just take off and travel and use her mom's house as home base. Being a teacher, Kathy had summers off. Maybe they'd take off and see the world next summer. She hadn't seen Linda in a while, but Kathy and Jess had been available making the loneliness bearable.

She missed David, but not in the way she anticipated. Cate wondered if she'd become so numb she had lost the capacity to grieve. The thought frightened her. It had opened a tiny crack in wounds that had taken so long to heal. She didn't know why she felt this way, David was a good man and she had loved him. Or at least some part of her loved him. Maybe her reaction was one of self preservation, she told herself, or the scars from the devastation Billy inflicted were just too thick. While she mourned David, it was not the way she mourned losing Billy which made her feel guilty; Billy was still alive. Maybe it was her life with Billy she mourned or perhaps the loss of her youth and dreams. Both seemed to have ended with the divorce.

"It's Friday night," Cate told herself aloud. She was about to do something she believed impossible a short time ago. She was going to the Homecoming Parade and football game with Ronnie and Kathy. Fight, fight for red and white, she half sang, half hummed . It was the first verse to the Cardinal Fight Song. She knew the remaining verses; the lyrics had been etched into her brain.

She'd missed the Snake Dance the evening before. It had been a tradition as long as Cate could remember. The last one she'd participated in was the fall of senior year but she remembered it like it was yesterday. Everyone gathered at City Hall

Episode 25

where the senior class president led the procession. Each person in line held the hand of the person to their right and left, which made it like a giant conga line, except everyone faced outward instead of forward. The students alternated boy girl. That night, Eric had been to her left. The line moved in a snake like fashion weaving in and out of the telephone poles along Oakwood Boulevard until it reached the open field next to Cardinal Stadium. A bonn fire was lit and a dummy, dressed in a football uniform of the opposing team's colors, was thrown onto the fire. As the player burned in effigy, the Cardinal Marching Band performed.

The concession stand was opened and everyone ate doughnuts and drank cider while the band played crowd favorites like Hang On Sloopy. After the concert, the students left to put the finishing touches on class floats. With less than twenty four hours to go until the parade, everyone worked frantically. The seniors would win, they always did. Finishing the float could last several hours. At least that's what parents were told, though a good portion of the time was spent necking in parked cars. Cate closed her eyes and could almost see their senior float sitting in the driveway at Kathy's house. That float had not been their best effort but had been the most fun. Eric had his dad's car that night and they'd snuck off for a couple of hours.

Cate always loved everything about Homecoming week. For small town kids in the sixties, it was like Christmas and Easter all rolled into one. Opening a corsage box had the tender suspense of gifts on Christmas morning, while shopping for a formal dress to wear was like being a ten years old girl again and picking out new Easter outfits. The football game was also exciting. The bleachers would be packed to overflow with raucous fans. Squeezed together, they would scream and yell for their red jerseyed Cardinals.

The dance followed on Saturday night. The girls wore formal dresses, their hair coffered and piled high like crowns of royalty. She had not been elected Queen senior year, that title had been won by a dark haired beauty named Helen. It really hadn't matter who was Queen, though, or who was on the Court; it was such an exciting night. She and her friends were young, dressed to the nines and escorted by handsome young boys carrying boxes of flowers. After the dance it would be off to a fancy restaurant like Carl's Chop House. It was a magical week for kids of blue collar parents.

Mothers fawned over the young couples and exclaimed how pretty everyone looked. Nervous fathers took pictures with Kodak cameras and swore under their breath about everyone being in such a damnable hurry as they changed scalding hot flash bulbs to get the next picture. They'd push silver colored bulbs, with little blue dots printed on the bottom, into giant flash attachments. The resulting flashes were slightly less intense than a ten megaton nuclear test and temporarily blinded excited young couples and left them seeing circular dots for several minutes. The couples knew it was hopeless to try and escape the photos because their parents always looked at them with special pride.

To working class parents, something as exotic as a formal dance, new dresses and driving to a fancy restaurant in a late model car would have happened to them only in dreams. Providing such opportunities made the long hours in sweaty factories and smoky mills worth it. Before the young couples scurried to their gilded carriages, fathers sternly reminded daughters they could stay out until one thirty only because it was a special occasion. The reminders were said loud enough to be audible to the young men waiting to whisk their little girls away.

And the Snake Dance was the official start of the festivities and Cate was sad she had missed it. She loved the taste of Michigan apple cider. The first swallow always made her salivary glands tingle and her lips pucker. The tart cider contrasted so well with the spicy sweetness of cinnamon and sugar doughnuts. The cinnamon always lingered on her tongue. The little round fried cakes were devastatingly unhealthy but no one knew anything about cholesterol back then. Maybe it was better that way, Cate thought, nobody wasted any time worrying.

After the Snake Dance, she and her friends would sneak a few cigarettes on the way to the float. While everyone knew smoking

Episode 25

wasn't good for you, no one ever paid any attention. A movie on lung cancer was shown at school every fall but the cancer patients were all always old. During their senior year she, Kathy, Jess and Linda made a vow to not worry about such things until they were fifty. The vow was made, cigarettes in hand, between incessant, hysterical laughter as they teased each other about how they would look at fifty. It all seemed so far away. Now, she'd like a chance to be fifty again. It was five more years to put into the time bank. Five years could be a lifetime; the divorce from Billy had taught her that lesson. The realization was reinforced when Bobbie had been wheeled to her nurse's station the week prior. It was more than a life time to Bobbie, it was several.

Episode 26

"Fucking asshole!" Ahmed spat the words as he threw the cell phone onto the passenger's seat. The phone bounced upward then fell between the door and the seat. Ahmed tried to calm himself. He leaned over and reached for the phone. When he opened the lid to the center console, Ahmed noticed a pack of Marlboros at the bottom. He'd been trying to quit.

"Screw it," he said then grabbed the pack. There were three left. Ahmed pushed in the lighter and waited. He speculated about the conversation with Mahmood as the lighter popped out. Ahmed took a drag and exhaled the smoke. He knew Mahmood wasn't calling to ask how things were going with Stacey or if he liked his job at the hospital. He might be calling to find out if I've discovered anything yet, or worse, it could be an assignment. The thought sent a shiver down Ahmed's spine.

Ahmed considered his alternatives. He could tell Mahmood about the blonde nurse who had stolen the vial, but what could he say. The vial had been in Raheem's room but he hadn't witnessed it being used on Raheem. Bringing up the incident could lead to questions about why he hadn't turned over the information earlier. Ahmed could tell Mahmood that Raheem had been moved to the mysterious eighth floor but Mahmood might already knew that. It was possible Mahmood and Raheem were connected but there also was the chance they were in separate cells. Maybe Raheem recognized me, Ahmed thought, which could lead to retribution for not passing the information along. Ahmed knew he was in a precarious situation and wouldn't be able to correctly evaluate the alternatives until he received Kamal's instructions at the mosque.

Also, telling Mahmood about Nurse Cassadea's thievery might endanger her life. Ahmed wasn't prepared to make that trade off. At some point he might have to do so to obtain his sister's freedom but telling Charlie about Nurse Cassadea's actions could also endanger her life. Ahmed had witnessed CIA agents doing things in Afghanistan the average American would not believe. This was a different situation, however, and unmerciful beatings of Taliban fighters or condemning them to death by packing them into shipping containers without food and water was not the same as violating the rights of an American nurse. For all he knew, Nurse Cate might just be a kleptomaniac who took objects of no value. Using her as a bargaining chip with Charlie might be the safest bet, but he'd have wait and see. Kamal's instructions at the mosque could tip the scales, it was a matter of timing. Ahmed finished the cigarette, threw the butt out the window and shifted the Pontiac into drive.

Episode 27

Cate added the finishing touches to her make up, then dressed. She selected beige corduroys, a black cashmere sweater and added a gold locket containing pictures of her daughters. Cate opened the locket. Heather was in sixth grade at the time and was smiling as only an eleven year old can. Erin was in fourth grade. She had lost her two front teeth. Heather had Cate's clear blue eyes while Erin had Billy's mischievous look. She had been a handful. Cate put on a pair of cashmere socks and slipped her feet into ankle high boots with squared toes. Cate could have moved into her mother's bedroom on the first floor and avoided climbing steps but that would be like taking Louis's place at the table. Some things were sacred.

Cate opened the front door. Ronnie would be along in a few minutes. It had been a surprise to see him at the hospital though she knew it hadn't been by chance. Bobbie had seen her on the patient's elevator on his way back from radiation. He'd looked very ill but managed to whisper her name. The next day she went to his room where he told her he might have a little surprise for her soon. She stopped in again the day after he'd gotten Ronnie to sneak him to her floor where Bobbie confided to her he never doubted his old friend would show up.

She'd heard they'd become estranged when Ronnie and Beth married. At the time, she was living with Eric in Miami and Melvindale seemed a million miles away. After the split with Eric, she'd been happy to keep it that way. From Kathy, she also knew Ronnie and Beth lived in the Pagoda House on Grosse Ile. Cate remembered the place because of its proximity to Looney Rooney's. Over a lunch at the hospital a couple of weeks earlier, Ronnie suggested the get together for Homecoming. It seemed a little silly at first, but Kathy, Linda and Jess had been excited about the idea. Cate could tell Ronnie still struggled with the loss of Beth, she could read it in his eyes. He'd also been very sympathetic about David's death.

Ronnie said he had a surprise after the football game. She tried to get the secret out of him over coffee, but he was unwilling to share. She'd told him she also needed to stop by the nursing home which might interfere with making the parade on time. Ronnie replied the parade didn't start until six and offered to accompany her. She accepted gladly because despite her best efforts, she usually left the place depressed. She arranged to meet Kathy, Linda and Jess at her mom's house after the nursing home, then drive to the parade. She hoped it'd be fun, but even if it wasn't, at least it was a night away from the hospital.

Cate glanced out the window as Ronnie pulled up in a tan Explorer and parked behind her Rivera. As he came up the walk, she noticed he no longer had the limp he had in high school and wondered how his gate had been corrected. He was not wearing metal braces, so she assumed he'd had some kind of surgery. She thought about asking him, but didn't want to appear intrusive. Ronnie saw her sitting at the kitchen table and waved.

"Come on in," Cate said opening the screen door.

"Thanks, Cate. Wow, this place brings back memories. This is just like walking into the house I grew up in," Ronnie said looking around the bungalow's small living room.

"Sorry I'm late," he added apologetically, "but my ex brother in law called. He's a freighter pilot and his boat was delayed at

Episode 27

the Edison power plant in Trenton. They were delivering coal and there was some kind of break down with the unloading equipment. He's going to spend a couple of days with me while the ship's in dock. I dropped him off at Beth's mom's. He and Carol still have a relationship of sorts and he's going to hang out there while we're visiting your mother. He'll meet us at the parade and go to the game with us if that's okay."

"No problem, will Carol be coming as well?" Cate asked. "Jesus, I haven't seen her in years."

"No, football isn't her thing. She's kind of a recluse now. Let's just say she has good days and bad days. I don't know which she's having today."

"Why should she be any different from the rest of us?" Cate replied as she walked to the hall closet and grabbed her coat.

The black leather was her favorite. It contrasted well with her blond hair, some of which was now silver. David had referred to them as platinum highlights. He always maintained there was something sexy about blondes and black leather. He liked the look so much he bought the coat for her last birthday. Spending that kind of money was uncharacteristic for him, but then again that was David. He could be such a tight wad about living expenses and then buy her an expensive gift. A pang of grief ran through Cate and for a moment she worried it might grow into a full fledged panic attack. She asked Ronnie to hang on for a minute then walked into the bathroom where she grabbed a small bottle of Xanax which she slipped into her coat pocket. Just precautionary, she said to herself. When she walked back into the living room, Ronnie was leaning against the door jam.

"We can sit for a minute if your leg is hurting," Cate offered.

"Oh, not a problem. I wear a plastic orthotic now. It gives my leg some support and corrects my walk. I don't limp so much anymore," Ronnie said in a matter of fact tone. "Well, not as long as I have it on" he added.

"That's really good. I kind of wondered, but didn't want to say anything."

"We're too old for modesty now, Cate. There were times, when I was younger, that it wasn't an open topic. Well, not to anyone but Beth. She'd let me have it all the time. In case you have forgotten, she was a straight at you kind of person."

"You don't have to remind me of that. We played at Melwood Park together every summer when we were little. I played softball with her. She was competitive to say the least," Cate added with a smile.

"What are you laughing at Cate?" Ronnie asked with a smile of his own.

"I was laughing about the time," Cate stammered unable to finish her thought.

"Come on. Now you've got to share. You can't keep this one to yourself, Cate. What's so funny?" Ronnie persisted.

"Okay, but let me catch my breath first," Cate said trying to keep herself together enough to finish.

"Okay, do you remember the time she beat the shit out of Clint Gunderson?" Cate asked laughing again. Her forehead crinkled up a bit as she struggled to finish her sentence. "Damn it. That was so funny. Do you remember Clint?"

"Well, no, I mean other than he was Toby's little brother. Toby was one tough customer. I didn't ever want the wrong part of him. He was one bad ass."

"Yeah, but one day, oh I think Beth was in about fifth grade. Anyway, Clint was in the same grade and he pushed her down at the bus stop. That's right, you went to Robert elementary so you wouldn't have been around. Anyway, Beth got up and that skinny little shit beat the hell out of Clint. It was unbelievable. We were all cheering her on of course. It was unmerciful. She blacked one of his eyes, bloodied his nose. Finally a couple of boys pulled her off of him. He went running home and didn't go to school that day. The next day Toby was waiting for her at the bus stop to get even for what she'd done to his little brother. We all tried to stick up for her but Toby was older. Damn, that girl took no shit."

Episode 27

"Never did. She had a short fuse, no denying that. After thirty years of marriage, I knew when to duck that Irish temper. I've heard parts of that story before, but never in its entirety from an eye witness. Whatever happened to Toby for beating her up."

"Well, Beth went on to school and tried to clean herself up. She was too proud to rat out on Toby, but some of the other kids did. He got suspended for three days, had to apologize. That was pretty much the end of it."

"Didn't Clint eventually die in 'Nam or something?"

"Yeah, that was bad. Stepped on a mine. Not much of him came back. Clint was an okay kid. He was just young and thought that he was his brother and could pick on everyone."

"Well, if he thought he could push Beth around, he was mistaken."

Cate began laughing again. "Yeah, that turned out to be a major mistake. We'd kid him about it every chance we got. He was better once he got a little older. Anyway we better get going. We don't want to be late for the parade, Kathy's all geeked about it. Then again, she's always geeked about something."

Ronnie opened the door and they stepped onto the porch. Cate stopped to lock the door. Before they went down the steps, Ronnie hesitated and looked around.

"Sometime, before the weather changes, I'd like to sit on this big ol' porch, open a Coke in a glass bottle and watch the traffic go by. Do the neighbors still come out in the evening to sit?" Ronnie asked.

"Yeah, but not as much anymore. Most of the old ones are gone, but you're welcome any time."

"Can I bring along a couple of Pall Mall's?"

Cate laughed, "Sure, but why would you want to do that?"

"Oh, my mom smoked Pall Mall's. When I was older, I'd sit on the front porch with her, we'd drink Coca Cola's or maybe a cup of coffee, and smoke those God awful rag weeds."

"If you can find 'em, we'll smoke them," Cate said as they walked to the street.

"Damn, I love your car," Ronnie said looking at the Rivera.

"Why don't we take it to the parade tonight? It'd sort of set the tone," Cate offered.

"Only if you let me drive it, Cate," Ronnie replied with a laugh.

Episode 28

Ahmed entered the mosque and found an open spot in the third row. As he knelt in silence, he looked around for anyone he might recognize. Several of the men kneeling around him looked familiar, but none were from the camps or Afghanistan. They were men he'd probably just seen around east Fairlane Hills. A few minutes later, Kamal entered and took a place next to Ahmed. After closing his eyes and remaining silent for a few moments, Kamal looked straight ahead and spoke in a whisper.

"Be at the New Lebanon bakery tonight at seven-thirty. Order at the counter. When you get your food, sit at an empty table. A tall man will sit down with you. You will be instructed by him."

"What do you mean I will be instructed?" Ahmed asked. He turned to look at Kamal while speaking and realized his mistake. He turned his head back toward the front of the mosque and waited for Kamal's reply.

Kamal didn't answer. Instead he closed his eyes again and began reciting the Koran. Ahmed knew it was useless to continue. His night with Ali and Stacey was in jeopardy, he'd have to call and make up a story. More lies.

Episode 29

Ronnie and Cate drove south on Allen Road. As they passed the Clark gas station, Cate asked him if he remembered buying gas there for nineteen cents a gallon and getting a free pack of cigarettes with a purchase of two dollars. Ronnie replied his mom made him buy gas at the Purple Martin because they gave away free dinnerware. His mom wanted the free plates and saucers though he never knew why. She'd never used them. Cate suggested they may have been for his sister's hope chest. Ronnie said he'd ask his sister the next time he saw her.

When they reached Southfield Road, Ronnie noted a change in Cate's demeanor, she had become quieter and introspective. When they passed Morey's Triangle Restaurant her mood lightened. He asked her if she'd ever had the corned beef and pastrami sandwiches there. With a far away look in her eyes Cate replied she and Eric went there often. Eric loved their fries. When Ronnie told her he and Beth were regulars, Cate smiled and reminded him how how they piled the cole slaw on the sandwiches between the slices of grilled rye bread.

"I always knew Eric was hot for you in high school, Cate, but I didn't know anything ever became of it?" he asked cautiously.

Book Two Home Again

"Oh yeah, something became of it," she replied looking out the window.

Ronnie didn't press for details. He didn't know if her gaze out the window was intended to hide the emotions spilling across her face; she appeared lost in reflection. He'd been lost in a few reflections himself the last two years. In them, he was usually wearing a red varsity jacket with white leather sleeves, a pair of pale blue Levis and a madras shirt. On his cheek were a couple of zits, partially concealed by a smear of Clearasil. Zits always seemed to pop out during Homecoming week; they emerged at the most inappropriate times. Ronnie wondered if drugstores still sold Clearasil. He hadn't shopped for any lately. He also hadn't shopped for Noxzema, Jade East or Trojans, but assumed they all were still available. For kicks, he had stopped at Save On Drugs before leaving the Island and bought a roll of fruit flavored Certs and a pack of Juicy Fruit gum. He was surprised Certs were still available in an age of Tic Tac's and more surprised they were still wrapped in aluminum foil.

When the light changed, Ronnie turned left. The nursing home was just ahead. It was a horseshoe shaped building with a court yard in the middle. The name had been changed recently to Metro Shores Senior's Center. The new name was an attempt to tune into a recent movement to improve Downriver's image. There had been an initiative to adopt Metro Shores as a catch all for the collective communities rather than Downriver. There had even been an attempt to merge them into one larger city to be named Metro Shores. The idea had been pitched as a way to reduce property taxes by consolidating police, fire and public works. The idea failed. Ronnie's father said consolidating the communities would be like combining the Roman Catholic Church with the Southern Baptist Convention.

"Good idea in theory, but ain't never gonna happen," Big Red put it. Then added, "while we agree on abortion and closin' filthy mouthed movies, we ain't ever gonna worship no Pope and they ain't never gonna get saved."

Episode 29

Ronnie told him that Catholics don't actually worship the Pope. Big Red countered by saying as long as Catholics believed he was infallible, they were putting the Pope on the same level as God. Ronnie replied Catholics only believe the Pope is infallible in areas of Church doctrine. Big Red said it was the same difference. Ronnie stated the term same difference made no sense and added it was an oxymoron. Things were either the same or they were different, but they couldn't be the same difference. Big Red said he'd never gone to college and didn't know what an oxymoron was. Before Ronnie could explain, his father quickly added anybody who couldn't see Catholics were idolaters, because they prayed to statues and thought the Pope was God, was some kind of moron. Whether they were the oxy kind or not, he couldn't say but they were morons just the same. Ronnie gave up the argument. Big Red ended the exchange by telling Ronnie sometimes separate ain't equal, sometimes it's better. Ronnie knew his father's Appalachian euphemisms were impossible to counter.

Ronnie parked the Explorer in the front lot. They got out and walked toward the entrance. Emma's room was on the second floor in the extended care wing. Ronnie's grandmother had been in a nursing home for the last nine years of her life in the long term care wing. Extended care was another clever play on words; it sounded better and hinted there was a sense of hope. It was false hope and everyone knew it; changing the name didn't change the outcome.

Ronnie hadn't been in a nursing home since his grandmother died. While The Metro Shores Senior Center was immaculate, it had the same smell as the place his Granny Harris served her life sentence. Nursing home smell was similar to a hospital's but had its own distinct undercurrent. Just like a wine connoisseur can differentiate the bouquet of a Pinot from a Burgundy, frequent visitors to hospitals and nursing homes can also describe the ever so slight aromatic differences. Hospitals always smell like a combination of antiseptic, medicine and quiet desperation. Nursing homes are a combination of urine, Lysol and despair.

Book Two Home Again

Cate led them to her mother's room. Emma was a tiny, diminutive woman. Her face was drawn to one side and she had difficulty articulating her words. She recognized Cate, but seemed unable to completely place her daughter. Cate told Emma she brought a friend with her, Ronnie Harris from high school. The statement registered some meaning but it wasn't clear Emma understood the relationship. Ronnie approached the bed and took her hand.

"How are you Mrs. Cassadea?" he asked in a sympathetic voice.

Ronnie struggled to not speak to her as he would a child, though he wasn't sure if she would realize it. If he was lying with one arm withered and drawn and his face slightly twisted, he wouldn't want to be talked to like he was a five year old. Then again, he thought, who knows what you'd be thinking after a blood clot lodged in your brain and starved it of oxygen. Maybe you'd end up thinking you were five years old. Cate's mom struggled to say something. Ronnie shook his head in agreement, though he had no idea what she had said. He asked Cate if it was okay to sit in one of the visitor's chairs. Cate said it was fine, then took her mom's hand and sat on the edge of the bed.

Ronnie looked at Emma's roommate. Though younger, it was obvious she'd suffered a more severe stroke. Ronnie felt a stab of guilt for feeling the woman's survival might not have been a blessing. It appeared she had been at the facility for a while, her side of the room had been decorated. There were pictures of her family in gold frames on the night stand next to her bed. Taped to the wall were several pictures drawn in crayon. Somebody named Ryan had completed a very intricate drawing of the Mayflower and the Pilgrims. The autumn pictures reminded Ronnie that Thanksgiving was nearing. He remembered similar drawings attached to the refrigerator with magnets. Next to the Pilgrims was a drawing of trees with branches filled with yellow and red leaves. Two stick figured children and a stick figured dog, that looked more like a pig, were playing under the tree. The picture was signed Chelsea and there was a note that read We Miss You

Episode 29

Grandma. As he sat looking at the pictures, Ronnie wondered if the Europeans were on to something with their euthanasia laws. Cate spoke to the woman in the bed next to her mother jarring Ronnie from his morbid thoughts.

"Marty, how are you this afternoon? Are they taking good care of you?" Cate asked in a pleasant voice.

Ronnie glanced at the woman but there was no response. He wondered if the woman named Marty ever responded to Cate. Talking to her appeared to be somewhat useless. Another shiver of guilt ran through him for harboring such thoughts. He reminded himself that Cate was a nurse and was much better informed on such issues. He concluded Cate most likely talked to the other woman because Cate was kind. He smiled at the woman then looked at Cate thinking about the load she'd carried the last few months. Before he could say anything more, a man about his own age walked into the room. He was large with a stocky build.

"Hi, Cate," the man said as he walked up to the woman lying in the bed. "How's my girl Marty doing today?" the man leaned over and kissed the woman on her cheek.

"Oh, Larry," Cate said, "this is a friend of mine, Ronnie Harris."

Ronnie walked over and shook hands. "Nice to meet you Larry," he said then returned to his chair.

"How's your mom today?" Larry asked Cate with concern.

"She's about the same. That's good I suppose," Cate answered.

"How are you doing Larry?" Cate asked. "Larry is an inspector for the city of Allen Park," she added looking at Ronnie.

"Really," Ronnie said. "My dad did the same thing for a while for the City of Melvindale. He was laid off from Ford Motors and worked for the city for about a year. He loved that job. How long have you been doing it?" Ronnie asked.

"I retired from Ford's myself," Larry replied.

"Really," Ronnie said. "What area?"

Larry took a seat at the foot of his wife's bed and the two men exchanged stories and spent a few minutes playing Six Degrees of Separation. After they had identified three or four Kevin

Bacons, Ronnie apologized to Cate for getting caught up in the conversation. She said it was okay, adding it was nice to just sit with her mom.

Ronnie asked Larry if it was easier working in the public sector. Larry answered it was but because the position was appointed, it was subject to the whim of the voters. He added some of the citizens were difficult to deal with and continually told him their taxes paid his salary. Ronnie said his father had voiced the same complaint. What Inspector Larry said next totally surprised Ronnie and Cate.

Episode 30

Ahmed's knees ached from the tile floor. He closed his eyes for the prayers and when he opened them Kamal was gone. A moment ago Kamal had been kneeling next to him but now had vanished. Ahmed realized closing his eyes during the prayers was a stupid mistake. When the prayer ended, Ahmed stood up and looked around hoping to catch sight of Kamal. Ahmed hurried through the crowd without embracing his fellow worshippers. He squeezed past two portly men with full beards by the entrance doors. Ahmed excused himself as he cut between the two men.

He burst through the double doors and hurried down the cement steps. Ahmed paused at the curb and looked down the street. He was about to give up when he turned and saw a young man get into the back of an older model Chevy Suburban. The man appeared to be the same height as Kamal. Ahmed walked in the truck's direction. When he was about thirty yards away, the truck stopped momentarily before turning right. Ahmed tried to get the license plate number. The first three letters were AGB followed by what looked like a seven, a three and a nine. He couldn't be sure because the seven could have been a one. His inability to distinguish the numbers wouldn't sit well with

Charlie, but how many green Suburbans could there be with a license plate that began with AGB.

****

Inspector Larry sat on the hospital bed next to his wife and held her hand in both of his. Ronnie had done the same with Beth. Inspector Larry paid keen attention to his personal grooming, his hair was neatly trimmed and perfectly in place.

"So your dad had the same problem with John Q. Public?" Inspector Larry asked.

He wore gold rimmed bifocals that matched the frames of the family pictures on Marty's night stand. The Inspector had on his official shirt with his badge pinned to his right breast pocket. The shirt was off white, heavily starched with his name printed in dark green letters above the badge. Big Red had worn a similar shirt. Ronnie was amused at Inspector Larry's reference to John Q. Public. His father had used the same expression, but surrounded it with four lettered expletives. Of course, that was before Big Red got religion. Since then, his language never got worse than an occasional dad burned and golly which was pronounced gaully. Big Red stopped cursing at the same time he quit drinking, though his Irish temper still surfaced occasionally. Ronnie found comfort in the outbursts. They were proof some part of his father's larger than life personality survived the conversion.

When his father used the expression gaully, it sounded straight out of Gomer Pyle USMC. The last time Big Red used the term, Ronnie had replied, "shazam Sergeant Carter," in a deep southern accent. His father stated the smart mouthed, Yankeefied impersonation hadn't been appreciated. Ronnie replied Yankeefied wasn't a real word to which Big Red countered by saying any word he used was real, as they were not imaginary. A two hour running debate on linguistics followed.

"Yeah, Larry, some of my dad's stories about how rotten some neighbors could be to each other were unbelievable," Ronnie replied coming out of his day dream.

Episode 30

"Well, you're dad was right. Pardon my French, but some of our fine citizens here in Allen Park are just plain assholes, with a capital a," Larry added with a smile. "Take today for instance. I've got these total moron's over on Keppen Street. But maybe I should watch what I say. I know Cate here is from Melvindale, but hell Ronnie, you might be an Allen Parker for all I know."

"Oh, go right ahead, Larry. I live on Grosse Ile," Ronnie leaned back in his chair and crossed his legs. The position made his right pant leg ride up revealing the white plastic brace.

Larry spotted the brace and asked Ronnie if he'd hurt his leg. Ronnie said the brace was needed because he'd had polio as a child. At the mention of Keppen Street, Cate's cheeks flushed and she sat up with a look of interest.

"So, Larry," Cate interrupted, "you were saying something about some morons on Keppen?"

"You don't want to hear about my work problems," Larry answered.

"No please, Larry go on," Cate pressed. "We grew up in Melvindale, though Ronnie now lives out on Fantasy Island, with all the other Downriver Yuppies."

"Well, one thing I've learned on this job is that there are some truly nasty people in Allen Park. Now I'm not one of those real preachy types, but a little compassion for those less fortunate shouldn't be too much to ask," Larry responded. "I guess I shouldn't be so harsh. There are some really nice people too. People who really look out for each other, but some of the folks on Keppen are really bad."

Marty shifted position and turned her blank stare toward a corner of the room where the ceiling met the wall. Ronnie followed her gaze to see what had attracted the woman's attention. He couldn't see anything and felt foolish. He turned his attention back to Larry and noticed a lock of hair had fallen across Marty's face. Larry tucked it behind her ear to hold it in place. It was a little thing, but was done with such tenderness it made Ronnie think of Beth.

"What do ya mean Larry?" Ronnie asked directing his thoughts back to the present. He knew Cate wanted to ask but was hesitant. He knew she wanted to know anything about Keppen Street.

"Well, you see," Larry said then paused. "Maybe I shouldn't say this."

A look of apprehension crossed Cate's face. It was obvious she was afraid Larry wouldn't elaborate his story. Larry lowered his voice implicating what he was saying was for their ears only. Ronnie was amused at Larry's demeanor thinking it wasn't like what Larry told them would be a state secret. There was just the five of them and for all practical purposes only three of them would comprehend anything he said. Emma and Marty certainly weren't passing any secrets. Ronnie wondered if maybe Cate and Larry were better off believing Marty and Emma could comprehend Larry's story. Maybe it personalized them. Larry lowered his voice to a near whisper. It was as silly as golf announcers on television talking in hushed voices when a golfer approached the putting green.

"But I will," Larry continued looking around to make sure no one had entered the room.

Cate looked relieved that Larry would continue his story.

"Well, there's this guy who lives on Keppen. A kind of reclusive type really. Anyway, his neighbors are just unmerciful. He's about our age, and the neighbors are in their eighties. Anyway, this guy has sort of a hard time, if you know what I mean," Larry looked at Marty's hair to make sure it remained in place.

"What do you mean, hard time?" Cate asked in a whisper, her eyes locked on Larry's face measuring every word.

"Well, he's like, I don't know how to say it, he's like, damn I can't find the right words to describe him. It's like he's on another planet at times, is the best way I can say it," Larry answered struggling to be discrete.

"When you say on another planet," Cate began probing Larry like he was the secret witness in a Congressional Hearing and she was the leading investigator. "What does that mean?" she added.

****

Episode 30

Ahmed hurried to his car. He'd parked in the mosque's back lot and the truck turned on Michigan Avenue, a four lane divided road. There were no major intersections for about a mile, but after that, there were several main roads where the Suburban could turn. If the Suburban turned down a side street, the lower speed limit would delay it enough to pick up the trail. It depended on how quickly Ahmed could get out of the parking lot. The lot was full so his chances were slim. Besides the number of cars, he had to factor in the skills of the drivers. Many would be older Arabs who had learned to drive after immigrating to the States, especially the women who for most of their lives, driving a car had been something beyond their imagination. With such little exposure, their skills were impaired making driving Fairlane Hills like driving in a bumper car pavilion.

Ahmed raced to his car. He started the Pontiac and backed out quickly almost hitting an elderly couple who wandered into his blind spot. The old man yelled something as Ahmed pulled away. At the exit he encountered a woman with her left turn signal on.

"What the hell," he swore in a low voice, "why would anyone try to make a left here!"

****

Larry looked at Cate.

"Well, like I said, it's kind of hard to describe," he finished.

"Does he just sit there, does he stare off into space?" Cate asked with rapid fire enthusiasm. "How would you describe his physical condition?"

"Well, he's rather unkempt; I guess is how to describe him. He doesn't bathe very often and I can't tell you the last time he had a hair cut. That's the odd thing, sometimes I'll show up and it'll be like he's pretty normal. I mean, his hair is still awfully long, but sometimes it'll be clean and his teeth, well they are in bad shape. Same with his clothes, some times they're clean, other times it's like he hasn't changed them in weeks."

"Yeah, yeah," Cate said as she got up and stood next to her mother's bed. She set Emma's hand down gently and walked toward Inspector Larry and pushed a chair up close and sat down. "That tells me a little more. How does he react to questions and other stimuli?"

"Other stimuli? Geez Cate, you seem pretty interested in this hermit on Keppen," Larry answered with a hang dog smile.

"Larry," Ronnie interjected. "Let me ask you a direct question, is this guy's name Eric, by any chance? Because that's where Cate's going with all of this. I'll save us all a little pain here, because Cate is dying to know if that's his name."

"Well, maybe I shouldn't say what his name is," Larry answered.

"Oh, it's for purely medical reasons. Larry, you know Cate is a nurse, so anything you tell her will be kept completely confidential," Ronnie stated with a quick laugh.

"So this is for strictly medical reasons?" Larry asked and winked.

"Hell, no," Ronnie interjected. "Larry, the truth is that if this hermit's name is Eric, and if his last name is Arnold, and if he lives on the second block of Keppen, on the west side of Allen Road, and if it's the third house from the corner, then he was a buddy of mine from high school, and an old flame of Cate's. A flame that burned very hot, I may add. So she's just about peeing in her corduroys to find out if he's the same guy."

"Well, his first name is Eric and yes, his last name is Arnold. But Cate, it looks to me like the spark went out on that flame long ago. To be honest with you, like I said before, sometimes he's there and sometimes there are a few aces missing from the deck."

"So tell me more, Larry," Cate continued. She was leaning forward in the chair with her legs crossed and her chin resting in her right hand. She didn't intend to let any detail pass her by.

"Well, it's like this. The old bag neighbors around him," Larry hesitated a moment then looked at Emma to make sure his comment hadn't caused offense. When no emotion registered on her face, Larry continued with his story. "The old bag

Episode 30

neighbors are really nasty to him. Now mind you, he doesn't cut the lawn regularly so I stop occasionally and remind him. And the leaves are never raked when they need to be. That's why I was there today. His leaves were blowing on the neighbor's lawn. There isn't an ordinance about raking leaves. It's not like keeping the lawn mowed where you can measure the length of the grass. Anyway, the old bitty neighbors were all upset about the leaves. Mostly they complain because they have nothing else to bitch about," Larry looked at Emma and Marty again.

"Sorry about my language. I have a lot on my mind lately and I just look at those neighbors of his and think, don't you have anything better to do than get on this man's case about some stupid leaves. I mean, he's a nice enough guy when he's with it and he really doesn't cause any problems even when he's not with it. The man's sick, know what I mean?" Larry patted Marty's hand.

"When you say with it," Cate asked, "what does that mean?"

"And please, Larry, use medical terms where possible," Ronnie added with a smile. He had not intended the comment to come off as a smart ass remark.

"Medical terms?" Larry asked a little befuddled.

"Pay no attention to him Larry," Cate answered. "He's just a smart ass. Some people never change."

****

After what seemed an eternity, the woman completed her turn. Ahmed made a quick right and headed for Michigan Avenue. He slowed, then turned his head left to check for oncoming traffic. Seeing the road was clear, Ahmed floored the Grand AM. The tires squealed as he turned onto the divided avenue.

Ahmed could see almost a mile ahead. There was no sign of the Suburban so he started checking the side streets. It was a slim hope at best, but it was the only one that remained. He had nearly given up as he pulled up to the corner at Cleveland Street, the last side street before Greenfield Road. If the Suburban turned at Greenfield, there was little chance of picking up the trail. Ahmed couldn't believe his luck. In the middle of the second block he saw a green truck parked on the right side of the street. Ahmed pulled to the curb and parked behind a blue Dodge. Gathering his thoughts, he considered his options if he located the Suburban.

****

"Medical terms?" Larry repeated, "You mean like is he on drugs or something?"

"No, just tell me how he acts, what he says. Does he recognize you, anything like that will help," Cate answered.

"Help you what?" Larry asked.

"Help me to understand what happened to him. At one time, Eric was brilliant. He could have done anything he wanted to. He came from some awful circumstances and I probably didn't help in that regard. But that's a different story; that happened a long time ago. Maybe there's something I can do now to remedy some of it. So whatever you can tell me will help."

"Well, like I said, sometimes he's with it, sometimes he's not. You're going to laugh at this, but sometimes we have lunch together," Larry replied.

"Lunch?" Cate replied and looked over at Ronnie who shrugged his shoulders.

"Yeah, I know it's kind of the dumbest thing you probably ever heard. But one day, I was at Celia's sub shop. You know over on Allen?" Larry looked toward Ronnie.

"Yeah," Ronnie replied, "great Philly Cheese Steaks. I've had occasion to explore the menus of most places Downriver. Not many I've missed. Being married to Beth, I think I've been inside every place that serves food Downriver. Well, I take that back, Kola's kitchen in Riverview might be the exception. I didn't exactly eat there."

"Is that the place that serves muskrat and all that wild stuff?" Larry inquired with interest.

"The one and the same," Ronnie answered.

Episode 30

"So, what about Celia's?" Cate asked.

"Oh, yeah, Celia's," Larry responded but wanted to continue the wild game topic.

"Got kind of side tracked there thinking about eating muskrat," he continued. "People really eat that stuff you know, what else do they serve there? Have you ever been in the place?" Larry asked.

"Yeah, I've been there. But only once, just after my wife died. They supposedly have great perch dinners. I bought a carry out," Ronnie answered, leaning back in his chair.

"So, how were they?" Larry asked, mentally kicking himself for not finishing his story.

"Oh, they were okay, but I like the fish at Lloyd's better. That's the little bar and grill on the Island," Ronnie answered.

"Yeah, I went there once. Marty has a childhood friend who lived out on the Island. We had the perch dinner there one Friday before bowling. They were good, but I have to admit, I like Fergie's better," Larry replied.

"Oh, yeah, Fergie's, the place over in Lincoln Park. You're right, they're good. But I think it was better before they sold it. We used to go there every year on Good Friday. You know, Fergie opened another place in Gibraltar," Ronnie answered.

"I didn't know that. When did they do that?" Larry asked then glanced at Cate.

"Hey, earth to Larry and Ronnie," Cate interjected, "can we focus here for a minute? I want to know about Celia's and lunch with Eric."

"Yeah, Celia's has great Philly Cheese steaks," Ronnie said.

"You guys are something. Can you please just tell me more about Eric?" Cate begged with exasperation.

"Oh, yeah," Larry said grinning, "sorry, we kind of lost track there. Anyway, I picked up Eric's mower one day last summer and took it in to have it repaired. It wouldn't run and the neighbors were complaining. So I dropped it at Marv's Mower next to Celia's. You know the place Ronnie?" Larry realized his mistake and jumped back to his story.

"Short story," Larry continued, looking at Cate, "I got a sub for Eric. Guess he'd stop at Celia's occasionally when his mind was right. Celia mentioned it when I was ordering lunch for Marv and me. I took it to him, Eric that is. Well, I took one to Marv too, but the ones I took to Marv's we ate in the shop," Larry realized he was drifting and refocused his story, "Anyway we sat on his back porch, Eric's that is, not Marv's because Marv really doesn't have a back porch. Anyway Eric, didn't say anything, but I knew he was pleased to have it. He ate the sub, and then it became sort of a regular thing. He still never says much, but you can tell from his eyes and how he's taken care of himself, if he's with us or in outer space. That's really about all there is to tell. I was there today because of the leaves. He wasn't doing too good. I told the old bag next door that with the leaves there's not much I can really do. Then she starts in with how she pays my salary and she knows the mayor. Hell, they all know the freakin' mayor; they're usually quick to point that one out. Sorry for the freakin' part, just sort of slipped out. Anyway, voting for the mayor and knowing him, are two different things. And shit, knowing him and understanding him, are another two completely, entirely different things. The mayor that is, not Eric, though you could say the same about him. Sorry about the language thing again."

"Well, saying shit isn't really swearing. Shit is really a shortened version of the Saxon word shite, which means excrement. It dates back to England when the Norman French conquered England, in 1066 or there about. Indigenous languages were considered inferior to Norman French, especially any Saxon words. Same with the F word. It originally meant plowing and planting the fields. It was a Saxon word, so to the Norman French, it was considered too low to use. The term was then generalized to husbandry then, to human intercourse. And not the verbal kind. Right Cate?" Ronnie asked.

****

Episode 30

Ahmed decided to drive past the Suburban and park on the next block. From there, he could look out his rear view mirror to watch the house. Ahmed knew it was risky. There would be lookouts spread around the neighborhood. As he drove by, he could verify the Suburban's license plate number. He needed something for Charlie and the address of the safe house would be valuable information.

Ahmed drove slowly up the street. He didn't see any sentries but knew they were there someplace. He read the street number over the porch then looked away again hoping none of the look outs had spotted him. If they did, he wouldn't know until it was too late. Ahmed continued driving, found a spot a third of the way down the next block and pulled over. He put the car in park but left the engine running. Ahmed opened the glove box and took out a road map.

Opening the map, he laid it against the steering wheel. On the back was a detailed street map of Fairlane Hills which he studied to get an idea of his position. He was familiar with the neighborhoods, but wanted to identify alternatives escape routes. Studying the map, Ahmed kept his right hand on the gear shift knob and his left on the steering wheel. He turned the front wheels slightly to allow a quick get away. Leaving nothing to chance, Ahmed knew the level of detail and preparedness of his adversaries. His only hope was to match them.

After thirty minutes, he knew time was drawing short. He couldn't stay much longer without drawing attention. He decided to wait a few more minutes. If nothing happened, he'd go home, change his clothes and drive to the New Lebanon Bakery. Folding the map, Ahmed glanced into the rear view mirror.

"Jackpot!" he said in a muffled voice.

****

"Right,' Cate answered. Norman French and Saxon languages; Cate wondered if she was in a game of Trivial Pursuit with the cognitively impaired.

"Cate was our class valedictorian, but I didn't realize she also was an expert in mid evil linguistics. Thought I might have had you there, Cate," Ronnie added.

"I wasn't agreeing with your analysis of the origin of the F word, though I believe you're right. I was agreeing with Larry's assessment of Eric," Cate said leaning back in her chair and biting her lower lip.

Ronnie remembered her lip biting habit from their Calculus class. It meant she was close to solving a problem no one else could solve.

"So Larry is right about what?" Ronnie asked with a chuckle, "That Eric is a recluse or that he loves Philly cheese steaks?"

"Morons," Cate said with chagrin, "I've got morons on my team. Larry's right about knowing Eric is not necessarily understanding him."

"Ahhh," Ronnie responded, "it appearth that the light from yonder window still burnith from a candle, or dare I say torch, that may have flickerith a few times low these many years, but shall never fade, nor be extinguished completely. Romeo and Juliet, act two, scene one."

Cate laughed, "You may know a little something, and the operative word here is little, about medieval linguistics but you do not know Shakespeare. Anyway, we better get going. We're supposed to meet Kathy and Jess for the parade.

"Larry, thanks for the information about Eric. See you tomorrow. Take good care of Marty," Cate walked over and kissed her mother on the forehead. "I'll see you tomorrow mom. I have to work Sunday. Frank will come then."

Ronnie thought he saw a glimmer of recognition in the old woman's eyes. Maybe those Europeans don't know everything, he said to himself. Hell, he added, maybe nobody really knows anything about anything. After hearing about Inspector Larry's shared Cheese steaks with Eric, maybe there was still a spark in Emma and Marty behind those drawn faces; whether that was a blessing or a curse was uncertain. Ronnie walked over to Emma and said goodbye.

Episode 30

"Nice meeting you, Inspector," Ronnie said extending his hand.

"Nice meeting you, too Ron. Hey by the way, next time pick us up some muskrat to go," Larry said with a down turned smile.

"Barb BQ'd or deep fried?" Ronnie asked with a laugh.

"Oh, Barb BQ'd of course, with extra sauce on the side," Larry answered.

"Extra sauce it is," Ronnie added with a wistful look.

It was the expression Beth used when he'd asked if she wanted carry out from Zukin's Rib Shack. She would eat two full slabs by herself. He'd seen her do it more than once. Extra sauce was a standing joke from an adventure they had shared as teenagers. At Beth's insistence, they'd gone to an art movie documenting strange customs around the world. The movie included a scene of nomadic tribal women castrating reindeer in the tundra using their teeth. The testicles were gathered and cooked over an open fire as part of a religious feast. At the time, such a graphic display had been shocking. Beth's knowledge about the movie was a mystery. He had reluctantly agreed to take her there after she'd called him a pussy for his reluctance. It was against his better judgment, but there was no negotiating with Beth when she set her mind.

During the scene, she'd leaned over and said, hmmm, barbecued with extra sauce on the side. They'd laughed hysterically, which drew stares and a flurry of shushing from the other patrons. After the movie they'd stopped at a Chinese restaurant near the art theatre where she ordered ribs. The waiter asked in broken English how she wanted them cooked. She answered barbecued with extra sauce on the side. They both began laughing. Thinking they were laughing at his English, the waiter had asked them to leave. Beth sensed his mistaken reaction and told the waiter, with great patience, about the reindeer scene. Though outspoken, Cate was very sensitive about people's feelings.

"Extra sauce on the side," Ronnie repeated softly as they left Emma's room. The expression summed up his life with Beth. When they went to A&W's for burgers, it was always extra everything on the burgers and extra ketchup on the side for the fries. Life was like that with her; extra everything.

Episode 31

Ahmed stared into the side view mirror. The warning printed along the bottom cautioned objects may be closer than they appeared. He wished the object he was looking at was further than it appeared. The tall Arab was dressed in khakis and wore an oversized blue wind breaker to conceal the Uzi sub machine gun Ahmed knew was strapped to the man's chest. The sentry had emerged from a two family flat not far from the Suburban. Ahmed studied the other houses searching for other look outs.

To get a better view, he turned in his seat. Ahmed placed the map on the passenger seat and pretended to study it. He had a clear view of the house through the rear window. Such tight security would not be expended for someone like Kamal. Someone more important was in the house. His suspicions were confirmed when two men exited the building. They hesitated on the large porch checking the street in both directions. Satisfied, they hurried down the steps and climbed into the Suburban. The tall guard opened the front passenger's door and got in just before the driver pulled away from the curb. Ahmed did not recognize the shorter man but there was no mistaking the other man. It was the ferret faced Mahmood.

Afraid that he'd be recognized, Ahmed turned forward. He slouched and looked into the side view mirror. He didn't have a good view, so he reached up and adjusted the rear view mirror hanging from the windshield. His eyes flittered between the two mirrors as the Chevy headed his way.

****

Ronnie and Cate walked from the nursing home in silence. Inspector Larry's comment about extra sauce cast a pall of melancholy over Ronnie. He'd looked forward to the parade and game and had a surprise planned for afterwards. Now, he wondered if he would be able to enjoy the evening. When he planned the outing, he thought it might be difficult to watch the floats without Beth. He'd become maudlin a couple of times the previous night at the Snake Dance and hoped tonight would be easier. Their first real date had been when Beth asked him to the Sadie Hawkins Dance in September 1965. Sadie's was in early fall to allow the girls to ask oft timid boys out first. The boys were expected to reciprocate and ask the girl to Homecoming.

Ronnie's mind drifted back to their first date. They wore paisley shirts with button down collars and matching suspenders. The shirts were brown with gold and black paisleys. They also wore matching beige corduroys. Seeing Cate's corduroys earlier had sent a small smile across his face. After Larry's comment, Ronnie's head had been a swirl of bitter sweet memories about being seventeen and in love.

Maybe it was all just hormonal, Ronnie reflected. It was a silly notion, but he wondered if the scientist who invented Viagra had gotten the idea after going back to his high school Homecoming. His friends who'd used the little blue pills said the psychological side was still missing. It seemed fitting, there were certain joys of youth that could never be captured and packaged in bubble wrapped, foil strips. At least not until a formula was designed to make a person laugh twenty times an hour, find pleasure in hearing the same song repeatedly and able to eat onion rings at

Episode 31

three in the morning. Even then, the magic would still be missing. There was no way to chemically erase the indelible marks etched onto a fifty year old's soul; all the shortcomings, secrets and separations.

Cate was lost in her own thoughts. Larry's revelations about Eric left her with overwhelming mind spins. Eric's times of lucidity narrowed the medical options to either a brain tumor or paranoid schizophrenia. If it was a brain tumor, Eric would have more consistent behaviors. Cate settled on schizophrenia. Unbelievable, she said to herself, you haven't seen Eric in over thirty years, yet here you are figuring it all out based on the fact that he likes to eat Philly cheese steaks on his back porch in silence. Cate was still mulling over Eric's behavior as she opened the door to the Explorer.

Ronnie put the key into the ignition, then looked over at her. "Ted Curtis?" he asked with a soft laugh.

****

The Suburban stopped just behind the Grand AM. Ahmed's heart felt like it was going to pound out of his chest. He slid his foot near the break and kept his hand on the gear shift knob. He just knew when the Suburban pulled next to him the windows would go down and a burst of gun fire would erupt from the monstrous Chevy. The Uzis would expel a blur of fire and smoke until his body was ripped apart by a flurry of bullets. Ahmed considered putting the Grand AM in gear and flooring it. He fought desperately to control his emotions.

Double checking the door locks, Ahmed took two deep breaths and looked in the side view mirror. The Suburban started moving toward him again. When it was a car length away, his cell phone rang. He was sure it was the Ferret. Ahmed reached into his pocket for the phone. As the Suburban pulled even, Ahmed knew all opportunity for escape was over. As his cell phone continued to ring, he looked frantically at the passenger door and pushed the unlock button with his foot. Ahmed was about to bolt from the car when he noticed Stacey's cell number flashing in the viewing screen. Ahmed wondered if by some cruel joke he was being given one last word with her before he was executed by the tall body guard. Ahmed flipped open the phone.

"Stacey," he said in a panicky voice.

****

"Ted Curtis?" Cate replied quizzically.

"Ted Curtis," Ronnie replied.

Cate wrinkled her brow in a questioning gesture. Examining her high school friend, she realized he'd become a fifty-five year old man. The last time she'd seen Ronnie his hair hadn't been as silver. He didn't have a beer belly and his skin wasn't weathered from working outdoors so he looked well kept for a fifty-five year old, but that's what he was. A fifty year old man who'd raised two sons, worked a full career and lost the love of his life. Ronnie noticed Cate was staring at him.

She was suddenly curious about Eric's appearance. He had been extremely handsome in high school with Hollywood good looks. He had a squared jaw and thick dark hair. With his high cheekbones and full lips he resembled a model in a Ralph Lauren advertisement she'd seen recently. Eric had worn braces in junior high and which gave him a killer smile. It saddened her to think a smile which had sent her reeling a lifetime ago, had been lost.

"Ted Curtis," Ronnie repeated, jarring Cate from her daydream.

****

As Ahmed whispered Stacey's name, the Suburban rolled past. It hadn't stopped and the tall body guard hadn't jumped out and opened fire. The truck had just continued down the street and stopped at the stop sign. Ahmed was perplexed about

Episode 31

his next move. He considered following the Suburban. Ahmed glanced into the rear view mirror while he contemplated his next move and what to say to Stacey. Two more men came out of the house and walked down the steps. One of the men was Kamal.

"Ahmed, what's wrong?" Stacey asked in a concerned voice.

"Oh, nothing," he answered, his voice sounding more controlled than it was. Ahmed had to get off the phone quickly.

"I'm on the road and some jerk just cut me off," Ahmed added. It was one of the things he learned early on; when you must lie, insert a bit of the truth.

"Be careful, you shouldn't drive and talk at the same time. It's dangerous," she answered.

"Okay," Ahmed replied keeping his eyes on the rear view mirror. Kamal and the other man walked in the opposite direction and got into a Dodge Neon.

"I was just getting ready to call you. I got called into work tonight. Can I call you later?

"Sure, call me later when you're not driving," she answered.

"Okay," he replied.

"Later," Stacey said.

"Later," Ahmed answered as the Neon pulled away from the curb.

****

"Ted Curtis," Cate answered with a smile. "What the hell does Ted Curtis have to do with anything?"

"He was your date for Homecoming," Ronnie answered.

"Jesus, I thought Kathy had a memory. You two should be on Jeopardy, you know that."

"Well, I could win if the categories were, let's see, something like, umm, Cardinal Red or Mrs. Haley's Comets or let's see, Abdon's Apples," Ronnie replied as he drove from the parking lot.

Cate began laughing. Cardinal Red referred to their school colors; the last two were school faculty members. Mrs. Haley was a certifiable lunatic who taught Civics. She was from Mississippi and gave meaning to the term crazed hillbilly. Numerous complaints were filed against her over the years but somehow Crazy Haley remained in the class room for forty years.

Bill Abdon, known as Apple Bill, was the assistant principal. He was the school's disciplinarian who also owned an apple orchard. His looks and demeanor were befitting of both occupations. An Ichabod Crane look alike, Apple Bill was the enforcer.

"How do you think of this stuff, Ronnie?" Cate had laughed so hard she had to wipe tears from her cheeks. "Damn, you made me smudge my eyeliner," she added.

"Sorry, Cate," Ronnie stifled a laugh, "in the future I'll try to be more droll."

"Please, it's going to be a long night, and I only have so many laughs. Don't want to use them all up at once you know."

"It still begs the question. Why Ted Curtis?"

"Well, why not Ted Curtis," she answered with a hint of annoyance.

"You mean besides the fact that he was a total psycho?"

"Well, that's not very nice. You're a psycho yourself," Cate added gazing out the passenger window. They'd just passed the Baskin Robbins. She thought about Eric's love of Rocky Road double dipped cones. They'd stopped there frequently during their magic summer.

"Yeah, true enough, but I was a fun psycho, still am I hope. Anyway, Curtis was a scary psycho."

"No, he was just a little misunderstood, that's all."

"Yeah, well so was Norman Bates," Ronnie answered with a laugh, "and at least good ol' Norman was good looking in a weird sort of way."

"Hey, Curtis was good looking."

"Dude, sorry, didn't mean to step on any toes," Ronnie replied hoping his character assassination of Ted Curtis hadn't put a damper on the evening.

"Your point is?" Cate asked.

Episode 31

"Well, you and Eric obviously had feelings for each other. But comes time for Homecoming and you go with TC?" Ronnie asked.

"TC, I forgot about that," Cate said with a smile.

"Yeah, stood for Totally Crazy," the words shot out of Ronnie's mouth before he could get them back.

"God, Ronnie, I didn't know you disliked him so much. What gives?"

"Oh, he did some stuff to Beth when we weren't going together. It was just before Beth started going with Bobbie."

"And you Scorpios never forget do you?"

"No, we're like terrapins"

"Like terrapins?"

"Yeah, we don't let go 'till it thunders."

"Don't get it?"

"It's an old hillbilly saying. If a terrapin bites you, he won't let go 'till it thunders, my dad says that all the time."

"Seems to me you're getting to be more like Big Red each passing day."

"Geez, Cate you know how to hit below the belt. That was Beth's biggest fear you know; that I'd turn into my dad as I got older. Guess you just confirmed her prognostication. She'd be pleased there's still someone down here busting my chops on Homecoming night. But don't try to change the focus. You were going to solve one of the biggest mysteries of 1966."

"Oh you mean who killed Jimmy Hoffa?"

"That was the 70s; you know that, you're just playing dumb."

"Maybe I'm not playing."

"Yeah, right, Ms. Valedictorian, Ms. Honor Society, and Ms. 1580 on her SAT."

"Now you sound jealous. Maybe it's not TC you're still mad at, maybe it's Bobbie."

Cate knew she had also struck a nerve. Ronnie was dumbfounded; this was not going as he had imagined. He needed to get some levity back into their conversation. Maybe she was right in her assessment about astrological signs. Though he never believed in them, Beth read their horoscopes out loud to him each month when her Vanity Fair arrived. It was one more little thing he missed.

"You really believe in that horoscope stuff, that surprises me?" Ronnie said changing the subject.

"No, I don't believe in them. If I didn't think that you'd take it so hard, I would have added dumb ass, but it appears I've roughed you up enough for one night," Cate felt relieved he hadn't taken her comment to heart. "Anyway, I have a feeling that's how Beth would have talked to you."

"Boy, I needed that," Ronnie said with a smile, "I haven't been kicked in the gonads by a female in two years."

"Hey, anytime I can be of help, let me know," Cate smiled as she looked out the passenger's window.

"Anyway, about Ted Curtis? Yeah, yeah, I know, I'm obsessive. I just can't let some things go. This has bugged me for over thirty years, you know."

Cate laughed at his persistence.

"So, let me see if I understand this, you've spent thirty years of your life wondering why I went to the Homecoming with Ted Curtis rather than Eric Arnold?"

"Well, I have wondered about a few other things along the way. Like why do we call it the 1967 Homecoming when it occurred in fall of 1966. And oh yeah, did Oswald act alone or was there a second shooter on the grassy knoll? And oh, yeah, here's another one, who really shot J.R., and did Paul McCartney really die before Abbey Road?" Ronnie replied.

Cate started laughing. They were about a mile from Keppen Street. Ronnie considered asking Cate if she wanted to drive by Eric's house but wasn't sure if she'd think he was being a smart ass again.

"Okay, but if I tell you the why about TC, I may have to kill you later," Cate added teasingly.

"In that case, just tell me if you think McCartney is really dead. It sounds like the safer option."

"Well, I do think it was really Paul McCartney who played with Wings. But the TC thing is really less of a mystery. I was

Episode 31

going to ask Eric to Sadie's but I heard Helen was going to ask him. They lived across the street from each other and I thought she kind of had first dibs."

"First dibs, I haven't heard that one in a while. First dibs, I'll have to hang onto that. I may even have to use it tonight if you don't mind."

"You really are obsessive compulsive aren't you," Cate laughed. "Here I settle this supposedly grand mystery that's plagued your life, and you obsess on my resurrection of the term first dibs."

Ronnie found her last dig funny.

"Oh, Beth would have loved that one, too. Anyway, so why did you let Helen get in first dibs."

"Because it was Helen Solenich. I mean come on, how do you compete with that?"

"Fishing are we, Cate?"

"Fishing, what do you mean?"

"Like in, fishing for compliments."

"I don't get it."

"Yeah Cate, like Helen or any other girl in our class was competition for you."

"What, I still don't understand?"

"Like you didn't know every guy in the class was totally hot for you. Don't get me wrong, Helen was knock down, drop dead gorgeous, but you didn't take a back seat to her."

"Well, she got elected Homecoming Queen, not me, so that must mean something."

"All it means is you were thought of as a little aloof, that's all. Helen was a sweet heart. Everyone thought you were just as good looking, though maybe a little too mysterious. Of course the intelligence factor only added to the attraction. Hell Cate, we were all hot for you. But most of us just figured Eric was the only one at your level."

"Really?"

"Come on Cate, like you didn't know?"

"I had no idea, really," Cate answered in a sincere voice.

"All right, I probably shouldn't tell you this story but I will," Ronnie replied. They were almost to Keppen Street, Ronnie thought again about asking her about a drive by Eric's house but decided against it.

"Okay RJ, tell me the story," Cate replied and rolled her eyes.

"RJ, what's that supposed to mean?" Ronnie asked looking over at Cate.

"Well, you called Ted Curtis, TC, which I thought was because those are his initials but then you so cruelly stated it stood for Totally Crazy. Well, RJ stands for Red Junior," Cate added with another laugh. "Cause I know you're going to tell me this story whether I want to hear it or not."

****

Ahmed had another decision to make. Whether to go home, change clothes and head to the New Lebanon Bakery or follow the Neon. Following the Neon was less risky than following Mahmood and might provide valuable information. Ahmed compromised, he'd follow the Neon for a short time but keep a good distance. Ahmed pulled away from the curb, drove to the stop sign and looked into his rear view mirror. The Neon turned right; heading toward west Fairlane Hills.

Ahmed decided to drive back to Michigan Avenue. After a few minutes his hunch paid off, the Neon was less than a mile ahead. Ahmed slipped behind a silver Saturn and kept pace, never letting the Neon out of his sight.

The Neon turn right on Monroe Street. Ahmed was familiar with the neighborhood from his soccer games. When it stopped on Hillbury Street, Ahmed pulled over and watched Kamal walk up the driveway. A toddler came down the drive and jumped into his arms. The woman he'd seen Kamal with at the restaurant walked toward the Dodge and embraced Kamal. From all appearances, Kamal was just another family man.

"Appearances can be deceiving," Ahmed said aloud.

****

Episode 31

"Geez, Cate" Ronnie said in feigned hurt, "now that was really unnecessary. Dude, that was just mean."

"Why," Cate replied, "your dad's a great guy."

"Yeah, I know, and I love him to death, but nobody wants to hear that. I mean my dad's a little over the top some times."

"Your point is?" Cate replied with a wry smile.

"Man, you are cruel. I don't think I'm going to tell you the story," Ronnie answered with more feigned hurt. They were almost to Keppen Street. At the last second he put on his turn signal, changed lanes abruptly then turned left.

"Where are we going?" Cate asked with surprise.

"Where do you think? We'll cruise the Arnold plantation to see how it looks since the North won the war and all the slaves have been set free," Ronnie added with a laugh.

"That's a hell of a thing to say," Cate replied.

"Hey, they had a housekeeper. How many people did you know growing up have a house keeper? Besides, Eric's mom could have been Scarlet O'Hara if she'd had been a brunette instead of a red head. She was from Alabama you know," Ronnie slowed the Explorer to a near crawl.

"She was also manic depressive, like Maureen O'Hara," Ronnie added. "Too bad it couldn't be treated back then like it is today. Do you think that's what is wrong with Eric, think he's manic depressive like his mom? He never acted bipolar to my knowledge. My cousin was bi polar. Eric never seemed to have those big mood swings like my cousin."

They were a near Eric's house when Cate answered.

"No, I think he's a paranoid schizophrenic, that seems to fit better. Believe me I know about being manic depressive. Well, I know more about the depressive portion. Lately I've managed to dodge the manic part. Takes more energy than I have," Cate answered with a nervous laugh.

"There's first dibs Helen's house. As I recall, Helen didn't go to homecoming with Eric, so what happened to the dibs?" Ronnie asked looking across the street. Tension was showing in Cate's face and he wasn't sure if the drive by had been a good idea.

"Well, the whole story is, Helen and Doug Simmons broke up when Doug went away to college. I heard she was going to ask Eric, so I asked TC."

"Totally Crazy, you mean?" Ronnie interrupted.

"You're the worst Ronnie Eugene. You're the one who wanted to hear this story, so let me finish."

"Yeah, but no more middle names, it creeps me out."

"Geez, you can be exasperating."

"Wow, Beth used the same word sometimes. That sort of creeps me out too, that you used her exact expression."

"I'm beginning to think everything creeps you out."

"Well, not every thing, mostly just middle names, and other terms Beth would use to tell me how annoying I could be," Ronnie answered with a laugh.

"This is just like high school, except we're fifty-five instead of seventeen," Cate said softly. "I can't believe I'm doing this."

"Well, you seem to be holding up pretty good. I wondered for a minute there, if bringing you here was a good idea."

"Well, I'm nervous as hell but I'm glad you did. I've been dying to come by this place ever since I moved back, but needed a brave pill. Thanks."

"No problem. There's Wes's house up ahead. You were the topic of many conversations in that basement between pool games and walking to Marino's Bakery for pizza."

Ronnie pulled over in front of Wes's house.

"Oh, really?"

"Yeah, like you didn't know. Don't go getting too big of a head, lots of girls made that hit parade," Ronnie added. "Sometimes I think I'd give about anything to be seventeen again and shooting pool in Wes's basement. Bobbie was always the funniest, though there were enough clowns down there to populate three or four circuses," Ronnie added with a pause. "I heard Eric took that one bad, when Wes died in California."

"Yeah, Kathy told me about that years ago, just after it happened."

Episode 31

"That was such a strange thing. I never really understood exactly how all that happened. Somehow he ended up married to Helen and then they moved to California. I think that whole thing came about from the ten year class reunion," Ronnie said looking at Wes's house again.

"I didn't make that reunion. I always wondered what happened," Cate replied not taking her eyes off Eric's house.

"I don't know all the details, I bumped into Wes just after the reunion. Beth and I were getting ready to move to Ohio. I was in a Kroger store the night before we were leaving. Wes walked in as I was walking out. He was married to a girl named Julie. He asked about Beth and I told him I'd been transferred and we were moving to Ohio. He said he had been transferred to California and he was leaving for L.A. the next day. We both laughed at the coincidence. I asked if Julie was excited and he said she wasn't going. I was shocked when he said Helen was going with him. Then I remembered they'd spent most of the evening together at that reunion. Go figure."

"So was Helen single then?"

"No, she was married to Doug. Anyway, two years later Wes dies in a freak car accident. Think that may have been the beginning of Eric's downfall. They were like Bobbie and me, friends from four years old. Wes was at a party after a softball game. He had his 'Vette for sale and some guy wanted to take it for a test drive. The guy drove it off a cliff into a canyon with Wes in the passenger's seat. The driver broke his legs and Wes ends up dead; another go figure."

"It may have been the straw that broke the camels back, but Eric's downfall began long before that," Cate replied.

"So what'ya think, how about we head back? Kathy's probably waiting on us. We don't want to miss seeing Mayor Dan in that convertible," Ronnie added, "and I have to meet my ex brother in law. If I'm late, he'll give me the business. Denny's one of those prompt people."

****

Kamal said something to the driver of the Neon then walked toward the house. Ahmed decided to follow the Neon though there wasn't much time. He still had to go back to his flat, change clothes and get to the New Lebanon Bakery.

Ahmed found himself on Michigan Ave again. When he passed Schaefer Road, Ahmed realized he would be in Detroit momentarily. Ahmed was about a half mile behind the Neon when it caught the light at Junction. He pulled over and looked around. This was not an area to be in after dark. To his right he saw a pawn shop with bars over the windows. The owner was closing his shop and was pulling a metal gate across the door. On the corner, a wino sat outside a party store pandering customers, mostly factory workers on their way home from shifts at the Ford Rouge Plant. Two men walked out of the party store with bottles of malt liquor tucked into brown paper bags. The men threw some coins at the panderer and walked away.

When the light changed, the Neon turned right. Ahmed glanced at his watch, he was cutting it close. He waited for a few seconds and then eased up to the traffic light. Looking right, he could see the Neon at the end of the block and continued his pursuit. Though the Neon made several turns, Ahmed remained patient.

The destination turned out to be a dilapidated house in a run down neighborhood in southwest Detroit. The houses were little more than shacks with tiny, weed choked yards. Ahmed examined the houses and noted most hadn't seen a coat of paint in decades. They were stained a faint shade of orange from the fall out of the factories surrounding the neighborhood. Some houses had fake brick siding with tarred backing visible where the siding had peeled and hung loose in large strips. Ahmed noticed the air smelled of sulfur and assumed he was near the Mobil refinery.

He watched the Neon turn into a drive way. Two heavily tattooed Hispanic teenagers wearing baggy jeans, that fell several inches below their waist, appeared out of nowhere. Ahmed

Episode 31

hoped they weren't sizing up his Grand AM. After a few minutes, he decided to head back home.

****

"So, what's the story you were about to tell me before we took the side trip down Keppen?" Cate asked reaching into her purse. She pulled out a pack of Big Red Cinnamon Gum. "Want a piece? The brand is kind of prophetic, don't you think?"

"Thanks, but no. I'm a Juicy Fruit kind of guy," he answered.

"Juicy Fruit!" Cate exclaimed. "Who the hell still chews Juicy Fruit?"

"Just us idiots who never grew up. Yeah, I know, it's juvenile but I still love it now and again."

"So go on with the story."

"Well, it's nothing really. Just another little tidbit to boost your already inflated ego," Ronnie jibed.

"Hey, I need all the help I can get. You can't start tell then not say what it is."

"All right," Ronnie answered, "though I'll probably regret it."

They were back on Allen Road and had just passed the Thunderbowl. Cate looked over at Celia's Sub Shop. "Maybe we should go there tonight and have subs after the game. What'ya think?"

"I think, you think Eric might stroll in. Could happen, not likely but possible. Anyway, I have something else planned. You'll like it, I promise," Ronnie replied pulling out a pack of Juicy Fruit.

"You want me to unwrap that for you, while you drive?" Cate asked.

"Sure," Ronnie replied, "remember when each piece had it's own paper wrapper?"

"No," Cate answered reaching over and plopping the stick in Ronnie's mouth. "But I bet Kathy will. Did you know she knows which pages of our senior year book her pictures are on?"

"Doesn't everyone?" Ronnie asked jokingly.

The gum was sticky and caught in his dental work. He couldn't remember the last time he'd actually chewed gum, now and again was really never and again. He'd forgotten how it tangled in his bridge.

"So, am I going to get to hear this story?" Cate asked. She popped her gum twice on purpose and laughed heartedly.

"Okay, here it is, but again, it's really a nothing story. A few years ago, maybe five, I'm not sure. Anyway, Beth and I were at the Hudson's store in Southland. It's Marshall Fields now, you know. How sad is that? Seems like Detroit can never hang on to the things that make it special. Do you ever think about that?"

"I'm beginning to think you may need Ritalin from the way you're telling this story," Cate replied.

"Ouch, you are a lot crueler than I remembered. You just want me to go on because you know this will feed your ego. Anyway, we're in the Home Furnishing Department, at the register waiting 'cause this sales woman has to re-ring up our entire order, and it was a big order."

"Why did she have to do that?"

"Well, Beth overheard one of the sales people say that a sale was starting the next day. She demanded the sale price, or she threatened to cancel the order and come back the next day."

"Smart girl," Cate popped the gum again.

"I forgot you did that," Ronnie said with a smile, "it always seemed out of place for the Valedictorian to pop gum. Sort of makes you out to be some kind of Valley Girl Valedictorian."

"Yeah, well I did a lot of stuff not very valedictorian like after I left here."

"Anyway Joey Miotti walks up while I'm standing there. You remember Joey? A little skinny guy, dark hair, think he had asthma or something."

"This is the short version of the story?" Cate interjected.

"I'll ignore that and continue, if I may, Ms. Cassadea. Anyway, Beth had wandered off to look at something while the sales woman was ringing up our stuff for the second time. So Miotti comes up, he's with his life partner, and they're picking out fur-

Episode 31

nishings. Miotti recognizes me and starts a conversation. The first thing he asks is if I've ever heard what ever happened to Cate Cassadea. I tell him the last I heard you were living somewhere in bum fuck Indiana but that's about all I know. Then he replies that he thinks about you occasionally. Then his boyfriend starts laughing. Tony says it's been nice talking and to take care and all of that happy horses shit and if I ever see you to say hello, then walks away."

"Yeah," Cate asked, "then what happens?"

"Well, Beth walks back and asks if that was Joey Miotti. I tell her, it was, and she asks what he had to say. I tell her that he wanted to know if I knew what ever happened to you. Then, Beth says very disgustedly, "Damn, that Cate Cassadea. She even got the gay ones."

Cate popped her gum twice as she looked out the passenger window.

"Well, if nothing else, this night has been an ego boost. Which is good, I needed one," Cate replied.

They were almost to Cate's mother's house. As they approached the bungalow, they could see Kathy and Jess sitting on the porch.

****

Twenty minutes later Ahmed was at his flat. After changing clothes he walked out on the balcony to grab a smoke. Lighting a Marlboro, he leaned against the railing and remembered he hadn't called Ali.

Walking down the stairs, he dialed Ali's cell number. When Ali answered Ahmed explained he'd have to work tonight. If he could get off early, he'd call. Ali joked Ahmed he was working too hard but understood; jobs were difficult to come by. Ahmed drove to Warren Ave and turned right. The Arabic deli was three blocks ahead on the opposite side of the street. After parking, he got out of the car and walked to the side entrance. Inside, the comforting smell of the freshly baked pita was mixed with the spicy aroma of skewers of lamb and chicken shawarma spinning slowly in open ovens. Display cases were filled with pastries and cakes brightly decorated with candied fruits. The counters were crowded with men dressed in dishdashas and prayer caps and women with covered heads.

Ahmed took a ticket from the dispenser and waited while other customers pointed to various Middle Eastern dishes as young men scurried behind the counter filling orders. After a few minutes it was Ahmed's turn. He hadn't eaten since lunch so he ordered a lamb shawarma sandwich, pickled beats, a side of potatoes with parsley and flat beans. The man filled the order then put a piece of pita on top. Ahmed walked to the cooler, selected an Orange Crush and headed to the cash register.

Ahmed paid his bill and walked into the dining area. He picked a table toward the back and sat down. He had just started eating when the tall body guard he'd seen earlier wearing the blue windbreaker approached his table. The body guard placed his tray on the table across from Ahmed. The man's plate was piled high with chicken, baba ghanoush and roasted vegetables. It was clear the man intended to eat quickly. Ahmed assumed he wouldn't have long to finish his own meal and began to match the man's intensity. When the tall man finished eating, he looked up.

"Let's go," he said and rose from table and with his tray.

Ahmed wiped his mouth with a paper napkin, grabbed his tray and followed the man. They threw their empty paper plates and plasticware into the trash and set the trays on top of a pile of other dirty trays. Ahmed started toward the door, when the man stopped him.

"Leave the bottle here, you won't need it," he said in a husky voice.

"What?" Ahmed questioned.

"The drink bottle, leave it here," the man said pointing at Ahmed's Orange Crush.

"Oh," Ahmed replied. He took the last drink and pitched the bottle into the trash can.

****

Episode 31

Jess and Kathy sat on aluminum lawn chairs separated by a snack table. Jess smoked a cigarette while Kathy raised a wine glass in salute as Cate and Ronnie approached.

"Started without you," she said smiling and took a sip of wine. Ronnie noticed a bottle of Pinot sitting on the snack table. "The kids have been a bitch all week; over excited about Homecoming. They're only in junior high, but it's still an exciting time for them. The excitement is contagious or something. Want a glass?"

"I'd love one. Ronnie says he's driving the Riv," Cate replied. "By the way, where did you get the wine glass?"

"Compliments of Kimmy's mom. I gave her some wine as a bribe," Kathy answered.

"Good idea. I gotta go let the dogs out. I'll grab a glass on my way back."

Ronnie looked at Jess hoping his surprise wasn't transparent. Though her face was drawn, she looked nice. She was wearing jeans, black boots similar to Cate's and a short black leather jacket. Her hair had been recently cut and tinted reminding Ronnie how good looking she had been when they were teenagers.

"You're looking good tonight, Jess," Ronnie said as he walked toward her.

Jess stood to give him a hug. He had also forgotten how tall she was. Cate returned to the porch carrying a wine glass

"I'll have to watch it," she said pouring a glass of the dark wine. "I haven't had alcohol since my meds were increased. If I start crying or get too maudlin, just throw my sorry butt out of the Riv and drive on."

"Not a problem," Kathy replied taking another drink.

They spent a few minutes making small talk about Inspector Larry's story regarding Eric. Kathy wanted all the details but Cate told her they'd better leave for the parade; they didn't want to miss Mayor Dan's grand appearance. Cate put the dogs back in the house and handed Ronnie her car keys. Kathy grabbed the bottle of Pinot off the snack table and they walked to the Rivera. At the last minute, Kathy handed her glass to Cate and told them all to wait while she ran to her car. Kathy grabbed another bottle of wine from her car then raced back to the Rivera.

"Thought we might need more refreshments for half time," she said hurriedly.

****

Ahmed followed the man to the parking lot where the green Suburban waited. Ahmed was instructed to get into the passenger's seat. The tall Arab started the truck and pulled onto Warren Avenue heading east. After a couple of miles, they turned on a side street and stopped in front of a house where two men waited by the curb. Ahmed was told to get into the back seat. He didn't like the idea, but knew he was in no position to bargain. One of the men got into the front passenger seat while the other man sat in back with Ahmed. Ahmed didn't recognize either man and made no effort at conversation. After riding a short distance, the man next to Ahmed spoke.

"We're going to blindfold you. Lie down on the seat. I'm going to put a hood over your head, I'll remove it when we get to our destination," the man ordered bluntly.

"Is this really necessary?" Ahmed asked. "You can trust me."

"Well, that may be true," the driver replied over his shoulder, "nonetheless, you must be blindfolded. Also, hand over your watch and cell phone."

Ahmed knew there was no negotiating so he did as told.

"Good," the man next to him said slipping a black hood over Ahmed's head.

****

Ronnie eased the Rivera from the curb and drove toward Oakwood Boulevard where they saw the marching band, political cars and floats lined up next to the police station. Shriners wearing their distinctive fez hats, with the little tassels hanging down, were buzzing around the intersection in miniature cars.

Episode 31

"So what's the deal with Shriner's?" Ronnie asked loud enough for Kathy and Jess to hear in the back seat.

"What do you mean?" Jess asked.

"Like, do you have to be over eighty to be a Shriner. I mean, have you ever seen a young one?" Ronnie asked.

Kathy told him he was being mean and added in a few more years, he'd be a shriveled up little old bald man driving around parades in a miniature Prune Mobile. Assuming of course that he could still see to pass a driver's test and his sons strapped a clean Depends on him. Ronnie dead panned saying he didn't see the humor. Jess said it would be okay as long as he didn't try to drive during the summer while wearing shorts. If so, his eighty year old saggy balls would fall out the side of his checkered Bermuda shorts and he'd run over his own nuts. Cate and Kathy laughed so hard Kathy nearly choked on her wine. Ronnie pulled into the Farmer Jack's parking lot on Prospect Street and turned off the Rivera.

Denny was waiting. Seeing Ronnie, he walked toward the car. As Ronnie and the three women got out, Cate and Jess were still laughing.

"Something must be funny," Denny said.

"Only to them," Ronnie replied with a grin. "Lesson learned, never ride to a parade with post menopausal winos."

"Oh, he's just being snippy 'cause nobody's changed his diaper yet," Jess said and the women started laughing again.

"It's an inside joke, Denny. They're men bashing, you don't want any part of it," Ronnie said with feigned disgust.

"Well, I would like to be part of that wine tasting. Time spent with Carol always reminds me why I drink," Denny answered sarcastically.

"Then let me help you out, mister," Jess said taking a bottle from the Rivera.

****

Ahmed realized it was pointless to try to memorize the number of turns or elapsed time between them to retrace the route.

Book Two Home Again

The driver of the Suburban was trained to make enough turns to prevent recreating it. Ahmed's only option was to keep track of time. He'd peeked at his watch before handing it over so he could affix that much. Ahmed counted off an hour of driving, when the Suburban came to a stop. Ahmed was told he could sit up. It was a relief, he felt nauseous from lying down during the ride.

"Any chance I can get a glass of water?" Ahmed asked.

"We'll be inside in just a minute. You can have a drink then," the man seated next to him answered.

Ahmed sat quietly. He heard the driver get out and the door slam. The door next to him opened and Ahmed was helped from the truck. He was led along a side walk then up five steps, then he heard two doors close behind him. When the blindfold was removed, Ahmed looked around. He was in the kitchen of an older house. The appliances were ancient but looked to be in operating condition. He was led to a kitchen table of light colored Formica with chairs made of tubular metal. The cushions might have been padded at one time, the foam had long since deteriorated. Ahmed was told to take a seat but the chair provided little comfort. The tall man picked up an Uzi lying on the counter. The dining area was connected to the living room by an arched opening. The tall man walked into the living room, pulled the shades apart slightly and peered outside. He closed the shades and remained next to the window. The man who had ridden next to Ahmed walked to the refrigerator. Norge was written in the vertical handle in gold letters but the N was almost worn away.

The man took out two bottles of water and handed one to Ahmed. Ahmed opened his bottle and took a long drink. The water tasted good and he began to feel better. After what seemed about fifteen minutes of sitting in silence, the door opened and two more men walked into the kitchen. One of them was Kamal and the other was Mahmood. They took seats at the table. Kamal sat directly across from Ahmed while Mahmood sat next to him.

Episode 31

"Sorry about the blindfold," Mahmood said, "but you realize it was necessary."

"No problem," Ahmed replied. He was tempted to add he was disappointed there was no piñata, but knew the joke would be lost.

"I will be direct, if that's okay with you?" Mahmood continued.

"Fire away," Ahmed answered, sipping his water.

"We have a problem. One in which you can be of assistance," Mahmood stated without emotion.

"What kind of problem?" Ahmed asked.

He knew cooperating was not negotiable, he had little doubt Mahmood would just put a bullet through his head. If he was lucky. Living through the next few hours would be tentative at best. Walking away in one piece was the objective Ahmed told himself. Mahmood could easily arrange for his head to leave in one direction, his body in another.

"I told you I'd be frank and direct and I will be. We have a demolition problem. Our explosive expert has become, let us say, very ill and is no longer available. We need you to take his place. Kamal trained with you. We understand from him and others that you can be very creative."

"Thank you for the complement. What, may I ask, happened to the other expert you had?"

"That's not your concern," Mahmood answered.

"I need to know. I don't want to repeat his mistake."

"He died of some kind of infection. He denied it, but we are sure he picked up something from some American whore, some kind of disgusting disease. Serves him right for interacting with some filthy western pig. He will certainly never see Paradise," Mahmood said. The words were spitted as much as said.

"What do you want me to do?" Ahmed asked.

"As I have said, we have a demolition problem. We want to show you something. Then we want you to devise a way to make it blow up at a precise time."

"And for helping, besides doing the work of Allah, what do I get, what about my family?" Ahmed asked quickly.

"You mean your sister? If all goes well, we will let her come here and live with you. Is that not fair recompense?

"You wont' hurt her? I have your word on that?" Ahmed asked.

"She is a Muslim child, we don't hurt Muslims you know that," Mahmood answered leaning back on his chair.

"Then I will do my best. But really, I would think Kamal would be as good at the task as me," Ahmed replied.

"Kamal will help, but as you know, his dexterity is a bit limited. He will be there to work with you. So the two of you are going to be a team so to speak. Your father would be most proud," Mahmood added.

"Yes, and if I make a mistake I will be joining my father," Ahmed replied.

"Yes, that is true, but because it's in the service of Allah, you will then be with him in paradise," Mahmood answered flatly.

"Show me the problem you are having," Ahmed said.

Mahmood rose from his chair and started toward the door.

****

"My name's Dennis but everyone calls me Denny," Denny said taking the glass from Jess. "I'm Ronnie's ex brother in law, but not ex friend," he continued with the same sly smile Ronnie had seen countless times.

This will be very interesting, Ronnie thought, even Denny was no match for Jess.

"My name's Jess," she responded and poured Denny a glass of wine.

"I had a dog named Jess."

"Really know how to flatter a girl," Jess said with a raised eyebrow.

"No, you don't understand. She was my favorite dog ever, a beautiful Irish Setter. I had her twelve years. I really loved her," Denny added taking a sip.

Episode 31

"Now that makes me feel a whole lot better, being compared to an Irish Setter," Jess looked at Ronnie.

A drum rolled in the distance signaling the parade was going to start. They walked to the corner. As the mayor's car approached, they cheered wildly and held their wine glasses up in a toast. Mayor Dan's wife Marie, who also graduated with them, sat on the rear deck of the convertible next to him. Cate, Kathy and Jess began chanting "The Queen". Marie stood up when the car stopped and bowed deeply. Cate and her friends curtsied. Denny made a joke about cutting them off, then quietly asked Ronnie why Jess wasn't drinking. Ronnie whispered she didn't handle it very well.

****

Ahmed followed Mahmood and Kamal outside to a dilapidated garage. With his hood removed, Ahmed could smell the night air. There was no mistaking the faint sulfur odor hovering in the hazy smog. Ahmed knew they were in the same neighborhood he had followed the Neon earlier. Just before they got to the garage, Ahmed caught a glimpse of three large letters from a lighted sign about a half mile away. The letters read ORK. He recognized them but couldn't place them. As they were walking into the garage, it struck Ahmed. The sign was on the front of the Hotel York. Ahmed knew where he was. Getting out would be a different matter.

****

After the parade, they followed the crowd toward the stadium. Denny poured the rest of the wine into their glasses then deposited the bottle into a trash can. Once inside, they took seats near the fifty yard line. Linda and her husband showed up just before kick off. Mayor Dan and Lady Marie found them in the crowd and sat down. After the game they agreed to meet in the parking lot.

****

Book Two Home Again

Entering through the garage's side door, Mahmood produced a mini flashlight and located the light switch on the wall. The garage appeared dilapidated from the outside, but was a different story inside. It was a workshop. There were two precision work tables, a lathe and welding and grinding equipment. All four walls and the ceiling had been sound proofed. The windows were securely covered so no light penetrated from the outside. On the larger work bench sat an automobile's gas tank. It had been neatly cut in two sections so that the top was neatly separated from the bottom. The fuel sending unit had been removed and lay beside the tank. A rectangular frame had been neatly welded into place next to the where the fuel sender had been located inside the tank.

"It looks like a gas tank," Ahmed said walking up to the work table. He felt impelled to say something. Ahmed had used fuel tanks in his drug smuggling in Kabul. He wondered if his expertise in smuggling was the reason Mahmood sought his services.

"It is. What we want you to do is install an explosive device into it," Mahmood answered.

"As Kamal well knows, that can be done easily enough, assuming we have the right equipment and ordinance. But you know those things as well," Ahmed said examining the fuel tank.

"Tell me what you need. If we don't have it, we'll get it. I want this assembled tonight."

"Tonight? Are you sure?" Ahmed asked incredulously. "That could be difficult."

"We heard you were very creative, so tell me. How would you propose to detonate it?"

"Well, that depends," Ahmed replied.

"Depends?" Mahmood asked. "Don't be, as the Americans say, cute, Ahmed"

"It depends on what you want to detonate and how you want to detonate it. Do you want to do it remotely, or will someone be in the vehicle?" Ahmed hoped it was to be done remotely. He hoped Mahmood wasn't going to tell him he was to be in the car. He'd had this fight with his father several times.

Episode 31

"Assume the primary objective is remote detonation, the fall back is on site. How would you engineer for such objectives?" Mahmood asked.

"Well, you could use plastic explosive denoted by a remote electronic devise or a timer. If you couldn't plan an exact time, you could gerry rig a cell phone to provide the electrical connection. The detonator could call the number at a precise time and set it off that way. You'd need some sort of electrical source, especially if a cell phone battery wouldn't last long enough between installation and detonation," Ahmed replied. The thought of setting up a bomb was not appealing, but Ahmed was intrigued by the logistics of the operation.

"Like, the fuel sending unit or the in tank fuel pump?" Kamal asked.

"Sure, see I told you that you don't need me to do this. From an engineering prospective, Kamal's way ahead of me," Ahmed said continuing to walk around the work table. On one end of the fuel tank he noticed a code number stamped into the tank. He made a note to remember the number EV 25S08.

"I'm going to leave. Work with Kamal to get this as ready tonight. He knows the details," Mahmood shut off the light switch then left the garage. Kamal produced a flashlight and switched the lights back on.

"Let's get to work," he said to Ahmed and walked to a storage cabinet at the back of the garage.

****

After the football game, the caravan made its way past Detroit Metro Airport then exited at northbound Middle Belt Road. They drove north until they came to Ford Road. Cate could see a large, brightly lit sign ahead that read Blazo's Drive In.

"Mother of god," she said sucking her breath in. "Tell me it ain't so. Blazo's still exists?"

"They closed the one on Michigan Avenue years ago," Ronnie replied. "It's a bank now, but they opened this one a few years back. A buddy at Ford told me about this place. What'll it be girls, a 'Country Cousin Get Together' or a 'Hammy Sammy?'" Ronnie asked with a laugh.

"No Melvindale Varsity Jackets allowed," Kathy added as they got out of the car.

Mayor Dan and Marie pulled up in their convertible. "We have surely died and gone to gastrointestinal Nirvana," Dan said with a wide grin.

"If only Beth could be here to get a load of this," Ronnie said to no one in particular.

****

Ahmed and Kamal worked diligently for nearly three hours. The rectangular box had been welded into place. Kamal picked up a metal cylinder out of the cabinet and pulled down his welding goggles. Ten minutes later the cylinder was welded next to the rectangular box Ahmed knew would be the bomb holder. Kamal's next action came as a surprise. From one of the cabinets Kamal carried three bricks of lead and set them on the work bench. He picked up one of the ingots and began melting lead onto the walls of the cylinder. Ahmed watched in fascination. He could not fathom a use for a lead lined cylinder. He wanted to ask Kamal but decided to wait. The less he knew, the better his chances of being allowed to leave the garage alive. The two men worked for the next four hours fixing the plastic explosives into place and installing the cell phone components. As he clipped the last wire into place, Ahmed realized what he was working on. The only reason to line the cylinder with lead was to shield the gas tank from any checks for radiation. A sickening feeling permeated his body, the cylinder was designed to hold a spent fuel rod from a nuclear power plant. This was not to be any regular car bomb. By planting the bomb in the gas tank, the odor from the gasoline would allow the vehicle to get past any bomb sniffing dogs while the lead lining would shield the contents of the cylinder from radiation detection.

Episode 31

Oh, my God, Ahmed said to himself as the realization sank in that he had been helping construct a dirty bomb. A feeling of despair ran though as he realized that unless he was willing to sacrifice himself and his little sister, there was nothing he could do to stop it.

Episode 32

Eating the double cheeseburger so late had been a mistake. Thankfully he had refrained from the onion rings. Ronnie wondered if Mayor Dan was in any better shape, he'd eaten a full order. Lying in bed, Ronnie remembered Denny and Jess were in the bedroom across the hall and wondered if they had heard him puking during the night.

The clock read eight-thirty. After ten minutes, Ronnie found the strength to stumble into the bathroom. Thirty minutes and half a pot of coffee later, he was sitting at the dining room table, reading the Detroit Free Press and gazing at the river. The sun was shining and the sky didn't have a depressing grey overcast an October Michigan sky can take. He'd promised Bobbie he'd come by the hospital and watch football. Both Michigan and Michigan State were playing. Ronnie doubted Bobbie would make it through both games. His pain was increasing and remaining lucid for more than three of four hours was a stretch, but they'd made a pact to watch the games anyway.

Ronnie heard movement up stairs. A few minutes later, Jess came into the kitchen and poured a cup of coffee. He had been impressed with her self control last night. She'd even driven them back to Grosse Ile.

"Any cream and sugar?" she asked from the kitchen.

"Sure Jess, check the fridge. Sugar's in the cupboard to the right of the stove," Ronnie answered.

"Thanks," she yelled back, "how's the stomach?"

"Oh, okay. Listen, there's cereal and some bagels if you're hungry. I could make some eggs if anyone's interested."

"Bagels sound good. No need to bother with eggs, don't think any of us feel like cleaning up," Jess answered.

A few moments later Ronnie heard the toaster pop and Jess came out holding a cup of coffee in one hand and a bagel coated with jelly in the other. She took a seat across from him and set the bagel down on a napkin. Her make up was gone and her hair was rumpled.

"Neat house," Jess said taking a bite of the bagel. She chewed the bagel then took a long drink of coffee. "I needed that," she said. "When we used to go to Looney Rooney's, I always wondered what this place looked like inside."

"And how does it look?" Ronnie asked setting his newspaper down.

"Just as I imagined. I love all the wood, and the view is really great. You can see in both directions. I could sit here for hours in the summer and watch the boat traffic."

Jess took another bite of the bagel and a little jelly stuck to the corner of her mouth which she dabbed with a napkin.

"Yeah, Beth loved to do the same. She'd sit on the balcony and wave at the boaters whether she knew them or not."

"You really miss her, don't you?"

"Does it show?"

"Only when you breathe," Jess replied.

"You want to see the rest of the place, Jess?" Ronnie asked to change the topic. It was too beautiful a morning to dwell on loneliness.

"Sure," Jess answered.

She got a kick out of the boat house and the tunnel that led to the garage in the clearing across the road. As they made their way back through the tunnel, Ronnie explained how Harry

Episode 32

Bennet had designed the place for quick get away. When they returned, Denny was sitting at the table staring into a cup of coffee. He looked haggard. His curly hair, longer than the last time he'd visited, was flattened on one side. After he declined Jess's offer of a toasted bagel, she made another for herself. When the bagel popped up, she added grape jelly and took a seat at the table. Ronnie told them he planned to visit Bobbie that afternoon and invited them along. Jess asked if she could take a rain check. Denny also declined, he didn't feel comfortable visiting someone at the hospital he didn't know. Ronnie said they were welcomed to stay and added Beth's car was in the garage. The keys were hanging on the key hook by the hutch. They sat at the table making small talk and drinking coffee for nearly an hour. At one point Jess started telling Denny about a house up the road.

"Let me guess," Denny interrupted in mid sentence, "there was an old recluse who lived there. He had a big covered porch, he'd play his guitar and everyone would drink and sing along with him. Kids would come from all over and stayed until the police would chase everyone away."

"So, how do you know about Looney Rooney's?" Jess asked.

"Because I've heard the story so many times, that sometimes, I swear, I was on that porch myself a time or two," Denny replied then got up to refill his coffee.

"You'll have to make another pot," Jess said as he got up.

"Geez, Ronnie what kind of boarding house are you running here?" Denny replied and headed for the kitchen.

"Well, you kids have fun," Ronnie said. "I'm going for a bike ride, then I gotta get ready to go see Bobbie. Y'all make yourselves at home."

"Got a spare bike?" she asked. "If so, I'll ride with you."

"Really, you want to go for a ride?" Ronnie asked eagerly, Jess's question had surprised him.

"Yeah, that'd be fun. I haven't been around the Island in forever."

"Well, you'll have to help me lift Beth's bike off the hooks. If the tires are okay, we'll add some air."

"Give me just a minute to get ready," Jess replied and headed for the stairs.

The bike ride cleared Ronnie's head and his stomach felt better. They rode along West River Road to Ferry then cut over to the bike path. When they reached the airport they headed back to Macomb and stopped at the bakery. Ronnie ordered two coffees and two glazed doughnuts while Jess took a seat at one a booth. After paying for the order, Ronnie took a seat across from her.

"The Island is such a nice place, I had forgotten. I used to come here all the time as a kid you know," Jess said between sips from the Styrofoam cup. Ronnie decided his stomach could handle another doughnut and walked back to the counter.

"I didn't know that," he replied sitting back down. "What brought you here?" Ronnie asked between bites.

"My dad belonged to West Shore Country Club. We came here all the time until I was a teenager. After that, well, my life really went south. Drugs and all that. I'm sure you've heard the stories."

"Hell, Jess, who am I to judge. I'm going to watch my best friend die a little more today. I'll do the same tomorrow and the next day and the day after that until he looks like one of those walking skeletons you see on CNN in some far off African country. And he'll lie there until God decides he's suffered enough for who knows what sins and grants him mercy to leave this planet," Ronnie replied. "I'll do all this knowing that I married the girl we were both in love with." Ronnie felt embarrassed about his tirade and quickly apologized. "Sorry, Jess, I don't know where that came from."

"Hey, you're losing your best friend. I know what it's like to lose somebody so close," she placed her elbows on the table and held the cup in both hands.

"Yeah, I guess. It's just so hard because, you know, we didn't speak for all those years. Now it all seems like such a colossal

Episode 32

waste of time. I don't understand your comment though. You and Linda are still best friends. She is doing fine, isn't she?"

"It's not Linda I'm talking about. It's my son, Justin. When I got so bad from the heroin and all, the state took him away from me. His foster parents adopted him and I haven't' spoken to him or seen him in ten years. Well, that's not entirely true. I've spoken to him, he just hasn't spoken back. I doubt he ever will. Someday, if I'm lucky, maybe it'll be like you and Bobbie, though I doubt he will ever have anything to do with me again. Can't blame him though. It kind of struck me when we rode by West Shore Country Club. Had things gone just a little differently, or maybe if I could had been a little different, maybe we could have been members at West Shore and Justin could have played golf there," Jess answered struggling to maintain composure.

"Hell, Jess. What'ya gonna do, you can't change yesterday. I mean you are right, things could have been very different but in some respects, those are just the genes you inherited. No one grows up looking to get addicted. Besides, the sixties were not a good time to grow up for anyone. I'm not saying everything you did was okay, but maybe some part of it wasn't your fault. Anyway, seems you've got things under control now. Who knows what the future will bring," Ronnie added.

After finishing their coffee and donuts, they decided it was time to head back and pitched their cups into the trash can. Ronnie said goodbye to Nadia, the owner, who'd made one of her usual crude remarks. When he paid for the second doughnut, she'd whispered to him in her thick Serbian accent, "Why you with such tall woman? She not like pip squeak like you!" then laughed a tawdry laugh.

On their way back, they stopped at West Shore Country Club where Jess asked if she could use the restroom. Ronnie knew club members would be arriving soon to watch football and take advantage of the club's amenities before it closed for the season. Ronnie told Jess he'd wait outside and was standing by the bikes when she emerged a few minutes later.

"Still look the same?" he asked strapping on his helmet.

"Yeah, guess it never changes, but then again, neither did the Judge," she answered.

"Maybe that's a good thing," Ronnie replied.

He handed her Beth's helmet and they left the parking lot for the five minute ride back to the Pagoda. Ronnie put the bikes away while Jess checked on Denny. Ronnie found them standing on the balcony. He'd put the patio furniture away a week ago and told them to take a couple of kitchen chairs outside if they wanted to. After his second shower of the morning, Ronnie returned downstairs. Denny and Jess were sitting on the balcony. Denny sipped a beer. Jess held a Diet Coke and was smoking one of Denny's Winston Lights when Ronnie ducked his head out of the sliding glass door.

"You kids don't wait up," he joked and closed the door.

Walking to the Explorer, Ronnie felt depressed. Cate had the day off so he wouldn't be able to sit with her in the cafeteria during her break and relive the previous night's events.

Ronnie arrived at the hospital at twelve forty. Kick off for the Michigan game was at one o'clock so he had plenty of time. Growing up, Bobbie had always been an avid Michigan fan and Ronnie had a surprise for him. In the plastic bag on the passenger seat was a maize baseball cap with a blue block M on the front and The Big House written in small blue letters on the back.

Ronnie parked the Explorer, grabbed the bag and walked into the hospital. He took the elevator up to the fifth floor. Bobbie was asleep. Ronnie set the bag down and walked to the nurse's station. The nurse said Bobbie's shot was a minimal dosage and he would be awake in an hour or so. Ronnie went down to the gift shop for something to read while Bobbie slept. He picked a Time magazine off the rack, selected a can of Coke from the cooler and took them to the counter. He paid the attendant then returned to Bobbie's room where he quietly eased into the visitors chair. He had nearly finished reading the Time when Bobbie woke up.

"Go blue," Bobbie said in a mildly slurred voice.

Episode 32

"Go blue," Ronnie responded taking the hat out of the bag and putting it on Bobbie's bald head. The hat sat lop sided with the bill pointing to the right like one of the hip hop artists Ronnie had seen recently on television. Bobbie lifted the hat off his head and brought it in front of his face.

"The Big House. Been there a few times," he said weakly. He was having trouble talking. "I'm really thirsty," Bobbie added, "suppose you could pour me a glass of water."

"Sure thing," Ronnie answered. As he walked to Bobbie's night stand, Bobbie pushed the adjustment button on his bed and brought the back into an upright position. When he released the button, Ronnie handed him the glass. His hand trembled as he took it. Ronnie grabbed a straw from the stand and removed the paper wrapping. He bent the flexible portion of the straw and inserted it into the glass.

"Thanks. Oh yeah, before I forget, thanks for the hat," Bobbie said between sips then set the glass down on the tray.

"The Big House, Big Red and Woody,' he said with a quiet laugh. "What the hell," he continued, "Red and Woody drinking those Pabst Blue Ribbons on the way. Seems like they also carried a little flask inside their coats when the weather was cold. Then it was two more PBR's for the ride home."

"Yeah," Ronnie replied, "and you and me in the back seat, no seat belts. Things were different then. No Mother's Against Drunk Drivers."

"If you did half that stuff today, Child Protection would put us in foster care," Bobbie added with grin.

"Yeah and stopping at the Mel Bar afterward for burgers and more beer, not to mention letting us play shuffleboard while they kibitzed with their buddies," Ronnie added.

"Oh, yeah," Bobbie said, "I'd forgotten about those shuffle board games. Big long tables with wooden boards with saw dust on top to make those little metal hockey puck thingies slide down the alley. Damn, I'd forgotten about them. Wonder what ever happened to them, you never see them anymore. Or pin ball games with metal balls and flippers; those are pretty much gone too. Anyway, add to that, Big Red hustling a few games of pool while we ate bar burgers and fries. You know, despite everything, including my dad deciding he didn't want us in his life anymore, my brothers, sister and I all came out okay. The four of us took different routes, that's for sure. But somehow we all came out okay."

"You all came out more than okay, Bob," Ronnie said sincerely.

"Anyway, we almost forgot the game. Slide that chair around here. I'll turn on this wide screen plasma television and we'll watch it in HD or Hospital Definition as it's known. Hell, we'll barely be able to see the damn thing," Bobbie replied with a weak smile.

Ronnie slid the chair around to the side of Bobbie's bed. It was the third quarter and Michigan was ahead by ten points over Purdue.

"Well, seems my boys seem have everything in control'" Bobbie added.

"Hey, speaking of football, how was Homecoming last night?" Bobbie asked.

Ronnie thought for a moment before responding. The night had been so much fun but he didn't want to make it out to be as good of time as it was because he didn't want Bobbie to feel bad.

"We had a pretty good time. They were really surprised by the Blazo's thing. Of course we all over ate. The greasy burger 'bout killed me. But you know, the stadium wasn't packed like when we were in high school. Guess people have other things to do now. That was kind of disappointing. Oh here's one for you, my ex brother in law Denny, spent the night with Jess. Go figure."

"Hey, to each their own," Bobbie replied.

"Oh yeah, after we ate, I told the crowd the story about Mr. Bowers' words of wisdom."

Ronnie watched as a smile spread across Bobbie's gaunt face.

"I almost forgot about that. Lot of truth to what old man Bowers had to say that day," Bobbie said with a far away look in his eyes. "I'll never forget the look on Gerry's face when his old man told us the most over rated thing in life was a piece of ass

Episode 32

and the most under rated thing in life was a good shit. Damn, thought I'd piss my pants laughing so hard."

"Yeah, too bad we couldn't appreciate it at the time. Damn, wasn't Gerry pissed at his old man," Ronnie replied with a soft laugh.

"Yeah, but you could hardly blame Gerry. I thought about telling him at least his old man was around to hand out such sage advice. But hell, everyone's got their own cross to bear. I suppose having an alcoholic father isn't an easy run at life either. By the way, did you ever wonder if Gerry's father was gay?"

"In retrospect, I'd say it was possible. Maybe that's why he drank so much," Ronnie replied.

The fourth quarter started. They continued watching the game though Bobbie looked fatigued. Ronnie asked if he needed another shot, but Bobbie declined.

"Oh, almost forgot to tell you. The weirdest thing happened yesterday, when I took Cate to see her mom," Ronnie said when the game went to commercial.

"What happened?' Bobbie asked. "Hey, but before you tell me, how about you run down to the nurse's station and get us some popsicles? I could use one now. I could just buzz the nurse."

"I can go, no problem," Ronnie replied. He left the room and returned with two popsicles. "What flavor you want, red or purple?"

"Red and purple are not flavors, Ronnie, they're colors. Anyway, I'll have the grape."

"Some things never change," Ronnie said handing Bobbie a popsicle.

"Maybe that's a good thing," Bobbie replied, it was the second time today Ronnie had heard the phrase. "So what happened at the nursing home?"

Ronnie told Bobbie about meeting Inspector Larry and his cheese steak lunches with Eric.

"Eric always had a thing for Cate; and her for him. She have any clue about what's wrong with him?" Bobbie asked.

"No doubt about that, the thing for Eric that is. She said something about him maybe being a paranoid schizophrenic."

"Guess there's a price to pay for everything, even being too smart. My payback certainly didn't have anything to do with being too smart. That was never my problem," Bobbie added. A cloud drifted over Bobbie's face. He looked down at his popsicle. He had sucked on the end of it until the juice was gone leaving the end just a pointed piece of semi clear ice. Ronnie remembered he did the same thing when they were kids.

"Did Cate say anything about trying to help him or anything like that?" Bobbie asked.

"No, we didn't get that far, though she seemed lost in thought during the evening."

When the game ended Bobbie turned the set off. Ronnie wondered if he had forgotten about the State game. Bobbie looked tired and bothered by something. Ronnie knew his friend would eventually tell him what was on his mind and decided to give him some time. If Bobbie wanted to just sit in solitude that was okay, too. Finally, Ronnie decided to break their silence. Something besides cancer was eating at Bobbie; it had been evident from the day Ronnie walked into the hospital room. It wasn't about Beth, they'd already settled that issue.

"What's on your mind Stick?" Ronnie asked softly.

"When I said that thing about everyone has a price to pay for certain aspects of their life," Bobbie couldn't complete his sentence and looked away as if he was trying to lift himself out of his cancer wracked body and travel to someplace else.

"Hey, Bobbie, I don't know where you are going with this, but don't do it if it's too hard for you. I'll listen to whatever you have to say, you know that. But whatever it is, if it's this hurtful, maybe you should just leave it alone for a while."

"I don't have a while," Bobbie said turning back to Ronnie.

"Okay then. Tell me what's on your mind."

"Okay, but first I want you to go to the nurse's station again and get a wheel chair."

"Why, where are we going this time? Cate's not on duty today."

Episode 32

"You're going to take me for another little ride."

"Will it be okay with the nurses?"

"I would say use your good looks, but given the circumstances, use your hillbilly charm instead."

"How about I go for the pity the old men routine? I think that's about what you and I have left."

"Whatever, just get the damn chair," Bobbie finished with a soft laugh.

Ronnie returned pushing a wheel chair with a nurse accompanying him.

"Reinforcements?" Bobbie asked.

"Yes," the nurse answered, "and the bailiff. You have ten minutes and that's it. Are you sure you're up to this Mr. Irwin?"

"No," Bobbie replied, "but we're going to do this anyway."

The nurse helped Bobbie into the wheelchair. He was in obvious pain from the move but the nurse knew her business and got Bobbie situated. She pulled an afghan off the bed and placed it over Bobbie's lap then reminded the two men that they had ten minutes and not a minute more. After the nurse left, Bobbie told Ronnie to sit down in the guest's chair across from him.

"Now, that we can look each other eye to eye, I'm going to go to confessional," Bobbie said quietly.

"Bobbie," Ronnie replied earnestly, "I'm no priest. You know I'm not even Catholic. Maybe I should get a priest for you."

"I don't want a priest," Bobbie answered quickly, "what good is it to bare your soul to someone who doesn't even know you. Where's the risk in that? No, what I have to say, I want to tell you because you've known me my whole life. I know you can't forgive me. Hell, neither can a priest for that fact. Only God can do that, and I'll be talking face to face with him soon enough."

"Don't talk like that Bobbie," Ronnie interjected, "who knows what tomorrow will bring?"

"I do and a cure for what I've got isn't going to come along by then. So for once, shut your hillbilly mouth and let me say what I've got to say. This will be hard, but I want you to hear me out. It's important that I tell someone about some things in my

Book Two Home Again

life that I deeply regret. God will judge me no doubt, so I'm just trying to unload some of the guilt. Just look at it as I'm practicing for what I'll have to tell him face to face. So shut up and listen."

"Will do. Oh, was I not supposed to talk yet?" Ronnie asked in an attempt to get his friend to smile.

"Very funny asshole," Bobbie replied. "here it is. When I was in the service, I did some things that weren't, let us say, in line with the Geneva Convention."

"Hell, Bobbie, if you're talking about 'Nam. I wasn't there, but I know that was crazy land, and it was so long ago."

"Just shut up and listen to me. It wasn't just 'Nam. It was 'Nam and other places. My last two tours in 'Nam weren't with the 101. I was in a special branch of Army Intelligence. We interrogated prisoners amongst other things and we didn't always do things in a manner that was exactly humane."

"Bobbie, are you sure you want to talk about this. I'm sure what ever you did, I mean you must have felt it was warranted and all."

"That makes no difference, and yes the situation required me to do things that were beyond what one human can expect another to do. Regardless, I did them anyway. We did them in 'Nam and we did them during the first Gulf War and other places. Then I got out and tried to live a different life. It now appears there's some baggage that refuses to be left at the door."

"Damn Bobbie, now I really feel bad. Maybe had the thing between Beth and I not happened, maybe you'd have gotten out after your first tour and all of this wouldn't have happened."

"And maybe you'd shut up for a minute. Anyway, that's not why I'm telling you all of this. I made my decision to be a lifer long before you and Beth hooked up that summer. I was just waiting to tell her. So don't go down some kind of guilt trip about all that. We were adults and made our own decisions. I made some after that, that I regret," Bobbie replied. He was looking so hard into Ronnie's eyes, Ronnie felt a part of his own soul was being bared.

Episode 32

"Anyway, this will sound very bizarre. I now believe that it wasn't just chance that I came down with this cancer. There's a reason I'm here and I want you to help me with it."

"Sure thing, Bobbie," Ronnie replied in measured words, "tell me what you need."

"Well, it's going to start with you wheeling me up to the eighth floor," Bobbie answered.

"The eight floor? Well, I know I can do that. Why up there?"

"This is what I meant when I said that thing earlier about Eric. You know, about his illness being a price to pay?"

"Yeah, so go on."

"Well, when I first came in here after that diagnosis of stomach cancer," Bobbie said in a tone as more a question than answer.

"Go on," Ronnie stated leaning forward.

Bobbie's voice cracked as he tried to speak. Ronnie asked Bobbie if he'd like more water. Bobbie said he did. Ronnie got up to pour them each a glass. He handed Bobbie a glass and returned to the visitor's chair. Sitting down, he held the glass in both hands and leaned forward again.

"The stomach cancer was payback for the Agent Orange we used all over 'Nam. I thought it was a just reward for the things I'd done there. I really can't say why, but when I was first diagnosed, I didn't want to go to the VA for treatment. I'd worked enough time in the private sector to qualify for hospitalization and told Amy I wanted to come here because Fairlane Hills is closer to her house and closer to Melvindale. I wanted to be close to my roots."

"Funny, Beth felt the same way. I begged her to go to Karmonos or Henry Ford, but she wanted to come here. Don't get me wrong, the care here is as good as anywhere, but Karmonos has such a great reputation. She wanted to be here for the same reasons."

"Well, all those reasons are true, but there was something inside me telling me that I had to come here. Yesterday I found out why."

Book Two Home Again

"Okay. Why was it so important for you to be treated here at Oak Grove?"

"Because it's my chance to right some of my wrongs."

"How is that?" Ronnie asked.

"Because there's something at this hospital that isn't quite right."

"Hey, we can get you out of here. Just say the word. We'll get you down to Karmonos tonight."

"That's not what I'm talking about. Listen, wheel me up to eight. When we come back, I'll tell you what I believe is going on."

"Okay," Ronnie said as he got up and walked behind Bobbie's wheel chair. He lifted the brake lever with his foot and began wheeling Bobbie toward the elevators. As they passed the nurse's station, Nurse Rachel looked at the two men. She held up both hands with her fingers extended upright, signaling they had ten minutes. She was twenty something with dark hair and eyes.

"Hard to believe anyone that young and cute is on her way to becoming Nurse Ratchet," Bobbie said in reference to One Flew Over The Cuckoo's Nest. "If you repeat what I'm going to tell you after we go to the eighth floor, you'll probably end up with a lobotomy like Nicholson's," Bobbie added as they boarded the elevator.

The elevator was empty, so Ronnie pushed the button for the eighth floor.

"What's on eight, Bobbie?" Ronnie asked after the door closed.

"If I'm right, not us for long."

The elevator emitted a soft hum. When they came to a stop, the door opened. Ronnie pushed Bobbie out. The floor was quiet and empty. They could see that the entry doors to both wings were equipped with locks. A sign that read "Infectious Diseases" over the nurse's station. A tall muscular male nurse walked toward them and asked if he could help.

"Oh, we were looking to visit a friend," Bobbie replied still wearing the maize and blue Michigan baseball hat.

Episode 32

"Well, the patients on this floor are quarantined," the nurse replied noting Bobbie's hat. "Did you watch the game today?"

"Yeah," Bobbie answered, "we won, only two more big ones left now. Anyway, we'll just go back to my room, my friend must be on another floor. Thanks anyway."

Ronnie turned and pushed the elevator button. Bobbie studied the male nurse as they waited. A female nurse came out from the locked door to the right of the station. When the elevator arrived, an elderly couple stepped to the rear make room for Bobbie's wheel chair. The man was wearing green wool pants pulled up nearly under his armpits. The elderly woman wore a feathered hat. Ronnie wanted to ask Bobbie when was the last time he'd seen a hat like hers, but decided he'd wait. Seeing the old couple sent a pang of grief through Ronnie, they reminded him he'd never have the chance to grow old with Beth. Nor would he and Bobbie ever be a pair of crotchety old men in a fishing boat. Both men remained silent during the ride back down to five. The elevator came to an abrupt stop and Ronnie wheeled Bobbie back to his room. As they passed the nurse's station, Nurse Rachel looked up from her work and gave the two men an approving look with her dark brown eyes.

"We should have hung out up there for a little longer or have taken some kind of side trip just so we could be a few minutes late," Bobbie said as they got to his room.

"If I didn't know better Bobbie, I'd think you're just trying to piss her off. What's up with that?"

"Just being a cranky old man. Pissed off at what I can't have, so I'm trying to spoil it for everyone else," he answered as a mischievous smile spread over his face.

"What'ya mean by that?" Ronnie asked.

"Well, if I give her a hard time, she'll go home in a pissy mood then take it out on her boyfriend. Then he'll retaliate. They'd end up in a big argument and he won't get any on Saturday night. Know what I mean?"

"Yeah, I catch your drift. There is a cruel side to you I didn't know existed," Ronnie replied, regretting his choice of words.

"You don't know the half of it. It's not that I was cruel as much as being able to detach myself. It made me good at what I did," Bobbie replied. Ronnie noticed a pall had set in again over Bobbie.

"Did you see what you needed to see?" Ronnie asked.

"And heard what I needed to hear." Bobbie answered. "Did you hear anything when the other nurse came out of the locked door?"

"No, should I have?"

"If it was indeed an infectious disease floor, there should have been a hissing sound when the door opened from the negative air pressure sucking air in. When you quarantine people, that sound should be heard when the doors are opened."

"Damn, didn't pick up on that. What do you think is going on?"

"I don't know for sure, but there is definitely something not right on the eighth floor. Coming from radiation earlier in the week, we ended at eight and two doctors I recognized got on the elevator. I was on the patient's elevator on a gurney. They didn't recognize me, but I damn well know them."

"Who are they, Bobbie?"

"One of them I knew by the name of Dr. Phil Morle, or Major Morle, I guess I should say. His name now is Dr. Midek. I read it on his name tag. When he was just out of med school, he helped me interrogate prisoners and perform other functions in 'Nam. He wasn't exactly Dr. Mingele, the Nazi doctor at Auschwitz, but he also wasn't, let us say Dr. Salk, the infamous doctor that cured the scourge that affected your life in such a big way."

"Who was the other?"

"Well, I couldn't read his name tag, but I knew him as Dr. Nagapa though he may have changed his name by now. I worked with him in the Gulf War. He also helped us interrogate prisoners amongst other duties."

"So what do you think they are doing here?'

Episode 32

"I don't know, but I will find out. It's part of my penance. Dr. Nagapa worked for an organization called the I.E.R. They're India's secret service, though their history goes back before India even became an independent country. Most of their work, from what I know, was against Pakistan. In the Gulf War, they helped us, mostly because they've had so much experience with radical Muslims."

"Jesus, Bobbie, are you putting me on? I mean you think there's something clandestine going on at Oak Grove. I mean that seems a little far fetched don't you think?"

"I have thirty years of far fetched experience. Besides, there are a lot of Muslims here in Fairlane Hills. It's the largest population outside of the Mideast. Buried in here somewhere you just have to know are some people who don't exactly hold a lot of reverence for American ideals."

"Are you talking about terrorists? Come on Bobbie, you don't believe there are terrorists here in Oak Grove Hospital do you? Anyway, not all Muslims are terrorists."

"Yeah, and all Italians aren't in the mob, and all hillbillies aren't in the Klan. But I bet if you go to Sicily you're bound to run into some mobsters, and if you go to Alabama, there are bound to be some Klansmen running around. Look, I'm not saying all Muslims are bad, I'm just saying that given a large population, you're bound to find some bad people."

"Why here at Oak Grove Hospital for god's sake?"

"Why not, terrorists get sick too you know. When they do, where do they go for treatment? They also have friends and relatives who get sick"

Ronnie knew Bobbie was correct.

"So what do we do now?"

"Keep an eye out, when I'm not too drugged up, and see what doesn't look exactly copacetic."

"Copacetic, now there's a Big Redism for you," Ronnie replied with a small laugh. "I haven't heard that one in a while."

"Yeah. Oh by the way, your dad called today, he may come by tomorrow for the Lions game. You in?" Bobbie asked.

"Yeah, I'm in. For now I think we better get you into the bed. Can you eat?"

"I'm never really hungry anymore."

"I'll get nurse Ratchet, I mean Rachel. We'll see if you can get her boyfriend cut off for the whole weekend," Ronnie said with a laugh.

"That sounds good because, if I ain't gettin' any, well you know the rest," Bobbie laughed and left the sentence dangling.

After Nurse Rachel helped Bobbie back into his bed, she brought a container of Jell-O which Bobbie ate reluctantly. When she came back a short time later, Ronnie was standing by Bobbie's bed.

"Good night, Ronnie," Bobbie said squeezing Ronnie's hand. The shot was fast acting, Bobbies eyes were already half closed.

"Damn," Bobbie whispered, "we forgot about the Spartan game."

"Next week, Bobbie," Ronnie replied, "next week."

"Yeah, next week," Bobbie repeated as he drifted off.

Ronnie released Bobbie's hand. He removed the Michigan baseball hat and placed it on the night stand before leaving.

Episode 33

Walking into the parking structure, Ronnie knew he should just go home, but Bobbie's revelations about a conspiracy made his empty house even less appealing. It seemed a burger and a beer should be the last thing he'd crave, but that was what he wanted. Ronnie knew it wasn't the food or alcohol he needed as much as familiar company. Miller's Bar was just up the road and it had been a sanctuary of sorts after visiting Beth. It was a chance to see Earl the bartender again and catch the second half of the State game. Ronnie eased the Explorer forward, lowered the window and handed the attendant two one dollar bills. A bored looking woman, wearing a powder blue I Love My Grandma sweatshirt, took his money. As the exit arm went up she handed him two quarters and told him to have a good day.

Ronnie was befuddled about Bobbie's confession. He wasn't sure how much was factual and how much was the result of too much morphine rattling around in a brain consumed by too many malignancies. It was all so confusing. Even if the allegations were true, there wasn't much that could be done.

Ronnie passed the Catholic church where Bobbie and his older brother Jimmy made their first communions. The communion party was the last time he had seen Bobbie's father.

Shortly after, Jim Sr. divorced Lisa; or Lisa divorced Jim Sr., the details were never clear. Nor did they make much difference to ten year old Bobbie. The results were the same. His mother's fierce accusations that day were followed by a heatedly intense argument. Lisa had screamed and cried; his father had yelled. In the end, Jim Sr. packed his suitcases and stormed out the door as neighbors looked on from their tiny front porches. Ronnie remembered that day. He was sitting on the step while his dad drank Phieffer's beer and his mom smoked Pall Malls. When they heard arguing from Bobbie's house, Ronnie was told to go inside just as Jim Sr. stormed out. It had been nearly forty-five years since.

The day of their communion party, Jim Sr.'s '57 Cadillac convertible was parked in the drive. It was a status symbol richly deserved by the Good Housekeeping Salesman of the Year. It seemed the Irwin's were on their way up and someday out. Lisa's days in Melvindale were numbered; her husband was selling appliances at a rate that guaranteed he'd have his own store soon. Then there'd be a brick house back in the Grosse Pointes, or at the least a house in Fairlane Hills.

As it turned out, Lisa's days in Melvindale were numbered but for different reasons. Selling appliances came naturally to Jim Sr. Big Red always said the man could talk a preacher's wife out of her under drawers. It wasn't a preacher's wife Jim Sr. had charmed, however, it was an attractive young bookkeeper at the store who was two months pregnant with his fourth son.

When the light turned green, Ronnie turned left and continued past Ford Motor's Research Center, where he worked part time. The campus of twenty buildings sprawled across both sides of the road. The job was effective therapy, though he missed some of his buddies. Most had packed their golf clubs and headed for the sun, an unlucky few found their way to funeral parlors. Ronnie vowed he wouldn't work much longer himself.

Ronnie passed the entrance to Greenfield Village. He could see the distinctive tower clock and the twin ponds. One of Eric's impossible missions had been throwing weighted cherry bombs

Episode 33

into the ponds and planting others along the perimeter with timed fuses. The police and fire departments had been called. The members of that Impossible Mission team thought it funny and exciting as they watched the commotion from their secret hiding spot.

Ronnie laughed softly as he turned on Michigan Ave. Miller's Bar was across the road from a bank building which at one time had been the original Blazo's Restaurant. Last night's gathering had been fun, but it would have been even better had they been able to eat at the original location. Ronnie thought it ironic a building that housed a million memories of his youth had been converted into something as sterile as a bank. He guessed none of the employees had any idea their commercial transactions were conducted at a yesteryear Nirvana.

Miller's had always been the in lunch place for Ford Motor's white collar employees and because of it's proximity to Fairlane Hills, Miller's was also heavily patronized by National Motor's workers. The flat roofed building is painted flamingo pink with Miller's Bar displayed in bright white letters along the side of the building. The building always reminded Ronnie of Jimmy P's tiny flat roofed pink home across the road from his childhood house. Ronnie asked Earl one time why the bar was painted pink. Earl had replied with a laugh that Mr. Miller maintained it was salmon colored, not pink. The tables and booths were full so Ronnie took a seat at the bar.

Ahmed and Stacey were seated in one of the booths along the wall opposite the bar. During the ride to Miller's, Stacey noticed Ahmed seemed distracted and asked if something was bothering him. He'd replied he was just concerned about his little sister. He certainly couldn't tell her he was worried about his part in helping a group of maniacal terrorists construct a dirty bomb. Reflecting on the previous night's events, Ahmed thought about the lead lined canister Kamal had so skillfully welded to the side wall of the gas tank. Ahmed had been amazed watching Kamal work with his damaged hand. Ahmed knew Kamal could have been a gifted sculptor, if he would have dedicated his talent to something creative and beautiful instead of wasting it on hate and destruction.

Ahmed had devised a detonation system that worked by delivering an electrical current to the plastic explosives using the circuitry from a cell phone. Ahmed still hoped to find a way to abort the device before it detonated. He could just reveal the plan to Charlie but it would be at the risk of his sister's life. Whatever decision he made, it would likely end his relationship with Stacy. The thought of not seeing her sent a wave of anxiety through him. As he turned his head toward the bar, he saw a short, older man take a seat. Ahmed recognized the man as a friend of Nurse Cassadea's. She had introduced the man one evening while he was cleaning. Ahmed concentrated, she had mentioned the man had retired from Ford Motor and worked in engineering. It was a long shot, Ahmed realized, but maybe he could provide information that might be helpful in thwarting Mahmood's plan.

Ronnie looked up at the television. Earl was at the far end of the bar pouring a beer for a customer. Earl was dressed the same, black trousers and a short sleeved white dress shirt with the sleeves rolled up. A narrow black tie and a gold watch completed the ensemble. He looked down the bar and signaled to Ronnie he'd be with him in a minute.

"Who's winning the game, Earl?" Ronnie asked as Earl approached.

"Well, your Spartan's were taking it on the chin at halftime," Earl answered.

Earl had lost an eye somewhere along the line and turned his head slightly to the right when he talked.

"I'll have a burger, well done," Ronnie answered.

"Of course," Earl responded, "and the usual to drink?"

It was the trademark of a born bartender, Earl still remembered his favorite beer.

"Oh yeah," Ronnie replied.

"Comin' right up, boss." Earl called everyone boss, except the female customers who he invariably referred to as mamn.

Episode 33

Ronnie glanced around the bar and saw a young couple in a booth near the front door. He recognized the dark haired young man. Ronnie had always been good at remembering faces, names and little details about other people's lives. He couldn't see the young woman's face but noticed her blonde hair was pulled back into a pony tail. Watching their interaction, Ronnie thought of Beth and how they'd sat in restaurants and bistros lost in their own world. The young man looked in Ronnie's direction. It was clear he also recognized Ronnie. Hoping he hadn't been caught staring, Ronnie turned his attention back to the game just as Earl walked up holding a glass and a LaBatt's bottle.

Ronnie took the glass in his left hand, set it at an angle and began pouring the beer. When he finished, he set the bottle down and took a drink. Ronnie thought how he'd come a far piece from that day in Gerry Bowers' living room. At that time, he thought the taste of beer might be one of the most overrated things in life. Now there were times when a cold beer tasted better than anything in the world.

Ronnie looked up at the television again, it was third and eight for Iowa. The two teams lined up and the center snapped the ball when Ronnie felt a gentle tap on his shoulder. He didn't want to miss the play and was about to put his hand up indicating he couldn't turn around just yet, but knew it would be rude.

"Your name's Ron, isn't it?"

Ronnie turned and saw the dark haired young man who had been sitting in the booth standing directly in front of him.

"Yeah, but everyone calls me Ronnie."

In his peripheral vision Ronnie watched the Iowa quarterback take the ball, drop back and launch a pass downfield. The Iowa receiver caught the ball a split second before the MSU defender put a vicious hit on him. When the receiver dropped the ball, the referee pulled a yellow flag out of his rear pocket and tossed it the air.

"Damn, that wasn't interference!" Ronnie snapped. "Oh, sorry. I'm a fan and that was just an awful call. Didn't mean to be so vocal" he added apologetically.

"That's okay," Ahmed replied, "I can understand. It's easy to get caught up."

"Your name's Ahmed, right?" Ronnie asked.

"Yeah, I didn't know if you'd remember me. We only met the one time, but I've seen you around the hospital."

"Yeah, you work with my friend Cate Cassadea," Ronnie answered.

Earl approached Ronnie and placed a steaming hamburger in front of him. The burger was sitting on a large square of waxed paper; Miller's never used plates, even plastic or paper ones. The burgers were served on squares of waxed paper though the fries came in little cardboard trays. Earl had joked one time how some younger patrons thought Mr. Miller was some kind of early day environmentalist who disdained Styrofoam and plastic. In reality, Earl elaborated, Mr. Miller was just a good businessman who cut costs where he could.

"Here's you burger boss," Earl said and turned away.

"Great burgers," Ahmed said. Ronnie looked in the direction of the booth and noted that it was empty.

"Yeah, best in town. Lloyd's has a close second, but most people never get a chance to compare."

"Lloyd's, never heard of that place. Is it close?" Ahmed asked.

"Not really, it's on Grosse Ile."

"Never heard of Grosse Ile either."

"That doesn't surprise me. It's where I live," Ronnie answered as he reached for a plastic tray sitting on the bar.

The tray contained mustard and ketchup containers and two small white bowls. One of the bowls was full of thinly cut onion slices, the other crinkle cut dill pickles. Ronnie grabbed the mustard container and squeezed several dribbles around the under side of the hamburger bun. He did the same with the ketchup. He piled on several slices of pickle and paused debating whether to add the onions slices. The voice of Beth whispered from the recesses of his memory, telling him to load the damn thing up. What the hell is a burger without onion, he could almost hear her say. Reluctantly, he added two slices.

Episode 33

"Where is it?" Ahmed asked.

The question jarred Ronnie from his internal debate about the onions.

"Where's what?" he asked.

"Grosse Ile," Ahmed answered.

"Oh, it's 'bout fifteen miles south of here." Ronnie added as he picked up the burger with both hands. Little droplets of grease fell on the wax paper as mustard dripped down one side. "Good burgers, but hard to eat without getting your hands a little messy."

"I lived here as a child then we moved away. I've only been back a short while," Ahmed replied.

Ronnie noticed Ahmed had only a slight accent. When Ronnie took another bite of the burger, mustard and ketchup squirted out of the back and plopped down on the wax paper after running over his fingers.

"Got to get a little dirt on your hands son, if you want to be a mighty big man," Ronnie said with a short laugh.

"What was that?" Ahmed asked.

"Oh, nothing," Ronnie answered. "It was just something my father used to tell me. I think of it when I get something on my hands," Ronnie grabbed several paper napkins.

"My dad used to have all kinds of sayings, too. Most of which I've tried to forget," Ahmed replied.

"Ha," Ronnie said then took a drink of beer. "I have two boys, the younger one's 'bout your age," he added. "My guess is they've also tried their damnedest to forget most of what I've told them over the years. It's a father's duty to impart knowledge to his sons. It's a son's duty to push it out of his mind until he has kids of his own. Then it just jumps out of his mouth in a most willful and annoying way. Anyway, looks like your girlfriend has deserted you," Ronnie looked toward the empty booth.

"Oh, Stacey," Ahmed continued, "she went to the restroom. She'll be here in a minute."

"In that case, I suppose you won't be pulling up a stool and hanging around to watch my football team blow it," Ronnie took another bite.

"Oh, no," Ahmed answered with a grin. "I understand from Nurse Cassadea, that you work at Ford Motor Engineering."

"That's true enough. I retired from full time work a couple of years back. I work part time now."

"Were you an Engineer?" Ahmed asked.

"No, actually I worked in Finance, though some folks described me as a frustrated accountant who wanted to be an engineer."

"Oh, well then you probably can't answer a question for me, then."

Ronnie could see Stacey coming toward them from the back of the bar.

"Well, you never know. Sometimes we Finance types can be a plethora of useless information. Or at least so I have been told that," Ronnie smiled then glanced at the television.

"Well, I was at a friend's house who works at National Motors, so maybe you can't answer the question. He had a part at his home that he was working on. I saw a number stamped into it wondered if you could tell me what it is that he's working on."

"Well, some of that stuff is sort of classified so your friend might not be able to talk about it. We used to get annual compliance notifications about not divulging competitive information. But what's on your mind, I'll do my best as long is it's nothing proprietary about Ford I can talk about it. Competitive spying and all that sort of stuff. Though I know you don't work for any of the competition, unless Oak Grove Hospital is treating Chevy Impalas," Ronnie winked and laughed again..

The blonde haired girl walked up and stood next to Ahmed and took his hand in hers.

"Oh, Stacey. This is Ronnie, he knows one of the nurses I work with at the hospital. He's a friend of Nurse Cassadea."

Episode 33

"A very old friend," Ronnie added. He extended his hand toward the young woman, after wiping it on a napkin. "Sorry about that, these burgers are a little juicy. Good, but kind of a mess."

The young woman let go of Ahmed's hand and shook Ronnie's.

"Yeah, but very good. It's nice to meet you."

"A pleasure, now tell me about this car part the friend of yours had at his house."

"Well, I don't know exactly what it was, but it had the number EV something 08 S stamped into it."

"Well," Ronnie answered picking up his beer glass. "That's easy enough. It's a coding system, we have one at Ford but it's different. If I were to guess, I'd say EV stands for Experimental Vehicle, 08 is the model year and S probably stands for Stallion, that's National Motor's muscle car. It competes with our Mustang and Chevrolet's Camero. Can I buy you two a beer?"

"No, but thanks," Ahmed answered, "we've got to meet some friends downtown."

"Well, it is Saturday night, I suppose. The new model Stallion is National's big deal new vehicle and will be featured next month at the North American Auto Show. You'll see pictures of the convertible model in the paper when the show starts. From what we hear, it's gonna put the Camero to shame and maybe our Mustang as well, but I hope not." Ronnie finished his beer.

Ahmed did his best to conceal his emotions. This was worse than he imagined. Mahmood had rigged a dirty bomb to be detonated at the North American Auto Show to shock the world. He planned to strike right at the heart of America's manufacturing just like September 11 had ripped at the financial heart.

"Are you okay, Ahmed?" Stacey asked. "You look pale."

Ahmed knew he had to recover quickly. "Yeah, I'm fine, I just ate too quickly."

"Do you want me to drive?" Stacey asked.

"No, no, I'll be okay. But we should let Ronnie get back to his football game."

"It was nice talking to you, see you at the hospital," Ahmed took Stacey's hand and turned to leave.

"Yeah, I plan to be there tomorrow."

"See you then," Ahmed said then walked toward the door.

Ronnie looked up at the television.

Episode 34

Cate woke up fifteen minutes before her alarm was set to go off. She looked at the two dogs snuggled next to each other. Gucci was a light sleeper and seemed to sense when Cate was awake. He opened one eye, noted his master was in her assigned place then closed the eye.

Cate looked at the ceiling, at least her head ache was gone. It had lingered most of the previous day. She would liked to have blamed the weather or her new glasses, but in truth she had drunk too much wine, not a smart thing to do. She had to drive to Indiana tomorrow, the county prosecutor scheduled a meeting about a pre-trial hearing. Cate couldn't believe she had to deal with such nonsense. David was gone, what was left to be done.

Besides packing, she had to get the dogs over to her brother's house. Kathy or Linda would have taken them, but they were leaving to chaperone the high school French club's trip to Paris. Cate had been invited but a trip abroad was out of the question. Jess had offered to watch the dogs, but she didn't have a reliable car.

Cate had also promised her mother she'd attend mass at St. Mary Magdalene's before leaving and she didn't want to let

Emma down. It had been ages since Cate had set foot in the church and Emma insisted Cate light a candle for her there.

Cate sat on the edge of the bed and put on her house slippers. She grabbed the yellow bath robe and headed down the steps with both dogs close behind. After putting them in the back yard, she returned to the house. She walked into the bungalow's tiny kitchen and turned on the coffee maker before opening the front door to get the Sunday newspaper. Sipping coffee, Cate read Susan Ager's article about an elderly man who had died and left over a million dollars to the Salvation Army. No one seemed to know the man had such wealth because he lived like a pauper. The story turned her thoughts to Eric again.

Cate heard Duffy yapping and set the paper on the table. When she opened the back gate, the dogs made a bee line to the side door where Duffy danced little circles as he waited for Cate. Back inside, Cate gave each dog a half of a can of food and poured her self a bowl of Cheerios. She munched on the cereal as she finished her coffee and the paper. Glancing at the clock, she noticed it was eight-fifteen. If she hurried, she could make nine o'clock mass and be back in time to finish packing before leaving for work. Cate rinsed her cereal bowl, set it in the sink and went in the bathroom to get ready.

Twenty-five minutes later she was dressed and driving along Allen Road towards the church. It was exactly nine when Cate genuflected and crossed herself before taking a seat in the long wooden pew at the back of St. Mary's. The priest and altar boys entered from behind the altar as the choir began singing. Cate looked around the sanctuary. The church was about half full, a stark difference from her childhood when the masses were so crowded the archdiocese spilt the parish and build a second church in the city.

She had forgotten how large St. Mary's was. Built in the twenties, the church had tall spires and a large belfry. Her mother said they didn't ring the chimes any more at early masses after some neighbors complained. Cate saw the complaint as a reflec-

Episode 34

tion of such changed times. It would have never been filed when she was a little girl, Melvindale was very Catholic. Cate had forgotten how beautiful the stained glass windows were. The morning sun seemed to set them aglow. Tuning out the elderly priest, she became lost in memories.

When the priest offered communion, Cate knew she hadn't done much to ready her soul but had promised her mother. When it was her turn, she stood up and made her way to the aisle. She hadn't recognized the priest but the lay assistant turned out to be Jenny Norello, a classmate. Cate took the Eucharist from the priest, dipped it in the chalice held by Jenny then made her way back to her seat. Jenny recognized her and had smiled and nodded. When communion ended, Cate watched Jenny take a seat next to a tall man with thinning black hair. After mass, Cate walked into the narthex and stood by the large entry doors. The doors had heavy brass handles and hinges. Each door had a small stained glass window with different colored crucifixes set in the center. Cate stopped to admire them before leaving when Jenny approached.

"Hey, Catie," Jenny said, "I thought that was you."

Jenny's hair was still very dark. She wore stylish glasses with narrow black frames.

"This is my husband Phil," she continued.

"Hello, Phil, nice to meet you," Cate smiled and extended her hand.

Phil took her hand and gave it a gentle shake.

"Well, you actually met him before at the twenty year class reunion, but that was a long time ago," Jenny interjected.

"You'll have to forgive me Phil, lately I can't remember what I had for lunch yesterday," Cate said apologetically.

"I know the feeling," Phil replied.

Phil was wearing gray wool pants, a blue blazer and a beige mock turtle neck. Another change Cate thought. Men wore suits and ties the last time she was a regular attendee at St. Mary's and the women wore dresses and hats.

"So, are you back in the area?" Jenny asked.

Book Two Home Again

"Yeah, at least for a while. I'm living with my mom. I was in Indiana a few years. My husband died recently and my mom needed some help. Sort of the big circle you know."

"We certainly know how that is, aging parents, grandchildren and all."

"Thought I might have seen you at Homecoming Friday night," Cate added.

"Oh, Phil went to Allen Park, and their Homecoming was Friday night, too. Our kids went to AP, so we have obligations there. We still come to mass here though, kind of a tradition. Did you see anyone from our class at Homecoming?"

Before Cate could respond, the entry door opened and two nuns walked into the narthex. They were not dressed in traditional habits but wore head coverings. Cate recognized the taller one.

"Well, I went with Kathy Mac and Ronnie Harris. We met up with Jess, Linda and Danny, oh excuse me, Mayor Killard and his first lady, Marie," Cate said with a laugh. The taller nun turned her way as she walked by and gave Cate a brief nod of recognition. A faint smile crossed the nun's face as she closed her eyes. It had been done in such a nun like fashion, Cate felt like she was eight years old and back in catechism.

"I know her," Cate said, though it was more of a question.

"You should, Cate," Jenny answered, "that's Margaret Bertilino. Of course she's Sister Maria now."

"Sister Maria," Cate said with a smile. "Sounds like something from a movie. What do you do about a girl named Maria?"

Cate could tell her line hadn't registered.

"You know, Maria, the Van Trapp family, Julie Andrews, the world is alive with the sound of music?" Cate continued.

"Oh, yeah," Phil said, "I get it now. Maria, I always got her confused with that flying nun."

"That was Sally Fields," Cate replied, "anyway, what a surprise to see Margaret."

"She teaches math at the grade school," Jenny added. "Our kids all went to St. Mary's through eighth grade."

Episode 34

"Well, small world. Anyway, I should get going. I have a shift at the hospital tonight and I need to get moving. It was nice seeing you Jenny," Cate put her hand on the door handle and pushed it open.

"We'll walk with you to the parking lot," Jenny said falling in step with Cate. Phil trailed a few feet behind.

"So how was Homecoming?" Jenny asked.

"Well, I haven't been to one in some time. I mean I have been to high school homecomings when my girls were in school, but not a Melvindale homecoming since let's see, umm, the fall of 1966," Cate answered. They crossed the street and were almost at the parking lot. "It was fun, we all went to Blazo's after and then to Danny's."

"Blazo's," Jenny said with a touch of excitement, "I thought that place closed years ago."

"We didn't go to the one in Dearborn. Ronnie somehow found out there's one left on, I think on Beech Daily out in Redford, I'm not sure."

"Was the menu the same?"

"Yeah, but our stomachs have changed or something. Maybe it's our tastes. I can't say for sure, let's just say once a year is enough," Cate replied with a laugh.

"It's nice to see you, Cate" Jenny added when they had reached the parking lot, "maybe we'll see you next Sunday."

"Maybe," Cate answered though her promise was for only one Sunday a month.

Episode 35

Cate pulled into the hospital parking structure at one forty-five. Her shift started at two so she'd have to hurry. Dropping the dogs at her brothers had taken more time than planned and finding a parking spot hadn't been easy. The first three floors were full. She finally found a spot on the fourth floor and castigated herself for being late as she walked down the stairs. Her break was at six and she planned to meet Ronnie in the cafeteria for coffee. At five fifty-five, she told one of her staff she was going on break.

Cate took the elevator to the main floor and found Ronnie waiting for her at a table near the back. He had a cup of coffee for her with a little container of half and half next to the cup. She walked to the table and took the chair opposite him.

"Thanks," she said peeling the foil top off the half and half. "My cholesterol doesn't need this," she added while pouring the entire contents into the cup. Little wisps of steam drifted up from the coffee as she stirred it, "but I sure do. I hate that artificial Coffeecream crap, it tastes so awful."

"You're welcome," Ronnie replied, "looks like you've recovered from Friday night. Me thinks maybe Cate hit the wine a little too hard?"

"Like you've got room to talk," she answered with a laugh, "if I remember right, it was Jess driving you and your brother in law home. What does that say about your state of being?"

"Ex brother in law," Ronnie said with a smile. "Please don't remind me. I paid a price for all that fun. By the way, just for your own personal info, Jess didn't leave until this morning."

"Well, well," Cate interjected, "do I denote a bit of envy in your voice?"

"No, it's not envy. If anything, it's irony you hear. I had to clean up after Kenny's last little dalliance, but this thing with Jess will probably turn out to be a role reversal."

"Careful now, Ronnie. You know she is one of my best friends. Course that's not a very exclusive club as of late."

Ronnie laughed, "You know I really like Jess, always have. I'm not disparaging her, but damn Cate, you have to admit, she's been places we've only seen on television. She's probably just what the doctor ordered for Denny."

"Hey, what do I know? I'm just a nurse," Cate answered.

"Anyway, I know we don't have much time, but there is something I want your medical opinion on, if it's okay?" Ronnie asked earnestly.

"Well, okay as long as it doesn't have to do with bed pans and enemas I'm all ears so to speak," Cate replied. "You have a serious look. What's up?"

Ronnie told her Bobbie's story about the two doctors and his suspicions. Cate listened without interruption. When Ronnie finished, she put her cup down.

"I've treated cancer patients over the years," she said, "chemo and radiation can cause emotional distress. Bobbie has more than one lesion on his brain, so that alone can lead to distorted thinking. My guess is he's experiencing some kind of end of life remorse. That's also not unusual. Do you want my recommendation as a friend or a nurse?"

"Both," Ronnie answered.

"Act like you believe him. There's really nothing to be served by trying to reason with him or telling him he's delusional.

Episode 35

Maybe he saw some doctors who remind him of a troubled past and he wants to make amends. The human mind is a funny thing without adding massive doses of poison. You know from your experience, it's a fine line those oncologists are treading. So listen to Bobbie, and go along. If you start believing his story, come talk to me and we'll decide what to do next," Cate looked at her watch. "Thanks for the coffee. I have to get back to the salt mines. I'll talk to you when I get back from Indiana. Then you can help me with a dilemma of my own."

"What's that?" Ronnie asked taking a sip of coffee.

"Eric," Cate said in a matter of fact tone then stood up. Ronnie walked her to the elevators.

"What about him?" Ronnie inquired as they walked.

"That's sort of the point, isn't it? That's what we need to find out."

At the elevator Cate pushed the up button and the door opened immediately. Several passengers got out. When the compartment emptied, she stepped inside.

"Have a safe trip to Indiana," Ronnie said as the door closed.

"I will," he heard her say as the door slid shut.

Cate had done her best to remain calm as Ronnie spun his story about Bobbie's revelation. While she appeared calm, her brain was spinning. Cate knew she could go to the hospital chief of staff and tell him her story of seeing Doctor Taj meeting with Dr. Nakshatra at the Hyatt and her subsequent theft of the vial from the trash. She could add her story about a friend from high school, a patient on the fifth floor, who had a nefarious history with Dr. Nak. Afterward, one of two things would happen. The hospital chief would test the vial, and confirm it was a standard medication, then fire her. Or the testing would confirm that patients were being injected with some lethal substance as part of a government sponsored anti-terrorist program. The FBI or CIA or whoever would then lock her away in some gulag. If she hadn't witnessed Doctor Nak's act of chicanery, she would have attributed Bobbie's tale to too much morphine

Book Two Home Again

She knew the eighth floor was off limits, so whatever was going had approval from the very top. Walking away was the smart thing to do. When the elevator stopped, she walked to her station and decided to put her run away brain on hold. First things first she told herself, which meant focusing for the next few hours on her patients. Cate sat at her desk and began reviewing charts. After a few minutes she noticed a chart was missing. She flipped through them again.

"Janine, where's the chart for Abu Caurdy," Cate asked. Janine was a thirty-two year nurse with flawless ebony skin who juggled a sixty hour work week with raising three young children. Cate admired her dedication.

"Oh, Doctor Nak took it out of the rack," Janine answered.

"Why would he do that?" Cate asked.

Abu Caurdy was a young Arab who had been in a motorcycle accident. He had almost lost a leg. He was recovering so well his pain medication had been reduced. Cate had given him a minimal dose before she left on break.

"Dr. Nak said that Dr. Wurtsmith asked him to look in on him and took the chart. He's down there now. He came on the floor just as you went on break. By the way, was that your friend from high school you were racing off to meet again?" Janine asked with raised eyebrows

"Yes, and he's just a friend, that's all."

"Hmmmm," Janine said, "I've had old friends like that. Only not too many of them come by anymore. They take one look at my kids and run off, as my daddy used to say, like a scalded dog."

"Really, Janine, he's just an old high school friend. His best friend is on five. He comes to see him."

"This friend married?"

"No, his wife died a couple of years ago. Cancer, she was on five, too."

"And you're just friends," Janine smiled as she left the station for the the storage area. "I have to go give Mr. Myers his meds."

"It's not that way, Janine," Cate said earnestly.

Episode 35

"Hey, I'm not saying nuthin'," Janine replied walking toward the hallway.

After Janine left, Cate began reviewing the staffing schedule for the following week when Dr. Nak walked up to the station and replaced the chart for Abu. Assured the chart was in place, he walked to the staircase and started up the steps.

Cate watched Dr. Nakshatra. When the stairway door closed, she went to the chart rack. She pulled Abu's chart and flipped it open. Examining the entries she noticed there were no notations from Dr. Nak. She replaced the chart and headed for Abu's room.

Dr. Nakshatra was almost to the sixth floor when he noticed his stethoscope was missing. He stood motionless for a moment mentally retracing his steps. He hadn't used it on the last patient; he'd only given the young Muslim an injection. He remembered he'd set the stethoscope on the table next to the young Arab's bed.

Cate walked into the Abu's room. The other patient was on a morphine drip and was out completely. She drew the curtain and quietly walked next to Abu's bed. She'd given him Demerol just before her break and he also was sound asleep. Cate lifted his left arm and looked at the injection site. There was a second puncture mark which hadn't been there earlier.

Dr. Nakshatra reached the doorway and lifted the metal handle. On his way toward Abu's room he passed the nurse's station and noticed no one was behind the desk. Just as he was at the door leading toward Abu's room he passed nurse Janine.

"Your station's unattended," he stated.

"I'm on my way there. Had to give some meds but we've got it covered, Nurse Cassadea's looking in on Mr. Caurdy, she just ducked in there for a moment."

He wondered why Nurse Cassadea would be in there so soon. The chart showed she had given him Demerol less than an hour earlier. Something wasn't quite right. He'd had that feeling the first time he'd seen her on the floor. He'd seen her someplace before, but couldn't place her. Feeling a sense of alarm, he hurried toward Abu's room.

Cate set Abu's arm down. She looked over and noticed a stethoscope on the table next to the bed. Cate looked around the room, everything seemed in order. As she stepped out from the curtain, she noticed the medical waste basket. Trying to resist her curiosity, Cate knew she would have to look inside.

Where had he seen her before, Dr. Nakshatra repeated to himself. He had a photographic mind; it was one of the assets that gained him admittance to the most renowned medical school in India. He would remember in time. Doctor Nakshatra's memory had unlocked many doors. He could have done other things with such a gift, but decided to dedicate its use to his country and religion. If everything went according to plan, the two would be one. India would be Hindu, and for Hindus only. That's why he'd joined the I.E.R., they understood the only national policy any true Hindu could embrace. There was no room for a Muslim presence in India, in their vision of what India would become. Even the great Mahatma Gandhi had erred in that respect. There was no sharing India with Muslims, ever. The only thing he intended to share with Muslims had been injected into a young Arab's arm minutes earlier. When the young man recovered and left the hospital, he would share it with someone else, and the gift would be then shared again with another Muslim. They had taken their battle half way around the world, because it served a Hindu only India. Abu Caurdy's room was just a few feet away now. He hoped Nurse Cassadea would not be a problem, but something in his head whispered she would.

Cate walked to the medical waste basket and pulled a pair of latex gloves from her pocket. She slipped them on before lifting the top to the container.

Dr. Nakshatra was just two rooms away from Abu's when Nurse Andrea walked out of the room on his right.

"Hello, Dr. Nak, I didn't expect to see you here so late on a Sunday night?" she exclaimed.

Episode 35

He'd always found Nurse Andrea to be pleasant despite her irritating voice.

Cate heard Andrea's voice from the hallway and froze.

"Damn," she said under her breath as she lifted the top to the waste container. When she heard Andrea's voice, she knew the stethoscope lying on the table was Dr. Nak's. Cate looked into the receptacle and saw a small glass vial lying on top of two bloodied dressings. She knew there was little time before Dr. Nak would enter the room. She quickly picked up the vial and dropped it into her uniform pocket. After replacing the top of the waste container, she spun around as Dr. Nakshatra walked in.

"Dr. Nak," Cate said in a voice that sounded very guilty in her head. She felt blood rush to her face and her cheeks felt warm. Cate felt like a child caught with her hands in the proverbial cookie jar. If Bobbie's allegations were true, getting caught with her hand in this jar would be something far worse than no desert after dinner.

"Oh, Nurse Cassadea, I've forgotten my stethoscope. I think I may have left it here. Have you seen it?" Dr. Nak stood in the middle of the doorway blocking her exit.

Cate realized there was no way of leaving the room, she had to think of something quickly. "Uh, yes, I mean there is one over on the table next to Mr. Caurdy. I was just about to take it up front."

"Well, I've saved you the trouble. Thank you anyway. I see you have your gloves on, is there anything going on with Mr. Caurdy?" Dr. Nak asked. The whiteness of his teeth was accented by his dark skin.

"No, I just like to be careful. Well, I have other patients," she continued, "your stethoscope is on the table."

Cate took a step toward the doorway expecting Dr. Nak to step aside, instead he continued to block the doorway.

"Yes, you've told me that already," Dr. Nak replied.

His eyes moved in a rapid up and down survey of her body stopping momentarily at the small bulge in her uniform pocket. As his eyes inspected her, his brain performed a separate retrieval.

The instant he saw the outline in her uniform pocket, Dr. Nakshatra's laser like memory locked onto the first time he had seen her. It had been in the Emergency Room when he treated the young Hezbollah terrorist. There had been an elderly woman in the room across from him who'd suffered a stroke. In a nano second, his neurons sent a follow up message. Wait a moment, his circuits shouted, there was an encounter before that. The entire record would come back to him, given time. Satisfied; Dr. Nak stepped slightly aside to allow Nurse Cassadea to leave.

"Thank you doctor," her voice cracked as she stepped toward him. Cate took another step, but he hadn't given her much room. To get by, she'd have to brush against him. It was probably her imagination, but as she did so, she could smell faint traces of curry emanating from his neatly trimmed mustache.

Out of the room, Cate walked briskly toward her station mentally kicking herself for taking the vial. She thought about the doctors visual frisking and concluded she hadn't been given a total body inspection like that since she was thirty-two and had been daring enough to wear a bikini to the beach. Cate wondered if the doctor noticed the vial in her pocket, it wasn't very big. Maybe once he got his stethoscope back, Cate reassured herself, everything would be okay.

As soon as Cate left the room, Dr. Nakshatra stepped behind the curtain and grabbed the stethoscope. He placed it around his neck and walked over to the medical waste basket. Assured he was alone, he lifted the top. The vial was gone. He cursed himself for such stupidity and left the room. As he neared the elevator he looked at the nurse's station. Nurse Janine was studying a patient chart but Nurse Cassadea was nowhere to be seen.

After what seemed an eternity, the elevator doors finally opened. Why had it taken so long he thought as he boarded the elevator and pushed the button for eight. The doors closed and the elevator began ascending. Two nurses got off at seven; Dr. Nakshatra was alone on the elevator as the doors closed. This is going to be a problem he muttered to himself. As the thought left his brain, another came screaming in.

Episode 35

"The Hyatt," he said aloud. "That's where I saw her."

Dr. Nakshatra's mind raced to retrieve other facts from that night. He'd met Dr. Taj for dinner where he received the latest case of vials. He'd seen Nurse Cassadea in the lobby and then again as he left the hotel. He closed his eyes and concentrated. When the elevator stopped at eight, Dr. Nakshatra got off. The male nurse at the station looked up and pushed a button unlocking the doorway. Inside his office, Dr. Nakshatra sat at his desk and dialed Dr. Midek's phone number. The phone rang twice.

"Ray Midek," the words were pronounced succinctly. It was the end of the first half on Sunday Night Football. He pushed the mute button on the remote and picked up the glass of Scotch from the end table.

Dr. Midek's tone indicated irritation about his evening being interrupted. No one called on Sunday night with good news, it didn't work that way. Not in either of the professions he'd chosen. Late night calls for a physician meant a patient was in trouble. Dalliances would have to be cut short, clothes would have to be changed and sleep would have to be foregone. For an agent, late night calls meant the same.

Dr. Midek had played football at the Academy and had an opportunity to play professionally but in those days that meant waiting until his four year tour of active duty was completed. After graduation, Raymond Midek entered Duke Medical School as a Second Lieutenant. Then it was Viet Nam and special missions. Doctor Midek had no regrets, it had been a lifetime of duty, service and honor that not many people outside of the Agency understood.

"We have a breach in security," the voice on the other end stated.

Episode 36

Doctor Midek closed his cell phone then took a pull on his drink. Doctor Nakshatra's call did not portend good things. Ray turned off the television, there'd be no Ravens game tonight.

In some ways, Ray Midek disdained certainty. It made life boring. It was why he was sitting in a condominium in Fairlane Hills, unmarried and working in the field again. At fifty-eight, he'd become bored with his desk job. The outcome of each day was too certain. There was no spark, there was no reason to look forward to the day. It had taken some persuading to get the Director to return him to the field, but it had been worth it. He felt invigorated and alive again. The idea for the operation had been his brain child. Recruiting Indian agents from Intelligence Evaluation and Research, or I.E.R. had been the icing on the cake.

Pulling the I.E.R. into the project had been his master stroke. Most Americans were familiar with the Russia's KGB or Britain's MI6, but few had ever heard of the I.E.R. Yet espionage, euphemistically called the second oldest profession of the world, finds mention in the Indian Vedas, one of the most ancient of human texts. Secret agencies in ancient India were not conceived as instruments of oppression but rather as a normal tool of governance.

A student of history, Ray understood the I.E.R. had been established to perform clandestine operations based on principles of deceit and guile. It successfully destabilized neighboring countries, disintegrated independent states and backed the most notorious guerilla organizations to achieve its ends. When compared to other intelligence agencies, it emerges as an aggressive, cold blooded and ruthless institution that engaged in the most macabre deeds. The I.E.R. had even enabled India to detonate an atomic bomb before the rest of the world had any idea the country was nuclear capable.

When Doctor Midek went to the Director, his oldest friend inside the Agency, and described his plan to use a hospital in the city with the largest Arabic population in the United States as a way to gather intelligence, the idea had been warmly received. In subsequent meetings with the I.E.R., Ray's basic operational proposal was refined and expanded. Six months later a completed plan had been approved at the highest levels. Known only by the Directors of the Agency and the I.E.R., the plan had been altered. It wasn't just hallucinogens and truth serum that was being injected to the Muslim patients. It was something more lethal and the primary reason the Director looked to the I.E.R. for assistance.

The Director had heard whispers the I.E.R. developed a strain of HIV genetically designed to be fast acting and resistant to available anti-viral drugs. Of course, the Agency had been working on their own strain, but developing and actually using the virus were two different things. The Agency Director also knew the virus was being tested by the I.E.R. in very limited cases against Pakistani Muslims taken captive in the fighting around Kashmir. The strain had shown great potential. The two Directors agreed to extend the testing to select patients in Fairlane Hills. This last wrinkle had never been revealed to Doctor Midek, so he had no idea the security breech included missing vials of the genetically altered virus.

This part of the operation was also not never revealed to Doctor Douglas Lange, the hospital's chief of staff. Doctor Lange

Episode 36

believed he'd only been doing his patriotic duty when he agreed to a meeting at a rustic villa in the Adirondack Mountains. He and the Board of Directors of Oak Grove Hospital had been briefed about the federal government's risk assessment for the presence of weapons of mass destruction in the Detroit area. It was no secret and not a slam against Arabs or Muslims, the Director maintained in his initial presentation, but there were suspected sleeper cells in Fairlane Hills. The board finally agreed with the Director's proposal and had signed documents to never divulge the content of the meeting.

According to the plan, one floor of the hospital would be designated a biological containment center and Agency personnel would be added to the hospital's staff as a link to the Center For Disease Control and National Security Office. The Agency doctors and staff would also examine and treat selected patients considered to be terrorist risks. The project would be given cover as an isolation wing established in the hospital in case SARs or Bird Flu epidemics struck. One side of the floor would be dedicated for such use, while the other side would house patients dedicated exclusively for use by the Agency. The Board of Directors left the retreat convinced they had accomplished three goals. They had prepared for a possible pandemic, helped their country in a time of need and obtained a Federal endowment virtually assuring a good bottom line for the hospital for the foreseeable future.

Episode 37

After leaving Abu Caurdy's room, Cate went to the storage room behind the nurse's station to compose herself. She had three immediate alternatives. She could pitch the latest vial and claim ignorance if questioned. She could hide the vial in the hospital and figure out what to do later. Or she could hang onto it and hope for the best. She opted to hang onto the vial. It was proof of Bobbie's allegations and her ticket out if the worst happened. What to do in the long term was another problem. If need be, she could give the police one of the vials then send the other to the newspapers. Cate realized she wasn't thinking clearly.

****

Doctor Midek walked into the bedroom and changed clothes. He stood just over six feet and weighed one hundred and ninety pounds. Other than the fifth of Scotch he spread over a week's time, Ray limited his vices.

He was confident he would resolve the issue in short order. Ray locked the back door and walked to his car. The condo was one of several new buildings on Hamilton Street in west Fairlane

Hills built in the brownstone style popular in D.C. Ray had considered property on Grosse Ile where his Cessna 170 sat in its hanger, but wanted to stay close to the hospital. After the Agency, flying and sports cars were his passions..

****

Cate left the storage room. She took a seat at the station and tried to focus on her job. The patient in room 448 needed attention. Cate told Janine she'd take care of it and when she returned Andrea was at the station.

"Cate, I saw Doctor Nak talking to you in Mr. Caurdy's room. Did he seem a little on the muscle or something tonight?" Andrea asked in her high pitched voice.

"Oh, yeah," Cate answered. "He left his steth there and wanted to know if I'd seen it."

"Did you?" Andrea added.

Cate didn't feel like talking, but didn't want to be rude.

"Yeah, good thing, you know how doctors are. Otherwise he'd have us tearing up the place until the damn thing was located."

"Agreed," Andrea laughed. "I was talking to Janine. She said on your break that you were having coffee with that friend of yours. The guy who's always stopping to visit," Andrea said with a wry smile.

"Listen, it's really nothing. I just know him from high school, that's all. Besides I've been widowed for all of four months now. I'm not interested at this point and doubt I ever will be," Cate added abruptly.

"Sorry," Andrea replied timidly.

"Listen Andrea," Cate apologized, "I just have so much on my mind. I have to go to Indiana tomorrow and I get a little wound up just before I go back. Memories and all, I didn't mean to be nasty. I'm sorry, really."

"Hey, that's okay. Anyway, how's you friend on five doing?" Andrea asked changing the subject.

"Not good. On my next break, I think I'll check on him."

Episode 37

"Why don't you go now? We've got it covered here. The rest of the night should be slow. I can always page you."

"Thanks, Andrea," Cate answered. "I appreciate that, maybe I will go see him now."

Cate patted Andrea on the shoulder as she walked toward the stairway.

****

Ray Midek pulled his Corvette into the doctor's parking lot. As he rode the elevator to eight he reviewed the protocol. According to plan, Dr. Nak hadn't gone into any details on the phone. So what had gone wrong? If one of the regular staff had somehow wondered onto the eighth floor undetected, security needed to improve. If the problem was within their staff, that was an issue requiring draconian measures.

Ray got off the elevator. The nurse pushed the unlock button and he continued to his office. Taking a seat on the leather couch across from his desk, Ray phoned Dr. Nak.

"My office," Ray said tersely.

"I'm on my way," Dr. Nak replied in his faint Hindi accent.

****

Cate took the stairway to five and walked toward the nurse's station. On a first name basis with the staff, she waived and continued to Bobbie's room.

"Hey Bobbie," she said. He seemed paler and was sucking a grape popsicle. A half eaten bowl of chicken broth lay on his tray.

"Well, now there's a pleasant face to wake up to. How's nurse Cate tonight?" Bobbie answered with a weak smile.

He looked into her clear blue eyes, one more regret he said to himself.

"Bobbie, I hate to be so direct, but I need to talk to you about something," Cate sat in the visitors chair.

Book Two Home Again

Bobbie set the popsicle on the tray.

"Fire away, Cate. At least my ears still work," a weak smile crossing his gaunt face.

"I'm in a bit of trouble. It has to do with what you told Ronnie."

"I tell Ronnie a lot of things. What did I tell him that is giving you so much consternation. How's that for a word Ms. Valedictorian. Not bad for a guy that barely graduated though I did need summer," Bobbie noted his humor was not registering.

"The stuff you told Ronnie about what you believe is going on here. The stuff about Doctor Midek."

"Ronnie would never have made it in my business," Bobbie replied seriously. "Secrecy seems beyond my best friend's capability."

"Look, he came to me as a friend and asked for medical advice. He wasn't really betraying any confidence; he's just worried about you."

"Well, I should have known better, I guess. He did offer to get me a priest. Guess he knew keeping secrets wasn't his strong suit. So what does this have to do with you Cate?"

Cate told Bobbie about her suspicions regarding Doctor Taj, the incident at the Hyatt, Doctor Naksharta and the two vials. When she got to the part about the vials, Bobbie tried to sit up. Cate could tell even the slightest movements were painful.

"Any idea what's in those vials?" he asked.

"No, but I've got one in my pocket and the other is well hidden."

"Listen to what I tell you Cate. These two men are very dangerous. Do not, and I repeat do not believe any thing they tell you. Now don't freak out on me, 'cause lord knows I can't be of much help. If they know you have one of the vials, they will not let you walk out of here. They'll try to get you to go with them, and they'll tell you that once they have it, you'll be in no danger. My guess is that they will find a way to get you out of the picture permanently."

Episode 37

A knot formed in Cate's throat. What was she thinking taking that first vial, she cursed herself and wished she could rewind the clock and undo the whole thing.

"Bobbie, I don't know what's in the vial. Can't I just give it back to them? Say I'm sorry and let it go at that?" She asked. Tears welled up in her eyes as she thought about her daughters and grandchildren she'd never see.

"Look just by knowing about the vials, you are a huge liability to them. At least I know if I were heading this thing up, you'd be removed."

Cate was astonished to hear Bobbie say something so cold and calculating. A shiver ran up her spine as she heard him talk so calmly about ordering someone's death like he was ordering dinner. Bobbie's emotions were mixed. He wondered how much was attributable to the medication. For some reason, all he could see was the young girl who was innocent and exciting inside the fifty-five year old nurse sitting across from of him. He knew what he'd just said had stunned her.

"Cate, I know you are frightened, but you are going to have to do exactly as I tell you. First, put all of those regrets aside; lock them out. You've been through some bad shit in your life but somehow you found a way to muck through it all. I assume you've been in the operating room and know how you sometimes have to block out everything that's going on around you and run on auto pilot. You have to do the same starting right now. First, as soon as your shift is over, get out of here as quickly as you can but do not go home. Is there someplace else you can go for the night?"

"Well, I could go to Jess's or Ronnie's I suppose."

"Don't go to Ronnie's, that's a last choice. The nurses you work with know him and so do the nurses on this floor. Go to Jess's, there's no known connection there. Listen, I'm going to give you a man's name and phone number. I want you to call him. He can help. We go back a long way and he owes me a couple of favors. If you can hold on for a week or two at the most, maybe we can get you out of this mess," Bobbie omitted his doubt about living that long.

"Give me a pen and a piece of paper. I also want you to memorize it. Don't call from the hospital. I want you to call the number from a disposable cell phone. Tell him you're a friend of Stick's. He'll know who sent you. Listen, I can't call him from here but if I can find a way to get a secure phone I'll call him. You're going to be all right Cate. One more thing, do not contact any of your family. They will be safe as long as the agents are certain you haven't contacted them. Have you heard every thing I've said Cate?"

"Yes," Cate answered. It was all she could do to voice the solitary word.

"One more thing," Bobbie added, "there's still a thing or two I can do even in here to help." It was meant as reassurance, but looking at Cate's face he doubted she would even make it out of the hospital.

****

Doctor Nak tapped on Ray's office door, opened it and took a seat in the chair across from him.

"We had a security issue tonight with a nurse on the sixth floor."

"How severe is the breech?" Ray asked sitting upright with his hands clasped under his chin.

"We may have to abort the project," Doctor Nakshatra said in a controlled voice.

"Abort!" Ray responded in a raised whisper, "Why the hell would we abort? Because some nurse witnessed you interrogating a patient?"

"It wasn't an interrogation she witnessed," Doctor Nak replied knowing some aspects of the project had not been revealed to Doctor Midek. It was protocol to keep certain elements compartmentalized to protect the mission and the agents. It also shielded higher levels, by preventing corroborative evidence. Doctor Nakshatra would keep knowledge of the injections of HIV from Doctor Midek unless it was an emergency. Their present situation certainly qualified.

Episode 37

"What exactly did she see?" Ray asked leaning forward.

"It's not as much what she saw as what she may have in her possession," Dr. Nak replied in evenly spoken words. He knew, as the Americans were fond of saying, the shit was about to hit the fan.

"Listen, Pradeeb," Ray replied using what he assumed was Dr. Nak's first name. "Please stop beating around the bush and tell me what is going on so I can assess the damage."

"I have been injecting Muslim suspects with a virulent strain of HIV," Doctor Nak added. Having rolled out the grenade, he now waited for the ensuing explosion.

"You have been doing what?" Doctor Midek asked standing up.

Doctor Nakshatra shifted his position to maintain eye contact.

"We have been working on a strain of HIV that is fast acting and immune to anti retroviral medications. You may have recalled there was an article in the New York Times recently about a Pakistani cab driver who was hospitalized with a rare form of HIV. He had been infected as part of our test program. The CDC said it was just a random occurrence and not the result of a new strain of the virus. Their response was part of our containment protocol."

"When you say our, do you mean my Agency?" Doctor Midek worked to control his rage. The fact that the CDC had been compromised from outside added to his anger.

"The people I am referring to work for I.E.R. We know you have your own people inside the CDC, but identifying them was not part of our primary objective."

"We'll talk about your primary objective in a minute. First tell me about the security breech."

"There is one breach for certain, and there may have been a second, but I will not be able to ascertain that until we take the subject nurse into custody."

"Take her in custody. Are you out of your mind? We just can't walk down there and arrest her. How will we explain that? Specifically, what happened?"

365

"There is a patient on her floor. A young Arab who was in an accident. As you know, we scan patient admissions for religious preference and Muslim names. Selected patients are interrogated. What you don't know is that I also select some for injection of the virus. After injecting them, I dispose of the vials in the standard biohazard waste containers. I believe Nurse Cassadea retrieved a vial from a container and has it on her person."

"Okay, that's the primary breech. What is the potential secondary one?"

"Remember a couple of months ago when we infected the food at those two Arab restaurants with an intestinal virus and we subsequently apprehended that Hezbollah terrorist brought into the hospital emergency room? I injected him with the HIV. Nurse Cassadea's mother was also in the emergency room. It is possible she could have retrieved that vial as well."

"Do you believe that she is working for someone or just a chance occurrence?"

"Well, it is possible she is employed by another agency. She may just be a drug addict and thought the vials contained a narcotic though that's unlikely. As a supervisor she has ready access to narcotics. She might have a political motive, it's just unclear."

"So what are you recommendations?" Ray asked.

"First, we must get the vial back, there's no doubt about that."

"I agree. We can make it look like a drug bust and play it that way. If she resists and things get really dicey, we can hold her stating security reasons and use the Patriot Act. We should avoid that avenue though, it might turn the spot light toward us. I'll make some calls to start that process just in case. We'll play it by the book and make it look like hospital security is busting her for drugs then take her to a safe house. In the mean time, I suggest you safeguard any remaining vials. Let's keep all of this in house until we get her in for interrogation. No need in going up the ladder until we are sure this isn't just some kind of drug theft gone awry."

"I'll see to the vials," Doctor Nakshatra got up from the chair and walked out of Ray's office.

Episode 37

"Damn," Ray said under his breath to an absent Director Walburn. "You should have told me," he added, "I could have taken the proper precautions."

Had he been the Director, Ray knew he would have done the same. He also knew his task had just gotten more complicated. Ray picked up the cell phone from his desk and dialed. When the phone was answered, Ray gave the coded instructions. The team would be at the safe house within the hour.

Episode 38

Cate studied statistics in college and understood probability theory. Though she'd never known anyone who had used statistical analysis in the real world, she knew that if there were fifteen red balls in a jar and five black ones, the probability of drawing a red ball was three out of four. She also knew the probability of drawing a red ball the second time changed. It was called Bayesian Theorem. But Cate also knew life wasn't static like twenty balls in a jar. In life, random events such as the jar getting knocked off the table disrupted probability theories. If the jar breaks and the balls scatter about the floor, the focus changes to the probability of not cutting your foot while you cleaned up the mess. Cate's textbook hadn't addressed such situations because clumsiness was outside the text's universe of existence.

Life wasn't lived in a controlled environment. Cate knew life was an open ended affair where random chance plays the major part in determining the course of a person's existence. Most people like to believe they are in control, while in truth events that determined their destinies were mostly random. Cate also believed simple things, like selecting a spouse or finding a job, were good examples. None of her friends married the person of their dreams. Some wondered what their life would have been had they not gone to that party or hadn't taken a job where they met Mister or Miss Wrong. The same was true of careers. Few people had the job they dreamed of when young. Random chance led them to a livelihood of selling insurance or changing bed pans or delivering UPS packages. Filling out their retirement papers thirty years later, they wondered what their lives would have been had they chased their dreams instead.

She had seen the same results in the medical field. A random bit of plaque lodges in the arterial wall and for that person life is never the same. A cell decides to mutate leading to events even more unpredictable. Or a person follows a strict dietary regimen and exercises regularly only to die in a car accident, while their sibling who chain smokes and lives on Tostitos and Budweiser arranges the funeral.

Life was a crap shoot and Cate accepted such randomness, like letting David drive home that night or accompanying her mother to the hospital and taking that first vial. What Cate didn't know, however, was that random chance was about to enter her life again and it would be triggered by something as innocuous as leaving work an hour early. It was only on hour, but that sixty minute change was akin to knocking the jar of balls off of the table. Mr. Bayes's theorem would no longer apply because the jar would cease to exist.

It was almost ten when Cate reviewed the last patient chart with Janine. Cate tried to remain calm knowing the next fifteen minutes would be decisive. If she could just get to her car and make it to Jess's house, she'd be okay.

****

Ahmed stood by the time clock watching the minute hand. It seemed to have stopped one hash mark shy of punch out time. The metal hands were painted black and matched the hash marks arranged in a circular fashion between the numbers. The clock looked so old he wondered if it was installed the year the hospital was built.

Episode 38

    His shift normally ended at eleven thirty but he had asked to get off at ten because he had an appointment at Wayne State University's Engineering School the next morning. Ahmed wanted to be well rested for the interview. Stacey had given him a student catalogue detailing the classes in the Electrical Engineering program and a publication listing available scholarships. Given his situation it was probably a waste of time, but she had gone to such trouble.

    When the minute hand finally moved, Ahmed slid the time card through the slot then removed the card, and replaced it in the rack. Taking the stairs to the first floor, Ahmed walked into the hallway leading toward the parking garage. He had to park on the fifth floor because Sundays were busy because of visitors.

    ****

    The four agents rendezvoused at the safe house thirty minutes after Doctor Midek's call. Three were men; the fourth a female. Doctor Midek began the briefing. Nurse Cassadea was to be taken into custody with as little force as possible. Two agents, dressed in Oak Grove Hospital Security uniforms, would be in place by her vehicle. Agent Ann would be the first to engage Nurse Cassadea. She would instruct the nurse to get into the white Ford Explorer with a Oak Grove Hospital Security sign displayed on the side. The agent would tell Nurse Cassadea she was being taken to the security office for questioning about missing drugs. If she resisted, Nurse Cassadea was to be tasered and loaded into the Explorer where she would be sedated for the ride to the safe house. A pair of agents would be posted at the exit to the parking structure in case she tried to run. All four agents were instructed to load their weapons with rubber bullets. Back up clips of conventional ammunition were to be kept on stand by.

    Nurse Cassadea's shift ended at eleven hundred so they needed to be in place by ten hundred. Her car had been located on the fourth floor. To not arouse suspicion, the first security vehicle would stay concealed on the ramp between the fourth and fifth floor. The driver would stay in the Explorer while Agent Ann positioned herself near the nurse's Buick Rivera. Once Agent Ann made visual contact, she would radio the driver to bring the Explorer into position. The driver would remain in the vehicle unless there was a reason to exit. Nurse Cassadea's car keys would be handed off to the second team who would drive the Rivera to the safe house.

****

The elevator door opened as Ahmed emerged from the stairway door. He was surprised to see Nurse Cassadea step out.

"Looks like I'm not the only one knocking off early tonight," he said with a smile.

Surprised to hear a familiar voice, Cate looked up apprehensively.

"Oh, hey Ahmed" she said attempting a demeanor of normalcy.

"You okay?" Ahmed asked noticing she hadn't smiled back. At times he had pictured Stacey would look like Nurse Cassadea when she got older. She'd have a great smile and keep herself fit.

"Yeah, I'm okay. Thanks for asking," Cate said forcing a smile. "Just have a lot on my mind."

"How about I walk you to your car?" Ahmed offered.

"That would be nice, but I had to park on four, so if you're on a lower floor, you don't have to go all the way up with me."

"Actually, I'm on five. I barely got here in time to punch in without being late."

"You seem excited," it was easy to tell when a young person was enthused. Her girls behaved similarly. She thought briefly about experiencing such manic moods then remembered the lows that inevitably followed. While the medication stopped most of the lows, she'd lost the highs in the process, a steep price to pay.

"I have an interview tomorrow morning at Wayne State. It's for their Engineering school," Ahmed answered.

He knew making long range plans was probably a waste of time but he was an optimist. While his situation was dire, Ahmed hoped he'd find a way. He had survived the camps, he had sur-

Episode 38

vived Afghanistan and he had survived Guantanamo. He would survive this as well.

As they approached the first set of steps in the parking structure, Ahmed looked out the stairway window at the entrance. He noticed two security guards in a white Explorer. He recognized most of the guards but these two faces were new. It struck him as odd there were two guards, usually there was just one in a vehicle. Ahmed put the thought aside and continued making small talk as they climbed the stairs. Cate told him it was wonderful he was continuing his education then added working full time and going to college would be difficult. Ahmed told Cate about Stacey and how she was encouraging him to continue his schooling. Cate now understood his air of excitement. When they reached the fourth floor, Ahmed told her he'd see her to her car and then walk to his own. As they entered the structure, Cate saw the white Explorer with Oak Grove Hospital Security on the side. It was parked on the ramp leading to the level where Ahmed had parked.

"You don't have to see me all the way to my car," she said, nodding her head toward the security vehicle.

"Okay, have a nice evening," he added then walked toward the ramp.

****

The two agents in the Explorer were caught off guard. They hadn't expected Nurse Cassadea for another forty-five minutes and hadn't expected to see her accompanied by the young Arabic informer. Maybe Doctor Midek had been mistaken, the driver thought, maybe this wasn't going to be as easy as it appeared. Her early appearance was a disruption to their plans. Agent Ann wasn't in place by the Rivera and the young Arab could present a problem if he was Nurse Cassadea's partner.

Agent Jeff spoke first.

"I think we should switch clips," he suggested, "if she's got back up, rubber bullets may be a mistake."

"No, stay with the plan," Agent Ann answered. Though she was younger, she had been with the Agency longer and outranked him. Pull around, I'll advise the other vehicle the situation has changed. When we get near her, I'll get out and we'll do the rest as planned."

****

Ahmed's car was a few yards beyond the security vehicle. He glanced into the truck as he walked by and didn't recognize the driver. The guard riding in the passenger's seat was a young red headed woman. He certainly hadn't seen her before. There was something wrong, he could feel it. He wondered if Mahmood or Kamal had been apprehended. He doubted the two fanatics would give him up, but everyone had their breaking point. Kamal had a wife and two children which was terrific cover, but also a liability. Ahmed had known fanatic Muslims who would consider it an honor to sacrifice their family for Allah. His father had been one of them. He hoped his concern about the second security vehicle was just his imagination. Maybe the hospital got a tip about an angry spouse showing up to confront an unfaithful wife. Still, he thought it odd the second set of guards weren't the typical overweight ex-police officers the hospital usually employed. There was something unusual going on, he could feel it in his bones. Ahmed hurried to his car as the Explorer moved forward. After unlocking the door, Ahmed got in.

****

"Go slowly, Jeff," Agent Ann said quietly. When you get close, stop and I'll get out before she gets a chance to get into her car. With his foot near the brake, Agent Jeff eased the Explorer forward.

****

An uneasy feeling settled in Cate's gut and the hair on the back of her neck begin to prickle. It was the same uneasiness

Episode 38

she got when she was ten years old after spending Saturday afternoon at the Mel Theatre watching Vincent Price follow an unsuspecting female victim down a dark alley in some class B horror film. The prickling would creep up the nape of her neck when her mom sent her down to the basement for a jar of home canned pickles or other items from the storage pantry. Even then she knew it was foolish, there really wasn't anything or anyone lurking under the basement steps but it felt creepy all the same. She would ascend the basement steps a smidgeon faster than normal.

Cate knew she wasn't being foolish now; Bobbie said she was in big trouble. That was how she felt, in big trouble and frightened. Cate increased her pace; the Rivera was just ahead. All she had to do was get to it. She pulled out her keys and slipped them into her jacket pocket. She returned her hand to her purse and pulled out the little canister of pepper spray Kimmy's mom had given her. At the time, she told Kimmy's mom it was an unwarranted precaution. Kimmy's mom reminded her she was in the big city now and made her promise to keep it with her always, especially in the parking structure at night. She had tossed the canister into her purse where it had stayed unused. You're not in Plymouth anymore; Cate could hear the warning reverberating in her head.

"This really ain't Kansas either, Toto," she heard herself whisper in an effort to remain calm.

****

Agent Ann watched Cate reach into her purse. "Looks like we might be in for trouble," she said to her partner.

"She just grabbed her keys," Agent Jeff answered. "The second reach must have been to make sure it was closed, because her hand came back empty."

Because of the dim light in the structure, both agents missed seeing the canister cupped in Cate's right hand. It was a gesture recalled from her high school days. Cate cupped her cigarettes the same way when she thought the neighbors might see her sneaking a smoke with Kathy.

****

Ahmed nerves were on edge. To calm himself, he reached into the console and pulled out a pack of cigarettes he had stashed away. At least the security truck had pulled away, a good sign he told himself. At Stacey's request, he didn't smoke in the car anymore but seeing the two security trucks convinced him this was an exception. Ahmed put the driver's window down and started the Grand AM. He pushed in the lighter and waited. He'd light his cigarette and then give the security truck time to get further ahead.

****

Agent Jeffery pulled the Explorer abreast of Nurse Cassadea, and stopped the truck as Agent Ann jumped out.

"Nurse Cassadea," Agent Ann said in a calm and clear voice.

Cate was a few feet from the big Buick and was tempted to make a run for the car. She realized the Explorer could easily block her way and froze in her tracks. She kept a firm grip on the pepper spray.

"Yes," Cate answered turning to face the voice.

"Get into the vehicle please; we want to talk to you."

Cate's mind was reeling. Should she get into the truck, she asked herself? Then she thought again about Bobbie's warning.

"Why do you want me to do that?" Cate was surprised at the calmness in her own voice. "You can talk to me right here."

"We just have some questions we'd like to ask you," Agent Ann responded taking a step closer.

"Question about what?" Cate asked. She spread her feet a little after noticing the female guard edging closer. Cate had taken self defense classes years ago at the YMCA. Assuming a defensive posture was the only thing she could recall now.

Episode 38

****

The lighter popped out. Ahmed lit the Marlboro and decided he'd smoke the whole cigarette before leaving. That would give the security truck plenty of time to move along.

****

"Questions about missing morphine at the hospital," the agent answered. Cate watched the guard take two more small steps in her direction. She countered by turning her body ever so slightly to the side, providing a narrower target. Cate surprised herself with remembering another lesson from the class.

"I don't know anything about any missing morphine," Cate answered.

The guard was now just a step away. Cate knew she had to make a snap decision to stand and fight or turn and run. The class instructor had told them to fight only as a last resort. Cate knew she didn't stand a chance unless she could scream and draw attention. She suddenly remembered Ahmed. He should have driven by them by now. The same thought occurred to Agent Ann, she knew the young man would be rounding the corner in a moment and would see his cohort in distress. Hopefully the young Arab informer would see their uniforms and continue on his way. Agent Jeff could neutralize him if need be, so Agent Ann decided to focus on getting Nurse Cassadea into the truck. Agent Ann wondered momentarily if the young Arab was armed. The rubber bullets could prove to be a fatal error. Agent Ann realized she had to act fast.

"Just get into the vehicle please, Nurse Cassadea," Agent Ann urged softly.

"Where are you taking me?" Cate asked, the air felt so thick she could cut it with a knife.

Agent Ann knew this was the point of no return. She also knew it wasn't going to be the cake walk as Doctor Midek predicted. She decided to make her move.

Book Two Home Again

"Please just get into the van," she repeated stepping forward and reaching for Cate's arm.

"No!" Cate screamed as she brought the pepper spray canister up. She pressed the button releasing a cloud of the acidic spray directly into Agent Ann's nose and eyes.

****

With the driver's window down, Ahmed heard the scream. He couldn't be sure, but it sounded like Nurse Cate's voice. If it was her, she was in trouble. He pitched the cigarette out the window, slammed the Grand Am into reverse and hit the gas. The Pontiac lurched to the rear and almost smashed into the cement buttress directly behind him.

****

"Jesus," Agent Ann screamed as she fell to the oil stained cement floor. Grabbing her eyes, she writhed in pain.

Not knowing what impelled her, Cate quickly delivered a swift and deadly kick directly into Agent Ann's face as she hit the concrete. Agent Ann's hands had initially flown to her face in reaction to the pepper spray that had permeated her eyes and nostrils. Her reactions had drawn the vapors into her lungs setting off coughing spasms redirecting her hands to her throat. Unfortunately for Agent Ann, but fortunate for Cate, the movement of her hands to her chest occurred just as Cate launched her kick. Cate's foot caught Agent Ann square on the nose sending tissue and cartilage from the bridge of her nose in several directions. The kick wasn't fatal, but Agent Ann's nose was shattered. Blood spewed profusely.

Cate looked on in momentary shock at the havoc her kick delivered to the young woman's face. Cate felt frozen in time, everything seemed to happen in stop action. She looked up to see the other guard open the driver's door of the Explorer in slow motion. Cate heard squealing tires coming from some-

Episode 38

where up the ramp then saw a blue car barreling towards her. The other security guard must have also heard the tires because he turned his head to determine the source. Cate watched the guard pause near the front of the Explorer. It was the momentary opportunity she needed. Cate turned and began running.

As Agent Jeffery cleared the front of the Explorer, he knew instantly he had a choice to make. Agent Ann was rolling around on the ground in extreme pain, her face and chest covered in blood. He could either tend to his downed partner or pursue Nurse Cassadea, there wasn't time for both. Believing the blow to his partner's face potentially fatal, he opted to attend her and radio the other team the nurse was on the run. She'd have to go to the first floor at some point where they would be waiting. As he bent over his partner, a blue Pontiac Grand AM came screaming toward him. Behind the wheel was the young Arab. Agent Jeffery wished he'd put the live clip into his weapon.

Hearing the second scream, Ahmed knew it was Nurse Cate. As he turned onto the fourth floor, the scene in front of him was beyond his wildest imagination. The hospital security vehicle was ahead to his right and the female guard was rolling around on the ground clutching her throat. Her face was gushing blood. The other guard was running around the front of the truck and to Ahmed's utter amazement, Nurse Cate was running toward the next turn in the structure's roadway. Ahmed wanted to accelerate but the lane was narrow; he'd barely clear the Explorer. As he went by the white security truck, Ahmed saw Nurse Cate run toward the turn in the roadway and duck to her right putting her on the next floor. Ahmed sped by the Explorer. With his window still down, he heard the first of two loud bangs. The next thing he knew, the rear window of the Grand AM exploded in a burst of flying glass. He recognized the noise that caused the window to shatter. The male guard who had been bent over the female guard was now visible in the rear view mirror and was in a firing position, He had shot out the back window. Ahmed didn't know where the next shot landed, but it hadn't been into his person and he considered himself lucky. The second shot hit his rear tire but had failed to completely penetrate the tire.

Ahmed rounded the curve in pursuit of Nurse Cate. He could see her running between parked cars to his right. He slammed on the brakes and brought the Grand AM to a screeching halt about ten feet from her.

"Quick, jump in," he screamed.

Cate stopped in her tracks. She thought it was the other guard and her life would be over in an instant. Hearing the two shots, she believed the guard was shooting at her. Cate was shocked to see Ahmed. It took a moment for her to register Ahmed had been the one barking the order to stop. In her dazed confusion, Cate couldn't comprehend what the young man in the blue Pontiac was saying. She wanted to scream at him she didn't have time to dawdle and chat. Crazy people with guns were chasing her for being so stupid as to trash pick in the wrong alley. Cate suddenly noticed she'd dropped her purse in her escape and was without her make up and other personal items. She knew given the situation it was a crazy thought, but her life had just entered the surreal.

"I've lost my purse," she heard herself say. She had no idea why she'd say such a thing but it was the only thing that would come out of her mouth.

"Get in the fucking car," the young man screamed. Cate was momentarily startled to hear such coarse language. Then it dawned on her. This handsome young Mediterranean looking man was here to rescue her like some kind of Saracen knight in shining armor. The thought of being a damsel in distress seemed so ludicrous, Cate was certain she had lost her mind and was having some kind of LSD flashback. She'd only used the drug a few times in college with Kelly and wondered why she'd be having a flashback decades later. She was trying to make sense of her last thought when the young man's voice broke through her mental fog again.

"Nurse Cassadea, for the love of god, please get into the car now!" he screamed at the top of his lungs.

Episode 38

Cate felt like she was in the Alice in Wonderland cartoon she'd seen as a child on Disney's Wonderful World of Color. Alice had spun down the rabbit hole into a world that was completely illogical. Getting a grip on reality, Cate realized she had better do as the young man instructed. Running to the Grand AM, she flung open the door and jumped inside.

"Put on the seat belt," Ahmed yelled as he jammed the gas pedal to the floor. Cate looked bewilderedly around the inside of the car. Broken glass was everywhere, on the seat, on the floor and in little piles along the dash board. She wondered where all the glass had come from. The Grand AM jumped forward with the sound of squealing tires. Smoke and the smell of burning rubber permeated through the rear window. The force of the Pontiac's acceleration pushed Cate back into her seat. Somehow she reached back and found the seat belt buckle dangling from the the pillar above her seat.

She heard the familiar click as she managed to snap the buckle in place. Her senses seemed to have gone into auto pilot because her body was moving without conscious effort. Maybe this really was just some kind of LSD flash back Cate thought again. Blurred images of parked cars flashed by her eyes like a kaleidoscopic image. Wasn't there a Beatles song with lyrics about kaleidoscope eyes. "I have gone totally insane," she said to herself between clenched teeth. In desperation, she closed her eyes and leaned back into the Pontiac's bucket seat.

Episode 39

Cate didn't know how long she'd been sitting there with her eyes closed. It could have been a minute or it could have been a week; time had lost relevance. She finally opened them to a continuously varying blur of reds, greens and blues interspaced with metallic shades of silver, gold and pewter. A panorama of parked cars zipped past her face. The constantly changing array reminded her of the artificial tree her father brought home one Christmas. It had shimmering branches of aluminum that reflected colored rays of light from a lighting fixture he'd placed under the tree. The fixture had a plastic wheel with panes of translucent colored plastic. As the wheel spun, the aluminum branches changed color from green to red to yellow. Her mom hated the tree and told him that next year they were going back to Scotch Pines, even if they did cost four dollars.

The image of the aluminum tree dissipated quickly. Cate realized she was still in the hospital parking structure which meant her last visit to reality had been minutes, not weeks. She felt chilled and noticed her window was down. Cold wind was rushing over her face. She looked down at the armrest, found the button for the power window and pushed it. The window went up, but there was still a draft coming into the car. It was streaming over the back of her seat, running up her neck and over her head. She glanced around trying to locate the source of the cold air. Her search stopped when she looked in the back of the car. There was only the remnants of a rear window. She thought it strange anyone would drive around without a back window.

"You don't have a back window," Cate heard her self saying.

"What?" Ahmed yelled without looking in her direction.

He was driving very fast and totally focused on the road. They were on the second level of the parking structure. The next turn would put them on the ground floor where Ahmed knew the other security vehicle was waiting.

"You don't have a back window!" she screamed.

"You're right," he yelled back, "they shot it out!"

"Who shot it out?" Cate asked.

She realized the broken window explained the bits of glass scattered around the car's interior. Her eyes zeroed in on one of the pieces, there were no sharp edges. Strange she said to herself, why wouldn't there be sharp edges.

"The agents," Ahmed replied.

He'd taken the last turn at such high speed the car leaned on two wheels. He was glad the sports coupe had a stiff suspension and high speed tires. If was a sedan, they would have rolled over.

"What agents?" Cate yelled again. She was losing her voice from screaming.

Cate's eyes caught site of another piece of shattered glass with rounded edges. She'd figure that anomaly out if she lived long enough. Cate suddenly realized living beyond the next few minutes was not certain. She felt a rush of adrenalin follow her panic attack and remembered a person's body did that when survival was in question.

"We don't have time to talk now. After I make the next turn, there will be another security truck waiting for us. They'll have the exit blocked," Ahmed screamed briefly looking her way.

"Take the Doctor's exit," Cate yelled.

"Shit!" Ahmed exclaimed, "Why didn't I think of that?"

Episode 39

When Ahmed completed the turn, they were on the first floor. A contingency plan began forming in his mind. If the doctor's exit was also blocked, it was game over. If by good fortune the entrance to the doctor's lot was not blocked, he'd drive through the security arm. The Grand AM would take a beating but the arm should be easy enough to get through. He hoped they were designed to be easily rammed. It seemed like they should be in case circumstances required the structure to be evacuated quickly. Ahmed made the final turn. The g-force caused his tires to squeal. Had he known about the bullet lodged in his rear tire, he would have slowed down. Completing the turn, he saw the doctor's lot dead ahead. Once past the security arm, they'd be in the uncovered parking area reserved for hospital physicians. There was another security arm where the doctor's lot exited to the roadway that served the Emergency Room. If they made it through the first security arm there was no reason they couldn't break through the second. They'd have a chance of getting away from the hospital. It was going to be a big if. Either way, Ahmed knew the answer would be evident in a few seconds.

"When we get up to this security arm, look behind us. See if that other security truck is blocking the main exit in case I can't break through the arm," Ahmed yelled.

"Okay," Cate yelled back. She turned in her seat to improve her view through the hole that was once the back window.

Ahmed slowed the Pontiac as he neared the yellow security arm. Cate could see the other white Explorer parked broadside blocking both lanes at the main entrance. Two uniformed guards had taken up firing positions at opposite ends of the truck. The agent at the front end had an elbow resting on the Explorer's hood and a large gun in his left hand. His right hand was clasped around the pistol's butt. Cate could barley see his head. The other guard was in a more upright position at the back of the Explorer.

Ahmed eased up to the yellow arm blocking the exit. He pressed the gas pedal and the Pontiac's front made contact with the arm. Ahmed gave the car a little more gas. The arm was putting up more

Book Two Home Again

resistance than he'd anticipated but finally gave way. Ahmed gave the Pontiac more gas and pushed the arm completely out of the way. He knew the front end of the Grand AM was dented and he could see a long crease and several scratches in the hood. His beloved Pontiac was beginning to resemble some of the cars at the end of a NASCAR race he'd watched on ESPN. He had been introduced to the sport by a couple of the custodians at the hospital who were so devoted to racing Ahmed initially thought Daytona was some kind of religious site.

"To hell with the car," Ahmed said as he punched the gas pedal. The Grand AM responded and he headed for the next security arm where he repeated the procedure. It took a few seconds for the agents guarding the main entrance to realize Ahmed's strategy. Understanding his intent, the agents jumped into the Explorer.

The agents would later realize following Ahmed had been a mistake. Had the driver just gone out the parking structure's main entrance and driven to Outer Drive Boulevard, he could have intercepted Ahmed. The chase would have been over at that point.

After breaking through the second barrier, Ahmed turned right on the service drive leading to the Emergency Room. Passing the Emergency Room, he headed toward the main entrance, driving fast but under control. Ahmed heard a siren in the distance. He assumed it was the police responding to a call for assistance. Calling for help was an action of last resort in Doctor Midek's disaster plan, the implications for damage control were enormous. There was no way he wanted coverage of tonight's events featured on the local news. It was going to be difficult enough explaining to the media why access to the parking structure had been shut down for thirty minutes. Doctor Midek had a story, complete with fictitious names and pictures, about an enraged and jealous husband.

It wasn't a police siren that Ahmed heard. It was an ambulance racing a seventy year old male with chest pains to the Emergency Room. As Ahmed reached the main road, Outer Drive Boulevard, he slowed and looked to his left. He saw the flashing

Episode 39

lights of the rescue vehicle and "Ambulance" printed backwards on the front end. Ahmed made a sharp right and heard the Pontiac's tires scream again. After the turn, something changed in the Grand AM's handling. The bullet lodged in the rear tire had partially separated the steel belts and the force of the turn completed the separation. A large bulge was now visible between the steel belts and rubber overlay.

The two agents were less fortunate. Assuming the service drive was clear, Agent John zipped through the entrance to the doctor's lot like he was back at the drag strip. After completing a hard left, he shot past the second bent yellow arm onto the service drive and floored the Explorer when he saw Ahmed turn onto Outer Drive Boulevard. He had also heard the siren and like Ahmed, assumed it was local assistance. Unfortunately, Agent John focused too long on Ahmed's blue Pontiac. When he looked back to the left, his eyeballs opened wide in surprise as an ambulance made a hard right directly into his path. Only a miracle enabled Agent John to turn the Explorer in time to avoid a head on collision. The Explorer careened right and nearly flipped before he corrected his over steer. The Explorer traveled almost a hundred feet perilously balanced on the two wheels along the truck's right side. To the few observers, who happened to be looking out the hospital's windows, it appeared the Explorer performed some kind of stunt driving trick. Agent John finally stopped the Explorer and looked back to assess the fate of the ambulance.

The ambulance driver was a forty-five year old paramedic everyone called Cal. It was an odd nickname considering he'd been born and reared in West Virginia and was not named Calvin. The nickname evolved from his penchant for listening to the Beach Boys. Unlike Agent John, he hadn't been distracted and was prepared when he saw the Explorer barreling directly at him. Having lived in Michigan since his discharge as an Army medic, Cal retained only a portion of his southern accent. He'd met his wife while on vacation at Virginia Beach where she'd been enjoying the sun with three teaching friends

Book Two Home Again

from Detroit. Two years later they were married and he'd taken a job with the Fairlane Hills Fire Department. His accent came back occasionally, especially when he was stressed. This was one of those occasions. As he swerved to the right just in time to miss colliding with the white security vehicle, he let out an epitaph that included a description of the Explorer's driver as a stupid Yankee son of a bitch. His partner had banged his head during the maneuver while the patient strapped into the stretcher turned a shade paler. The old man's wife somehow managed to escape unscathed. Satisfied everyone survived; Cal gave the driver of the security vehicle the finger. Agent John, however, misread the salute and assumed it was a high sign meaning everyone in the ambulance was okay. He looked over at his partner. As usual Agent Bradley was the picture of calm.

"You gonna go after that asshole or just sit there," Agent Bradley said with quiet repose.

It may have been adrenalin or dazed confusion because Agent John wasn't sure if his partner was talking about the driver of the blue Pontiac or the ambulance driver. Agent John pulled the Explorer off the lawn and back onto asphalt drive where he gunned the Explorer. The truck's wheels spun momentarily as dirt and clumps of grass lodged in the heavily knobbed tires flew from the wheel wells. When the tires cleared their packed debris, they screeched loudly and the truck jumped forward. Agent John barely slowed as he approached the intersection. The agents looked right and saw a set of faint tail lights in the distance.

Ahmed checked his speedometer. The needle was just past eighty. He stole a glance at Cate as the wind poured through the back of the car. The rushing air caused her hair to stand up on her head, reminding him of riding the giant roller coaster at Cedar Point amusement park. When their coaster car flew down the first hill, Stacey's her hair had stood on end just as Nurse Cate's did now. He and Stacey had laughed, stuffed themselves on French fries and drank freshly squeezed lemon aide. Ahmed wondered if he'd ever see her again. Dwelling on such things was not good and he forced himself to concentrate on driving.

Episode 39

He had no idea where he was going so he took the first left on Rotunda Drive then a right on Oakwood Boulevard. He passed the entrance to the Southfield expressway not wanting to get trapped on a limited exit highway. He'd have to make a turn soon though and get off of Oakwood to lose the pursuing agents. He had no clue as to which way to turn as they whizzed past a sign saying Welcome To Melvindale. There were other things written on the sign but he didn't have time to read them. In the rear view mirror he saw a pair of headlights in the distance and assumed they belonged to the security vehicle. Cate turned her head and saw the headlights.

"Oh shit!" she exclaimed. "Turn at the next side street."

"Okay," Ahmed replied and made a sharp right. The street sign said Hanna. As he made the turn the rear tire on the passenger's side blew with a loud bang when the treads separated completely. The tire disintegrated leaving nothing but the metal rim. Ahmed fought hard to control the Grand AM.

"Damn it!" he exclaimed slowing the car. He hoped the noise hadn't awakened the neighborhood. All they needed was for some local to call the police.

"Pull the car over!" Cate yelled desperately.

Ahmed continued driving. He slowed at the stop sign but didn't come to a complete stop. The steering was compromised from the blown tire and the car pulled left. He corrected the steering and continued forward.

"What?" he asked Cate.

"Pull over and let me out," she replied, "you don't need to be involved with this. Tell them I forced you to drive me from the hospital."

"Do you really think they'll let me go Nurse Cassadea?" Ahmed replied and kept driving. He turned off his headlights and chastised himself for not doing so earlier.

"Call me Cate."

"What?"

"I said call me Cate, I think Nurse Cassadea is a little too formal considering the circumstances. And let me out of the car.

They won't hurt you. They want me. I can take care of myself, so just let me out and turn yourself in. Tell them I had a gun or something and forced you to help me escape."

"Why are they after you Nurse, I mean Cate?"

"Look it's really better you not know. The less you know the better. So just let me out, turn yourself in and get to your interview tomorrow morning."

They traveled two more blocks when they saw headlights coming up from behind. Ahmed's curiosity was piqued and he pressed Cate again.

"Look, I'll let you go, but first you have to tell me why the Secret Service or the CIA or who ever the hell they are, are after you. If they take me in, I need to know what they are after so I can protect myself," Ahmed asked. "Sorry about the language,"

"This is probably a mistake," Cate answered, "but they are after me because of this." Cate pulled the tied off rubber glove out of her pocket.

"They're after you because of a rubber glove?" Ahmed laughed.

He knew it was no time for being funny, it was his natural reaction to laugh after life threatening situations. He'd experienced the same kind of exhilaration smuggling hashish out of Afghanistan or contraband into the country.

"Look we don't have time for a long explanation, there's a vial of something in the glove. I don't know what it is, but I saw a doctor injecting it into young Arab men at the hospital. So now let me out, I can take care of myself."

Cate's revelation hit Ahmed like a thunderbolt.

"Fucking Charlie," he heard himself say.

He looked into the mirror; the headlights were getting closer. He knew with the blown tire, he couldn't outrun whoever was following them. He made a quick left at the next street. The Pontiac's handling was so askew it was all he could do to make another right at the next street. After turning, he pulled the Pontiac up a drive way and continued beyond the front of the house almost to the garage. Parking the car out of sight might throw off their pursuers long enough to give them a few seconds head

Episode 39

start. He shifted the Grand AM into park and quietly opened the driver's door.

"Don't slam the door," he said to Cate in a low voice. "The less noise the better."

Cate got out, closed the door gently then ran around the back of the vehicle where Ahmed waited.

"Thanks for the help," she whispered and began running down the sidewalk.

Ahmed caught up with her after several strides. He was surprised at how fast she could move.

"What the hell are you doing?" Cate asked between shallow breaths.

"Coming with you," Ahmed answered.

"I told you, go, turn yourself in. You don't want to be involved in this."

"I already am," Ahmed replied. He looked back. "Damn it," he added, "the assholes didn't take the bait."

Looking back, Cate watched the headlights stop near the ditched Pontiac. She increased her pace into a dead run. She couldn't keep going long at this speed and was ready to stop and give up when she saw the familiar outline ahead. She knew the building was their only chance. It would be close.

****

Agent John knew it would be sheer luck to pick up the trail of the Grand AM again. The two agents arrived at the location where they believed the vehicle turned. They weren't certain which side street the car turned on, so Agent John took a chance. He turned on Wood Street but after failing to see any taillights stopped.

"This is the wrong street or that asshole turned off his lights. What'ya think?" he asked his partner.

"If he's turned off his lights, then we won't see him anyway, go with the wrong street. Double back one street."

"Roger that one," Agent John turned the Explorer around, made a left at the first cross street and stopped at the corner of Henry Street. They looked in opposite directions. Agent Bradley strained his eyes looking back toward Oakwood Boulevard but saw nothing. Agent John looked the opposite way and thought he saw a car pulling into a driveway. He wasn't sure, but it was the only option available. Agent John turned left.

"See something?" agent Bradley asked as he leaned forward straining his eyes.

"I'm not sure what it is, but I saw something up there," Agent John replied pointing up the street.

****

"Follow me," Cate said dashing across the street. Ahmed could see a large building fifty yards or so ahead. Looking up, he saw a huge spire with a belfry and realized they were running toward a Christian church.

****

Agent Bradley assumed it was his Irish luck that led them to double back to Henry Street. They were close to where he'd seen the car turn up a driveway. Looking up the street, a flash of movement caught his attention. Agent John was searching the driveways furtively when he saw the vehicle with a missing rear window. He was about to jump out of the Explorer when his partner elbowed him in the triceps.

"Check it out," Agent Bradley said pointing up the street.

****

Cate and Ahmed watched the headlights stop where they'd ditched the Grand AM.

"They've spotted the car," Ahmed said running up the steps toward the large double doors. "Damn, I hope these are

Episode 39

unlocked," he continued between gasps for breath, "if not, we're cooked!"

Cate's thoughts were identical to Ahmed's. She prayed the doors were open. If not their only hope would be to run across the street and try the Rectory. She doubted there was time, however, to check both buildings.

****

"Oh yeah, we've got those assholes now," Agent John said pressing the gas pedal.

The Explorer's tires spun and squealed as it shot toward the two figures crossing the street. Agent Bradley hoped the noise wouldn't awaken anyone. If so, he prayed the neighbors would attribute the screaming tires to some teenaged boys. He didn't want the local police involved, seeing the situation had just come back into control. In moments the two Muslim extremists would be sitting in the back seat of the Explorer, if they came peacefully. If not, they'd be lying in the back. Agent Bradley reached into the back seat and lifted a small case into the front. He opened it and pulled out two silencers. He screwed the end of one onto the barrel of his pistol.

"Give me your weapon," he said to his partner.

Agent John withdrew his pistol while steering the Explorer with his left hand. Agent Bradley placed his own weapon between his legs, took his partner's weapon and fitted it with the other silencer. Agent John felt his anticipation build, they were within a hundred yards and closing rapidly.

****

Ahmed looked at the metal sign affixed to the side of the church. It read St. Mary Magdalene Roman Catholic Church, Dedicated July 2, 1934. Cate ran up to one of the doors and jerked frantically on the handle; the door wouldn't budge.

"Damn it!" she screamed reaching over for the other double door. It was also locked.

"Son of a bitch," she said in a guttural voice.

Cate realized she had nearly blasphemed on the church steps. What would Emma think if she heard her daughter swearing on the steps of St. Mary's. Cate knew a reprimand from her mother should be the least of her worries but found it difficult to dismiss her lifetime of Catholic upbringing.

"Sorry," she apologized.

"It's okay," Ahmed said forgivingly.

"I wasn't apologizing to you," Cate said moving to the second set of doors, She grabbed the handle. "Why would you lock a church, for God's sake!" she added frantically.

They looked up the street. The white Explorer was now less than fifty yards away and closing fast.

"Go to the end and work backwards toward me," she told Ahmed.

"Got it!" Ahmed exclaimed and ran to the last set of double doors.

****

"Oh, we got these two just where we want them," Agent Bradley said stifling a laugh.

"Your asses are ours now," Agent John added wheeling the Explorer to the curb. He brought it to a quick stop.

****

Sister Maria wanted to continue as St. Mary Magdalene's Social Outreach Administrator even though she was now principal of the grade school. Father Jude thought it too much, and delegated her Outreach responsibilities to Sister Agnes. Sister Agnes, a younger nun, now ran the programs but Sister Maria helped as time permitted.

It was St. Mary's week to host Downriver Christnet, a cross denominational effort to care for Downriver's homeless. Fifteen to twenty indigent souls would be provided a warm place to sleep

Episode 39

and hot meals this night in addition to bag lunches and transportation to day labor jobs tomorrow.

Sister Maria had walked to the basement of the Rectory where twenty cots had been set up. The room was partitioned with curtains to separate the men from the women. Father Jude would split the shift with Brother Brian, one of the deacons. Sister Agnes would share her shift with Sister Judith. It appeared Sister Agnes had everything under control, Sister Maria said to herself, and then headed to the kitchen.

****

Ahmed grabbed the large brass handle and felt a rush of unbridled joy when the heavy door gave way.

"It's open!" he exclaimed.

Cate let go of the handle and darted toward him. As he held the door open, they ducked inside.

"Now, what?" Ahmed asked. He had no idea as to the next part of the plan. He looked around. They were standing in a large antiroom of some kind with several interior doors in front of them.

"Follow me," Cate said heading toward the second set of doors.

****

Outside the church, the agents' elation suddenly turned to confusion.

"What the hell?" Agent Bradley said looking at his partner.

"You stay outside," Agent John said opening the driver's side door. "Give me my weapon," he continued reaching out his hand.

"You can't go in there with a gun!" Agent Bradley replied, having gone to Catholic schools his whole life.

"Watch me," Agent John said taking the weapon out of his partner's hand. "You stay out here in case they exit the building. I'll stay in contact with the radio. Reaching into the Explorer's console, he grabbed a headset and removed his Oak Grove

Security baseball cap. The mouthpiece extended around his jaw and fit closely to his mouth. He tossed a second headset to Agent Bradley.

Agent John slammed the Explorer's door and ran toward the Church's entrance.

"This isn't right," Agent Bradley said before turning on his headset. In a few seconds he heard Agent John's voice, "I'm going in." Agent Bradley watched his partner open the door to the church and dart inside.

****

Hurrying through the narthex, Cate and Ahmed entered the sanctuary. Ahmed looked around in silent wonder. There was a small alcove to their right where several rows of candles burned. In the middle of the alcove there was something that looked like a basin.

"What's that?" he whispered.

"It's a baptismal font," Cate answered. They passed the alcove and walked quietly to the rear of the sanctuary. Cate thought it ironic she had been sitting in the last row of pews a few hours earlier.

"What's it for?" Ahmed asked again.

Cate thought she heard something and stopped. She put her forefinger to pursed lips indicating to Ahmed to be quiet. Ahmed stopped and held his breath. It was deafeningly silent in the church. Looking around, he was struck by the sanctuary's enormity and lavish adornment. It was much bigger than any mosque he'd ever been in. There were several statues near the altar and the stained glass windows looked as if they would be beautiful when the sun back lit them. He looked closer at one of the statues. In the dim light he could see it was a woman holding an infant. Ahmed assumed it was the Virgin Mary holding the baby Jesus. As a Muslim, he believed Jesus to be a prophet but not the messiah. He also recognized Jesus's virgin birth, which

Episode 39

seemed an inconsistency. Ahmed had admitted such to Stacey when they had been discussing religion recently. Christianity has its own inconsistencies, he thought looking at the front of the church. Behind the altar was a giant crucifix with a statue of the crucified Christ. He had his arms outstretched and a wreath of thorns on his head. There were some words written in large gold letters above the crucifix. Ahmed knew they were Latin. Cate signaled to continue moving forward then increased her pace. Ahmed had no idea where she was taking them, but during the silence he heard what sounded like a door closing. He assumed their pursuers had entered the outer doors and were now in the narthex. He wondered what Cate's next move would be. When she broke into a run towards the altar, Ahmed knew she'd also heard the door.

****

Agent John went through the outer doors and saw a second set. One of the doors was held open by a small door stop at the bottom. He glanced at the little metal stopper as he brought the pistol level to his chest. With his arms outstretched in front of him, he slipped to the side of the open door, stopped and held his breath. He could hear muffled noises coming from the sanctuary. He pirouetted around the door opening in time to see two figures disappear through a solitary wooden door to the right of the altar.

****

Knowing at least one agent was now somewhere in the narthex, Cate ran toward the door next to the altar. She prayed it was unlocked. If not, it was game over. She looked for some place to hide the vial but nothing looked promising. She reached for the door knob and gave it a turn.

****

Sister Maria walked into the kitchen where Sisters Agnes and Judith were making lunches. At times like this, when her church fed the poor, Sister Maria knew her life of servitude had been the correct choice. She'd had moments of doubt over the years, even before the child molestations scandals rocked her church and challenged her own faith. She wished the Catholic bashers, as Father Jude called them, could come into her church right now. Then they could witness the assistance the Church provided to helpless mothers with small children. Women who had fallen between the cracks in a society of plenty. They could see the hope offered to those escaping a life of physical abuse the judicial system found no way to prevent.

"Need some help, Sisters?" she asked with a smile. Loaves of Wonder Bread spread on the work table were being topped with slices of bologna. Three packages of American cheese sat next to the partially completed sandwiches.

"Oh, Sister Maria," Sister Agnes said washing a large knife in the sink. "We ran out of mustard. Jake is getting us some out of the pantry. Maybe you could help him finish making sandwiches." Sister Agnes knew Sister Maria missed helping in the preparations.

Jake was one of the homeless men who'd stayed at the church several times. He'd also come by occasionally to do odd jobs for Father Jude. Jake was a hopeless alcoholic who'd stay sober for extended periods but back slid frequently. Father Jude let him work for food. No one knew how old Jake was, his life had been one of physical and mental hardship and it showed. He was missing teeth, and had to be reminded to bathe when he showed up but he was a good soul. He had proven himself trustworthy when not drinking. A look of pride had shown on his face when he'd been asked to go into the store room alone. It was a reward for his latest efforts at sobriety.

****

Cate and Ahmed bounded through the door next to the altar.

Episode 39

"Where the hell are we going?" Ahmed asked as they hurried down the short hallway. There was another door at the end with a stairwell to the right. "Sorry about the language again," he added.

"To the rectory," Cate answered in hurried breaths. She turned right and flew down the steps two at a time.

"To the Rectory?" Ahmed answered. "Isn't that the building across the street?"

"Yes," Cate said over her shoulder, "there's a tunneled hallway that leads under the street. It connects the church with the Rectory and the school. When I was a little girl, we were led through it during catechism classes when the weather was bad or for tornado drills."

"What's a tornado drill?" Ahmed asked amazed how fast she was taking the stairs.

Cate looked at Ahmed, "You don't know what a tornado drill is?" she asked incredulously.

"We didn't get many tornadoes in Afghanistan," he answered.

When they reached the bottom of the stairs, a windowless hallway lay directly ahead. Hearing a door above them slam, they knew the agent was getting closer. The tunnel extended about a hundred yards with no visible avenues of escape. Ahmed knew if the agent got to the bottom of the stairs before they made it to the rectory, they were sitting ducks. Cate took a deep breath and broke into a full sprint, Ahmed followed closely behind.

****

Agent John watched the pair of fugitives go though the door next to the altar. "Spotted 'em," he said into his mouthpiece. "They've gone through a door at the back of the church. I don't know if it leads outside, so be ready." Agent John ran toward the door hoping it didn't lock from the inside, if so he'd have to call Doctor Midek because they would be out of options.

When he reached the door by the altar and turned the knob. The door opened into a short hallway where there was another door ahead and stairway to his right. He stopped and held his breath to hear if the nurse and her young friend had gone through the door directly ahead or were headed down the stairs. After a second, he heard feet pattering on the stairway below and ran toward the stairs. Reaching the steps, he began running down them at a sprint. "I'm on a stairway," he said into the microphone.

****

Cate and Ahmed were three quarters of the way along the tunnel when Ahmed looked behind them. The agent had just reached the bottom of the stairs.

"Halt," the agent shouted, "I'm an agent of the United States Government. Stop where you are."

Cate couldn't remember many details about the hallway's interior. There was more than one door ahead and she couldn't remember which door led to what. They'd have to take the first exit available. Her legs were tiring and her back ached. Cate scolded herself for sitting on the bleacher's at the Homecoming game with Ronnie and Kathy. She found it difficult to believe that only been two nights ago; it felt like years. Damn them, she thought, for talking her into sitting on those stupid bleachers without any back support. Where were those two jerk offs now, she asked herself. Kathy was in Paris on a school sponsored boondoggle. Ronnie was probably sitting in his cozy house on the Detroit River watching the lights on the water with a nice log burning in the fire place. Neither of them were running for their lives with a back that felt like two ice picks were lodged in their spine.

Cate looked over her shoulder. The agent was gaining on them. He was about thirty yards behind them and from the sounds of his foot steps, appeared to be closing fast. Cate looked ahead and saw a doorway on her left. A sign just below the security light said Kitchen. Time seemed to stand still again as she took a deep breath and reached the door and pulled on the

Episode 39

handle. Cate flung the door open and flew through the doorway with Ahmed so close she could feel his warm breath hitting the back of her neck. They burst into the kitchen where Cate stopped so quickly, Ahmed nearly ran up her back. He bumped into her with such force it knocked her forward and she stumbled. A nun tried to catch her but barely broke her fall. Ahmed also lost his footing but managed to regain his balance. Out of breath and panting heavily, he helped lift Cate.

"Margaret Bertilino?" Cate replied getting to her feet and looking bewildered.

"It's Sister Maria now. I haven't seen you in twenty years and look, God has delivered you to me twice in one day Cate," Sister Maria replied with a startled look.

The other two nuns appeared confused at the sudden appearance of two visitors. Sister Agnes was about to voice her surprise when the door flew open again and a tall man in a police uniform burst into the kitchen holding a large pistol. Sister Agnes dropped the kitchen knife she was holding and raised both hands.

"Everyone just remain calm," the officer said. "I'm a federal agent."

"Please put the gun away," Sister Maria said calmly. "You're in a house of God, there is no need for weapons here."

Jake heard noises from outside the store room. Sent into the pantry for mustard, his attention had been captured by a commercial sized can of Campbell's Chicken Noodle. He had picked up the can planning to take it out to Sister Agnes. He'd been fixated on the label. There was a picture of a blue and white china bowl filled with delicious looking noodles floating in deep yellow broth. Wisps of steam wafted up from the bowl reminding him of a time that now seemed far away, a time when he had a home and a family. A cup of hot soup before bed seemed a good idea. He was carrying the can toward the kitchen when he heard the commotion. Jake wasn't sure if what he saw was real or another vision from his alcohol damaged brain. As he approached the doorway, he was befuddled to see a nurse and a young man standing next to Sister Maria. He was even more confused by the uniformed security guard pointing a gun at them. Sister Agnes and Sister Judith had looks of terror in their eyes.

"I've got them," Agent John said into the mouth piece. "Radio Doctor Midek and tell him everything is."

He intended to say in control when pain exploded in the back of his head and his knees buckled.

"Don't worry Sis, Sis, Sister Maria," Jake stammered as he walked out of the storage room and brought the large can of chicken noodle soup down on the agent's head.

Jake never held much love for police officers or security guards; they'd been mean to him more than once. When lucid, Jake would be the first one to admit it sometimes had been warranted. Other times they'd roughed him up needlessly. Having been sober three months, he knew there would be a price to pay for conking the guard on the head.

"I better go now Sister, before he wakes up," Jake said starting toward the doorway leading to the room with the cots. Jake raced through the door before Sister Maria could stop him.

"I have to go stop Jake before he runs off," Sister Maria said noting the officers arm patch said Oak Grove Hospital Security. "I don't know what all this is about, Cate, but if you intend to leave, you should go now. The stairway leading up to the Rectory is at the end of the hall."

"Thank you Margaret, I mean Sister Maria. Don't believe what they tell you," Cate added as she grabbed Ahmed and followed Sister Maria through the swinging double doors. Ahmed looked over his shoulder and almost laughed thinking the two nuns looked like a pair of marble statues with expressions of astonishment etched into their faces.

****

Agent Bradley opened the driver's door when Agent John failed to complete his transmission. Agent Bradley pressed the earpiece into his right ear to improve his hearing. He heard garbled voices along with what sounded like moaning. He pressed

Episode 39

the earphone into his ear but couldn't make out what the voices were saying.

"John are you okay?" Agent Bradley asked. There was no reply. "Listen, John if you can hear me, I'm coming in. Hang on." Agent Bradley ran to the front of church and disappeared behind the door.

****

Cate and Ahmed ran past Sister Maria as she followed Jake into the room full of cots. The stairway was directly ahead. Running up the stairs, they found themselves in the lobby facing the street. They could see the Explorer across the street from them.

"What now?" Ahmed asked panting from climbing the steps.

"There's a door at the back that leads to the school. We can go out from there, we'll be shielded from their view," Cate answered. "Follow me."

"You've said that a lot tonight, Nurse Cassadea," Ahmed said with feigned sarcasm then fell in line behind her. He was impressed with Cate's stamina; his own legs were beginning to cramp.

"I told you," Cate said over her shoulder, "you don't need to come with me. Give yourself up now and blame it all on me. I still don't understand why you're doing this."

"I have my reasons," Ahmed replied.

When they reached the doors to the grade school, Ahmed noted one set of double doors led into the school while another opened to a small court yard between the rectory and the school building. The court yard was open at the far end. Cate grabbed the door and was about to open it when she stopped in her tracks.

"Why are we stopping?" Ahmed asked trying to catch his breath.

****

Agent Bradley entered the church then ran to the far end of the narthex. Standing next to the doors that led to the sanctuary, he stopped to listen. Hearing nothing, he went through the doors with his gun pointed ahead. Looking around, he spotted the door next to the altar. Dropping the gun to his side, he ran towards the door.

"I'm in the building, John," he said into the microphone. "I'll be there in a minute just hang on.

Reaching the next door, Agent Bradley brought his gun up again. He opened the door and headed toward the stairway. When he eased around the corner he saw no one. He ran down the steps and into the tunnel. Once there, he continued down the hall at full speed until he came to a gray metal door where he came to a full stop. He looked into a small wire embedded window in the door. His partner was sitting on the floor with a nun bent over him holding an ice pack against the back of his head.

Agent Bradley opened the door, holstered his pistol and bent down to look at his partner. Agent John had a glazed look to his eyes. Agent Bradley guessed his partner had a concussion, but other than that, appeared to be unharmed.

"You okay?" Agent Bradley asked.

"Yeah," his partner replied, "just a splitting head."

"We've called 911," the nun said.

"Not necessary, Sister," Agent Bradley interjected before she could finish her sentence, "there'll be somebody here in a few minutes to take him to the hospital. Call 911 back and tell them they're not needed."

"Can you walk?" he asked his partner.

"Yeah, I just need a few minutes to clear out the cob webs," Agent John answered.

"I'll go back up and radio Doctor Midek. He'll send help. I'll see if I can figure out where the suspects went," Agent Bradley added opening the door to the tunnel.

****

Episode 39

Cate pulled the rubber glove from her pocket.

"There's a vial of something in here that they are willing to kill me for. I understand that. What I don't understand is why you'd be willing to risk your life for it, or for me for that matter. Now, tell me why you'd risk everything?" Cate demanded.

"Nurse Cate," Ahmed replied, "we don't have time for this. We need to get out of here now."

"I'm not moving an inch until you tell me what's going on. Maybe somebody else wants this vial and that somebody else might be you or who ever it is you work for. I'll be damned if I'm going to risk my life only to find out I'm a target for somebody else," Cate stated with conviction.

"Okay, okay," Ahmed answered, "I'm an informant for the CIA. It was my only way out of Afghanistan. At the hospital I look for terrorists. That vial you have may be the bargaining chip I need to get my little sister out of Afghanistan." Ahmed omitted his part in a dirty bomb planned for the Auto Show.

"Are you telling me everything?" Cate asked. After Billy she could smell a half truth as good as she cold smell a lie. There was something this young Arab was leaving out.

"Yes, now where ever it is you're taking us, take us now," Ahmed said earnestly.

"I hate to say it Ahmed, but follow me," Cate answered running into the courtyard.

Ahmed fell in step as they raced through the courtyard. The double doors had opened to a large stone patio with wooden benches. Burning bushes and neatly manicured beds along both walls surrounded the courtyard. During autumn, their leaves turned a deep crimson. In the spring tulips and irises bloomed in the beds. The Flowering Crab and Weeping Cherry trees had been saplings when Cate last saw them. When they reached the end of the rectory, Cate turned left and followed the building's wall slowing her pace to a fast walk. Near the end, Cate moved closer to the side of the building. With Ahmed close behind, she pressed so close to the brick wall it felt like sand paper was rubbing across her cheek. At the end of the rectory, Cate eased her face around the corner to observe what was happening at the church. She expected to hear multiple siren's and flashing lights as police cars joined in pursuit, but the front of the church was eerily quiet. The Explorer hadn't moved. Cate looked up the block and saw another pair of headlights approaching. She assumed it was the police but was surprised there were no red and blue lights flashing.

"What do you see?" Ahmed whispered anxiously.

"Nothing's changed. There's another car coming up the block. Take a look for yourself," Cate answered crouching down.

Ahmed inched a little closer to Cate. He put his left hand on the wall for support then peered around the corner with his head about two feet above hers. Cate thought how ridiculous they would appear to someone viewing them from across the street and emitted a muffled giggle. They resembled the characters in the Little Rascal's episodes she watched every morning before school. When Spanky, Alfalfa and the gang hid from Butch and the other bullies, curiosity eventually get the better of them and they would peer from around a building in a column of stacked heads just as she and Ahmed appeared now.

"What's so funny?" Ahmed asked. Given their predicament, he wondered what could strike Nurse Cate as funny enough to laugh out loud.

"You're too young to understand," she replied. When the oncoming car stopped, a heavy set man with dark curly hair got out and ran into the church.

"Shit, that's Charlie," Ahmed exclaimed in a muffled voice.

"I don't know who Charlie is," Cate replied, "but this may be our only chance. Let's go."

Cate took off in a dead run toward the road beyond the parking lot. Ahmed caught up when they were at the road's edge. Across the road a hill rose sharply and a rail road track ran along the top. To his left, a major intersection lay at the bottom of the hill. Above the intersection a large railroad bridge with trestles spanned the distance across the diagonal corners. A Clark gas station sat on the corner closest to them but Ahmed's view of

Episode 39

the opposite corner was obstructed by the railroad bridge. On Cate's signal, they sprinted across the road and climbed the hill. At the top, they paused to catch their breath and Cate looked back toward the Church.

****

Agent Bradley was coming back through the door next to the altar when he saw Agent Charlie coming through the door with his gun drawn.

"Charlie," Agent Bradley yelled in warning.

Charlie stopped by the doors and waited.

"We caught the 911 call on the box. What's the situation?" Charlie asked.

"John's down with a head injury. Go through that door and take the stairway to the bottom, follow the hallway to the kitchen. He'll need help getting back to the car. There's a nun attending him, she called 911. I told her to cancel the call, but the locals will probably be showing up soon. Listen, you handle this situation, I'll pursue the suspects."

"Roger that," Charlie responded and headed to the door. Agent Bradley ran through the narthex and burst through the exterior door. He planned to drive the Explorer to the far side of the Rectory and school building. Outside of the church, he looked left to survey the area. His eyes caught movement across the street and saw a figure disappear over the hill. Deciding to follow on foot, Agent Bradley sprinted towards the hill.

****

Ahmed looked back toward the church. From the top of the hill, he watched the agent emerge from the door and look in their direction.

"Shit, Cate," he said between puffs of breath, "one of the agents just spotted us."

Climbing the hill had been an aerobic event and Cate's lungs were screaming as they made their way over the railroad tracks. At least she wasn't wearing high heels, she thought, and wouldn't twist an ankle like the helpless women in the movies. It seemed a small victory.

"Hell," she panted, "I'll probably die of a heart attack before they shoot us anyway."

Cate increased her pace as they entered a small copse of poplar trees just past the railroad tracks.

"Where are we going?" Ahmed asked. The trees still held their leaves and it became noticeably darker.

"The trees will end in a minute, there's a small field and beyond that is Thunderbowl Lanes. We used to sneak to the bowling alley after Catechism class. I've been on this path a thousand times, though it was a lifetime ago."

"I don't think we have time for bowling, Cate," Ahmed said jokingly. He hoped she had a plan, they were now out of his comfort zone. He was lost regarding their next move.

"Don't be stupid. There'll be a lot of people there and there are multiple exits from the building. As long as that agent doesn't call for assistance right away, we may have a chance to lose him. He can't guard all the exits, we may be able to get away yet."

At the edge of trees, Ahmed saw an open field. Their chance of success depended upon crossing the field and getting to the bowing alley before the agent caught up. In the open field, they were dead meat. He took several deep breaths trying to get as much oxygen into his bloodstream as possible.

****

Agent Bradley reached the top of the hill and was sprinting across the tracks when his right foot caught a patch of loose gravel. As the gravel gave way, his foot lodged on a railroad spike that had jarred loose. His foot gave way and his left knee came down hard on one of the steel rails.

Episode 39

"Mother fucker!" he screamed grabbing his injured knee. "Damn it," he gasped while getting back on his feet.

He could feel blood trickling down the front of his leg. Reaching down, he felt a hole in his pants and knew the gash needed stitches. The fall only delayed him momentarily, but it was a precious amount for Cate and Ahmed. They were at the side door of Thunderbowl Lanes before Agent Bradley cleared the trees.

Looking back through the open door, Cate could not see the pursuing agent.

"Let's go," she said to Ahmed hurrying toward the far end of the bowling alley.

"This place is huge," Ahmed said as he looked at long wooden aisles with vinyl upholstered booths interspersed between them.

Ahmed was intrigued by the sights and sounds enveloping him. About half of the long wooden aisles were occupied with people wearing matching shirts. Others wore everyday clothes. He heard thumping sounds as heavy looking balls landed on the brightly polished wooden aisles. A low pitched drone followed as the balls made their way toward chalk white pins. A sharp crack would sporadically follow as the pins exploded and whirled when the brightly colored balls struck them. The place stirred Ahmed's senses. The air smelled like a mixture of cigarette smoke, sweat and stale beer. Waitresses wearing bright red blouses carried trays of beer bottles to the booths. If he survived the night, Ahmed vowed he would take Stacey bowling. The thought sent a pang of sadness through him, knowing he'd likely never get that opportunity.

"There's over a hundred lanes in this section alone," Cate answered. "in the arena there's another twenty or so. At least there used to be. At one time it was the largest bowling alley in the state."

Cate kept walking with Ahmed at her side. They passed a counter where a young man was sliding pairs of shoes towards a couple of teenaged boys. Ahmed could see a rack where numerous pairs of shoes were neatly stacked.

"What are they doing?" Ahmed asked as they passed the counter. He and Cate were about halfway to the end of the building.

"You have to wear bowling shoes while on the lanes. If you don't have any, you can rent them," Cate answered. She turned and looked at her young companion, "You've never been bowling, have you?"

"No, but it looks like fun," he answered looking around in wide eyed wonder.

"Listen, if we get through all of this," Cate said, "I'll take you and your girlfriend bowling."

When a sad look passed across Ahmed's face, she regretted her choice of words.

"That's a big if," he answered.

"Life's a bunch of big ifs," Cate replied.

She had no sooner gotten the words out of her mouth when she saw Inspector Larry sitting at a booth with a couple of other men. She stopped in mid stride.

"I've got an idea. We've got to get out of here before our friend arrives," she added looking over her shoulder.

Ahmed saw a set of doors at the end of the aisle. Beyond the doors, there appeared to be another hallway. Cate opened the door and went thorough with Ahmed beside her. Ahmed saw more bowling lanes and rows of elevated theatre seats. He assumed they were in the arena. Ahmed followed Cate as she turned down another hallway that led to the left. They were at another set of entry doors. She opened them, took a step outside and looked around. Assured it was clear, she motioned Ahmed to follow. Once outside, Ahmed saw a high rise apartment building. They ducked through a large hedge row that separated the parking lot from the apartment building. Next to the high rise was a large church with a sign that read Inter City Baptist Church. Cate turned left after they were on the other side of the hedge and headed toward the street.

"Are you sure of what you're doing," he asked Cate, "maybe we should stay clear of the road?"

Episode 39

"It's a risk I know, but I have something in mind. It's obvious they aren't going to call for help from the local police because they're afraid I might start waiving this vial around. That might create some questions they don't want asked. That agent will be searching the bowling alley long enough to give us time for what I have planned. Besides the bowling alley, there's a bar, the arena and a pool hall upstairs," Cate answered, "searching all of them should keep him occupied."

The pool hall was one of Eric's favorite hang outs. She wondered what it looked like now. Another time, she thought and headed toward the street. Not waiting for the walk sign, they ran across Allen Road toward a building with a sign that read Celia's Sub Shop.

Ahmed stayed next to Cate as they entered Celia's. Several people occupied the booths next to the window. Most of the men had on matching shirts with various advertisements embossed on the back's of their shirts. Cate took a seat at the counter across from two men who had brown shirts with G&L Collision written in cream colored letters. A young woman with a patch of brightly dyed red hair scrunched on the top of her head and a nose ring came over to take their order.

"Three cheese steaks to go," Cate said. "With everything and three cokes, too."

"It'll be a few minutes," the woman answered and walked back to the grill. She threw shredded steak, onions and mushrooms onto the grill then picked up a plastic squeeze bottle. Ahmed watched as the nose ringed cook drizzled sauce onto the shredded steak. The sauce emitted a sizzling sound when it hit the grill. A small cloud of steam shot up. Cate reached into her uniform pocket and pulled out a leather credit card case containing her driver's license, two credit cards and a couple of folded twenties. She'd slipped the case into her pocket before going to the cafeteria to meet Ronnie. Cate took out a twenty and handed it to Ahmed.

"I've got to use the rest room. If she comes back before I'm out, pay her. Oh, yeah, stay away from he window," Cate said and walked to the back of the sub shop.

411

Cate opened the door marked Ladies and went inside. Ahmed thought about telling her he had a training in this area and knew better than to put his face in the window. In fact, according to his training, coming into the sub shop hadn't been a good idea at all. Before the young girl with the nose ring returned with their order, Cate came out of the rest room.

"I think I need to do the same," Ahmed said and handed Cate back the twenty. He walked into the men's room, urinated then washed his hands and splashed water on his face. What the hell is this Nurse Cate up to he asked himself. Waking back, he could see Cate holding two bags. She handed Ahmed the drinks and they left by the same door they entered. Turning away from the street, they headed down an alley behind the buildings. Ahmed was impressed, it was a smart move. They walked up the alley two more streets then turned back toward Allen Road on a side street named Keppen. Heading toward a major road with good lighting was the last thing they should do, but he didn't have a better alternative. They could call someone to pick them up, but who to call was a problem. He didn't want to involve Stacey nor did he want to jeopardize Ali. Following Nurse Cate seemed his only choice.

Crossing Allen Road, they walked quickly for another block then paused at the third house. Cate walked up the side walk and onto a small porch with Ahmed beside her. She handed Ahmed the bag of Cheese Steaks and opened the aluminum storm door. When Cate began pounding loudly on the wooden entry door, Ahmed became concerned. He was about to tell her whoever she wanted to talk to wasn't home when the porch light flicked on. It took several moments for whoever was inside to unlock the door. Ahmed heard considerable fumbling from inside and prayed it wouldn't take much longer. Their exposure on the open porch was not good. Ahmed heard the interior door unlock. When the door opened, Ahmed almost dropped the bags of cheese steaks and Cokes.

Episode 40

Ahmed could not believe his eyes. Growing up in Afghanistan he had seen more destitute people than he cared to remember. To see someone in suburban Detroit as ragged and filthy as the pan handlers around Kabul seemed beyond comprehension. The man looked to be in his late fifties; it was difficult to tell. Traces of silver ran through the matted black hair hanging over the man's ears and extending mid way down his back. There was less silver in his beard, but in the dim light Ahmed could see it was greasy and unclean. The man's eyes were wide set and dark. His skin was pallor and his face had an oily sheen. Body odor drifted through the open doorway. The man wore tattered blue jeans frayed at the hems and a black sweatshirt with several holes. The neck of the sweat shirt was stretched and Ahmed could see a dingy tee shirt beneath.

Ahmed was uncertain how long they stood transfixed on the porch. The man stared only at Cate, making Ahmed feel invisible. Cate returned the man's gaze but said nothing. Ahmed waited for one of them to speak but the silence continued. Glancing sideways, he saw tears welling up in Cate's eyes. Ahmed turned his attention back to the man in the doorway feeling their situation was becoming more tenuous by the minute. If the agents drove by, they were totally exposed. Ahmed stole another glance at Cate; tears were now running down her cheeks. She was trying to speak but couldn't. Ahmed gave her a gentle nudge. Cate looked at Ahmed then back at the man.

"Oh, Eric," she said in a soft voice, "what's become of you?"

Cate couldn't believe the broad shouldered handsome boy who had captured her heart years ago had become the man standing in front of her. Ahmed waited for the man to reply. He knew the man recognized Cate on some level; there was some kind of connection. It seemed other worldly though, as if some kind of telekinesis was taking place between them. It reminded Ahmed how he and his little sister sometimes communicated with only expressions and gestures, especially during family celebrations. A thought could pass between them without a single word being spoken.

"Eric, can we come inside?" Cate asked softly.

Her voice sounded shaky as she struggled to maintain her poise.

"We have some Cheese Steaks and Cokes from Celia's. Inspector Larry says you like them. So can my friend and I come inside? Please Eric."

"Okay," Eric answered in a hoarse whisper stepping backwards.

Inside the foyer, Ahmed closed the door. Looking around the living room, his sense of relief faded. Ahmed was speechless. There were the stacks of newspapers, magazines and computer reports everywhere. They were piled chest high in the living room and dining room. Narrow paths led around the stacks. The carpeting was worn bare and the padding visible. Ahmed's eyes followed the little trails. To his right they provided passage to the kitchen. To the left, they led to a hallway providing access to other parts of the house. He stood next to Cate trying to fathom what he was seeing.

Eric sat down on a heavily soiled couch and slumped forward. Putting his head in his hands, he began rocking rhythmically back and forth. Muffled cries came from his down cast head. Cate walked to the couch and sat next to him. Ahmed

Episode 40

took a seat in a threadbare chair that had seen better days. He was still holding the two paper bags and was at a loss what to do with them. Finally he set them on his lap. Ahmed wondered why Cate had led them here. It was obvious they had been involved at one time. It was also obvious Cate still had deep feelings for the man. It was difficult to read anything about Eric, his mental state seemed so precarious.

"It's her," Eric repeated over and over.

Cate put an arm around him and pulled him close.

"Who is her?" Ahmed asked softly.

The question startled Cate. She looked at Ahmed in surprise not knowing his query had been a natural reaction from helping the traumatized children at the orphanage. He'd seen this behavior before. Eric lifted his head. Tears were running down his cheeks and dropping onto the couch making tiny dark spots where they landed.

"Who is her?" Ahmed repeated gently.

"The girl," Eric answered.

Ahmed was relieved. He had made a connection; sometimes the children remained mute. Ahmed knew in some ways Eric was little different from the dirty, undernourished waifs his father brought home from the villages around Kabul. Though not homeless in a physical sense, Eric was abandoned emotionally. The next few minutes would be crucial, he'd seen orphaned children have similar reactions. Sometimes they curled up into little balls and totally disconnected. Some recovered; others never did and died. Their deaths would be attributed to infection or disease, but Ahmed believed the real cause was isolation and despair. Their spirits were mortally wounded rendering their little bodies unable to sustain life.

"What girl, Eric?" Ahmed persisted.

Cate looked in silent amazement at the young man sitting across from her. He surely couldn't have had any formal training in psychology, yet somehow he managed to get Eric to respond.

"The girl from a long time ago," Eric stammered.

"How did you know this girl?" Ahmed continued.

"She's the girl in the book."

"That's right, Eric. She's the girl in the book. But which book, Eric? Which book is the girl in?"

"The green book, with the gold lettering," Eric answered in a voice that made him sound like a child. Ahmed glanced at Cate and noted she had stopped crying.

"Do you have this book?" Ahmed asked again.

"No, not here," Eric answered softly, "it's in the bedroom."

"Can you get it, this book. Eric, can you get it for us to look at?"

"Yeah," Eric said very slowly.

"Tell you what, you get the book and show it to us. We'll wait right here, or if you want, maybe Cate can go with you. Would that be okay?"

"Yeah, that's right Eric, I can go with you. Would that be okay?" Cate asked.

"Okay," Eric answered and rose from the couch. He wiped his cheeks with the sleeve of his sweat shirt leaving smears of grime on his shiny cheeks. Cate stood up with him and they walked toward the hallway.

Ahmed remained seated. Looking down at the bags, Ahmed saw grease had leaked from the sandwiches and a dark spot was forming on the bottom. He hurried through the stacks of papers toward the kitchen hoping the bottom wouldn't give way.

"Holy shit,' he said in a low voice as he entered the kitchen.

Though surprised at the mess in the dining room, Ahmed was unprepared for what he saw in the kitchen. It was an unbelievable mess. Dirty dishes were stacked everywhere. Green and black patches of mold were growing on several plates. Open cardboard food containers and empty cans were lying everywhere. Ahmed made room on the counter by pushing several pots and pans into one corner. He set the two bags down and hurried back to the living room. He returned to the thread bare chair and waited for Eric and Cate to return. Ahmed had no idea what to do next, it would just have to play out. When Cate and Eric returned to the living room, Cate

Episode 40

carried a large book with a green cover and gold lettering along the outside.

"Is this the book with the girl in it?" he asked Cate.

"I think so," Cate answered as she and Eric sat down on the couch.

"I've never seen a book like that, what is it Cate?"

"It's a high school year book. Eric and I went to high school together. It's an annual. It records one year of school with pictures and commentary. This one is for 1967."

"This is the book with the girl in it, Eric?" Ahmed asked again in a soft voice.

Eric shook his head yes.

"The girl in the book is Cate who's sitting next to you?"

"Yes," Eric replied in a low voice.

"What about this girl, Eric. What about Cate?"

"She went away," Eric answered with great effort. "They all go away,"

"But now she's back, isn't she Eric. She's back and she's right here. Sitting next to you on the couch."

"And I'm not going to go away again, Eric," Cate answered placing her arm around him.

"You said they all go away Eric. Did other people go away?"

Eric shook his head yes.

"Who else, Eric, who else went away and didn't come back?"

Eric didn't answer. He sat staring off into space. Ahmed could see Eric's throat move up and down as he struggled to swallow. Tears began running down Eric's cheeks in great rivers and his chin quivered as he tried to talk. Little threads of saliva had gathered at the corners of Eric's mouth making it look as if his upper and lower lips were connected by thin strands of spider web. The webs would decrease in diameter as Eric opened his mouth in feint attempts to speak.

"Who else went away?" Ahmed prodded gently.

He knew from the orphans, if they could articulate the horror they'd experienced, it brought their terror to the surface. It allowed them to accept the comfort and compassion needed to ease their shattered souls. From there it was a long road to healing, but some of them made it. The ones who failed to confront their fear and pain eventually just gave up.

"Who else Eric?" Ahmed asked again.

"Nancy" Eric said in a whisper and collapsed into Cate's lap. He pulled one of the couch pillows to his face and cried in muffled sobs. Cate put her other arm around him. She whispered it was okay, everything would be all right now, she was back. They sat that way for several minutes. Believing they needed to be alone, Ahmed whispered he needed to use the restroom. Cate motioned her head toward the hallway. Silently Ahmed got out of the chair and walked to the hallway.

He assumed the bathroom would be like the rest of the house and was not disappointed. Walking by the sink, he could see it was ringed with stains. Articles of clothing were scattered about. Two mildewed towels were on the floor next to the bathtub which was as filthy as the sink. Ahmed walked to the toilet. The seat was down and as was the cover. Ahmed lifted the toilet cover first.

"Mother of God," Ahmed hissed jumping backward in reflex. The toilet bowl was filled with what looked like blood.

"Holy shit," he added taking a step forward. His eyes had not deceived him. Ahmed hurried back to the living room where Cate still held Eric.

"Cate, I think you need to see this. I'm sorry, this may not seem to be the time for an interruption, but you need to see this anyway."

"Eric," Cate said in a soothing voice, "I have to use the bathroom. You lie down on the couch for a moment. I'm just going to walk down the hall."

Cate lowered Eric onto the couch. Eric drew his knees up to his chest and wrapped his arms around his legs. Ahmed knew it was not a good sign.

"Who's Nancy," Ahmed whispered as they neared the bathroom.

"His mother," Cate replied.

"I thought as much. What happened to her?"

Episode 40

"She died. That happened after Eric and I split up. I never knew her, but she was unstable. She was institutionalized off and on after Eric was born. His folks divorced and she eventually remarried. Eric lived with his dad."

"Guess he's had it tough."

In the bathroom, Ahmed pointed toward the toilet.

"Take a look in there, your friend Eric might need to go to the hospital."

Cate walked over and looked into the toilet. Stepping back quickly, she sucked in her breath and put her hand to her mouth.

"Jesus," she gasped. "That can't be blood."

She looked into the toilet again. The bowl was full of a reddish looking liquid that looked like blood but wasn't the normal crimson color. On closer inspection, it was plum colored and looked like a bottle of wine had been poured into the toilet. Cate studied the contents of the bowl and saw dried spots around the rim that were not consistent in color to dried blood. She looked for some toilet paper but the roll was empty.

"Get my purse from the living room," she said. Ahmed went to the living room but couldn't find it. Noting Eric was where they left him, Ahmed walked back to the bathroom.

"Cate, I couldn't find your purse."

"Damn it," she said disgustedly, "I dropped it while running in the parking structure. Damn it all, I look like hell and don't have any make up. See if you can find any napkins or paper towels."

"There's napkins in with the subs. The girl stuffed a few into the bag." Ahmed replied.

"Great, those'll work."

Ahmed returned and handed the napkins to Cate. She put on one of the rubber gloves she'd stuffed into her pocket to conceal the vial and took the napkin from Ahmed. After dipping it into the toilet, she lifted the napkin out and examined it closely. It had a wine colored stain.

"Just as I thought, it's not blood," she said, "but you're right about Eric needing to get to a hospital. I've seen this before, but only twice. I think he has a blood disorder called porphyria. It makes his urine very dark when he's having an attack. We need to get him there soon; it also might explain his erratic behavior."

"Good, I hope there's some kind of explanation," Ahmed replied, "'I mean this dude is really messed up."

Cate looked sharply at Ahmed

"Sorry Cate, I didn't intend for it to come out that way. But you gotta admit, looking at this house and all. I mean, could this whatever it is, blood disorder, account for all of this?" he asked raising his eyebrows.

"I really don't know much about it. Like I said, I've only seen it in two patients in all the hospitals I've worked at. But it can make the patient delusional, and it can be life threatening, so we need to get him checked out."

"Yeah, but where are we going to take him? Oak Grove's the closest hospital, and we certainly can't go back there."

"You're right. There's Taylor General but they're part of the Oak Grove system. Some of the doctors work both locations so we might be recognized. There's Waterside Hospital in Wyandotte. I don't know if they are affiliated with anybody. Go call them and make sure they're not part of Oak Grove. If Waterside is still independent, we can go there."

Ahmed headed to the kitchen to use the phone. Peeling off the latex glove she remembered she was supposed to call Jess.

"Damn it," she said aloud.

Sitting down next to Eric, she took her cell phone out of her uniform pocket and accessed the directory. After scrolling to Jess's number, she pushed enter. The phone rang twice.

"Hello," Jess answered in a raspy voice.

"Jess, it's Cate."

"Where the hell are you?"

"Listen, I'm at Eric's."

"Eric's what the hell are you doing there? Wait, don't answer. I don't want to know," Jess replied with a laugh.

"It's not like that. Listen, Eric's pretty sick."

Episode 40

"You didn't have to tell me that," Jess interjected, "you've forgotten, I've seen him at the store."

"No, Jess, he's physically sick. I have an idea, though, what's wrong with him."

"Hang up now, Cate," Ahmed frantically interrupted.

"Who's that with you Cate? Is that Eric? Cate, Cate, you are a constant source of surprises," Jess laughed.

"What'd you say, Ahmed?" Cate looked up.

Ahmed had a look of anguish on his face.

"Ahmed," Jess interjected, "now Cate, don't even tell me you have two men there."

Before Cate could answer, Ahmed grabbed the phone from her hand.

"Sorry, she'll call back," he barked into the mouthpiece and flipped the phone closed.

"What are you doing?" Cate said looking surprised.

"Your cell, they'll track us!"

"Oh, my god!" Cate replied. "I'm sorry I forgot. Can they do that?"

"Yes, they trace by your account and they can pinpoint the geographic location by satellite. We need to pull the battery out of the phone right now. It sends a signal even when it's turned off. They'll pull your call record and pick up your friend no doubt, we gotta tell her she's in real danger. She's going to have to come with us wherever it is we're going. We'll stop at the first pay phone we see and you can call and warn her."

Ahmed pulled the back off the cell phone and removed the battery.

"What'd you find out about Waterside Hospital?" she asked when he finished.

"They're not affiliated with Oak Grove, so we're okay there. We gotta move now, we have about two hours before they can trace your call and fix the location. It'll just confirm what they already know, that we're in this area. We need to find out if Eric has a car and get him ready to go. Think he's up to it?"

Book Two Home Again

Ahmed looked over at Eric who was still lying on the couch in a fetal position. It didn't look promising.

"This isn't going to be easy," Cate looked at Eric, "but we need to get him there somehow. Let's hope he trusts me enough."

Cate gently pulled the pillow away from his face.

"Eric," she said.

Eric looked up at her. She could see his teeth were badly decayed. What a shame she said to herself.

"Do you remember when we were in Florida together?"

Eric's shook his head no.

"Well," Cate continued, "we lived together for a while in Florida. You remember Florida don't you?"

The last question elicited more negative head shaking Cate looked at Ahmed.

"This is not going well. Can you think of anything? Seems like you have some experience in this," Cate asked.

Ahmed doubted he could help but decided to try one last thing before giving up. He was about to look in the garage for a car. Where they'd go after dropping Eric at the hospital was still unresolved. Ahmed looked at the stacks of reports.

"What do you think he's doing with all of that stuff?" Ahmed asked pointing at the stacks.

"Hard to say," Cate answered.

Ahmed walked over to one of the stacks and picked up a report.

"It's some kind of census report, or at least that's what it says," Ahmed looked closer at the computer print out.

"It's for the election," Eric said, his voice cracked as he sat up.

"Jesus," Ahmed said in amazement. He glanced at Cate who looked as bewildered.

"Eric loves politics," Cate replied with a forced smile.

"What election?" Ahmed asked.

"The election for President, of course," Eric replied.

Ahmed had seen this with some of the traumatized children. They'd occasionally latch on to the most obscure facet of their

Episode 40

prior lives, as if somebody had thrown them a life line to prevent them from totally drifting away.

"Who's running?" Ahmed let his arm drop to his side but he continued holding the report.

"George, of course," Eric said wiping his cheeks with the backs of his hands.

"George Bush?" Ahmed continued.

"No," Eric answered. "George McGovern."

Ahmed shrugged his shoulders. Looking at Cate, he saw a look of astonishment cross her face as she reached over and took Eric's hand.

"Senator George McGovern is running against Richard Nixon for president," Cate said to Ahmed, "and Eric works on his campaign. Eric works for Senator McGovern in areas of strategy and demographics. That's why he left Florida, to work on the campaign."

Eric looked at Cate. He tilted his head to the right and gripped her hand tighter. She hoped he would say something in recognition of their lives together in Miami. He remained silent and Cate knew it was now or never.

"Listen Eric, we need to take you to see a doctor. You're sick and the doctor can help you," she said in coaxing voice.

Eric dropped her hand and stood up.

"No doctors!" he stated loudly.

The sudden outburst caught Ahmed and Cate by surprise.

"Okay, okay, easy Eric," Ahmed said. "No one's going to make you do anything you don't want to do."

"Okay, Eric," Cate repeated standing up next to him. She put her arms around him and held him close. "Listen no one's going to do anything that you don't want. Let's just sit down again. It'll be okay."

Sitting on the couch, Cate took Eric's hand and pulled him down next to her. She had an idea.

"Ahmed," Cate looked over at the young Arab, "are you hungry?"

"Not really. I've seemed to have lost my appetite," Ahmed answered.

"Well, I am," Cate arched her eyebrows letting Ahmed know his answer had not been the correct one. "and I know how much Eric loves Cheese Steaks. Inspector Larry told me. You do like them, don't you Eric?"

Eric went mute again and just nodded his head yes.

"Okay Eric, I'm going into the kitchen and get them ready for us. You sit with Ahmed for a few minutes while I get them ready."

Cate got up from her seat and walked into the kitchen. Sucking in her breath, she felt a wave of guilt run through her. Why did I ever make him leave she started to say, but she knew given the same situation she'd do it all again. Cate found the bags of sandwiches and Cokes on the counter. She looked around for clean plates and realized the search was useless. She took the bag of Cokes, removed one of the Styrofoam cups and lifted the top off. She reached into her pocket and took out the credit card holder. The holder had four slits. The first held her driver's license and voter's registration. The second slit held the remaining twenty dollar bill, the third her Visa card. Cate reached into the last slit and removed a small piece of folded aluminum foil which held three Xanax tablets, her emergency stash. She took one tablet out of the foil and put it back into the credit card holder then closed the aluminum foil around the other two. Digging through a stack of dishes, she found a tablespoon. Cate placed it on top of the foil wrapped pills and pressed down until the pills were crushed. Opening the foil, she hoped Eric would not taste the medication. She scraped half of the ground pills into the Coke and swirled the drink around with her finger. None of the particles floated to the surface. Satisfied she'd done her best to make them dissolve; she licked the soft drink off her finger and removed one of the sandwiches from the bag. Opening it up, she sprinkled the remaining ground Xanax on the sandwich and rubbed it into the shredded steak hoping it would go unnoticed. She rewrapped the sandwich and placed it into the bag. Carrying both bags into the living room, Cate made her

Episode 40

way around the stacks. Eric had laid down on the couch while Ahmed sat in the chair massaging his neck.

"Everyone hungry?" she said in a cheery voice and took a seat next to Eric. "Okay,, here's yours," she added reaching into the bag. Eric sat up slowly as Cate handed him the sandwich. Seeming to not care the wrapper was greasy, he placed it onto his lap. Cate then handed Ahmed a sandwich.

"Okay, Cokes now," she said. Eric set his Coke on the floor. Ahmed did the same.

Cate took out the remaining Cheese Steak and after unwrapping it, took a bite. Surprisingly, it tasted good. She took a drink of the Coke and wondered if some of the Xanax had stuck to her fingers causing her sudden appetite.

"Eat up boys," Cate said lifting her sandwich. Ahmed had no idea what she was up to but knew he'd better comply. He unwrapped the Cheese Steak and took a bite. He had difficulty swallowing and took a drink of Coke to wash it down.

"Come on Eric," Cate pleaded. "It'll be like a picnic we used to have at the beach. Do you remember the beach Eric?"

Shaking his head in agreement, Eric unwrapped the sandwich and took a small cautious bite. Cate wondered if something had registered in his brain because he leaned back and seemed to relax. Eric picked up the Coke, lifted the plastic top off and dropped it on the floor. After taking a drink, he looked into the Styrofoam cup and a perplexed look crossed his face.

"Is the drink okay?" Cate prayed he hadn't tasted the Xanax.

"It's not Diet," Eric replied.

The response caught Cate and Ahmed off guard. Ahmed had just taken a drink of Coke when Eric gave his unexpected reply. Ahmed start choking and bent forward in a coughing fit. Cate set her sandwich down and started to get up but Ahmed indicted he was okay. Cate saw little streams of Coca Cola running down from his nostrils and thought how funny Ahmed's choking would have been if they were all young, stoned and sitting on a beach in Florida again.

"It went up my nose," Ahmed uttered. As he wiped his face with a napkin, Eric surprised them again.

"Maybe you should switch to something not so strong," Eric said taking another bite.

Cate dropped her sandwich. The cheese steak landed in the wrapper with a plopping sound. It was what Eric always said to her when they smoked pot on the beach. They'd roll a couple joints and pick up a bag of burgers or tacos then watch the sunset. She habitually choked on the first couple of puffs and would often comment between coughs that the weed was a bit harsh, then pass the joint back to Eric. He'd say she should switch to something not so strong and laugh. They'd feast and listen to the ocean. The scene had played out countless times. Cate wondered if a small part of Eric's memory that had slipped into obscurity had suddenly resurfaced. She also felt the night had turned into a Looney Tunes cartoon and she had become Daffy Duck. Looking over at Eric, she saw an almost smug look on his face. She remembered that look. Cate glanced at Ahmed and then back at Eric. He had finished almost half of his sandwich. She felt guilty but knew drugging him was their only recourse.

"You okay?" she asked Ahmed again.

"Yeah, I think so."

"Well, better finish your sandwich, as my dad used to say, you don't know,"

Before she could finish, Eric interrupted.

"When you're going to eat again."

He'd slurred his words and she hoped she hadn't over dosed him. It was a large amount of medication, but she wasn't certain he'd eat the whole sandwich or even drink the Coke. As it turned out, he nearly finished both. Eric yawned and set the Coke down. Swallowing the last bite of the sandwich, he leaned back. When his eyes batted several times, she knew the drug had kicked in.

"Feel shleepy," Eric said leaning his head on the arm of the couch. His body went limp and his breathing became deep and regular. Cate felt his pulse. It was slow, but not dangerously so.

"What the hell?" Ahmed said looking at Cate.

Episode 40

"I drugged his Cheese Steak and Coke with Xanax. He'll be out until we get him to the hospital that's for sure." Cate replied. "Let's look for his car or call a taxi."

"Damn Nurse Cassadea, you are full of surprises," Ahmed replied.

Cate gave him a disapproving look when he set his sandwich on the floor.

"A stain on this carpet will hardly make a difference," he added.

"Let's look in the garage," Cate got up and led the way to the back door. Ahmed followed her onto the driveway. Because they had approached the house from the other direction, they hadn't seen the full sized van parked in front of the garage.

"Bonsai!" Cate exclaimed.

"What the hell does that mean?" Ahmed asked.

"It's Japanese. Again you're too young," Cate answered.

"What does it mean?" Ahmed asked.

"It translates as, now we need to find the bloody keys," Cate replied walking up the steps leading back to the kitchen. Reaching the top step, she saw a hooded sweatshirt hanging on a wooden pegged coat rack. "He always kept them in his coat," she added reaching into the pocket.

Cate found a set of keys and jingled them. She felt excited and fatigued at the same time.

"Think that thing will even start?" Ahmed asked.

"Only one way to find out," Cate tossed him the keys

Episode 41

Outside a twenty-four hour pharmacy, Ahmed waited in the van while Cate used the pay phone. Ahmed left the engine running, he wasn't sure the clunker would start again. When he looked to his right, Ahmed saw an L shaped row of stores that looked like a cross between a strip mall and an enclosed mall. There was expansive side walk in front of the stores that was covered by a large overhang. At the entrance was a brightly lit sign that said Sears Lincoln Park Plaza

Cate noticed the sign as she deposited two quarters into the phone and dialed Jess's number. Growing up, The Plaza had been the only shopping nearby. As teenagers, she and her girlfriends were regulars. While waiting for Jess to answer, she looked over at the Plaza again. Sears and Roebuck remained open but most of her favorite stores were now gone. Mary Ann's had been replaced by a Dollar Store and Albert's was home to a GNC. She wondered if Meyer's Jewelry was still in business.

She knew the Cunningham's Drug Store had closed years ago. Cate thought nostalgically about the times she, Linda and Jess had walked to the Plaza. They'd hang out at Cunningham's soda fountain sipping cherry Cokes and eating fries. Sometimes they'd stop at the Sander's Ice Cream shop for an egg salad sandwich or a hot fudge cream puff. In late August, the plaza was a bustle of activity with everyone shopping for new school clothes. Chance meetings with boys from neighboring high schools always added to the allure.

Christmas was her second favorite time at The Plaza. Cherry Cokes were replaced by hot chocolates and there was a phone booth inside Cunningham's where she'd call home for a ride if the weather was bad. Sometimes Kathy and Linda would wedge themselves into the booth and their incessant giggling would make her mom's voice barely audible.

"Jess, this is Cate again," Cate said but before she could finish, Jess interrupted.

"Cate what the hell was that last call about, are you okay?" she asked in a concerned voice.

"Well, yes and no," Cate responded. "Listen I have to be brief. Ahmed, I'll explain him later, and I are on our way to Waterside Hospital in Wyandotte. We are taking Eric there. This may sound strange, but there are some things going on and it may not be safe for you to stay where you are. I shouldn't have called you from my cell, it was a mistake and I'm so sorry. Listen, I didn't want to drag you into any of this but I screwed up royally and now it can't be helped."

"What the hell are you talking about Cate? Are you sure you are okay, you didn't take any drugs or do anything stupid like that did you?"

"No. Now listen. After we get Eric to the hospital, I'm going to send Ahmed for you. He'll bring you to the hospital. I'll explain when you get there and we can figure out what to do then."

"Okay," Jess replied, "but are you sure you're all right, Cate? You're not having a meltdown or something?"

"Well, that's hard to answer, but yeah, for the time being, I'm okay. You can be the judge after I explain what's going on."

Cate walked back to the truck. It had taken every bit of their energy to load Eric into the van. His body had gone limp from the Xanax. After throwing a blanket over him, they'd held their breath as Ahmed turned the ignition key. After a couple of anx-

Episode 41

ious minutes, the engine finally came to life. The gas tank was even half full; Cate hoped their luck would hold.

"Did you get a hold of her?" Ahmed asked as Cate climbed into the passenger seat. She adjusted the seat belt before answering.

"Yeah, I told her that you'd come pick her up."

"Does she have a car?" Ahmed asked.

"Yeah," Cate answered looking out the passenger window, "but it doesn't run. Anyway, get back on Southfield and turn right. Take it all the way 'till it ends, that'll be West Jefferson, then turn right. You can't miss the turn, if you do, we'll end up in the Detroit River. Maybe that's our best option anyway," Cate added.

After riding in silence a few minutes, Cate took off her seat belt and climbed into the back. Assured Eric was okay, she returned to the front. A sign told them they were entering the city of Ecorse. Cate noted the small houses along the river still had well tended front yards. Passing several marinas, Cate thought about the summer she and Eric spent cruising on his friend's antique cabin cruiser.

As they neared Wyandotte, Cate could smell the faint odor from the chemical complex. When they passed the red brick buildings she noticed the sign that used to read Wyandotte Chemicals now read BASF. She and Eric went to the movies a couple of times in Wyandotte before moving to Florida. When they passed the theatre, Cate saw it had closed and felt maudlin.

"Another Downriver casualty," she said aloud. She could see the hospital ahead on their left.

"Pull into the Emergency entrance. I'll go in and tell them about Eric."

"Better take off your hospital identification card," Ahmed advised.

"Good point," Cate replied slipping it into her pocket.

"Are you going to sign him in? I don't know about using you're real name?"

"I don't see an alternative. If he doesn't have coverage, I'll have to sign for him. We'll play it by ear. Listen, when we get him inside, you head for Jess's. I'll write the directions for you."

"So when does sleep fit into the equation?" Ahmed asked with a passing smile.

"Maybe next week," Cate answered as Ahmed turned into the entrance.

****

Cate sat next to Eric's bed. After she explained her suspicion of Porphyria to the doctor, he'd ordered a blood test and a catheter. The doctor then disappeared as emergency room doctors seem to do. Cate closed her eyes for what felt like only a moment and was awakened by Ahmed's gentle shaking.

"I've got Jess in the car, any idea what to do next?"

Cate was about to answer when the doctor returned.

"We've got the results back from the lab. Eric's PBG counts were off the chart. He's most certainly porphyric. I've spoken to the Hematologist on staff. He's coming in to look at your friend. You said he didn't have any stomach pain, but the Xanax may have dulled that. There's a new treatment, it's called Porphozym, it's administered in a 12 hour drip. It won't cure your friend, but it will stop the attack and stabilize him. Sometimes it prevents attacks for a year, depending on the patient. Anyway, Doctor Singh will administer it. You can stay with your friend or go home. If you go, can you leave a number where we can reach you?"

"Yeah," Cate answered, "I'll leave it with the registration people. I need some sleep. Thank you Doc."

Ahmed followed her to the registration desk. The woman ahead of them was looking for her health care card in a purse the size of a small suitcase. The delay was annoying and Cate turned to Ahmed.

"Go to the truck and tell Jess I'll just be a minute."

"What number are you going to give them Cate; you can't give them your cell phone number."

"I'll give them Ronnie's number."

****

Episode 41

Ronnie had stayed up late watching a movie. After an hour of tossing and turning he was almost ready to give up, turn on the light and read. He finally dozed off and had dreamt he and Beth were out on their boat floating down the Ganges River in India. In his fever like dream, he was steering the boat and heard ringing. After a few moments he realized it wasn't a dream, the doorbell was ringing.

Ronnie looked at the clock. The green digits read two-twenty. The doorbell hadn't rung at that hour since the boys were teenagers and misplaced their keys. Ronnie's head was spinning. He wondered if everything that transpired the last few years had also been just part of some bizarre fever dream. Maybe the boys were still teenagers and Beth was still lying next to him. He reached over with his left hand and felt the empty, cold spot on the bed. Two years ago he would have felt the warmth from her body long before his hand touched her. There was no warmth now, just an empty place. The door bell continued to ring.

"Shit fire," Ronnie said in a low voice, "who the hell could that be."

It was a southern expression, the only profanity his mother ever uttered. Ronnie wondered how it sprang into his head, he never used the euphemism.

At least the dog isn't barking, Ronnie mumbled putting on his slippers. Biscuit had died just before Beth was diagnosed. She was half Golden Retriever, a gentle soul who lived to fourteen. She seldom barked unless someone came to the door at night. Few things stirred Beth's temper more than Biscuit barking because of the boys' forgetfulness. Ronnie looked down at his slippers. If he was lucky, the right one would stay on his atrophied foot. The odds were better than fifty-fifty it'd slip off by the third step. Ronnie shuffled to the stairs and swore softly as the slipper fell off before the first step.

"All right, all right, I'm coming," he yelled making sure to put his bad foot down first and follow with his good leg. It was the only way to make sure he didn't go ass over elbows down the stairs. Ronnie reached the foyer and turned on the porch light. For a minute he thought he was back on the Ganges River, the apparition before him made about as much sense.

"What the hell?" he said out loud opening the storm door. He'd taken the screen out the week before and replaced it with the heavy glass. Standing on the porch was Cate and the young Arab janitor. Jess was on the step. Ronnie gazed at the unlikely trio with blinking eyes. He hadn't put on his bath robe and was relieved he didn't have what Beth used to call his piss erection, an infrequent event lately. It was one of the very few advantageous of being over fifty. Ronnie brushed aside his analysis of male aging and opened the door.

"Uh, Cate," he heard himself mutter holding the door open, "come on in."

"This is a surprise," Ronnie added as he led them into the living room.

Cate flopped down on the sofa. Ahmed took a seat at the end of the couch while Jess walked over and sat on the love seat.

"Can I get you guys something to drink or eat? Maybe a beer or Coke or something?"

"A beer sounds really good," Ahmed answered.

"Just a glass of water," Cate added.

"I know my way around, Ronnie. Why don't I get the drinks while Cate lets you know what we're doing here? You might want to sit down for this. Oh, yeah, do you want anything while I'm up?" Jess asked.

"You know, put some water on for tea. There's some Lipton decaf in the pantry and the tea pot is in the cupboard next to the stove. It's white with pink roses."

"I'll have some too," Jess added walking toward the kitchen.

"Put some on for me," Cate yelled into the kitchen.

"I'll make enough for three then, unless you've changed your order Ahmed," Jess yelled back.

"No, bring me the beer. You might want one too, Ronnie after Cate tells you what's going on."

Episode 41

"So what is going on Cate?" Ronnie asked. "Wait; don't answer that until I get my glasses." Ronnie started toward the stairway then hesitated when Cate began speaking.

"Bobbie's story wasn't a figment of his imagination or from too much chemo. We're in big trouble!" Cate blurted out. "I needed to get that out, now go get your glasses."

"I have the feeling this may get complicated," Ronnie replied and headed up the stairs. He returned a few minutes later wearing his glasses and a bath robe. Remaining bare foot, he sat in the chair across from the sofa. Cate noticed his limp was more pronounced without the plastic brace.

Ahmed sipped beer from a long neck bottle.

"The tea will be ready in a minute," Jess said from the kitchen." She brought out three cups and placed them on the glass coffee table.

"Nice house, Ronnie," Cate said in tired voice, "I always wondered what this place looked like inside."

"Remind me to give you the grand tour tomorrow morning. Now tell me about Bobbie's story."

Cate gave an account of everything that happened. Jess came in, poured their tea then sat on the love seat. Ronnie listened to Cate's tale interrupting her twice for details about Eric. Ahmed broke in occasionally to embellish the story. By the time Cate finished telling her story, it was nearly 5:00 a.m. The sun hadn't risen completely, but the birds began chirping and the sky was getting lighter. Ahmed got up and looked through the window facing the River. He noticed the lights on the bridge didn't stand out as much in the morning light. He yawned heavily, his eyelids felt like they weighed fifty pounds. Ronnie noticed the yawn.

"I think you two need some sleep," he said setting his cup onto the coffee table.

"I'm really sorry to bring you into this, Ronnie," Cate said apologetically.

"Nonsense, Cate," Ronnie answered, "you didn't bring me into anything. Bobbie did that, not you. Hell, if I hadn't stolen

Beth back, he'd never have stayed in the damned Army to begin with. So this had nothing to do with you. I'd have been involved whether you worked at Oak Grove or had stayed in Plymouth."

"Thanks," Cate answered in a shaky voice. She was spent and could fall asleep where she sat.

"Jess, take Cate upstairs and put her in the room you and Kenny used. Ahmed can take the other room. You can use my room Jess, think I'll stay up for a while.

"Hey, get in your own bed, Ronnie," Jess said clearing the dishes. "I can flop on the couch. I snoozed on it watching the game with Kenny, I'll have no problem."

"Okay, listen, there's an afghan in the little basket in the dining room."

"Already know where it is, come on Cate, let's get you to bed," Jess had a dish towel still draped over her shoulder.

"You get them up there, Jess, I'll be up in a minute," Ronnie replied.

Ronnie sat in quiet reflection for a few minutes then headed upstairs as Jess was coming down. They met each other half way between floors where Jess thanked him. Ronnie told her it was really nothing then looked in on Cate and Ahmed. Both were fast asleep. Ronnie walked into his room. The birds were chirping and he doubted he'd be able to sleep. His worries were short lived.

****

The phone rang, jarring Ronnie from a dream filled sleep. He rolled over and looked at the clock. This time the dial read eight-twenty. He grabbed the phone quickly hoping it hadn't woke the others.

"Hello," he said groggily.

"I am calling for Cate Cassadea please," it was male voice with a slight Hindi accent.

"Yes," Ronnie answered, "may I ask whose calling?"

Episode 41

"This is Doctor Singh, at Waterside Hospital. She left her name as a contact for a patient."

"Sure, I'll have to wake her up, give me a minute."

Ronnie carried the phone with him and knocked gently on Cate's door.

"Cate, there's a doctor on the phone who wants to talk to you," he said softly.

"Okay," Cate's voice was weak. Ronnie heard her walk towards the door.

"Sorry, to wake you," Ronnie said handing her the phone. She looked dreadful. Her hair was scrunched to one side and there were dark rings under her eyes. She still had on her nurse's scrubs which were wrinkled and smudged. Though blood shot, her eyes were still the deepest blue he'd ever seen.

"It's okay," Cate answered taking the phone. Ronnie walked back to his bedroom and grabbed his bathrobe from the chair. He heard Cate talking to the doctor as he walked to the stairs. When he got downstairs Jess was already awake, lying on the couch with the afghan pulled up to her neck.

"Hey, Jess," Ronnie said as he walked past, "you want some coffee?"

"Yeah, sounds good."

Ronnie put on the coffee and walked back into the living room. Jess was up and sitting on the couch putting on her tennis shoes. She had faired the night's events better than the rest of them.

"I'm heading up stairs for a shower. Think I better get one in quickly before the rest of you decide to get up and going," Ronnie said as he walked to the stairway.

"Next dibs," Jess answered.

"Dibs, ha, haven't heard that one in two weeks," Ronnie replied.

An hour later, they were sitting at the kitchen table attempting to eat scrambled eggs and toast. Ahmed and Jess had no problem finding their appetites. Ronnie managed to finish one egg and a piece of toast. Cate made an effort and in between bites, relayed what the doctor told her. Her diagnosis had been correct, Eric was porphyric. Cate admitted she knew only what the hematologist told her. It was a very rare disease. During an attack, Eric's hemoglobin formed incorrectly which prevented his liver from cleaning his blood. Eric's blood would fill up with porphyrins making him disoriented and delusional. Jess asked if there was a cure. Cate said no, but there was a new treatment that they'd started Eric on. Cate looked despondent.

"What's wrong?" Jess asked.

"Oh, I was just thinking how awful I was to Eric in Miami. He was acting so weird, it was part of the reason I broke it off. All the time it was just this dreadful disease. I feel just awful about how his life turned out. If I'd only known."

"How could you know?" Ronnie asked. "The doctor said this was very rare. Don't beat yourself up Cate. You were fighting your own demons then. Do you really think everything would have worked even if Eric didn't have this disease?"

Cate took a deep breath. "No," she finally said. "Maybe it was as much me. The doctor said Eric's disease sometimes progresses with age. He said there was a movie a few years ago, The Madness of King George. It was about King George of England, the one who was king during the Revolutionary War. He was porphyric."

"Oh my God," Ronnie said, "Beth and I saw that movie. That's tough, let's just hope this new treatment works. If Eric was acting like King George in the movie, that's really sad. Anyway, did the doctor say anything about Eric being schizophrenic? You seemed to think that was the problem, because his mother was schizophrenic."

"I asked the doctor about that. He said Eric could have both, but the porphyria could be enough in itself to cause Eric's strange behavior. He said he would know more when the treatment was complete. Eric became lucid a while ago and the doctor explained to him what happened. Eric's okay, a little confused, but okay. I told the doctor I'd visit Eric today."

"Guess now we have to figure out what we can do about all of this," Jess said lifting a coffee cup to her lips.

Episode 41

"That's not going to be easy," Ronnie replied. "We have some time, but not more than a day or two, three at most. The agents will eventually come here after snooping around the hospital. They'll back track to Bobbie's floor, the nurses will give them my name and they'll be here. What do you think Ahmed, you're the expert here?"

Ahmed was sitting in the chair that faced the window, his thoughts alternating between Stacey and his little sister. He still had a card to play but didn't want to divulge his hand just yet. By now Charlie probably knew he was involved. Unless they figured out a way to use the information about the conspiracy at the hospital, they'd all sit in jail cells until they rotted. Ronnie was right; they had at most three days to figure a way out.

"What do you think, Ahmed?" Ronnie repeated.

The question jarred Ahmed from his thoughts.

"We need a plan, but what to do is unclear. We could go to the newspapers, we might get some protection there. We need to know is what's in those vials but I don't know how to get that done," Ahmed looked out at the County Bridge again knowing they could be trapped on the island once Charlie figured out where they were. They didn't have a safe house and he didn't want to head to a hotel or motel.

"I can help there," Cate said pushing her plate away. She looked down at her cup of coffee, it was still half full. Her stomach was upset and the coffee was not sitting well.

"What'ya mean?" Ronnie asked.

"Well, I have a friend in the lab back in the hospital in Plymouth. I could Fed Ex the vial to her and then we could find out what's in it. Once we know, we can go to the authorities for protection."

"What authorities?" Ahmed asked.

"I don't know, maybe like a Senator or something. Someone who could offer us protection."

"What if the vial gets lost or something, Cate? Or what if your friend gets nabbed and the vial suddenly comes up missing?" Jess asked.

"I have a back up," Cate answered.

"Okay, how about this," Ahmed interjected. "We ship the vial to Plymouth. In the mean time, we get as much cash as we can before Charlie freezes us out and we need to get disposable cell phones. We wait here till we find out what's in the vial, then decide whether we go to the authorities or the newspapers."

"I need to see Eric today," Cate interrupted. "I need to make sure he's okay."

"Okay Ahmed, that will work," Ronnie agreed. "I'll take out what I can from the bank here, they're not looking for me yet. Cate, I'll take you to a Fed Ex store and a bank across town. We'll ship the vial and get cash from the bank. Jess, you and Ahmed get us the phones. Cate and I will go see Eric. We'll all meet back here later, say five o'clock. Cate and I will take my Explorer. Jess, you and Ahmed can drive Beth's car."

"Ronnie, I'm really sorry to have involved you and Jess. I really am," Cate said. A small tear trickled down her cheek and her hand was trembling.

"Cate, I would have been involved anyway. We still haven't talked about Bobbie. You know he was ready to blow the whistle anyway. This will all be over when we know what's in the vial. We'll have a big laugh about this someday," Ronnie said putting his hand on her shoulder.

"We need to do something with Eric's car. If they triangulate our location last night from Cate's call, they'll be looking for his vehicle," Ahmed added.

"Okay, when you and Jess go get the phones, take the van someplace and dump it in a mall parking lot. Go to Somerset in Troy. We'll go to a bank branch in Birmingham. That may divert them to the north side of town. It may help buy time," Ronnie offered.

"That's it then?" Ahmed asked.

"Unless there's something that anyone wants to add," Ronnie replied.

"Just one thing," Cate interjected, "I need some make up and a change of clothes. I have to get out of this filthy uniform."

Episode 41

"Sure," Ronnie replied, "I saved some of Beth's stuff, it'll probably fit you. At least it will get you by until we can stop later on. Ahmed, some of my older son's stuff is still in the closet in your room. I think there are some jeans that will fit you. The rest, underwear and socks and stuff like that, use mine. What about you Jess?"

"I brought some stuff. It's in the van, I lived on the streets so long, I know how to pack in a hurry," she said with a sharp laugh. "I'll clean up the kitchen while Cate and Ahmed shower."

"Okay, I'll go to the bank. Come upstairs Cate, and you can pick out what you want from Beth's stuff."

Ronnie headed to the stairway and began his one legged assent. Cate followed behind.

When they reached the bedroom, Ronnie opened the closet. He'd never been able to clear out all of Beth's clothes. As long as some of them still hung in the closet, he felt a part of her was still in the house.

"Listen, Ronnie," Cate said looking at Beth's clothes. "You don't have to do this."

"I know, but you have to understand how Beth was about sharing. She scared people with her temper, but inside, she was the most caring person I ever met. If you don't take something from here, she'll kick the crap out of both of us when we see her next," Ronnie added with a laugh.

"You sure?" Cate asked.

"Absolutely, pick out something. I'm heading to the bank, be dressed and ready when I get back. I think Eric will like these, Ronnie said pointing to a pair of Ralph Lauren blue jeans and a yellow sweater. They are U of M's colors. It might bring a grin to Eric's face. Lord knows that boy needs every boost he can get," Ronnie smiled as he walked to the door.

****

It was twelve-thirty when Ronnie and Cate pulled into the hospital parking lot. Black smoke spewed from the brick smoke stacks at the power plant next door. Wisps of smoke drifted across the river toward the Canadian shore line.

"Not a good thing for the asthmatics," Cate said looking up at the smoke.

"Oh, the power plant got a permit a couple of years ago to burn old tires in addition to coal. Go figure, only in Downriver. I think the EPA gave up trying to regulate us," Ronnie answered with a laugh.

Standing by the elevators, Ronnie noted how much better Cate looked. She'd borrowed make up from Jess and Beth's clothes fit her well. Beth's pale blue windbreaker accentuated her eyes. Beth had worn it on the boat and seeing it reminded Ronnie of better times.

"I'm nervous," Cate said. She still had a Xanax left and was tempted. Her antidepressants were in her purse. She'd have to do something about that very soon.

"You look great Cate, I think Eric will be pleased."

When the elevator arrived, they got on with a young couple and their daughter. The little girl had curly hair and large brown eyes. She was shy and pressed herself close to her mother. Ronnie glanced at Cate and wondered what was going through her mind. His own world had certainly been turned upside down since Beth's death. Ronnie had no idea what to say to Eric, it had been so long. He wondered if Eric would even remember him. Mulling it over, he decided to follow Cate's lead. It was obvious Cate still had deep feelings for Eric. How Eric would respond was any body's guess. They got off at the third floor and stopped at the nurse's station for directions. Outside Eric's room, Cate stopped and turned to Ronnie.

"I don't know if I can do this," she said with a look of panic. Ronnie could see she was inches from falling apart.

"Cate, you already have done it. Listen, you saved Eric's life. Just ask yourself what's the worst that can happen. I don't mean to sound like Dale Carnegie, God knows I've not been the tower of strength, but you have to ask what's the worse that can happen. Even if he walks out of here tomorrow, and returns to being

Episode 41

Allen Park's answer to Howard Hughes, at least you've given him a chance. The rest is up to him. If he gets his life back, maybe it's a chance for you to get yours back as well. What the hell, after we're all locked up in some gulag, Eric might be the only one smart enough to get us out."

"Yeah, and maybe he'll hate me for dragging him back into a hospital where they'll make him even worse."

"Worse than living the way you described it. Worse than being trapped inside a mind that won't even allow him to leave his house. Screw it, Cate what could be worse than that? If he hates you for dragging him out of that world, he can crawl right back into that hole."

"I never knew you could be so harsh."

"Ask my boys sometime, you ain't seen the half of it," Ronnie added with a laugh. Turning her around by the shoulders, he gave her a gentle shove. "Remember Kemosabi, Tonto is right here behind you."

"Coward," Cate said over her shoulder.

"Eric ain't my long lost love. At least not that I'm going to own up to," Ronnie added giving her a little push.

****

Cate walked slowly into the room. Eric was asleep. He looked better than when she'd last seen him. Even with an IV coming out his arm, his face seemed to have color. They hadn't done much to clean him up, but it appeared they'd taken a wet cloth to his face. His hair was still matted and his beard long and scraggly.

"Geez," Ronnie hadn't intended to say it out loud; it seemed to just slip out. The sound woke Eric. Neither Cate nor Ronnie knew what to expect.

"Hey, Eric," Cate said as she walked to his bed. Eric's mouth opened in a small smile. With a look of recognition crossing his face, he brought his hand up to his mouth to hide his teeth.

"Hey yourself," Eric answered softly. Though Ronnie hadn't heard the voice in years, it registered instantly.

"I don't see you in thirty years and you drug me and bring me into this place and then drag this sorry asshole along," Eric added with a hidden smile.

"Bite me, Eric," Ronnie responded using one of Eric's favorite retorts in Wes's basement.

"Ha," Eric answered. "You gonna hide behind Cate's skirts here, or are you going to step over here where I can see your ugly face."

"I will for just a minute. Then I'm going to go to the cafeteria, can I get you anything?"

"Bottle of Ripple would be nice," Eric responded.

"Yeah, but they're out. All they have is Boone's Farm."

"I'll pass for now. Allergic to apples. Anyway, nice to see you. It's been a while."

"Yeah, a long while. Listen, I'll be back in a few minutes. I think you two need to catch up." Before leaving, Ronnie shook his old friend's hand and gave Cate a hug of encouragement.

"Did I do good, Ronnie?" Cate whispered.

"Real good," Ronnie whispered back. "She's a nurse Eric, you're in good hands," Ronnie said and left. Looking back from the hallway he watched Cate pull a chair next to Eric's bed.

****

It took a couple of hours for the hospital to discharge Eric. As they drove through downtown Wyandotte, Eric examined his new clothes and the bags from Chelsea's Men's Store and began crying. The doctors told Cate that Eric might experience some depression.

Eric wanted to go back home but Cate persuaded him to come with them to Ronnie's. Eric brightened when Cate told him Ronnie lived in the Pagoda House on Grosse Ile. He had even asked if Looney Rooney was still alive. Ronnie told Eric that Rooney'd left the Island years ago. Eric said he understood Rooney a lot better now as he sat looking out the side window. After they crossed the toll bridge, Ronnie glanced into the rear

Episode 41

view mirror. Eric seemed to be all eyes, as if he was trying to take in everything.

"I always loved this place," Eric said as they turned onto Meridian Road. "Hey, Ronnie, before we go to your house, can you drive around the Island one time. It's been so long since I've been here."

"You bet Eric, but please tell me you're not on a reconnaissance mission and plan to cook up some Impossible Mission for us," Ronnie replied jokingly.

Though said in jest, Ronnie wondered if they'd need one shortly. Thinking of the uncertainty ahead, Ronnie knew Eric needed time and wondered how much they had to give to him. It appeared Cate was going to be at the center of whatever direction his life took.

"I nearly forgot about this place," Eric said seeming to enjoy the ride. He leaned forward in his seat taking in the sights.

"Is the Wishing Well still open?" Eric asked. "Some fireworks would be nice."

"That's right, you and Wes went there, too." Ronnie replied, "I tend to forget Bobbie and I weren't the only Melvindale boys who frequented the Wishing Well."

"Wes and I used to go there when his dad used the airport here. He'd take us by the Wishing Well on our way home. Wes's folks also belonged to West Shore Country Club. By the way, whatever happened to old man Swann who owned the Wishing Well."

"That place always reminded me of something out of a Steven King novel," Ronnie answered enthusiastically. "You know with the sulphur smell permeating all over the place from that artesian well and the nitrate smell from the gun powder Old Man Swann used to make his fireworks. And those big spooky ol' pine trees and that big scary looking pond behind the place, man it was right out of one of King's nail biting thrillers. Jesus, I'm scaring myself just talking about it." Ronnie answered.

"I don't know who Steven King is," Eric replied. "but it was a creepy place all right. I remember old man Swann would stand

Book Two Home Again

behind that counter full of his homemade fireworks. He never moved an inch. He looked like some kind of erie statue from a Boris Karloff movie. When you heard him speak the first time, it would make your skin crawl and send shivers up your back. You're right, the inside of that cinder block building reeked from nitrate. Remember, he'd pay you a nickel for empty orange juice cans, you know those little cans of ready to drink juice you could buy from vending machines. I haven't seen those in years, or I guess I should say decades. Funny how I can remember something from forty years ago and I don't know shit about what happened last week."

Eric's eyes clouded over.

"Can you believe that old maniac showed my boys how to make a pipe bomb, one time? I asked one of the Island cops why they let that geyser keep running the place. They said he was grandfathered, he made his own fire works before they were outlawed. Anyway, he was ninety-five when he died which is hard to imagine, he looked ninety-five when we were kids. The place is closed. Dig this, when he died, the artesian well stopped flowing. The largest artesian well in the Midwest just stopped dead for a week. Talk about spooky. My boys still talk about the place."

"Wesley sure loved it. He's gone now, too," Eric added looking sadly out the window. "Take me by there tomorrow if you can, Ronnie."

Passing the airport there was a row of small single engine airplanes by the hangers.

The planes reminded Eric of flying with Wes's father, during a time when life was simpler. Ronnie knew the Island had a melancholy effect on people who'd been away for a while. At East River Road he turned left. As they passed palatial houses with manicured yards, a peaceful look settled across Eric's face.

"I always thought we'd live here one day, Cate," he said. She put her hand to his forehead and stroked his hair.

"I did too, Eric. I did too."

Episode 41

Ronnie pulled the Explorer to the front door. Cate sat in the backseat next to Eric. She opened the door and walked around to his door to help him out.

"Really Cate, I don't need any help," Eric insisted as she opened the door.

While in Wyandotte, Cate had bought Eric two pair of jeans, two shirts, a sweat shirt and underwear and socks. She added a Tommy Hilfiger jacket and a pair of Nike sneakers. Apart from his waist length hair and overgrown beard, Eric was beginning to resemble the boy she remembered. Ronnie knew a bit of porcelain would restore Eric's smile but wondered if his fractured spirit could be as easily restored.

"There's a couple of other people staying with me Eric, just for a day or two," Ronnie said apologetically. He knew the old Eric was free wheeling, but wondered if that was a different and more confident person as a look of apprehension shot across Eric's face.

"Do I know them?" he asked stopping where he stood.

"You know one of them. Jess Olsen, she's also had a rough time Eric. I'll tell you more later, but she was homeless for a while. The other person is a young man named Ahmed who's also had it tough."

"He got out of Afghanistan just before the war," Cate interjected.

"Afghanistan? What about Viet Nam?" Eric asked.

"That ended a long time ago," Cate replied.

"Oh, yeah," Eric answered, "I knew that. Sorry."

Ronnie wondered if Eric knew about September 11, though it really didn't matter. Eric seemed okay, he hadn't freaked out with the idea of other lost souls staying at the Pagoda. Maybe he'll be okay, Ronnie thought leading them to the front door.

****

Dressed in his new clothes, Eric looked better. Cate and Jess cut his hair and trimmed his beard. At Cate's insistence, Eric kept a goatee.

Book Two Home Again

It was an almost balmy autumn evening, following a warm Indian summer day Michigan sometimes displays as a tease before the arctic snow and cold hit. They'd decided to have a picnic on the balcony, so folding lawn chairs were brought up from storage. Ronnie went to Nate's Market and brought back fried chicken breasts, potato salad, baked beans and freshly baked Italian bread. On his way to the register, Ronnie added an apple pie for desert. They moved indoors for desert and Jess brought a pot of coffee into the dining room. The aroma filled the room as she poured steaming cups for everyone. Cate and Ronnie decided to tell Eric everything that had transpired. After hearing their story, he could either throw in with them or go home. Eric listened intently and seemed to absorb every word.

"So what are your thoughts?" Jess asked Eric when Cate finished.

"I think I need some time to digest it all," Eric said taking a sip of coffee. "I'm not leaving you again Cate, that's certain. Sounds to me like the contents of the vial will determine the next step. We won't know that until tomorrow, but it's clear our time line doesn't end there. They'll make the connection to Bobbie and when that happens, they'll be here. We need to make sure we aren't. Deciding whether to go to the authorities or to the press will be difficult but I don't see much of an alternative to either option."

****

It had been a long night for Bobbie. His pain increased daily and so had the morphine. He hadn't heard from Ronnie; it was not a good sign. He remembered most of his discussion with Cate and wondered if she had called the phone number he'd given her. He'd asked his sister to bring him a disposable cell phone, but she hadn't as of yet. He guessed Amy wrote off the request to the morphine. He thought about telling her why he needed it but didn't want to involve her. Keeping her safe was the least he could do.

Episode 41

From the light coming through the window, he knew it was almost sunrise. He considered reaching over for his watch on the table but the effort required too much energy. Time didn't make much difference, he wasn't going anywhere. The day before he had tried to get one of the nurses to wheel him up to the eighth floor. He had a present for Doctor Midek, but the nurse ignored his request. Today he would make one more attempt. It was the only way to give his best friend and one time heart throb a chance. Bobbie gathered his strength and reached under his pillow. The present he intended to deliver was still there. If he couldn't get up to eight, he'd ask one of the nurses to see if Dr. Midek would come down to his room. It was his last option.

****

Sunrise found Ronnie awake. The fried chicken had put his stomach into a knot. Ronnie was heading to the bathroom when he heard a car door close. Diverting his path, he walked to the window at the end of the hallway and looked out the window. Two cars had pulled into the parking area across the road. Three serious looking men got out of the cars. Ronnie hurried to Eric and Cate's bedroom and rapped on the door.

"We've got company," Ronnie said in a loud voice. "Grab your stuff and get downstairs. We're got to leave now."

Ahmed heard the commotion and opened his door. Hearing Ronnie's warning, he grabbed his duffel bag. Ronnie ran to the stairs and made his way down as fast as he could. Jess, like the rest of them, had slept fully dressed. They'd devised an exit strategy the previous night and had taken some preventive actions. Ronnie's Explorer was parked three streets away. They would split into two teams to improve their odds. Jess and Ahmed would take Beth's car parked in the garage. Ronnie, Cate and Eric would use the Explorer and they would all meet up at Pegasus Restaurant in Detroit's Greek Town.

Ronnie looked out the window again. One agent stayed near the cars, the other two were walking toward the front door. As planned, they grabbed their duffel bags and headed down the stairs to the tunnel. The tunnel led under the road and had two exits. One came out inside the garage where one of the agents stood. The other came out in the woods beyond a fence near the property line. The exit beyond the fence was concealed from the house and garage by a row of pine trees. With the agents' cars parked near the garage, Eric suggested they all to go to the Explorer. It limited their alternatives but there was no choice.

The door bell rang just as they closed the door leading to the lower level. They were passing Ronnie's boat on it's mooring straps when the the doorbell rang again. The boat could have provided a waterway escape but it was still winterized from the previous year. Seeing it, Ronnie thought of the times he and Beth had enjoyed on the River. Grabbing a flashlight from the shelf, he wondered if he'd ever see the boat again as they made their way to the door to the tunnel. Spare flashlights had been one of Eric's additions to the plan, as well as moving the storage shelves in front of the doorway. They had drilled holes and strapped the shelves to the door for camouflage. It wouldn't take the agents too long to figure where they'd gone, but five minutes could make all the difference. Ronnie looked over at Eric. It was like they had entered a time warp and had been thrown back forty years. Eric always loved this cloak and dagger stuff but this time they weren't stealing chemistry tests or planting cherry bombs by the police station. The men outside were not the local boys in blue, either. These guys were serious and meant to take possession of the vials at whatever cost. When they discovered one was in a Fed Ex truck heading to a diagnostic lab in Indiana they were not going to be happy.

After they were all in the tunnel, Ronnie closed the door. Ahmed and Eric pulled on ropes tied to the metal storage rack pulling it next to the doorway. They'd put heavy tools and other items on the shelf that would not easily fall off. They pulled slowly to make sure everything stayed in place. Cate looked down the passage. It was much darker than the tunnel at St. Mary's. They'd walked the length last night but Cate still felt claustrophobic.

Episode 41

"Damn it," she muttered in a low voice, "two stinking tunnels in less than a week."

Ahmed glanced back at her. He'd felt the same way at the training camps. The key was to imagine being someplace else and had mentally put himself back on his balcony with Stacey. He imagined she was worried sick having not heard from him but the less connection she had with him now, the better. Jess seemed unfazed by the prospect of escaping through the narrow passage way or anything else about their situation. Having spent so many years on the streets, she was beyond fear. As Jess rushed down the passage, a lyric from an old song popped into her brain, something about freedom being just another word for nothing left to lose. Until she found a way to reconcile with her son, Jess believed she really did have nothing left to lose.

****

When Bobbie awoke, he was surprised to see the tall Indian doctor standing next to his bed. It took him a moment to focus on what the doctor was doing. As the doctor emptied a syringe into his IV, Bobbie recognized his face but couldn't make out the name on his identification tag. He knew it was the doctor with Doctor Midek in the elevator. Bobbie had no idea what the doctor had injected, but guessed it wasn't something to make him better. Bobbie knew there was little time. Though the doctor didn't know it, he'd just given Bobbie a divine gift and Bobbie was ready to reciprocate. Realizing he had only a few seconds to live, Bobbie wanted to thank the doctor for giving him the opportunity to see Beth again. Moving his lips, Bobbie spoke in a soft whisper. When Doctor Nak leaned over to hear Bobbie's last words, he was unprepared and equally shocked when the steak knife hidden under Bobbie's pillow pierced his jugular.

Bobbie had asked his sister Amy to bring him a letter opener, saying he hated the way the envelopes looked all tattered and raggedy when he opened them without one. She'd brought him a steak knife yesterday along with his mail. She apologized for being unable to find his letter opener. Though Bobbie was sure he left the opener in the top drawer of his desk, he was elated knowing the knife would be better for what he intended to open.

Bobbie knew the blow he struck into the doctor's neck had been very lucky. Hitting a major artery was mortal, as both he and the doctor were aware. The large artery had been totally severed sending great spurts of blood flying through the air. The dark red liquid landed in little puddles on the tiled floor. The doctor's right hand shot up and groped for the knife's black plastic handle. His initial reaction was to remove the instrument of death as quickly as possible. It was his second mistake of the morning. His first had been to underestimate a dying patient named Robert Virgil Irwin. The good doctor wouldn't live to make a third.

Bobbie watched as the doctor took two steps then collapsed into the curtain. The crash woke his roommate who pushed the nurse's call button. A nurse arrived within moments, but was too late to help either of the two men. Bobbie hadn't been able to reach Doctor Midek but knew his message would be received all the same. A smile crossed Bobbie's face as he felt himself beginning to drift away. The hospital room began to fade and recede into a dense fog as a feeling of peacefulness permeated his body. Strangely, he felt no fear. Life had become a burden that thankfully was about to be lifted.

Episode 42

The tunnel way was wide enough for two people to walk abreast. Harry Barnett had personally overseen its design and wanted to allow two body guards to emerge from the escape exit before exposing himself to an assassin's bullet.

Cate stayed next to Eric as they made their way along the dark passage. Jess and Ahmed brought up the rear. The tunnel was narrower than the one at St. Mary's. Even with flashlights, Cate was getting more claustrophobic by the moment. When she squeezed Eric's hand, he looked over and assured her everything would be okay. She managed an awkward smile then turned her eyes back to the tunnel's floor. If they survived, Cate swore she would never let Eric out of her sight again. Life's brevity had taken on a new meaning.

The tunnel was equipped with lighting and ventilation systems; wired to separate circuits. Ronnie had pulled the fuse to the lighting, another of Eric's insightful ideas. Ronnie was amazed Eric had retained his gift for planning and strategy. Telling them their escape should be made in the dark, Eric advised nothing should be made easy for any pursuing agents.

****

Agent Brad rang the door bell again and waited on the porch with Agent Nelson. They didn't have a search warrant. As Doctor Midek told them, there wasn't time for jumping through the hoops required by a federal judge, then added the people they were chasing were terrorists who hadn't flinched at arranging Doctor Nak's death. He maintained they also wouldn't think twice about killing anyone who stood in their way.

Agent John stood by the garage and looked inside the window again. A Ford Taurus was parked in the center facing the door. The positioning indicted the car had been readied for a quick escape. The agents knew there should be two vehicles, the other was a Ford Explorer which was unaccounted for.

Dr. Midek managed to keep the deaths of Doctor Nak and Bobbie Irwin out of the news. Dr. Midek assumed Al Qaeda had operatives in the hospital, so it was possible Nurse Cassadea and the young Arab already knew of Mr. Irwin's death.

Standing by the garage, Agent John double checked the safety on his weapon. Looking at his partners, he watched Agent Nelson produce a small tool and pick the lock to the front door. They could communicate by radio but decided to stay non vocal as long as possible. The young Arab had training in electronics and might be able to intercept their radio conversations. Agent Bradley hand signaled they were going inside.

****

Cate wished they were out of the damned tunnel but knew there was at least fifty yards more to the exit. Even with ventilation, the air was musty and stale. In the practice run, Cate had seen a very large wolf spider scurry along the concrete floor. She had tried to step on it but it had slithered into a crack where the floor met the wall. Jess told her they were better off that she'd missed, killing spiders was bad luck. Cate imagined getting trapped in the tunnel and having to sit in the dark while the insidious beast stalked her. She fought hard again to catch her breath and realized she was beginning to hyperventilate.

Episode 42

She tried to slow her breathing and pulled the neck line of her sweater up over her nose so she'd breathe in some of her own exhaled air. She'd have brought along a paper bag to breathe into if she had thought ahead. She realized berating herself served little purpose, so she focused her attention on the dimly lit cement floor.

****

By the garage, Agent John kept his eyes on the house. Everything seemed quiet; almost too quiet. He decided to change his position to improve his sight line. Inside the house, Agent Bradley and Agent Nelson searched the first floor providing defensive cover for each other as they moved from room to room. Satisfied the first floor was secure; they made their way to the second floor. After inspecting each bedroom they went back down the stairs where Agent Bradley decided to break silence.

"We've finished searching the first and second floors. They're empty. The suspects haven't been gone very long, one of the beds was still warm. We missed them by a few minutes at most. They may have posted a look out somewhere. We're going to inspect the basement, they may be hiding down there. Over."

"Roger that, I've moved my position to get a better view of rear of the building. Over."

"We're heading downstairs. Over and out."

****

Ronnie knew they were near the tunnel's secondary exit. The tunnel widened at the end leading to a small hexagonal shaped room with a cement staircase leading up to the trap door in the ceiling. The door was metal and heavy. Ahmed had oiled the hinges during their practice run. Ahmed and Eric went up the steps first. Ronnie thought of the pictures he'd seen at The Henry Ford Museum. In his mind's eye, he could see heavily armed guards dressed in 1920s suits leading Harry Barnett up the stairs. He could picture the guards emerging from the trap door holding Tommy guns with large round ammunition clips. If there are agents waiting for us up there with guns, he thought, we don't have a chance. He held his breath as Ahmed lifted the heavy door.

****

Agent Nelson found the doorway leading downstairs. The agents made their way down the steps very slowly. When they reached the bottom, Agent Bradley inched his way forward in the darkness. At the stern of the Four Winns he whispered to his partner that he'd provide cover. The agents strained their eyes looking for a light switch. Agent Brad produced a small flashlight from his pocket and moved the pencil thin beam of light methodically around the room. Locating the light switch, he quietly made his way to it then flipped the small lever. Nothing happened. The agents realized the fuse for the basement lights had been pulled.

The agents made their way around the dark room quietly. They found the small window in the far corner had been covered with pieces of cardboard and duck tape. Someone had gone to great effort to conceal their escape path. When Agent Nelson removed the cardboard, light streamed in through the small rectangular opening.

****

Eric and Ahmed were careful to not let the metal door slam against the ground. They lowered it slowly, gripping the chains attached to each side. When the door touched the ground, Ahmed eased himself out of the exit and inspected the grounds in all directions. After climbing out of the hole, Ahmed hand signaled Eric. Eric climbed the steps, then signaled Cate, Jess and Ronnie. When they were all safely out, Ahmed and Eric lifted the trap door and set it in place.

****

Episode 42

Agent Nelson watched the last piece of cardboard fall on the basement floor. With the improved visibility the agents inspected the walls. It didn't take them long to find the door hidden behind the metal shelves leading Agent Bradley to break their radio silence.

"We've found an exit from the boat house. There's an escape door and we're about to open it. Keep your eyes open out there, they may already be outside. Over."

"Roger," Agent John replied.

****

Ronnie took the lead. A short distance from the opening disaster struck. His good foot caught in an exposed root of a willow tree, When he fell, Ronnie's knee struck a dead branch lying on the ground. The branch snapped in two emitting a sharp cracking sound which Agent John heard. He thought the noise came from behind the line of pine trees and wondered if it was a deer, he'd seen several deer crossing signs on the Island. It was a dilemma, if he went to check the noise and it proved to be a deer, the suspects could escape from the back of house and he'd miss seeing them. Agent John began walking side ways looking alternately in both directions as he made his way toward the pines.

****

Recovering from his fall, Ronnie stood up.

"Sorry," he whispered to Eric.

"I see you're no less clumsy," Eric whispered back suppressing a wry grin.

Though he knew they were in a dangerous predicament, Eric felt invigorated. He had his mind back and was matching wits with law enforcement agents. Looking at Eric, Ronnie knew his old friend saw the world differently; he always had.

****

Inside the house, the agents saw the shelves were tied to the doorway and looked for something to cut the rope. Agent Nelson raced to the workbench by the far wall and rifled through tools looking for something sharp.

"Damn it," he swore.

"I'll go up to the kitchen," Agent Bradley said running up the steps. He returned brandishing a large serrated knife and began hacking at the ropes. After what seemed an eternity, he cut through the final strand. The two agents threw the metal shelves aside creating a loud crashing sound as the items stacked on the shelves bounced off the concrete floor. Agent Bradley grabbed the door knob and gave it a turn.

"It's locked," he said in a loud voice.

"Shoot the bloody lock," Agent Nelson responded. He'd been stationed in England with MI6 for two years and liked to flaunt his acquired accent. They backed up and Agent Nelson pointed his pistol. Taking aim, he pulled the trigger twice. The large pistol emitted a muffled swooshing sound as the bullets struck the lock. The two agents raced towards the door and pulled the knob. The door opened revealing a dark hallway. Agent Brad pointed his tiny flashlight into the opening.

"Damn," he exclaimed, "it's an escape tunnel. A fucking Chinese house, complete with an escape tunnel. What the hell kind of place is this?"

They hurried inside the doorway. From the footprints visible on the dusty floor, it was obvious the tunnel had been used recently. They took a few steps then stopped and listened for sounds coming from the other end. They heard nothing. Listening to the conversation between his two partners, Agent John realized the snapping sound had not been a deer.

"They've made their way out," he said into the mouthpiece and took off in a dead run toward the pine trees. He nearly stumbled as he picked his way though the pines but recovered his balance as he came into the clearing.

"I've marked their exit, we need to do something fast," Agent John said waiting for orders.

Episode 42

"Get back to the cars as fast as you can. Head for the county free bridge, I'll head for the toll bridge. Agent Brad will follow the tunnel to its end to make sure it's not a rouse. They may have sent a decoy out to throw us off. Over," Agent Nelson replied.

"Roger that, I'm heading to the cars now."

****

Ronnie and Jess were out of breath when they reached the Explorer. The other three fared little better as Ronnie unlocked the door. Ronnie's hands shook as he put the keys into the ignition and started the truck. He shifted the lever into drive and pressed on the gas. The tires squealed loudly as the SUV shot forward.

"Keep it under control," Ahmed said. "We don't want to get into an accident or pulled over. Those are the last two things we can afford. Take a breath, get control of yourself, and then drive fast but under control."

"Okay," Ronnie replied slowing the Explorer. He had parked about a half mile from Meridian Road and decided to use the county bridge; this was no time to wait at a toll booth.

****

Agent John sprinted back to his car, got into the driver's seat and started the big sedan. He didn't want to show his badge unless forced to but the Explorer had a sizable head start. He'd have to make up for lost time. Agent John drove the Chevy Impala along West River Road towards the county free bridge. He'd gone about a quarter mile when he saw the Road Closed sign. At the next street Agent John made a sharp left. It was a side street but he floored the Chevy anyway and reached sixty-five as he approached the turn onto Meridian Road. He prayed traffic was light.

****

Officer Matt was in his usual hiding spot just south of Meridian Elementary School. He had taken the top off the Styrofoam cup and set it on the dashboard. He picked up the little container of half and half and was pulling the tab when he glanced at the radar screen. The display registered 50 mile per hour. Steam from the coffee had gathered on the inside of the windshield partially obscuring his vision. If this dead beat didn't slow in time to comply with the reduced speed limit, Officer Matt knew he'd have to pull him over. It was a trade off. Giving a ticket would take the pressure off filling his quota, but he was really looking forward to his first cup of coffee. He'd also bought a glazed doughnut while at the bakery and it was still warm when Nadia handed him the bag.

Ronnie remembered the speed trap and braked the Explorer. Sitting in the back seat with Eric and Cate, Jess turned her head toward the front. She'd was responsible for the rear window while Eric and Cate watched the sides.

"There's a car coming up on us like a bat out of hell," Jess said calmly. "either someone is really late for work, or they figured out what we have in mind. Ronnie, I don't think this is the time to slow down,"

"Well, there's an officer just up ahead who will slow him down for us," Ronnie replied as they came abreast of the black and white cruiser.

Ronnie looked to his left, caught Officer Matt's eye and waved. The officer waved back in recognition. Once he was beyond the speed trap, Ronnie floored the SUV.

****

Agent John spotted the Explorer and radioed his partners. He gunned the Chevy and was doing eighty-five and accelerating as he hit the speed trap. Office Matt was relieved when the Explorer had slowed down allowing him to finish his coffee and doughnut. He also didn't want to pull over Ronnie Harris. Ronnie had been a regular customer at the Shell Station and was very earnest in his

Episode 42

congratulations when Matt made the force. Taking a sip of coffee, Officer Matt saw the radar display flash eighty-five.

"Fucken A," he exclaimed as the Impala came into view. "You're mine asshole," Officer Matt continued slapping the lid on the Styrofoam cup. After turning on his flasher, he gunned the cruiser into a U turn and was behind the Impala in an instant.

Agent John hadn't seen the Police cruiser until he was on top of it. He'd slammed on his brakes to decelerate, but knew it was too late.

"Damn it," he said into his microphone. "I'm being pulled over by one of the locals, should I ignore this Barney Fife? Over."

"No, I'm not far behind you," Agent Nelson answered. "Just string it out as long as you can. Show him your ID but tell him little. When I pass by, tell him we're teamed and I'm giving chase. Over and out"

Officer Matt pulled along side Agent John with his siren going and his lights flashing. He motioned the Impala to pull over. Agent John complied. In the distance he saw the Explorer slow momentarily at the traffic light then turn right towards the county bridge.

As Officer Matt got out of his car, another gray Impala blew past him. He started back to his car when the driver of the first Impala got out of his vehicle. Befuddled by the two speeding Impalas, Officer Matt drew his service revolver. The man getting out of the first car put his hands up holding something in his left hand.

****

Jess kept her look out. She told them the squad car had pulled from the side of the road with his lights flashing in pursuit of the agent chasing them. Ronnie asked Ahmed to take the cell phone out of the storage compartment and dial the number he was about to give him. Ahmed wondered what Ronnie was up to as he punched in the numbers. Ronnie listened as the phone rang three times.

"Sisification!" Ronnie said in a loud, high pitched voice. The greeting surprised everyone except Jess. She knew who was on the other end.

"Fucking Sisification yourself," Denny answered with a laugh. "What's up puss face?"

"Denny listen, I don't have much time to talk. Jess is with me and we're trying to evade an overzealous police officer. I need a huge favor. Can you to call your buddy who operates the bridge and ask him to open it when we pass over and keep it opened for a few minutes to give us time to lose this cop? I wouldn't ask but we're in a real fix here. You could say it's urgent. Call me back when you know. We're in my tan Explorer. If you can you do this for me Denny, I'll be forever in your debt."

"Ronnie Harris running from the cops, this is one for the ages. I didn't think a big puss like you had that in him, especially now you old shit. I don't know if my buddy will be working, but I'll call anyway. I know some of the other operators but whether they'll do it or not, I can't promise. If the cops call the control booth he'll have to comply. Anyway, I'll call now, you big sissy."

"What the hell was that all about?" Jess asked without turning her head.

"Denny has some connections with the bridge operators. Some of them are retired river pilots. He had them open up the bridge one time to impress me. If he can do it again, it might be the break we're looking for."

****

After getting out of his police cruiser, Officer Matt approached the man with caution. Keeping his service revolver drawn, he took his portable radio from his belt with his left hand.

"This is Officer Davis; I have a man pulled over who was speeding in a grey Chevrolet Impala. He's holding up what looks to be some kind of identification. Another late model Chevrolet just passed me heading south on Meridian at great speed. Send

Episode 42

a car in pursuit while I find out what's going on here and send back up to my location. I'll leave my radio on. Over."

"Matt, you are the only car on patrol. I can send the Sargent as back up if needed or I can call Trenton, the State Police or the Wayne County Sheriff's Office. Over."

"Best send the Sargent first, he can make the call. Over"

"He's on his way. Over."

With so much new home construction on the Island, gravel trucks were a regular site along Meridian Road. The trailers are supposed to be covered to prevent gravel from spilling but as most Islanders knew, the covers were useless. The driver of Rockway Truck 15 had done a less than adequate job of tying his cover that morning. As a result, there was a trail of loose gravel where Officer Matt pulled over the speeding Impala. Morning traffic scattered most of the gravel to the side of the road but a patch remained in the center of the north bound lane. Normally the gravel would have posed little danger other than a minor ding or cracked windshield but this was not a normal morning, as Officer Matt was about to find out.

Through simple misfortune, a motorist driving a late model Jaguar north on Meridian saw the squad car's flashing lights. Being a good citizen, the driver slowed and veered to the right side of his lane just as Officer Matt placed the radio back onto his belt. When the left front tire of the Jaguar struck one of the quarter sized rocks, the compression caused the rock to shoot out sideways with a loud popping sound. The flying gravel struck the agent directly into the rib cage causing him to drop his identification. Simultaneously, his right hand reached for the spot struck by the rock.

It was bad luck for both the agent and Officer Matt. The popping sound and the agent's quick hand movement proved to be a lethal combination. Officer Matt stood transfixed after firing his revolver. He'd mistaken the popping sound for a pistol shot and had mistaken the agent's hand motion as reaching for a weapon. It took Officer Matt a moment to realize the sequence of events had been reversed. The popping sound had come before, instead of after the hand movement. He watched in horror as the agent flew backward, seemingly suspended in mid air as a red stain appeared on his mid section. Officer Matt's eyes knew he'd just shot the man, but somehow his brain refused to register the fact. He also realized he'd fired in error. Oddly, the only thought running through his mind was he'd no longer be Officer Matt. He'd soon be Oil Change Matt again.

"The police just pulled over the agent. Uh oh, hang on," Jess hurriedly exclaimed. "There's another car coming. Shit, it's that other fucking agent and he just blew by the police car. I hope this Denny thing works, Ronnie, otherwise our ass is grass."

****

In the rear view mirror, Ronnie saw the second Chevy about a half mile behind. After stopping momentarily at the light at Grosse Ile Parkway, Ronnie turned right toward the county bridge. Seeing the iron girders rising skyward ahead, Ronnie reduced his speed. From experience, he knew that once the pavement stopped and the steel grating of the bridge began, controlling the Explorer would be difficult. It was a delicate trade off. He had to go fast enough to maintain his lead from the Impala but slow enough to avoid skidding into the curb on the narrow two lane draw bridge. If Denny was successful, the middle section of the bridge would soon rotate ninety degrees blocking the pursuing agent from crossing the river.

Ronnie braked, slowing his vehicle to forty-five just as he hit the metal approach. The tires emitted the familiar low pitched hum as they made the transition from asphalt. He felt the vehicle slide right and avoided the natural reaction to brake harder. Even with antilock brakes, skidding was possible on the metal roadway. He let off the gas and the Explorer came back into control. Glancing into the rear view mirror again, he saw the Impala barreling towards them like a freight train. Ronnie held his speed and steered as straight as possible. As they passed the mid point marker, Ronnie felt a sense of relief when the red

Episode 42

warning lights came on. The bridge was about to swing open and in a moment, the guard arms would drop.

"Holy shit!" Ronnie exclaimed as he looked into the rear view mirror again. They all felt a minor thump when the Explorer left the moveable portion of the bridge. Ronnie knew the road would return to regular pavement in a few moments.

"What the hell is that asshole thinking?" Ronnie added as his Explorer hit pavement again. Ronnie brought the vehicle to a complete stop on the Trenton side of the river. They all turned and watched as the draw bridge swung open.

****

Agent Nelson pressed the accelerator to the floor after turning from Meridian Road to Grosse Ile Parkway. The Explorer appeared to be half way across the bridge. If he could catch them, he'd shoot their tires, take the nurse and young Arab and leave the others for the locals. His plan depended upon not losing the Explorer. Agent Nelson looked at the speedometer. He was doing over ninety when he saw the flashing red lights. When the guard arm dropped a moment later he had reached one hundred miles per hour. Agent Nelson jammed the brakes just as the Impala passed from pavement to the metal surface of the bridge. The Impala skidded sideways, then swerved as his tires fought the latticed metal roadway for traction.

****

Older pilots flying out of Grosse Ile's municipal airport often remarked how the county draw bridge looked like something they'd built from erector sets as boys. Ray, the bridge operator on the morning shift occasionally thought the same thing. After climbing four flights of steps to the booth on top of the bridge, he had taken his seat at the control panel and was a little blurry eyed from staying up late watching football. His wife had reminded him twice he needed to get to bed because he had to work the next morning, but it had been an exciting game.

He had just made an entry into the daily log when Denny Warner called and asked him to open the bridge immediately after a tan Explorer passed by. Ray assumed Denny had some bar maid or waitress he wanted to impress, it wasn't the first time he'd made such a request. When the tan Explorer reached the mid point of the bridge, Ray pushed the buttons to start the opening sequence and walked to the window. He hoped to catch a glimpse of Denny's companion as they passed under the control room. He'd been so fixated at getting a view of Denny's latest conquest, he didn't look back toward the Island until it was too late.

As the gray Impala approached the bridge's steel grated roadway, Ray knew the driver was going too fast to stop. The Chevrolet skidded and turned sideways just before crashing through the guard arm and sliding over the end of the stationary part of the bridge. The car seemed to hover in mid air for several moments before it dove straight into the swift current. Picking up the phone, Ray felt like a marionette whose arms and hands were controlled by some hidden puppeteer. When the 911 dispatcher answered his call, Ray was certain his lower jaw was attached to a set of strings as it moved up and down. After hanging up, Ray continued his Howdy Doody impersonation and walked down the steps to the guard rail as if he was being maneuvered by remote control. He saw himself grab the life preserver and rope from the glass covered emergency box and race toward the end of the rotated section of the bridge. In panic, he threw the preserver into the swirling water but there was no one there.

****

Ronnie watched glassy eyed as the Impala flew off the open end of the bridge. Mesmerized by what they'd witnessed, Cate was the first to speak.

"Holy hell," she said softly.

Episode 42

Cate thought about the time she'd crossed the bridge with Kathy and the girls after graduation and wondered if she'd just become loonier than Rooney.

"Get the hell out of here!" Eric shouted.

Surprised by Eric's voice, Ronnie wanted to laugh at the shear insanity of their situation then remembered the agent in the car.

"Oh, man," Ronnie muttered, "should we stay to see if we can help?"

"Yeah, we can pull him out, so he can level his big pistol at your head!" Ahmed exclaimed. "Or during the confusion, we can get the hell out."

Ronnie didn't need any more coaxing. Moving his foot off the break, he jammed the accelerator. As they reached the end of Grosse Ile Parkway, Ronnie heard sirens and turned left on West Jefferson Avenue. When they reached Van Horn Road, the flashing blue lights of a Trenton police car flew by them from the opposite direction. After turning on Van Horn Road, they passed two other police vehicles. Ronnie knew the county sheriff's police boat moored at the foot of the bridge would be in the water within minutes so maybe the agent still had a chance.

"Oh, shit, you better call Denny," Jess said from the back seat.

"Damn, you're right," Ronnie replied. He flipped open the cell phone and pressed redial.

"What's up now Sisification?" Denny asked cheerily.

"Where the hell are you Denny?" Ronnie asked.

"On a shit bag ore boat docked in Toledo," Denny answered.

"Listen, you need to get off that boat right now. I'm on my way to pick you up."

"Why the hell would I want to do that?"

Ronnie quickly told Denny what had happened. When Denny agreed Ray would tell the police everything, Ronnie told Denny he could throw in with them though he really hadn't done anything other than do a favor for an old friend. After hearing the story about the vial, Denny said he'd take his chances with them.

Episode 43

Eric stood in the parking lot of National Motor's Experimental Vehicles Building. Employees coming through the doors looked different from when his father worked there. The men were casually dressed in kakis and open collared shirts, as opposed to the dark trousers, white shirts and narrow ties required when his dad worked worked in the building.

In his chinos and golf jacket, Eric blended in. The only thing differentiating him was the 9 millimeter pistol tucked inside his jacket. The gun, one of four purchased at a run down house in Detroit's Cass Corridor, hadn't come cheaply. Jess had laid down five thousand dollars in crisp one hundred dollar bills to buy them and the silencers. She wondered if some portion of her life on the streets hadn't been a total waste.

It had taken them twenty minutes to locate the car. Kamal's wife had verified it was his white Focus. Kidnapping Kamal's family was not something Eric wanted to do, but accepted as necessary and had convinced his team there was no alternative. He had devised a simple solution to their complex problem. Going to the authorities or newspapers was not going to be as simple as they had hoped. Cate's contact at the Plymouth medical lab had suddenly disappeared. When Cate phoned posing as a nurse

Book Two Home Again

checking the status of a lab order, she was told her contact had called in sick and would be out indefinitely. When Ahmed suggested the vial sent to the Center For Disease Control had most likely been compromised, Cate was distraught about her friend. Eric reminded Cate that her action had save many lives. Cate reluctantly accepted his rationale. Without the vial, they all knew success now depended upon exposing Doctor Midek with the spare. As the group discussed their options, Ahmed told them there was another complication.

The others sat dumfounded after he told them about the dirty bomb planned for the Detroit International Auto Show. When he finished, they looked at each other in disbelief. They were speechless until Jess said the bomb might be their way out. Ahmed reminded her he'd be prosecuted for his part in the plot and wouldn't get much sympathy about trying to save his little sister. The CIA wouldn't accept a trade off that endangered thousands of American lives in exchange for a twelve year old Arab girl ten thousand miles away. Ahmed maintained that any plan to expose Mahmood, would require assurance his sister's freedom be part of the deal.

Eric sat in silence. When he finally spoke, he told them he had the skeleton of a plan that might accommodate everyone. After listening to him, they had agreed and were now in the execution phase.

Ahmed sat quietly in the back seat of the Explorer holding a cell phone to his ear. Eric stood close to Kamal's car with his cell phone. After Ahmed identified Kamal, Eric would make the initial contact. Showing Kamal the gun under his jacket, Eric would instruct Kamal to look down the aisle where his wife and children sat in a car with Jess. Eric would assure Kamal his family would come to no harm if he simply got into the Explorer. After being drugged, Kamal would be taken to a secure location. His family would be held in a hotel room nearby until the plan was completed. There was risk of traumatizing Kamal's children, but it was a small trade off to prevent several thousand deaths from a dirty bomb.

Episode 43

Later that day, Doctor Taj would find his family held hostage in the parking lot of Plymouth Memorial Hospital. He would also be put into a rental car, then injected with enough heroin to render him semi conscious.

****

From Detroit, there are two crossings into Canada. The Detroit Windsor Tunnel runs under the Detroit River while the Ambassador Bridge spans the river at it's narrowest point. Eric and Cate were at the midpoint of the bridge where the arching suspension of steel girders, thick cables and concrete roadway rises a hundred and sixty feet above the water. Looking down, Cate saw several fishing boats scattered across the aqua colored water. They looked like the toys her daughters played with in the bath tub as little girls. Looking to her left, Cate could see downtown Detroit. A haze of smog clung to the top of the four high rise towers of the Renaissance Center. Looking further up river, she saw Ford Auditorium and thought about high school graduation. She'd sat in the auditorium with three hundred other eighteen year olds, dressed in caps and gowns, and had given the valedictorian's speech.

Driving across the mammoth structure reminded her of the time she told the customs officials her place of birth was Russia. It seemed a good joke to an eleven year old; her parents and the customs agent had failed to see the humor. Their station wagon had been searched and the whole family questioned. It was a frequent topic of conversation during ensuing trips to the cottage.

When they passed the bridge's zenith, Eric noted there was a line of cars at every custom's booth. Eric followed Ahmed's car into a line for the middle booth. With his goatee and bad teeth, Eric hoped to pass for just another American whose gambling addiction was a higher priority than dental care.

Eric's plan assumed the customs agent would be so attuned to Ahmed in the vehicle ahead, they'd pass his and Cate's car with only cursory questions. If Eric was forced to open the Crown

Victoria's trunk, they were in trouble. It would be difficult to explain the two men blindfolded and drugged.

Ahmed prayed Eric's plan would work. It seemed logical. As Eric explained, their only hope was Canada. Once there, he'd make a phone call. If his request was denied, they'd drive to Toronto, tell their story to The Toronto Star then ask for asylum. It was a huge risk, but their only alternative.

Ahmed had his fake identification ready and reminded himself his name now was Salah. The ID was good considering the time they had to procure it. Jess's connections again proved invaluable, though the passport, weapons and other identification had been expensive. Denny's friends Candice and Eddie were waiting in hotel rooms back in Detroit guarding Kamal's and Dr. Taj's families. Ahmed was doubtful at first about how reliable Candace and Eddie would be in completing their parts of the mission. After hearing who was pursuing them and the risks they faced, Ahmed believed they'd give it their best effort.

Ahmed took several deep breaths. There was one car ahead of him. He doubted he'd ever see Stacey again but his sister's freedom was worth the gamble. When the car ahead of him was waved on, Ahmed looked in his rearview mirror. Cate looked nervous but Eric seemed as cool as ice. Ahmed knew Eric had missed his calling and should have been a CIA or FBI agent. Even with no formal training, Eric could plan circles around some of the buffoons he'd been in contact with since Afghanistan. Glancing left, Ahmed saw Denny and Jess in the next lane. Ronnie was by himself behind them. Having split up to minimize their risk, the plan assumed Ahmed would be searched and thereby improving Eric and Cate's odds of being waved through without being searched.

The agent in the customs booth signaled Ahmed to pull forward. He put the Malibu in gear and eased ahead.

"Citizenship?" the agent asked.

"United States," Ahmed answered.

"Do you have a passport and driver's license?" the agent asked. Hearing Ahmed's accent, he looked into the back seat.

Episode 43

"Yes," Ahmed answered. He'd kept the inside of the car hot to maximize his sweating. Ahmed wanted to look nervous to entice the custom agent.

"How long will you be in Canada?" the agent asked.

"The rest of the day."

"What is your destination?"

"Vivaldi's restaurant," Ahmed replied, "I hear it's one of the best restaurants in Little Italy".

"Why are you going there?"

The question was unexpected. To eat, Ahmed thought to himself, why else would someone go to a restaurant. He felt taken back at the question.

"I'm meeting friends there for dinner. Afterward we might go to the casino."

"Are you bringing in any firearms or alcohol?"

"No sir."

"I'm going to ask you to pull into that lot," the customs official pointed to a covered area next to a brick building.

Ahmed knew he'd just been profiled.

"Yes, sir," Ahmed answered pulling the car forward. When he reached the indicated area, another agent came out to meet his vehicle. Ahmed looked back and saw Eric pull the big Ford up to the spot he'd just vacated. He saw Eric's mouth move, then stop. The agent must have addressed Cate because she begin talking.

'Okay, go ahead," the agent said to Eric.

Eric pulled away from the booth and drove by the inspection area as Ahmed opened the trunk of the Malibu. Eric watched a customs agent in a baseball cap and beige uniform begin searching the trunk. As planned, Cate and Eric stopped at the first gas station. They would wait for the others to show, then drive to Cate's family cottage at Point Pelee.

Eric pulled into the British Petroleum station and checked his watch. He and Cate changed seats. Denny and Jess showed up five minutes later and said Ronnie should be along shortly and they'd seen Ahmed being taken into the customs office. While they were talking, Ronnie arrived. After updating him, they drove

Book Two Home Again

to Highway 401. Eric took a disposable cell phone from the glove box and dialed while Cate drove. The phone rang twice.

"Senator Gary Martin's office, may I help you?" the receptionist said in a monotone voice.

"Hello," Eric replied sounding business like, "my name is Eric Arnold. My father was a very close friend of the Senator's. His name was Alan. The Senator will recognize the name. I need to speak to him; it's a very urgent matter."

"The Senator is involved in a hearing right now and is unavailable," the receptionist replied.

"Okay, do you have a pencil and paper handy?" Eric asked.

"Yes, I do," the receptionist answered.

"Good, now I want you to write this down; it is very important," Eric replied curtly.

"I'm ready."

"My name is Eric Arnold, that's spelled ARNOLD. My number is 734 – 822 – 4338. I have information about a national security issue. Tell Senator Martin to call Homeland Security Director Stoynoff. Unless Senator Martin and the Director contact me within thirty minutes I am going to the Toronto Star and tell them about a Doctor Midek and a covert operation at Oak Grove Hospital in Fairlane Hills, Michigan. Tell him my story also will include information about the vials. I want Director Stoynoff on the line as well because I also have information regarding a separate terrorist threat. There are certain conditions that I will request in writing. I am holding an agent of Hezbollah and an agent of the I.E.R. hostage to corroborate my allegations. Do you have all of that?"

There was silence on the line.

"Yes, sir I believe I do," the receptionist replied.

"Oh yes, tell Senator Martin that I'm doing much better now. I've been diagnosed and treated for a blood disorder by a Doctor Singh, at Waterside Hospital in Wyandotte. If he doubts this authenticity of what I've said, I'll have the editor of the Toronto Star give him a call. This is no joke. Also, may I have your name?"

"My name is Ms. Fenbert. Is there anything else?"

Episode 43

"No."

"Thank you Mr. Arnold," the receptionist said and hung up.

****

Ahmed sat on a metal chair. He'd been the interrogation room for twenty minutes when a customs agent walked in. The agent looked to be somewhere in his mid forties and was wearing pale blue uniform pants with a darker blue strip down each leg and a white uniform shirt, starched and pressed. He had a receding hairline and ruddy complexion. The agent took a seat across the table.

"Okay, Salah. While we continue to search your vehicle, we've decided to perform a full body review."

It was a very diplomatic way of saying he was to be strip searched.

"If you have anything to tell us, make it now. Otherwise, the search will be done immediately. You also should know, we have X Ray facilities and since you are not female and with a risk of pregnancy, you will be X Rayed."

Ahmed managed to keep a straight face. They suspected him of drugs, did they think he'd swallowed condoms full of cocaine. At least they hadn't challenged his identification. A strip search was nothing after Guantanamo.

"I have nothing to tell you. So if you need to search me, I won't like it but there is nothing I can do."

"Okay, then Salah, come with me."

An hour later Ahmed put his clothes back on and was shown to his car. He wondered how the agent would feel the next day when he read how a covert operation had been uncovered by a group of Americans who had made their way into Canada. He'd like to be there when the agent found out the Arab he'd given a near colonoscopy to was part of the group. Ahmed got back into the Malibu and started the engine.

****

Eric's cell phone rang.

"This is Eric Arnold," he answered, again business like.

"Hello, this is Robert Stuckey, Senator Martin's chief of staff," the man said perfunctory.

"I was expecting Senator Martin," Eric said.

"The Senator is tied up at the moment."

"Listen, I gave Ms. Fenbert very precise information."

"We are verifying that right now. The Senator needs a little more time."

"You need to understand something, Mr. Stuckey. You don't have much time. My father was a close friend of the Senator's. My dad was his campaign organizer when he was running for State Representative in Michigan. Look, I realize the Senator may have reason to believe that I am mentally ill, however, I gave Ms. Fenbert the name of the doctor who will verify that I am not. Listen, I want to do the right thing here, but you are not leaving me many options. There's something you need to tell Senator Martin. I know of plans to detonate a dirty bomb. You need to start taking me seriously right now."

"Mr. Arnold, we are taking you very seriously, but The Department of Homeland Security gets hundreds of false threats every day. Now if you tell me where you are, I'll direct you to the nearest FBI office."

"No. Now listen to me. I'm recording these calls, and if this thing happens before I get to speak to the Senator and the Director, many people are going to look stupid. You've got fifteen minutes to get Senator Martin and Director Stoynoff on the phone with me. Tell the Director we have one of the vials in our possession and access to a medical lab. This time the lab won't send it to the CDC again. We are also holding two agents."

Eric hung up and looked at Cate. They would have to make a decision soon, either to head to the cottage or to Toronto.

"That didn't sound good," Cate glanced at Eric.

"We've done as much as we can," Eric replied looking back at her, she'd always be the shy girl with the deep blue eyes who had stolen his heart. He desperately wanted to recapture some of their lost time. He thought about telling her to pull over. They'd dump the two maniacs in the trunk and just drive west to Vancouver and steal as much time as they could. Ten minutes later, Eric's phone rang again.

"Eric Arnold," Eric said.

"Eric, this is Gary. It's been a long time. How are you?"

Senator Martin's voice sounded the same as the countless times Eric had heard it at the house on Keppen Street.

"I've been worse," Eric answered.

"Listen, if it's okay, I'm going to put you on the speaker phone. Director Stoynoff is here with me. We're in his office. We've checked out the information you've given us. As you know, this is a very grave matter. We're prepared to do whatever it takes but you realize, what you and your friends have done amounts to kidnapping and crossing international borders to commit a felony."

"I understand that. I didn't know holding international terrorists was a crime. That's part of the reason I called. We are prepared to give you and Director Stoynoff all the information we have, but we have certain conditions. We want a pardon, agreement to immunity and placement for certain members of our team in the federal witness protection program."

"That can all be done," Director Stoynoff interjected, "assuming everything you tell us is true. You said something about the Toronto Star. Are you in Canada now?"

"I assume you know the answer to that, or will in few minutes when the Director uses his satellite to triangulate our location. I could just hang up now and call back."

"Eric," Senator Martin cut in, "there's no reason to do that. If you are in Canada, that will complicate things a bit. That's all the Director was getting at. Of course you already know that, or you wouldn't have gone there."

"Okay," Eric cut in, "here's the deal. My dad trusted you, I'm willing to do the same. You get us what I've asked for; we'll give you the information. Call me back when you are willing to put your political life on the line. Can you do that in thirty minutes?"

"We will do everything in our power Eric, you can trust me about that."

"Okay, when you're ready to provide what we're asking, call me." Eric added and hung up.

"Take the exit for the cottage," Eric told Cate. She looked at him with a nervous smile.

****

William Clay Junior looked up from the agenda. The son of William Clay Senior, he looked more like his uncle Henry Clay II. After firing Gerald Roberts, National Motor's CEO, Bill Clay Jr. had taken a more hands on role. As CEO, Bill's days began at seven and seldom ended before ten at night. He thrived on running the business and despite the stress, managed to keep his youthful looks.

As Chairman of the Finance Committee, his opinion carried great weight. Tom LeBlanc, the Chief Financial Officer, sat to his right. LeBlanc, a thin man in his early fifties with salt and pepper hair, worked even longer hours. He was presenting the first item when Ms. Tillman walked into the room. Conversation stopped immediately. After the Board of Director's Meeting, the Finance Committee meeting was the most important event on the Company's calendar. Interruptions were a rarity. The other members of the Finance Committee looked at each other for any hint as to the cause for interruption. Some assumed it may concern the health of Bill's father who was in his eighties. Ms. Tillman handed Bill a note and remained next to him.

The Executive Conference Room is on the twelfth floor of National Motor's World Headquarters. The Green Palace, as it was referred to, is a thirteen story monolith on Michigan Avenue in west Fairlane Hills. When it was built in the 1950s it was unlike any other office building in Detroit. Passers by would stop and gawk at the exterior's pale green reflective glass.

After reading the note, Bill Clay rose from his chair and told the committee there was a security issue. LeBlanc and the other

Episode 43

members knew what that meant. The Company was under a terrorist threat. There was a protocol for such an event and each member knew the protocol. Bill Junior took the stairway to his office on the nineteenth floor. Ms. Tillman climbed the stairs at his side.

"Is the Homeland Security Director on the phone now?" Bill Clay Jr. asked.

"No, sir, it's the President himself."

They walked briskly to Bill Clay's office where Fred Calloway, National's Director of Security sat waiting. The two men hoped this day would never come, but were prepared if it did. Bill Clay had great confidence in Calloway. He was an ex Navy Seal, former FBI agent and a former Assistant Director at the CIA. Bill Clay took a seat behind his large desk. Looking out the window, he could see Company buildings sprinkled around Fairlane Hills. Further in the distance, he could see the Fairlane Hills Proving Grounds with it's oval shaped test track and the Engineering Research Center. From the one word coded message Ms. Tillman handed him, he knew somewhere the family empire was under attack. He wondered which building had been selected. The answer would be known momentarily. He pushed the lighted button on the phone and spoke clearly into the mouthpiece.

"This is Bill Clay, Mr. President."

****

Killard's Cutter Grinding sits directly across the street from the White Castle hamburger stand. Considered Melvindale landmarks, both businesses had been in operation as long as anyone remembered. Mayor Daniel Killard left his shop shortly after one p.m.. While the shop was Danny's full time occupation, his mayoral duties were part time. Lately it seemed the other way around.

He was on his way to a meeting with Lyle Pinkowski, the city treasurer. They planned to review the budget proposal before tonight's council meeting. Danny said hello to Barb, the office

Book Two Home Again

manager, then made his way to Lyle's office. Lyle stood six four and weighed a little over three hundred pounds. He was a noon time regular at the Mel Bar and Grill where he ate a medium rare cheeseburger and fries for lunch. Before his heart attack, Danny had joined him regularly. At doctors orders, it was now chicken breast sandwiches and a solitary beer.

"Do you want to do this in your office Mr. Mayor?" Lyle asked in his deep baritone voice. At city hall, Lyle insisted on formalities.

"Na," Danny responded. "This is fine. Unless you tell me the numbers will get better if we look at them there. Otherwise I'll just suffer my pain right here."

"Sorry, Mr. Mayor, not much has changed."

"In that case, we should have just done this at the bar," Danny joked.

"No, this is better," Lyle replied, "at least if we both have heart attacks and die, it'll be on the job and our wives will get a better settlement."

Lyle got up from his desk and walked over to the table. He took a seat across from Danny and handed him the financial summary. Danny smiled at Lyle's joke.

"Did you get any more information on that salt mine thing?" Danny asked. "Maybe we can get some relief there."

"Sorry, no help," Lyle answered. "You know it takes forever for anything to make it's way through the bureaucracy of Detroit. If they started blasting tomorrow, then just maybe Detroit would get around to notifying us in about three years."

All of the Downriver communities had been notified the Global Salt Mine property had been sold and the new owner intended to reopen the mine. Danny thought about his high school friend Tom Auten whose dad worked in the mines. As boys, they'd listened to Mr. Auten's stories about driving a truck so big it had to be disassembled on the surface, shipped down on the elevator and then reassembled below. He'd added the tires were taller than the roof of a car and as big as the car itself.

Episode 43

Though Mayor Danny had never been inside the mines, he knew they ran for miles under the Downriver communities. Even though several hundred feet below ground, anyone who lived above the mines would never forget the punctual blasting every morning and night. The tremors felt like mini earthquakes and were very unsettling the first time experienced. After a while, the blasts went unnoticed. When residents occasionally filed formal complaints about cracks to basement floors and walls, government officials just shrugged their shoulders and quoted laws about ceded mineral rights.

"Seems we should be able to get something from them," Mayor Danny commented. "Those damn caverns are right below us. They should have to pay some kind of tax. They told us three months ago that they might start blasting again as early as next January."

"Well, maybe we'll get lucky and they'll blow up half of Detroit in the process," Lyle said with a smile.

Danny didn't know how to respond to Lyle's joke. It was no secret all the suburbs had terrible relations with the City. Most viewed the sprawling monstrosity as the prime example of urban decay and everything that was wrong with big cities. Danny thought about the sermon he'd heard the previous Sunday.

"You know Lyle, that's not so funny," Jimmy said looking over his half glasses, "there are a lot of good Christian people who live by that mine."

"Sorry," Lyle apologized. While Danny had gotten on his high horse occasionally over the years, he seemed to get on it more often since his heart attack. Lyle toyed with asking Danny if it was okay to blow up the non Christians, but decided against it.

"Besides, the entrance to the mine sits a little too close to us if something goes wrong," Danny added with a wry grin.

"Amen brother," Lyle responded then looked at the report.

****

Book Two Home Again

The transport plane's tires emitted a high pitched squeal as it touched down at Selfridge Air Force Base thirty miles north of Detroit. Two men de-boarded the plane and walked toward a black limousine parked on the tarmac. Military guards held the rear doors open as Senator Martin and Director Stoynoff climbed into the back seat. Satisfied the men were properly seated, the guards slammed the doors shut. The driver and guard in the front seats were Secret Service agents. Another vehicle with four heavily armed agents would escort the limo to the Ambassador Bridge. The trip into Canada was to be kept low profile. The President had phoned the Prime Minister of Canada and the ambassador and given them a joint briefing. The limo would be whisked through customs where an escort vehicle containing four plain clothes Royal Canadian Mounted Police would accompany the American escort.

A contingent of Royal Canadian Mounted Police had also been dispatched to the small cottage on Lake Erie. Their captain had delivered faxed copies of the documents Eric requested. Eric and the four others would be taken back to the United States, accompanied by Senator Martin and Director Stoynoff. Ahmed's sister had been taken into protective custody during the middle of the Afghan night by a squad of Army Rangers and was in route to a military plane. She would be in the United States by the next day and had spoken to her older brother by satellite phone. They would enter the witness protection program along with Denny's friends Candice and Eddie. Having his best friend disappear for who knew how long would not be easy but was better than bidding Eddie farewell in a hearse. Denny knew they'd see each other again in time.

****

Eric and Cate walked down to the beach. With most of the cottages closed for winter, Point Pelee was a peaceful place. It was sunny and unseasonably warm for November. Walking along the shore line of Lake Erie, they were never far from two Royal

Episode 43

Canadian Mounties standing guard. Cate looked at Eric and thought about the times she'd sat on the beach dreaming about the coming school year. She thought about fish dinners with her family after her brothers and dad returned from a morning on the lake. Cate vowed she would find a way to spend endless summer days on the beach with Eric.

She'd contacted her brother, Frank who was relieved to hear from her. Because she and the rest of the group had signed an agreement to not divulge anything about the vials or bomb plot, she told her brother a story about running into Eric and getting him into rehab. Frank wasn't enthused about her reconciliation with Eric but when Cate told him emphatically this was her second chance at happiness and she didn't intend to let it pass her by, Frank reluctantly wished her well.

****

Bill Clay Jr. recognized the voice, he'd met the President several times during the last election campaign. He listened as the President told him Director Stoynoff and Senator Martin were on their way to Detroit. An anti-terrorist team was on its way to the Experimental Vehicles Building where they would take possession of the vehicle scheduled for display at the upcoming Auto Show. The President asked Bill Clay if the team had permission to enter the building without a warrant. They both knew the request was perfunctory, Bill Clay told the President all of National Motor's resources were at his disposal.

The President asked if Fred Conway could be there to help direct the team. Director Conway said he would. The executive of the building and the employees would be told it was part of a State Police bust of a stolen parts theft ring. Any press releases would say the vehicle was being held as evidence. The President said the plan was to keep everything low profile. He assured Bill Clay that everything was under control and that an evacuation of the area would not be required. Bill Clay asked if there was anything else he could do to help. The President replied the best thing he could do was stay by the phone and to stay in touch with Mr. Conway. The situation would be handled quickly and with minimal exposure. The President emphasized the goal was to keep everyone calm and to not induce panic. The knowledge of any terrorist attack was to remain in his office. Bill Clay assured the President he could count on confidentiality.

****

Mayor Danny Killard left his shop at five-thirty. The Council Meeting was scheduled to start at seven and he wanted to review his presentation one more time. As he waited to turn into the city hall parking lot, a large moving van with Preston Brother's Moving and Storage passed him. Mayor Danny noticed nothing unusual about the truck or its drivers. If he stepped inside the vehicle, however, he would have noticed the walls of the trailer had been reinforced with armored steel and were lead lined. The drivers were enclosed in an air tight cab equipped with special filters connected to a remote oxygen source. It was no ordinary truck and it carried no ordinary cargo. The truck had been airlifted to Selfridge Air Base and was headed to The Global Salt Company mine in southwest Detroit. The Company was owned by a shell corporation which was owned by a series of other shell corporations. Following any paper trail back to the Agency would be near impossible. The idled salt mines were an ideal location for storage of nuclear waste. The idea to use them for commercial storage of spent nuclear rods had been floated several times. There had been public outcry of resistance, however, because of the mine's close proximity to a densely populated area. It had been decided that storage would now take place in rural Nevada.

As Mayor Danny reviewed the agenda, preparations were in full swing at Global Salt. The sleek looking convertible was unloaded and placed into an elevator car. It would be unloaded several hundred feet below the surface then loaded onto the bed of the same truck Tom Auten's father drove for thirty years. Once it was placed in the designated cavern, there would be a detona-

Episode 43

tion but it wouldn't be a dirty bomb exploding. The convertible would be sealed behind several hundred tons of rock salt.

Mayor Dan ate a turkey sub and sipped a Diet Coke while he prepared. He was almost finished when the Chief of Police knocked on his office door.

"Come on in George. What's up?"

"Listen, I know you're busy getting ready for tonight's meeting," George answered, "but we just got a call. They're planning on doing a test blast tonight at Global Salt. We put a notice on the local cable station and I've prepared the dispatch desk to handle any added phone calls. Some of the residents might think it's an explosion at the Ford Rouge Complex. Anything else you can think of?"

"Yeah, tell those bozo's at Global we want some tax revenue," Danny replied with a smile.

The Council meeting started promptly at seven. After standing for the pledge of allegiance, the council members took their seats. As usual, the meeting was covered by local cable television. Danny said he had an added item to the agenda then announced there would be a test at the salt mine. At 7:15 p.m. the floor of the Melvindale City Hall vibrated noticeably. Mayor Danny looked around the table and then into the television camera.

"Ahh, just like old times," he said with his best politician's smile.

Epilogue – Nine Months Later

It had been a difficult year for the Stalters. After Pete was diagnosed with Lou Gehrig's disease, they'd sold the Grosse Ile Hardware Store to a man from Rhode Island. The store had been in their family for eighty-years. Pete was ready to retire but had always pictured himself sailing his vintage cabin cruiser to Florida.

Timbo Dickenson stepped from under the car hoist and looked across the street at the hardware store. Because his two daughters had married men with no interest in cars, he wondered if the same fate awaited his business. Timbo didn't relish the idea of turning the station over to a stranger. The new owner of the hardware seemed a decent person, but Timbo couldn't get used to the idea Pete wasn't running the place. Timbo believed the Island was losing its character and he wondered where it would end.

Looking across Macomb Street again, he saw Pete and Maureen making their daily pilgrimage to Lloyd's Bar and Grill. Maureen was walking next to Pete as he guided his electric scooter down the side walk. Lloyd's was about four city blocks from their house next to the hardware. They'd have lunch together today, the same as always. Maureen would have a burger with everything and a beer. Pete would forgo the burger; he was now on a feeding tube. Sandy, who ran the place, would still serve him a short draft beer. He'd fill a syringe with the amber colored liquid and inject it into his feeding tube. Pete had always been an optimist and would not let something like Lou Gehrig's deprive him of his noon time ale. Life was too short. Timbo knew it was going to be even shorter for Pete.

Though he knew it was silly, Timbo still expected to see Pete's '56 Chris Craft navigating the waterways around Grosse Ile. The thirty-two footer was a classic. Aside from his wife and children, it was the love of Pete's life. They'd sold the boat much sooner than expected. Timbo understood friends of Ronnie Harris bought it.

****

Ronnie walked out on the balcony. Eric would be docking the Chris Craft in a few minutes. Cate called from her cell to say they were running a few minutes behind because Kathy had been late getting to the dock. That was Kathy, Cate remarked on the phone with a laugh, she'd be late to her own funeral,.

****

The twenty-eight foot Boston Whaler pulled up in front of the condominium complex on the east side of Aruba Bay. It had been chartered for a day of scuba diving. As the captain eased his craft slowly toward the white planked dock, he could see the American waiting on the dock. The man was tall with thinning black hair and looked to be in good shape for his age. The American had signed the contract as Doctor Rick Martel and had a passport to prove his identity. Unknown to the captain, Doctor Martel had passports in several names including one issued to a Doctor Frank Midek. When the Whaler reached

Epilogue – Nine Months Later

the dock, the American disdained the offer of help and jumped aboard unaided.

"All set?" the Captain asked.

"Take her out," the man replied.

****

It was shortly after eight in the morning in northern California. Ahmed had just dropped his sister at school and was on his way to a chemistry lab. His sister was still adjusting to the move but otherwise was doing well. In three short years, Ahmed promised her, he'd be done with engineering school. She would be in high school by then. Though he missed Stacey, Ahmed accepted the loss. His only regret was there had been no opportunity to explain.

****

It was nighttime in Kashmir. Doctor Taj hadn't slept well, but he didn't complain. Compared to sitting in an American prison, deportation back to India was a minor inconvenience. Knowing the Muslim terrorist Kamal would never come to trial, Darpak contented himself with being the only surgeon within a hundred miles as the war with the hated Pakistanis continued.

****

Ronnie looked up the river. Lifting the binoculars to his eyes, the cabin cruiser was about a half mile away. Eric was behind the wheel in the enclosed bridge. The dentist had done a marvelous job restoring Eric's teeth. The porcelain caps were flawless and Eric had regained his irresistible smile.

Denny stood next to Eric drinking a beer. Panning the binoculars to the boat's stern, Ronnie saw Cate sitting across from Linda, Kathy and Jess, who was wearing florescent pink retro

Book Two Home Again

sunglasses. She and Denny had moved in together. Though she hadn't heard from her son, she still held hope. Roy, Kathy's new husband, was sitting next to her. They'd met while chaperoning students to Paris. She'd gotten much teasing about their teenaged like doting on each other, but Eric and Cate were not much better. Linda's husband would meet them tomorrow at Cate and Eric's cottage at Point Pelee, Canada.

Ronnie could see the women were singing because their mouths were moving in unison. As the boat came abreast of the dock, Ronnie heard the lyrics. The four girls who had crossed the county bridge in the summer of 1967 were singing together again. Ronnie recognized the song, it had been one of his favorites in high school. As they neared the dock, Cate looked over and smiled. She lowered her sunglasses and Ronnie saw her deep blue eyes. They seemed to have a special light in them now; it was nice to see her happy. Ronnie grabbed the rope Denny tossed as the women finished the last verse of Go Now by the Moody Blues. When they finished, they laughed hysterically. Sometimes fifty-six year old girls do that, too.

Made in the USA
Columbia, SC
28 November 2023